WHITEWALLS

by CHRISTINE RICHARD

Published in 2009 by New Generation Publishing

Copyright © Christine Richard

First Edition

British Library C.I.P.

A CIP catalogue record for this title is available from the British Library

Acknowledgements

Many thanks to all those people who have encouraged me in the writing of this book. These include not only my family but also Maggie McKernan, Ian Rankin and Mo Elliott who have provided much-needed guidance and encouragement. My thanks, too, to the writersscotland on-line group, who are always encouraging of each others' literary endeavours.

The book is dedicated to my late husband, John, to Fiona and Andrew and to all my extended family.

Chapter 1

Whitewalls

Every spring and summer morning for as long as she could remember, Rosie had woken up to the sounds of wood pigeons cooing against a sweet chorus of small songbirds.

"Whitewalls" had been her childhood home. Her marriage to Jamie had seamlessly changed it into theirs. It was here that the children, Polly and Charles had been born. They still came here as often as they could. Whitewalls was the heart of the Douglas family.

The house had been built in the 18 century and was a solid construction in the Scottish Baronial style, with crow-stepped roof and a rounded turret in the centre which housed the main staircase. The outside walls had been harled and painted white, for as long as anyone could remember. It stood in around 10 acres of garden set back from the River Tweed.

There was a backdrop of blue tinted hills and the house seemed as if it had been there for ever. Polly and her husband Richard came from Edinburgh regularly, bringing with them the twins, Minty and John. Charles was in the Army, in his grandfather's old Regiment but he, too, gravitated home to the Scottish Borders whenever the chance arose.

This Friday morning in late May, Rosie stretched out her arm to find the pillow next to hers in the old brass double bed cool and empty. Jamie was always up before her, no matter how early she awoke. She glanced at the crystal clock on her bedside table. Six o'clock. And so much to do today. Rosie started to make a list. She liked the sense of order the list writing and ticking off tasks gave to her life. It defined her progress. It made her feel grounded. She sat up and the movement wakened the Empress who slept in a small basket at the bottom of the bed. The miniature sleeve Peke bustled round to the side of the bed and looked appealingly at Rosie.

'Oh all right, five minutes then'. Rosie scooped the little dog into her arms and onto the quilt. She put on her spectacles and once again picked up the pad and pencil as the Empress snuggled in. No sooner had she begun to write "spray the roses, take pheasant and gooseberry fool out of deep freeze, make apple pie for Saturday ...." than the telephone rang. 'Hello Rosie, I'm not disturbing you am I? Her mother's voice came crisply on the line. I thought I'd come over today with some more geranium plants for the tubs outside the gates. If you plant them now they'd be just right for the Garden Opening, make the entrance look welcoming.'

'No, Ma, wide awake, trying to write a list and not getting very far. What colour are the geraniums? Do you want to come for lunch? Richard's coming later; he's bringing the twins down straight from school.' Richard, her son-in-law, was an Edinburgh lawyer who loved nothing better at the weekends than pottering around the stables, going for long walks with the dogs and enjoying the gentle pace of country life. Rosie was so fond of him. His quiet manners greatly appealed to her. Then she realised her mother was still talking to her.

'Right I'll bring a variety of colours of geranium' her mother replied briskly. 'Won't be able to stop for lunch. Molly's coming to clean the silver this afternoon and I need to lay it out for her but see you around half past eleven. Bye.' and with that Betty hung up.

Selkirkshire

Lady Betty was a small woman with a huge appetite for life. This had sustained her well into her late seventies through many turbulent events. Her marriage to Sir Alistair, Rosie and her brother Hugh's father had begun in passion and ended in acrimony. Shortly after they married Alistair had developed what later became a habit of casual, and some not so casual, affairs. Betty had tolerated it whilst the children were growing up. But there had been one scandal too many. The minister's daughter became pregnant by him and Betty had had enough.

Alistair had been generous. The divorce settlement had given her Whitewalls, the family home and farm situated on the banks of the River Tweed in the Scottish Borders. Later when their son Hugh had married Virginia from the south of England

4

and acquired his own substantial house, High Wynch Park in Gloucestershire, Betty had settled a generous sum of money on him and given Whitewalls to Rosie. The Tower, where she had lived with eccentric flair ever since Rosie's marriage to Jamie had been bought using much of the remainder of the capital.

Thanks to a Trust Fund, set up by her own father and sales of her paintings and tapestries she had lived as she pleased for a long time.

All of this seemed now to be under threat.

The day before, Andy the postman had handed over a registered letter from her lawyers which had created an unaccustomed anxiety. He needed her to make an urgent appointment to discuss a problem with the long-ago divorce settlement, which could have far-reaching consequences if not properly resolved. The substance of the letter was that Alistair was attempting to reclaim ownership of Whitewalls. It appeared that the divorce settlement had been incorrectly registered and there was a legal argument that it could be nul and void.

Betty had decided not to bother Rosie about the letter. Rosie, in her mother's opinion, had quite enough on her plate at present and Hugh was wrapped up in the excitement of a film being made at High Wynch Park.

After letting her peke, Emperor, out in to the garden, Betty went to her studio-cum-office at the top of the tower and sat quietly for a few moments at the mahogany campaign desk she had inherited from her father and which always reminded her of him.

After a few moments, Betty gave herself a shake. She had better find out what it was all about. There was really only one person she could phone. It was John Prendergast. She picked up the receiver from the handset and dialled.

He answered quickly, 'Hello, Stitcholme 8476 John Prendergast speaking.'

'John, dear, it's me, Betty, there's something I need to talk to you about. It may be serious.'

John Prendergast was a retired Army Colonel of the "old school". He and his late wife, Beatrice, had no children. When he retired they had chosen to live in a pretty cottage in the village of Stitcholme. Betty and the Prendergasts had built up a solid friendship over the years and when Beatrice died John had found Betty's strength and support a great comfort. Now they often enjoyed companionable meals together and it was natural for Betty to turn to him for advice.

'Whatever it is Betty I will be happy to help if I can', he readily responded. Briefly she told him about the letter and outlined the problem. They agreed Betty would have supper with him that evening and discuss what this might mean.

Whitewalls

Abandoning her list for the moment, Rosie slid out of bed putting an indignant Empress on the floor and went off to the bathroom. From the brass bedstead to the white painted wicker dressing and bedside tables and the comfy sofa under the window, strewn with patchwork and cushions embroidered by Lady Betty to the sheepskin rugs on either side of the big bed, the effect of the master bedroom at Whitewalls was soothing. Family photographs, some in old silver frames, were displayed on every available surface. Jamie's watercolours were arranged round the walls. From the window you could see across the gardens to the river beyond. The overall effect was the gentle country style, which was Rosie's hallmark.

Before long she was back, her long legs thrust into their daily uniform of cord trousers. She shrugged on her checked shirt and slid her feet into brown leather loafers. Pausing only to throw back the patchwork quilt, she went downstairs followed by Empress to start her day.

As it was still early, the room was calm and peaceful. Later it would be humming with activity as Molly crashed around cheerfully, as she had done for the last 30 years, baking, laundering, cleaning and simultaneously dispensing the homespun homilies for which she had become - often irritatingly - famous. The Douglas family was Molly's life. She had never married, and never regretted it.

'Men are more bother than they're worth' she replied when anyone asked why she had never married. In fact, there had been a young farmer, Tommy, many years ago but he had got another girl into trouble and that was that.

The sayings included such gems as "God gives us all the strength to bear whatever life throws up". "Clean pyjamas, a hug and hot chocolate give anyone a better night's sleep than all the new-fangled sleeping pills in the world" and mysteriously "No good ever came of flighty ways". This latter had often been used of Polly before, to Molly's profound relief she had married Richard who himself had been the mildly startled recipient of "Keep a firm hold on her, now you remember that. She could be a bolter if you take your eyes off her."

At this calm early morning of what promised to be a lovely day, only the ticking of the old clock above the pin board and the purring of Dundee, the ginger cat, in his basket in front of the Aga disturbed the peace.

Rosie lifted the heavy lid on the Aga hotplate and brought the kettle quickly to the boil. She had just sat down at the scrubbed pine kitchen table, which had been in the centre of the room for at least fifty years when Jamie came in.

'Oh is there no peace?' she cried with mock exasperation. 'You can smell tea from a hundred yards away!'

He put his hand on her shoulder and kissed the nape of her neck.   After thirty-five years of marriage, his touch still moved her. From the first fumbling kiss after a long-forgotten hunt ball to now, he made her feel complete.

'I'll have a quick mug of tea. Dad's a bit worried about Princess, she's not due to foal until next week but she's had a very restless night. Horses!'

Rosie smiled ruefully. 'I expect he's been up with her for at least half of the night himself. Ring him and invite him over for breakfast.'

'I already did.' Jamie grinned ' I knew you'd want me to. He's coming around half past seven.'

'Right, that gives me an hour to finish my list and get ....'

'Organised' laughed her husband

'While you start cooking breakfast' she finished.

The kitchen at Whitewalls, as in most 18th century Scottish country houses the kitchen faced north. Even so, Rosie's powerhouse was bright and sunny with yellow painted walls, clear turquoise blue doors and white gauze curtains which today were flapping gently in the spring breeze. The slate floor was worn smooth by generations of feet. Rosie had put sisal mats in front of the Aga and a dresser, giving the traditional room a look of the warm south.

Over the years Jamie had learned to be a good simple cook. With eggs from his own hens, bacon from the home farm and mushrooms from the fields he made very tasty breakfasts. He appreciated Rosie's praise glowed in her approval. He knew she was the go-getter in the partnership and although he looked after the farm and the estate with skill and care he would have been just as happy in a cottage, with a small studio, painting all day.

The kitchen door opened and Roddy, the Major came in followed by Empress, who had been left out in the garden for long enough.

'Well, it wasn't an easy birth' he announced 'but Princess has dropped her foal. It's a lovely filly.'

Rosie got up and kissed her tall, slimly built father-in-law.

'I'm so pleased Roddy. You wanted a filly, didn't you, to carry on the line?' She was fond of him and knew he had been very lonely since her mother-in-law, Lorna, died ten years ago. It was not Roddy's nature to complain.

Jamie turned round from the Aga with a tea towel slung over his shoulder. He slapped his father on the back.

'Well done, Dad, but you should have called me to help. You're getting on a bit for all-night stints.' The older man smiled and said,

'I did cheat a bit. Young Christine from Tony's practice came out to help. She's thrilled. It was her first foal delivery.' She may be small but she's certainly strong.

'Where is she now?' asked Rosie 'you didn't just leave her to find her own breakfast, Roddy.' She hoped that her father-in-law wasn't losing his faculties with age!

'Don't get excited, she had to go on a difficult case at Dodie Thomson's. One of his cows is in a bad way. She's a tough young lady. I did say you'd make her welcome but she said to thank you and could she come another time.' Roddy loved to tease Rosie, she was so kind but could take everyone and everything a little bit too seriously in his view.

'Right' said Jamie, 'stop chattering you two and eat.' He, too, loved his father dearly but like many Scotsmen of his age found these feelings hard to put into words.

The two men tucked into the huge spread. Rosie just had a boiled egg and some of her home-baked brown bread. She was proud of her slender figure at the age of 54 and worked hard to ensure it stayed that way.

'Are you going to keep the foal?' she asked. 'You said if it was a filly that you might. It would be hard to replace Princess but, like me, she's getting on a bit now!'

Roddy was not a man who spoke without first thinking. He smiled at his daughter-in-law, whom he loved very much though he, unlike his son, would never ever put that feeling into words. This was particularly so because of the "stiff upper lip" of his army background.

'Well' he said slowly 'I'd be tempted to keep her and let Princess retire. But why don't you come and see for yourself and let me know what you think?'

Jamie laughed. 'Dad, you know Rosie hardly knows one end of a horse from the other. I would take her advice on many things, but not this.' Roddy smiled then and Rosie thought how alike they were. Jamie would look and sound just like his father in 20 or so years' time. It was a good thought. Roddy wanted to get Rosie away to speak to her about something totally different. He wanted to talk to her about his will. He knew her knowledge of horses was minimal.

'That may be Jamie, but she has a good eye and I value her instincts.' Jamie smiled, shrugged his shoulders and went on eating his breakfast.

Later as Roddy and Rosie completed the short journey to the stables in the landrover Roddy said 'I meant what I said about valuing your instincts, Rosie. Part of me wants to start all over again with a new breeding line, and then I think maybe I'm getting a bit old for this game.'

He was a young-looking eighty-three year old with a lean tanned face and a shock of white hair and a wiry frame and Roddy Douglas most certainly didn't look his age. He had seen active service in the Second World War and bore the physical discomforts of old scars stoically. He never spoke of the two days and nights when he had lain paralysed in a ditch behind enemy lines before being found and carried bodily out to safety by his sergeant.

Rosie laughed 'thanks for the compliment. As for you being too old you certainly don't look it if that's what's worrying you.'

Together they entered the immaculate stable yard and immediately went into the airy loose box, which housed Family Princess and her foal. Talking quietly and gently to the chestnut mare, Roddy led the way. The filly, also chestnut with a white blaze on her forehead was sprawled on the sweet straw that thickly covered the floor of the Edwardian loose box. As they went in, she scrambled to her feet, ungainly yet already beautiful in the vulnerable way of all newborn creatures.

Rosie stretched out her hand and gently caressed Princess who placed herself protectively between her foal and the human visitors. The mare soon relaxed, though, and allowed Roddy to run his large capable hands first over her head and back and then allowed him to do the same to her foal.

Roddy cleared his throat.

'There's another reason why I wanted to get you on your own, Rosie.' She smiled enquiringly.

'I'm no longer a young man ....' seeing Rosie was about to protest he smiled,

'No let me go on. I've decided I want to leave the lodge and the stud to Richard'

Rosie could stay silent no longer. 'To Richard, but why not to Polly, or to Charles? In fact, why not directly to the grandchildren? Anyway, as you know Richard's a lawyer doing well in a busy practice in Edinburgh ...'

By now Family Princess had decided that she'd had enough of her visitors and pushed her head gently, but firmly against Roddy to show she'd welcome her privacy again.

16

'Come into the Lodge for a while and I'll try to explain.'

Over a pot of strong Indian tea and seated at the oak table in Roddy's spartan kitchen he expanded on his theme.

'The way I look at it is this. Charles will eventually have Whitewalls and whatever you all decide should be kept of the farm. Hugh's family is taken care of so I want to leave this place to Richard. He is very interested in horse breeding and loves the country, too, so why not?'

For Roddy this was a long speech. Rosie had listened intently and without interruption. She paused, and then spoke thoughtfully,

'I can see maybe Minty and John are too young, but if you want to do it this way why, not Polly?' He replied, pausing to choose his words carefully 'I love and like my granddaughter, Rosie. But to be honest she's not really a country girl and, I hate to say this, I'm not sure if she and Richard are really right for each other in the long term.'

Rosie stared into her teacup for a few moments before responding. In a way Roddy was putting into words thoughts she, too, had harboured.

'Does that mean you don't think Polly is worthy of being your heir?' she asked with a note of disapproval in her voice. After all she could criticize Polly but wasn't sure that she cared for anyone else to do so – not even Polly's grandfather.

'No, that's not what I mean at all. I've probably put this very badly. It's more to do with stability and continuity if you like. So it can eventually be handed on in a good state to the little ones.' Damn it, he thought, if only Lorna were still here, she'd do this much better than I can.

Now Rosie said 'I'm not sure what you mean and, frankly, it's a bit of a shock. What does Jamie think about it?'

Roddy spoke again:

'I haven't talked to him about it yet. I wanted to sound you out first. Now it looks as if I've made a mess of it.' He looked wretched and old. Rosie got up and hugged her father-in-law fiercely. For the moment she set aside the fact that Roddy had seen fit to talk to her before he discussed this with his only son. She would think about that aspect of it later. After all Roddy might change his mind. And he seemed to be in good health.

'No, I know you mean to do the right thing. I've been concerned, too, about Polly. She's become so brittle and edgy. In fact coming here, which she used to love, now seems like a chore when compared with tennis, the health club and her cooking business. The latest is talk of golfing lessons. Perhaps she's still trying to break away from what she sees as our influence. I'm not sure. I am troubled, though.' "Yes," Roddy thought "she looked worried which was so unlike her."

Glancing at her watch, Rosie jumped to her feet. She gave her father-in-law another hug. In her view he didn't get enough hugs and even though he had upset her, Rosie's affectionate nature did not hold back now. It couldn't be much fun growing old on your own. A shiver ran through her as she even for a moment contemplated being without Jamie.

'Sorry, Roddy. I must rush, there's so much to do and it's nearly half past nine already. I'll think about what you've said and talk it over with Jamie. Will you come and have supper with us evening? It's just pheasant casserole, I'm afraid - I'm using up the frozen birds from last season.' Everyone laughed about Rosie's parsimony and, in truth, her pheasant casserole had an undeservedly bad reputation. She was a good cook and prided herself on her ability. 'Yes, thank you, I'd like that. Let me drive you back to the house.' He was relieved he had got the idea out into the open. Now he wanted the solace of the horses and time to think.

She kissed him lightly on his cheek.

'No need, honestly. The walk will do me good. Besides I think best when I'm walking.' And with that, she was gone.

The day was getting warmer with a pleasant breeze and the sun on her back felt good. Rosie loved this time of year when, even in the Scottish Borders, the signs of the late, short spring were still around and the first promise of summer flowers was filling the hedgerows. All around Whitewalls the late narcissi were still showing their pale gold colours, whilst in the long herbaceous border the first flowers were opening with plump peonies and the ever-reliable pulmonaria and violets showing their purple coloured flowers.

Rosie loved her garden though she had no pretensions about it unlike some of her more competitive neighbours along the Tweed who had changed garden opening into either an art form or a moneymaking business. So she was fairly relaxed about the planned Open Day in aid of research to help find cures for cancers affecting children.

There was a great deal of work to be done. She quickened her step through the white-painted gate leading from the back drive into the kitchen courtyard.

Dundee was sunning himself, stretched out on the warm flagstones. Empress shot out of the open kitchen door looking reproachful at being left behind. From deep inside the house came the sound of the vacuum cleaner signalling Molly's presence. Of Jamie there was no sign. "Damn" Rosie thought, she had so wanted to share Roddy's proposal with him. Jamie, in his quiet way, could always put a calmer perspective on events. This time she would just have to wait until later when they could be alone.

Later that morning with a pan of home-made vegetable soup simmering gently on the Aga Rosie and Molly sat down at the kitchen table enjoying their mugs of coffee and the desultory gossip which characterises the easy familiarity built up between two women who for many years have used their combined talents to keep a household running smoothly. Most of the time Molly observed the unspoken parameters of their relationship and if she did go too far with her forthright comments on family matters, Rosie found it easy to forgive her.

'What time are they getting here from Edinburgh?' Molly asked.

'Richard is bringing the twins straight after school but Polly is cooking for a dinner party in Edinburgh so she won't arrive until Saturday lunch time.'

'H'm. If you ask me she's spending far too much time on this cooking business, heaven knows what she's getting up to.'

Rosie smiled, but was troubled. She couldn't put her finger exactly on why she felt uneasy, she just did.

'Molly, I didn't ask you but yes, I guess she is getting more and more involved. Richard really doesn't mind, he's very supportive of her business. I don't think we should interfere. Polly is a grown woman, after all, not our little girl needing to be looked after all the time.' "I shouldn't have to justify myself to Molly" she thought.

Molly only sniffed and, unusually, made no further comment. Instead she got up from the table as quickly as her ample frame and stiffening joints allowed and confined herself to saying:

'Well, I can't sit about here gossiping all morning; I've got work to do.' With that and much clattering of mugs Molly signalled that, for the moment, her contribution to the conversation was at an end.

'Hello, hello' The kitchen door was flung open theatrically and a small whirlwind of a woman dressed dramatically in black trousers and a brilliantly-coloured smock came into the kitchen. It was Rosie's mother, Lady Betty.

'Good heavens, are you still having morning coffee? Hello Molly, remember that you're coming to me this afternoon to do the silver. I'll collect you at 2 30.' Rosie was struck afresh at her mother's energy and exuberance, despite her age. She was tiny with a neat head of white curly hair. Her practically unlined face had a light tan, which made her blue eyes look brilliant. Betty's zest for life seemed undimmed by the passing years.

'The geraniums are in the car. Come and help me unload.' She addressed Rosie after exchanging brief but affectionate greetings. She was determined to be cheerful and not give her daughter any inkling of what was troubling her so much.

'You said not red ones so I've brought pink and white. They'll flower in good time for your garden opening.' With that she sped out of the kitchen again to her ancient, though immaculate, Morris Minor traveller. The wood was gleaming from its annual spring coat of varnish. The car was one of Betty's favourite possessions.

Rosie followed her, reflecting, not for the first time, how much sheer energy and vitality her mother possessed. This was largely owing to the fact that she had always led a thoroughly self-confident life expressed in behaving exactly as best suited her at all times, or so it seemed.

It didn't immediately occur to Rosie to share with her mother the unease she felt about the conversation with Roddy and his desire to leave his home and the stud to her son-in-law rather than to Polly or Charlie. Betty had always treated life as a series of events, which contained not problems but alternative solutions. She considered introspective thoughts and most emotions to be a complete waste of time. Therefore, she was not the ideal confidante about matters, which might, or might not cause difficulties at some future time. Just for once, though, Betty might have welcomed Rosie confiding in her to give an opening to share what was on her own mind.

"See you at supper this evening even though I expect it'll be pheasant casserole yet again!' Betty's voice interrupted her introspective thoughts.

'Oh, Ma don't be unkind you know it really is quite good with red wine and herbs and mushrooms in it!' Rosie replied in defence of her signature dish. Betty only smiled lovingly at her and departed with a flourish.

She waved good-bye to her mother then Rosie gave herself a mental 'shake' and resolved not to give in to the feeling of deep unease which had threatened to engulf her since the morning's talk with the her father-in-law. Sometimes she felt she hardly knew Polly at all. Even though she loved her dearly. Still, she must stop all this and get on. There was, as always so much to do.

Edinburgh

Richard was whistling tunelessly as he unlocked the dark green front door of the house in Murrayfield Gardens. The two Norfolk terriers, Pixie and Pod ran excitedly to meet him. Polly was out shopping for the dinner party she was doing for a client this evening. She wasn't coming down to Whitewalls until tomorrow. He couldn't wait to get out of his blue pinstripe suit, into cords and an old sweater. It was three o'clock. The children would be out of school in half an hour. He would collect them and drive straight down to the Borders. Edinburgh was a great city in which to live and work but at his in-law's comfortable and relaxing country house he felt most at home and at peace with himself and the world.

Richard quickly changed into fawn cord trousers and pulled a yellow cashmere sweater over his business shirt, picked up the holdall, which he had packed early that morning and dashed into the children's rooms to collect their belongings. All the family kept a number of items of clothing at Whitewalls - jackets, boots riding hats and anoraks so there was no need for over-elaborate packing. Just as well, he reflected, as Polly was off again doing her own thing. Though, to be fair she had left the rucksacks ready on the bottom of each child's bed. He wished she were coming with them today. Lately she'd seemed different. Half the time she was charged up with excitement and the rest down in the dumps. Richard resolved to talk to Rosie about it all and immediately felt better.

Wasting no more time he ran downstairs again, collected Pixie and Pod who were now wild with excitement and in no time at all he was driving the unglamorous but highly sensible Volvo estate car down the hill to St George's school to collect Minty. From there he would go across the city to his old school, the Edinburgh Academy, and collect John. Then driving out of town on the A72 they would go through the pretty Borders town of Peebles and down the Tweed valley past Cardrona House and on to Whitewalls.

Minty was at the school gate hopping up and down when he appeared. Unlike her brother John who always looked as if he had slept in his clothes Minty was extremely neat and well organised. Her pale blond plaits were as tidy as they had been at breakfast. The school tie was still in place and her white knee socks unbelievably clean.

Waving goodbye to her equally neat and pretty friends, Minty got into the back of the car.

'Hello daddy, where's mummy?' His own disappointment reflected in his voice Richard replied.

'Remember, she's not coming until tomorrow.'

'**Why** isn't she coming 'til tomorrow?' demanded Minty, her voice echoing his own disapproval.

'Because, darling, she's doing a cooking job for one of her clients this evening and she's gone shopping to buy the food, I expect. Now we'd better get a move on, John will be waiting for us and think we've got lost.'

With that he pulled out into the heavy post-school traffic to repeat a similar collecting operation at the Academy. When Richard had been a day boy he'd either walked or got the 23 bus from Morningside where his parents still lived. Nowadays, though, the school run was the norm at least for younger children. John's acceptance of Polly's absence was even less willing than his sister's.

'She's **always** cooking for David McLean. It's not fair. Why does she have to do it? I don't like him anyway!' "Why can't he leave my mum alone?" John thought. "She gets all silly when he's around and then she had the cheek to get him to meet me at school!"

Richard replied rather absently as he was concentrating on the traffic.

'You can't say you don't like someone you don't even know.'

'Yes I can, and I do anyway. He picked me up from rugby for mummy last week. So there, I do know him and I **don't like him**.'

'OK that'll do, John. Now think what you're going to do when we arrive at Granny's' Richard was to remember his son's throwaway remarks later. But for now he was just keen to get out of the city and into the countryside.

'That's easy,' cried John, quickly diverted.

'We'll catch Snowball and Butterball, tack them up and ride along the river bank.' The Palomino and Welsh mountain ponies were a huge attraction and Roddy, had bought them in the hope the twins would take to riding whilst still young. They thought the ponies were the best Christmas present they had ever had and hardly complained at all about the more mundane tasks of mucking out and grooming, as well as cleaning tack, which they had to do whenever they were at Whitewalls.

Whitewalls

Tumbling out of the car without a backward glance the twins raced off into the house taking their rucksacks with them. Minty's was carried neatly over her shoulder whilst John's bumped along the ground behind him. The dogs, after briefly stopping to pee on the nearest bush, ran barking excitedly at their heels. Richard followed more slowly. He was reflecting on what the children had innocently revealed.

What did John mean? Polly had said nothing about David McLean collecting them from school. Had it been just the once or was this happening often? He was still frowning when he walked into the empty kitchen. Dundee lazing by the Aga briefly opened his eyes, yawned widely and closed them again.

The room was quiet in the lull before the late afternoon's activities began. The sun was shining softly through the gauzy-clad windows; the kettle was steaming gently on the hob. With the familiarity of family membership Richard dropped his own bag on the floor, pulled a large mug from the dresser and made himself tea. He was standing at the window, which looked out into the walled vegetable garden when Rosie came into the room.

'Richard, you're here. Where are the twins? When is Polly coming?' she asked looking pleased to see him. Not for the first time she thought how fortunate she was in her daughter's choice of husband. He was an ideal son-in-law.

Richard hugged her and replied.

'Polly's not coming until tomorrow morning. She's cooking for a business dinner this evening. The twins have gone to catch their ponies. Where's Jamie?' he asked wondering if he would have a chance to talk to Rosie on his own for a while.

'Out getting some more trout for the fishing pond, I think. But I'm glad to get you to myself for a little while. I've something really important to tell you.'

Although Rosie had not yet had a chance to share fully with Jamie her father-in-law's bolt from the blue delivered that morning, she felt so strongly that she must tell Richard at the earliest opportunity. At first she found it difficult to explain but then it was easy. Quickly she outlined Roddy's plan, finishing by saying,

'So you see Richard, part of me thinks it is the most wonderful idea and yet part of me feels that, somehow, it's not fair to Polly or to Charles, either.'

When she had finally finished. Richard looked pleased and yet troubled simultaneously. Out of the blue it seemed as if, in future, there might be an alternative way of life for him for Polly and his family, away from the demands of living and working in the capital city. He responded thoughtfully, saying

'I don't really understand why Roddy wants to do this; apart from leaving Polly out of it what about Charles. He's the grandson and surely, after Jamie, the heir?' Richard could hardly take in the news that his wife's grandfather, of whom he was very fond, thought so much of him he had decided to make Richard the main beneficiary of his will.

Rosie sighed. She had not felt as troubled as this for a long time.

'Maybe I didn't explain it very well. Probably it would be best if you and Roddy spent some time together and talked about this. I think I understand why, but I want you to understand why, too. I know, Roddy's gone to Hawick this afternoon but he's coming for supper this evening. Why don't you go over there at drinks time, see the new foal and come back with him? That should give you plenty of time to talk privately.'

Richard gave her a brief, warm hug. He heard other men talk in disparaging tones about their mothers-in-law. With Rosie there was no problem. She was warm and affectionate towards him – more than his own mother to tell the truth and he really admired the way she made everyone's lives seem to run so smoothly.

'Yes,' he smiled I'll do just that. Now I'd better go and make sure the twins have caught those ponies and tacked them up properly. I'd better take Pixie and Pod along as well, they're dying for a run around."

'And I must go and do something about supper or we'll all starve!' The last thing anyone ever did at Whitewalls was become mildly hungry, let alone starve. Rosie, though liked to nurture a mild air of muddle and eccentricity, whilst ensuring that there was no part of her life, which was not, in fact, lightly but firmly under control. She ruefully reflected – at least it had been until now; until this business over Roddy and Polly. It troubled her deeply, for her family was her life's work and she liked things to go well for all of them.

She switched on her little radio, permanently tuned to Classic FM and began to peel carrots, shred spring cabbage and prepare the mushrooms and onions for the pheasant casserole she intended to serve for supper. A gooseberry fool from her amply stocked freezer would be the pudding with the remains of the homemade elderflower syrup from last summer. In less than two months it would be time to make a fresh batch. She would give the twins their supper early and had already made a cottage pie with cheese topping; it was one of their favourites.

Rosie had always believed the seasons of the year and the fruits and vegetables that she grew in season gave a certainty to life. Anything to do with food preparation and cooking usually soothed her and Rosie tried to put the Polly situation on one side to deal with later. But she felt angry and tearful.

'Damn, damn, damn' she cried and sniffed hard.

Jamie came quietly into the kitchen. He was so neat and soft in his movements she hardly heard him but, as always, immediately sensed his calming presence.

'What's up love?' he asked putting an arm round her shoulders and dropping a kiss on to her bent head. He thought as he folded her in his arms how rarely she showed any feeling that was not positive and upbeat. In fact, he was sure that if there was a nuclear explosion she would marshall her family together under an upturned sofa and tell them all would all be well very soon.

'It's not like you to get in a state about cooking supper. Anyway it's only family and Tim and Anne, isn't it?'

'Jamie, it's nothing to do with cooking supper.' Then she wanted to shed the burden to be weak instead of strong, irrational and silly instead of the perfect wife and mother.

Gratefully Rosie turned, hugged her husband and felt his strong arms holding her, keeping her safe. Hot tears welled up again.

'Oh, Jamie, I don't know. I'm so pleased about the foal and Richard and twins are here, but not Polly. She's cooking for some magnetic magnate in Edinburgh and I don't like what your father's going to do and yet I see why ....'

She stopped as suddenly as she had begun and started to laugh shakily. She must sound like a complete idiot.

'Oh dear, how silly of me, you don't even know yet what I'm talking about do you?'

Gently, yet firmly he pulled her away from the sink.

'Leave this. Let's go out to the summerhouse for a while and you can tell me all about it there. Then I'll help you to get organised. Richard's with the twins and the ponies, they'll be good for another half hour at least.' Jamie always tried to deal with things before they gave any possibility of growing into dramas.

Hand in hand, followed by the bustling Empress and Jamie's bounding Labradors they left the kitchen and walked through the walled kitchen garden. They went through the little gate set within the wall and on to the first of a number of the "rooms" which Rosie had created in the gardens using hedges of beech and low edgings of box. In the corner of the second one was a wooden summerhouse with a west-facing veranda situated to catch the afternoon and evening sun.

As long as anyone could remember the summerhouse had been the place to which any member of the family could retreat to find peace, wrestle with problems or simply to enjoy a solitary snooze over a book whilst lounging on the old but still comfy steamer chairs on the verandah or inside in one of a comfortably cushioned, but shabby selection of basket chairs.

As it was a warm and sunny early evening they sat on adjacent chairs outside with the big dogs contentedly at their feet and Empress ensconced on Rosie's lap.

'Do you want to tell me about it?' asked Jamie gently.

Rosie took a deep breath. It was not often she found a situation with which she found it hard to cope, or a problem she could not solve. It was a new sensation and she did not care for it at all.

Jamie was a good listener and heard Rosie out without interruption. When she had finished he didn't immediately respond. This did not surprise her so she waited quietly then asked,

'Jamie, don't you agree with me your father is being very hard on Polly? After all she is his granddaughter. Richard, much as I love him, is only related by marriage. Then there's Charles, what on earth is he going to think about all this?'

She stopped. Jamie cupped her chin in his hand and turned her face very gently towards him.

'Rosie, I think Dad's right.' Astonished and angry she jerked her face away from him. This was the last reaction that she had expected to get.

'No, please listen. It's my turn now. Hear me out.' He spoke firmly.

'I'm sorry,' said Rosie immediately contrite. Jamie went on.

'You see, in many ways Polly is a mixture of sophistication and complete naiveté. You have never been able to see her faults, only her virtues. She's a lovely girl, or should I say, woman - but sometimes I think she missed out on a whole chunk of growing up. She and Richard were so young when they married and Polly went straight from one safe and sheltered home to another without any of the usual dramas most young people go through. There's a repressed restlessness, even wildness about her that I think will surface sooner or later.'

Rosie could keep quiet no longer. She simply did not recognise this description of her dearly loved, though sometimes exasperating, daughter.

'Jamie, she's our daughter. We love her. Certainly I love her. Polly is generous, open and caring. I really don't know what you're talking about. Anyway, we were young too when we got married and it didn't hurt us. Or perhaps you're saying I'm not grown up either!' This was not exactly true but Jamie knew in his heart that she, too, had always been sheltered from the harsh realities of life, firstly by her mother and later by him.

'Rosie, I love Polly just as much as you do but may be I'm not as blind to her faults. Yes, we were young but times were less complicated and we were different people. You never hankered after a career, and a life of your own which excluded the rest of us. You've been the heart of this family for so long we sometimes take you for granted. You **are** my life and that applies to all of us to a greater or lesser extent. But this means you've never really let Polly and Charles go. To you they're still the children and not adults in their own right. You can't go on trying to shape and influence them as if they were still youngsters.' He did not really expect her to agree with this criticism but had to voice it anyway.

This was a long speech for Jamie and he wasn't sure that his wife accepted what he said to her or of the relevance of Polly's lack of maturity in relation to his own father's decision.

Again the uncharacteristic tears welled up in Rosie's eyes and a lump formed in her throat. It was a few moments before she could say anything at all. Then she didn't know what to say. The silence lengthened.

'Jamie will you or Richard tell her over the weekend, please. I don't think I can bring myself to do it. Or do you think it's best if your father takes it on?' Jamie thought and then replied.

'Probably yes. It doesn't have to be this weekend, though. I think he wanted to sound us out first. It might be better to let it rest for a while.'

This didn't suit Rosie's temperament, which naturally made her want to find tidy solutions, but she felt so troubled, for once, it seemed easier to do nothing. It was not that Jamie was an indecisive man but he believed often issues, which seem problematic, turn out alright if you leave them alone for a while. He gave his wife a reassuring hug. Rosie took a deep breath and stood up, dislodging an indignant Peke. The Labradors, Heather and Tweed, sensing departure, hoping for a walk eagerly jumped up and nudged Jamie. The discussion was over and they went their separate ways again. Rosie refused Jamie's offer of help and went back to the kitchen to continue preparations for a family and friends supper which she felt she did not really want. Jamie went to his studio in the grounds accompanied by the two Labradors who were still hopeful of a romp by the river.

The dogs soon realised that wasn't where they were going but even a walk to the old stone steading whilst not quite as good as the river was better than nothing.

Although it was rather grandly known as 'the studio' Jamie's retreat was really a farm steading with its clear north light streaming through the enlarged skylight. There was an easel, paints and all the other artist's paraphernalia. This was Jamie's own place and generally recognised as such by the rest of the family

Jamie sighed. Like Rosie he preferred life to be smooth-running without dramas. A farmer by upbringing, an artist by inclination and talent, he believed quietly yet passionately in the rhythm of the seasons in nature and in life. One of his favourite biblical quotations was from Ecclesiastes, *'To everything there is a season, and a time to every purpose under the heaven: a time to be born, and a time to die: a time to plant and a time to pluck*

up that which is planted: a time to kill, and a time to heal: a time

to break down, and a time to build up: a time to weep, and a time

to laugh, a time to mourn, and a time to dance: a time to cast

away stones, and a time to gather stones together: a time to

embrace, and a time to refrain from embracing: A time to get,

and a time to lose; a time to keep, and a time to cast away: a time

to rend, and a time to sow: a time to keep silence and a time to

speak: a time to love and a time to hate: a time of war, and a

time of peace. "

He sat down in the shabby leather chair placed in front of the old but tidy desk. Heather and Tweed who were disappointed at the absence of the walk they had so eagerly anticipated flopped at his feet. Jamie felt he had not handled the Polly situation very well. He loved his only daughter but, unlike his wife, he was not blind to her faults and he had an uneasy feeling cracks were already beginning to appear in her marriage to Richard.

Really it would have been so much better if his father had not raised the inheritance question now - but everyone, including him tended to forget how old Roddy was. Like his son he was an orderly-minded man and he would want to feel his affairs were settled. Then, again Rosie should not have blurted it all out to Richard. He felt very troubled.

It was important to Jamie to have this physical space not only because he painted there but also for the chance to be alone, which was a rarity in his busy life.

He thought of how lucky he had been. He had a wife whom he loved deeply and who was the rock of his existence, a loving and talented family, a home where life and light, happiness and laughter were daily blessings and he earned his living in an immensely satisfying way from the land. Also Jamie's painting had developed from a boyhood hobby into almost a parallel career and provided not only artistic expression but also a useful source of additional income.

He had not had the chance yet to tell Rosie but the Edinburgh-based art gallery run by a friend of his who had already sold pictures for him wanted to put on an Exhibition of Jamie's paintings later that summer. At first he had rejected the idea having mostly sold his work locally but then reflected that farming produced a less reliable income now than in the past and as Henry McLucas had said:

'It really is time to have a big Douglas exhibition. I'm sure we'd sell a lot of pictures for you. There's a big demand for your style right now, it would be a shame not to cash in on it.' Henry might be an old-fashioned Edinburgh picture dealer but his commercial instincts were pretty accurate.

Initially Jamie had pushed the idea to the back of his mind but now it seemed like a great possibility. He had plenty of paintings already available, landscapes mostly, and there was time to do more. Rosie would be delighted and the challenge of another new project to add to the garden opening would be a welcome distraction to the family problems, which were looming up in the wake of his father's decision. Right, he would do it. With new energy and resolve he jumped to his feet and followed by the bounding dogs went out of the studio towards the river bank hoping to blow away the thick feeling in his head.

Edinburgh

The crescent of Georgian houses and flats called Moray Place in the Edinburgh New Town is one of the best addresses in Edinburgh. David McLean's double flat was in the centre, facing the immaculately kept communal gardens to the south with magnificent views of the firth of Forth and the Fife coast to the north. David was unmarried.

In contrast to the elegant surroundings, but with great style David had furnished the large double drawing room with a soft cream carpet, massive squashy white sofas at either side of the Adam fireplace and carefully placed low glass tables with two deep armchairs covered in coral providing a splash of colour. The coral colour was repeated in the ribbon bindings on the otherwise starkly white heavy curtains. Three large, modern and colourful landscapes were hung on the walls. David, who was a highly successful interior designer, and was unmarried, took a deep and sensuous satisfaction in the near-perfection of the room.

Through the folding double doors into the dining room the modern scheme continued with a glass dining table and surprisingly comfortable stainless steel chairs. Here the floor was of polished blonde wood and a large mirror over the built-in serving table reflected not only the dining room but also the drawing room.

The galley kitchen with its brushed stainless steel work surfaces continued the modern theme. It was here where Polly, still dressed in her chef's whites was putting away the last of the white china with gold rims and the hand-washed thin Rosenthal glasses which were too delicate even for the German-made built-in dishwasher to deal with.

David had loosened his tie and rolled up his sleeves. He came quietly into the kitchen and stood for a moment behind Polly. She didn't turn or move but was acutely aware of his presence. A shiver of excitement ran through her.

Very gently he laid his hands on her shoulders. She tensed. He dropped the lightest of kisses on the back of her neck. Heat spread through her whole body. Slowly he turned her towards him. This was crazy but she wanted him.

'No, David, please' she said, without conviction.

'You mean yes David, please,' he replied softly but insistently as he propelled her gently from the kitchen. In the hall he stopped and lifted her chin towards his face. The message in her eyes was unmistakable. David had come a long way from his council house roots in the notorious Craigmillar district of the city and the challenge of this cool, privately educated and, even better, married woman was proving irresistible.

'But not now, I smell of cooking' she protested, weakly. He laughed and said,

'You smell simply wonderful' and led her unprotesting up the staircase into his bedroom. Polly heard the door gently click behind them. The room was warm and softly lit. The floor was covered with the same deep cream carpet as the drawing room. The large bed was piled with white pique cotton pillows and a soft brown fur throw was folded across the bottom of it.

Polly stood, almost childlike, whilst David undressed her. He picked her up and laid her on the bed. Afterwards she couldn't remember him taking off his clothes but she would never forget the heat of his naked body against her as his hands and mouth moved urgently over her. She yielded willingly. He felt

triumphant, but also curiously tender towards her.

Fleetingly, she thought how different he felt from Richard

whose body was slim and boyish and whose lovemaking was

gentle and tender. David's chest was covered with crisply curling

dark hair; his limbs were muscular and very strong. He was

demanding, athletic and very passionate, urging her on to ever

deeper and wilder movements. She cried out and he smiled

exultantly at her response. She was his.

CHAPTER TWO

Whitewalls

Jamie took another log from the basket beside the drawing room
fireplace and threw it on to the dying embers. He had taken off
his shoes and his feet were resting on a tapestry-covered
footstool, one of his mother-in-law's creations. He and Rosie
were alone now.

Tim and Anne had departed to their cottage nearby and
Betty to her Pele Tower outside the Border town of Selkirk,
driving slightly unsteadily away. Roddy had taken Richard off to
the Stud to continue the conversation they had started before
dinner. Minty and John who demanded to see the foal, which
they had immediately christened 'Cinderella', had interrupted
them.

'So she can marry Prince Charming and have lots of baby
foals,' Minty had announced after they had duly inspected,
admired and sighed over the new arrival.

Richard had taken the Norfolk terriers with him so the twins would settle down to sleep. He would then put them into their shared basket in John and Minty's bedroom.

Rosie was stretched out on the sofa facing the fire. She also had kicked off her shoes and propped herself up with a collection of soft cushions.

'That was a good supper party, love' Jamie said, 'even the pheasant was edible and you know it's not my favourite.'

Rosie smiled. Jamie had never liked eating game, even though he was a good shot and had run the small shoot at Whitewalls for many years. She felt some response was needed and said, I know it's not a treat but in a casserole with wine and herbs it is a good supper dish ' Her voice trailed away. For once she couldn't care less about food or the success of her dinner party. She was tired and anxious. She turned to the subject really troubling her.

'Did you think Richard was quiet at supper?' she asked worriedly.

'Rosie, do stop. You're getting all worked up again about Dad and the Stud. Please don't. It will all turn out for the best, you'll see!'

'But what will Polly say when she finds out that Roddy has disinherited her in favour of Richard? It's all very well for you to say it will be 'for the best' I think she will be very upset.'

Seeing that his wife would not easily be placated Jamie went over to her and put his arm round Rosie's shoulders and hugged her. She could be very stubborn once she got an idea into her head.

'Come on,' he said, and taking her hands pulled her to her feet and into the familiar comfort of his tight, warm embrace.

'Let's go and give the dogs their night-time walk then I suggest we both go to bed together.' Now she smiled.

'I know, I'm just being silly like a mother hen!' Jamie just said   'Come on, let's go.'

He put the brass-rimmed guard in front of the fire and arm in arm they left the room.

Soon Heather and Tweed were watered and settled down for the night with biscuits to stave off any hunger pangs. They curled up together contentedly in the big basket at the side of the Aga. Dundee was out hunting for mice and shrews, which he regularly brought into the house, as his feline thinking demanded, to supplement the family diet. This was considered to be an endearing habit by all the family. Everyone, that is except Molly, who had been known to attack the cat surreptitiously with a broom when she thought no one, was looking. Empress fussily followed Rosie and Jamie upstairs to settle in her basket at the foot of the bed. When they reached the bedroom Jamie kissed Rosie and said, softly

'Are you very, very tired?' She smiled at him thinking how attractive he was still. Even after all their years together Rosie still desired her husband as much as he still wanted to make love to her.

'Not too tired. I think I need to have a bath, though, I'm sure I smell of cooking.' Probably she didn't but she was so attracted by the idea of a lovely scented bath.

'Why not have a bath. I'll come in too.'

Bathing together had been one of the early pleasures of their marriage, which they still enjoyed though less frequently. This invariably set the scene for making love.

The bath did not last for very long. Soon, with the curtains left unclosed and the moonlight shining through the open window they turned to each other with a sensuous passion and delight which would have surprised their family and friends had they ever dreamt that well into their fifties the initial surging, sexual need which had gripped them both at the start still remained so strong.

Later, as she drifted off to sleep Rosie heard Richard coming into the house. It was quite late. She hoped that things were sorted out with Roddy. Perhaps Richard would talk to Polly when she came down tomorrow. Snuggling closely to her husband Rosie relaxed into a deep and dreamless sleep.

Richard quietly let the two little dogs into the twins' bedroom. He saw they were both fast asleep. Minty, as usual, was lying neatly on her back in the centre of the bed. The patchwork quilt was still neatly folded back and her teddy bear, equally tidily, tucked in beside her. John, by contrast, could hardly be seen at all under the untidy heap of bedclothes, which had become loose and his teddy bear was perched precariously on top whilst John's right arm trailed down to the floor.

Resisting any attempt to straighten up his untidy son, which would possibly have woken him up, Richard lightly kissed his little daughter and briefly, affectionately patted John on the only visible part of him, the top of his tousled head. He plonked Pixie and Pod into the basket in the corner and they settled down happily enough. They were tired after not one but two long walks that day.

In Edinburgh the twins each had their own room but at Granny's they insisted on remaining together, enjoying their own special bond and the language of twins which, at 8 years old, still enabled them to slip into the magic world they inhabited almost at will, especially when they were at Whitewalls.

Richard looked at his watch. It was only just midnight. He felt wide-awake. If he drove quickly on the deserted roads back to Edinburgh he could be home with Polly just after one o'clock. Then he could try and explain to her the bombshell, which Roddy had dropped. They could drive back together in the morning and the worst would be over. He would leave a note for Rosie in the kitchen. The twins would be fine.

Once he had resolved to go back to Edinburgh, Richard lost no time. He ran quietly back downstairs to the kitchen and motioning to Heather and Tweed to stay quietly in their baskets he quickly wrote a note for Rosie and pinned it where she would see it in the middle of her message board.

'Five to twelve - have gone back to Edinburgh to talk to Polly about things; we'll both be back after breakfast! Hope you understand. Love R.'

Letting himself out equally silently Richard started the Volvo and went down the winding drive. Only then did he stop to think a little more rationally.

"Damn" he thought "she'll be tired out after cooking and probably in bed. I'd better call her so she won't be scared when I turn up."

He dialled the home number.

"Please leave messages for Richard and Polly Graham after the long tone." Where was she? He spoke to the answering machine.

'Hello, Poll, it's me. Look everything's all right but I'm on my way back. I'm on my own. I know it's late but I've something to tell you, something important. We'll talk about it and both come back to Whitewalls together, tomorrow. Lots of love.'

With that he drove as quickly as he could back to Edinburgh, to break the news to Polly. He had not paused to think a late-night homecoming might not provide the best atmosphere in which to discuss something as important as Roddy's bombshell decision. Sometimes, for a lawyer, Richard did not always think things through in his private life. This was in sharp contrast to the extremely careful and cautious approach that he brought to his profession. His character was one of contradiction and his careful Edinburgh upbringing often fought with a more unconventional way of looking at life. Richard was good at hiding this.

Edinburgh

Polly awoke with a start to find David once again lying on top of her. His knee was moving between her legs, parting them, his mouth caressing hers. She responded, quickly feeling a surge of renewed need. She caught his hand away briefly then tightened her arms around his neck.

Then she saw the time on the bedside clock and pushed him away from her.

'David, it's midnight. I have to go home.'

He pulled her back into his hot embrace.

'No you don't. Richard and the twins are safely in the Borders. You told me. Stay all night Pollyanna. I want you so much and I want to wake up with you beside me in the morning.' He was determined she should stay. He would make her stay.

'You don't understand. Richard's quite likely to phone me before he goes to sleep, or at least call first thing in the morning. He'll just get the answering machine and know that something's wrong. I must go!'

Switching on the soft white lights David looked intently at Polly, who by now had struggled into an upright position and swung her long bare legs over the side of the bed.

Not wanting to lose her by being too insistent David changed his mind, propped himself up on the pile of pillows and laughed indulgently,

'Alright, Pollyanna, this time I'll let you go. But you and I are going to see a lot more of each other.'

She felt relieved. Then turned and kissed him swiftly before hurrying into her clothes. He made no attempt to get out of bed, watching her until she was ready to leave.

'Will you be happy to drive home or shall I get a taxi organised and you can collect your car tomorrow?'

'David, I've no time to wait for a taxi. Besides I haven't had a drink apart from one glass of champagne. I have to go.'

He held her a moment longer, lifting her chin so she looked up at him.

'No regrets?' he asked softly.

'No regrets.' she replied and was gone.

It was a lovely moonlit night with, for once, an absence of the famous Edinburgh North East wind. She could smell the late-flowering narcissi in the gardens outside the flat. The street was quiet. As Polly climbed into her four-wheel drive Rav for the short drive home she felt a sense of unreality. It was as if her body belonged to someone else. What had she done? She brushed aside the thought. Richard wouldn't find out; where was the harm?

Richard had reached the Edinburgh City Bypass only a few miles from home. He was rehearsing how he was going to break the news to his wife that her grandfather intended to disinherit her in favour of him.

'So you see, Darling, it's keeping it all in the family and for the twins ...' - not convincing...'maybe 'Roddy thinks it would be too big a burden for you'... equally weak.

'Oh hell!' he said aloud. He'd just have to see what sort of mood Polly was in and proceed accordingly.

Meanwhile Polly parked the Rav in front of the darkened house. Not bothering to unpack her cooking things she ran up the path to the front door, unlocked it, dashed to unset the burglar alarm and went back into the hall. She saw the telephone answering machine blinking, showing there were 3 messages waiting.

"I'll listen tomorrow," she thought.

Not troubling to do more than lock the door and she made her way upstairs to the large bedroom, which she and Richard had decorated with such care and enthusiasm to recreate the country-house style of her childhood home.

The heavy curtains were still drawn back and the moonlight was streaming in through the windows. Polly closed them and went into the adjoining bathroom. She turned on the shower and stood under the strong hot jets, soaped herself vigorously with her favourite Floris Stephanotis soap and shampooed her short, curly blonde hair. Her body ached and she felt as if she were living in a dream. Had she really spent hectic passionate hours in David's bedroom making love with an intensity she had never experienced during the nine years of her marriage to Richard? Would she do it again? Yes she would.

She heard a noise downstairs. It sounded like the front door opening. Burglars didn't have keys, did they? Jumping from the shower a she hastily put on her pink towelling dressing gown. Her heart was beating rapidly as she crept from the bathroom, through the bedroom and to the landing outside. At that moment the hall light went on and she saw Richard.

Anger and guilt combined and she spoke very sharply,

'What the hell are you doing here Richard?' she demanded.

'Has something happened to the twins, or Ma and Pa, Betty, Roddy what's going on, you half scared me to death?'

'Darling, I'm sorry. I did ring and I left a message on the answering machine. Didn't you hear it?'

By this time, Polly had joined her husband in the oak-panelled hallway.

'Oh let's go into the kitchen and I'll make some tea.' she said regaining some of her composure then you can explain what's going on.'

When she switched on the light in the kitchen Richard saw her hair was wet.

'Polly, have you only just got back in - or did you fancy a late-night beauty session?' he asked in a singularly unsuccessful attempt to lighten the atmosphere.

They looked at each other. He sensed a coldness in her and something else that he could not quite work out.

'Richard, I've been out working, alright? I'm tired. I needed a shower. I know it's one o'clock in the morning - any objections'

'Sorry, ' he said, putting his arm round her very tense shoulders. He thought to himself "this cookery business is getting out of hand if it's making her so tired and jumpy!"

'I'll make us some tea and then if you're not too exhausted I'll tell you the news.'

So they sat in their "country kitchen" with its warm scarlet Aga whilst Richard told Polly about her grandfather's decision to make him heir to the Stud and Lodge House. He didn't do it very

well and Polly didn't help him. She heard him out in silence.
When he had finished she said

'Well, that's that. Grandpa is entitled to do what he wants
with his property. I can't think that Charles will be any more
pleased than I am.' Inside she felt furious though she was
determined not to show it.

This was not the kind of response Richard had expected.

'Darling, it won't make any difference to us now will it?'

She shrugged but her eyes were bright with anger and
unshed tears. He went to the other side of the kitchen table and
put his arm round Polly. She stiffened and brushed him away.

'Look, Richard. I'm tired out. You all seem to have
decided that this is alright, including Ma and Pa so I really don't
think there's any point in discussing it any more. I'm off to bed.'

She ran from the room, upstairs and hastily yanked back
the patchwork bed cover, pulled on her full-length white lawn
nightdress and got into bed, turned on Richard's brass bedside
light and immediately closed her eyes.

He soon joined her and tried again to take her in his arms, but she pretended to be asleep and he turned away. They lay back to back, each lost in their own troubled thoughts dozing until the early dawn light crept round the curtains. Then, at last they both slept.

Richard woke suddenly, with a start. Why wasn't he in his and Polly's cosy bedroom at Whitewalls? Then he remembered. Polly was still asleep with her head pushed into the pillows and her back still turned towards him. Quietly, so as not to disturb her, Richard slid out of bed went as silently as he could to go to the adjoining bathroom.

His head ached. The business yesterday had really got to him. Yes, he would love the Lodge and the Stud eventually but not if it was going to cause conflict and a rift with Polly. Her reaction had been inexplicable. Why had she not raged at him? It was so unlike her to take news like that with hardly a comment. He thought her family and its way of life meant everything to her. They would need to talk more. Maybe over breakfast? Richard believed he knew his wife inside out but this hardness was, different and he did not like it one little bit. He would need to think carefully what to do next.

He went downstairs. The house was quiet without the twins and their excitable little dogs. The kitchen clock showed it was half past seven. Too soon to phone his in-laws, though he knew Jamie would be up but was almost guaranteed to be out of the house with the dogs, round the farm or even in his studio. Perhaps a cup of tea would help to ease Polly into the day.

'Polly, wake up. I've brought you some tea.'

There was no response. Putting the pretty china mug carefully on the bedside table Richard gently stroked Polly's face. After what seemed ages she opened her eyes and looked sleepily, yet coldly at him.

'Thanks very much.' she said politely, formally as if to a hotel waiter. She felt awkward talking to her husband, the father of her children, the man she loved and had chosen to marry. It was like being polite to an acquaintance whom you weren't very sure about. Her feelings were, of course, compounded by the guilt beginning to creep in over the starting of her affaire with David.

'That's very kind of you.'

'Move up darling' Richard said and tried to put his arm round his wife's shoulders. She slid out of his tenuous grasp and dashed off to the bathroom. Polly was close to tears. Looking in the mirror she was sure she looked different - almost as if she had "adulteress" tattooed on her forehead. Don't be ridiculous, she told herself, no one need ever know and you don't have to do it again. She shivered although the room wasn't cold and thoughts of David, the greedy passion to which she had responded so willingly. Polly didn't know where it would lead but she knew she wanted to continue, to take risks to feel wanted, desirable and alive! She pulled herself together and splashing her face with cold water Polly returned to the bedroom to drink her tea and face her husband.

Whitewalls

John woke up first with Pixie and Pod on top of his bed and dive-bombing him. Although they were not barking, the little dogs clearly meant to get out of the bedroom to start their day.

Usually either Richard or Polly came into the children's room to wake them up and take the dogs out into the gardens for their first run of the day.

'Get off me you horrible little dogs,' he cried, 'go away, I'm asleep.'

That was a mistake. When they heard his voice the terriers became even more active yapping and bustling about. This roused Minty who sat up in bed - still as neat and composed as when she had gone to sleep the previous evening and she added her voice to that of her brother.

'Yes, do be quiet; you'll be let out very soon.' She looked at her watch with its brightly patterned dial. It was a new and prized possession.

'It's only seven o'clock. I expect Daddy's asleep and Mummy's still in Edinburgh'.

'I know,' said John, excitedly, 'let's take the dogs downstairs and let them out ourselves. Then we can make tea for Daddy and Granny and Grandpapa!'

'Don't be silly, Grandpapa will be up already. We'll just do it for Granny and Daddy' she said decisively. John was the noisier of the two but in her quiet way Minty was the leader and generally got her own way with her twin brother.

John, however, was in a hurry to put his plan into practice.

'Let's not get dressed. We'll just put on our dressing gowns and slippers and go!'

Minty smiled and got out of bed putting on her Winnie the Pooh dressing gown and slippers. With John dressed in his superman dressing gown and slippers they each paid the quickest of visits to the bathroom next door and tumbled downstairs accompanied by two excited terriers. Pod and Pixie bolted through the kitchen door and into the walled garden.

They made the tea with great enthusiasm and Minty insisted on setting two trays, one for Daddy and an extra-pretty one for Granny. With great care and some giggling the twins each took a tray upstairs. They came first to the double bedroom usually occupied by their parents. John opened the door after putting his tray on the floor to let Minty into the room with Richard's tea.

'Daddy, we've brought you some tea and we've let the dogs out ...' her voice trailed away uncertainly as she saw the bed was empty, with the quilt pulled up and the curtains still drawn across the window.   She felt a bit scared, where had he gone? John followed her into the room. He looked round and decided to take charge.

'He's been kidnapped' John announced importantly. 'There'll be a ransom note soon I expect.' "I'll have to be very brave and rescue him" he thought and tried not be scared at the prospect.

Minty was composed again and answered prosaically.

'Much more likely he's gone out to see the horses or with Grandpapa to the farm.'

'Let's go and see Granny,' she continued, 'She's sure to know.'

Rosie had not been awake for long. Jamie, as usual, was already out and about with the dogs, including, for once Empress though not Pixie and Pod as it was Richard's job to let them out. There was a brief rap on the bedroom door. It burst open and a very excited John dashed into the room followed by a quieter Minty who was carrying a tray on which were precariously balanced a china mug of very strong tea and a plate of Rich Tea biscuits.

'Granny, Daddy has disappeared. We think he has been kidnapped. We took him some tea, too, but he's not there.'

Rosie laughed.

'I expect he's gone out early, maybe he's with Grandpapa.'

'Well, his bed hasn't been slept in' said Minty as she gingerly set down the tray on the sofa at the foot of the bed.

'Where's Empress?' John asked. 'Perhaps she's been kidnapped too.'

'John, for goodness sake calm down. She went off with Grandpapa. Now it's very kind of you to bring tea for me. I'll drink it whilst you two go off and get yourselves washed and dressed. Where are Pixie and Pod? Not still in your room crossing their legs, I hope.'

'No, Granny' Minty replied, 'they've gone out into the walled garden, but we'll go and get them and give them their breakfast as soon as we're dressed. And, Granny, dogs don't cross their legs, they'd fall over.'

Rosie sighed and got out of bed. She would never drink such strong tea but it was sweet of the children to make it. Where on earth was Richard? He was not usually such an early riser. She had better get up and find out what was going on. Already she had the beginnings of a headache. There had been more of these recently.

As soon as she went into the kitchen Rosie saw Richard's note. A sense of foreboding filled her. What on earth had happened? Once she had read the note Rosie felt a little happier though she doubted if Polly would have welcomed the sudden arrival of her husband, late at night and with such momentous and controversial news. Richard could be impetuous at times. Rosie often wondered if his real nature was entirely suited to the Law. Maybe school, Edinburgh Academy, followed by Edinburgh

University had conditioned him and steered him into the legal profession without too much conscious deliberation.

His father worked in middle management in one of the city's large insurance companies and his mother an Edinburgh matron who did charity work and held "competitive" coffee mornings where the unwary newcomer, if admitted at all, would be quizzed on her children's school closely followed by her husband's career to ensure that she was "suitable".

Still, the important thing now was that Polly would be arriving later and they would make time to discuss the whole wretched issue in calm and considered fashion.

Perhaps she should telephone Polly and speak to her before she and Richard left Edinburgh. No, she thought, it would be easier to deal with the issue face to face. Rosie felt, and then quickly dismissed a feeling of apprehension, amounting almost to a fear of facing her daughter.

"It's just that you don't like rows and unpleasantness" she told herself "leave things to sort themselves out."

Then John and Minty came running downstairs again, carrying their riding helmets. Jamie came in from outside, leaving his muddy black Wellington boots in the small lobby and padding into the kitchen in his stocking feet. Pod and Pixie, still wriggling and barking with excitement closely followed him.

'Is Daddy with you, Grandpapa? If he isn't we think he's been kidnapped!' cried John.

'What's all this about?' asked Roddy. 'I haven't seen him yet this morning. Maybe he's still in bed, worn out I shouldn't wonder by you two!'

"No, no he isn't' Minty said 'we took tea for him, and he wasn't there and I don't think he went to bed at all last night.'

Rosie had not really been listening to the twins burbling but when she heard Minty's last comment she said, sharply for her,

'Now please stop this nonsense. Daddy went back to Edinburgh late last night after the rest of us had gone to bed. He wanted to see Mummy and they're both coming down after breakfast, so don't keep going on about it.'

There was a small shocked silence. Rosie **never** raised her voice or shouted at **anybody.** Not that she had shouted but this wasn't like Granny. With a small tremble in his voice John said with an attempt at bravado, though he actually felt quite scared,

'I suppose that means no ransom note either...' "This isn't very exciting after all" he thought, suddenly worried.

Seeing his wife's stony expression Jamie jumped in.

'Who wants a bacon roll?' This diverted the twins who at once set about getting plates and knives and their own mugs. Minty went over to her Granny who was busy writing another list and gave her a sympathetic hug! Rosie felt a rush of love towards her grandchildren and smiled at the solemn little girl.

'Minty, while we're having breakfast let's make a plan for today.'

'Well, we're riding Butterball and Snowball this morning' John announced 'those ponies are getting **far too fat.'** Now it was Jamie's turn to smile at his grandson.

76

'Indeed they are, John. They need a lot of work; but take it slowly and warm them up properly before you go galloping.'

Whilst the twins were tucking in to their bacon rolls, Rosie nibbled a piece of brown toast and planned the day. She turned to Minty with what she hoped was a reassuring smile.

'I have to go to Great Grannie Betty's later this morning to collect a painting for your mummy to take into Edinburgh to the picture framers. Do you want to come with me?' Rosie thought that it was important to keep Minty busy so she would not be too upset at the non-appearance of her mother.

'Oh yes, please' replied Minty at once. She loved the old tower house with its funny shaped rooms, one of top of the other. Especially she loved the room at the very top with the chests of dressing up clothes. John was less keen. This was all girls' stuff and boring.

'I would rather like to stay here or go to Great Grandpapa and help with the horses' he replied. That seemed to him a much better idea.

This did not suit Rosie's plan. She wanted Polly and Richard to go and see Roddy together and John would be a distraction. Jamie came to the rescue.

'Well in that case would you like to come with me to the pond after your ride and we'll fish for trout? I think Granny would like to have some to cook for supper this evening.'

'Oh, yes please,' cried John. He was an obliging little boy and it was easy to generate his enthusiasm. Fishing, he thought, was nearly as good as helping with the horses.

As they were finishing breakfast the telephone rang. Jamie was nearest and picked it up. His voice was even and calm.

'Oh sorry to hear that, Richard. Are you going to stay there with her? We can cope perfectly well with the twins.'

There was a pause whilst he listened during which Rosie got up and gesticulated to him to hand her the telephone. He frowned and shook his head.

'She doesn't want to speak to either of us at present. Alright, Richard. We'll see you later. It will just be boys for lunch. Rosie is taking Minty off to her mother and you'll find

Jamie and me fishing in the trout pond. The children are both
going for a ride before that.'

'Jamie, what is going on?' cried Rosie. She was bursting
with impatience.

'I wanted to speak to both of them.' She added sharply.

'What's the matter, Granny, you look cross again.' said
Minty worriedly.

'Is there something wrong with Mummy, is she ill?'

Rosie replied sounding much calmer than she felt.

'No darling, Mummy is fine. She's just very tired and
wants to have a rest today. She might come down tomorrow.'

Before anything else could be said Jamie asserted himself.
He wanted everyone to calm down. Things would sort
themselves out, they always did.

'Come on you two. Let's clear away the breakfast things
and get those ponies ready.'

The breakfast dishes were quickly loaded into the
dishwasher and, happy for the moment, the twins scampered off,

followed by the two terriers. Jamie gave Rosie a quick hug and said,

    'I'll explain later.' With that she had to be satisfied, though she was far from content.

Chapter 3

Edinburgh

It was quiet when Richard had gone. The morning sun was streaming in to the kitchen through the open window and the cuckoo clock , a souvenir from a Swiss skiing holiday in Wengen, ticked fussily. Polly sat, still wearing her pink dressing gown at the kitchen table, nursing a rapidly cooling mug of China tea.

'Damn' she said out loud and banged the mug down on the pine table. Running her hands through her short blond, curly hair she said it again, three times,

"Damn, damn, damn.' Why hadn't she just agreed to go to Whitewalls with Richard? It was, after all, hardly her fault Grandpapa had thought up this weird plan to leave everything to Richard. In fact, the more she thought about it the more convinced she was that her grandfather was acting from the purest of motives. He probably realised that Richard had always felt at a little inadequate because of his lack of land or capital.

Richard's parents were from Edinburgh's middle-class. They were respectable, professional people but without inherited wealth or property. Richard was making his own way in his chosen profession and working hard to give Polly and their children the kind of life he believed they deserved.

Last night with David had been unplanned on her part, which did not mean totally unexpected. She had known for some time that he was attracted to her, both physically and mentally. Sex with him had been amazing to her, exciting, tumultuous and overwhelming. David was a very different kind of man to Richard. He was self-educated, certainly self-made and had a strong and dominating personality. In spite of that, she felt he understood her. Polly had a need to explore other worlds and conventions that were different from the assured, gentle ways of the country-loving Douglas family.

Sometimes she envied her parents. They loved and cherished each other. Their lives were busy and fulfilled. Always, it seemed to her, they dovetailed in whatever they thought, believed or did. Polly was, of course, too young, too sheltered and in spite of marriage and motherhood too inexperienced in life to realise that only the patina of years of loving compromise had led Rosie and Jamie to their present state of "oneness".

Her reverie was interrupted by the intrusive sound of the telephone. Automatically she reached behind her to the dresser and lifted the phone from its base.

'Well, Pollyanna. I hope you're feeling good. You were so wonderful last night I wanted to speak to you before you went off to play happy families in Peeblesshire.'

All at once she wanted, no needed, to see him. David knew that she was not a flighty daughter, or unreasonable wife, or even simply loving mother. With him she felt that she was herself, pretty, fun, exciting and sexy. Before she could help it Polly said,

'David, I'm so glad you 'phoned. I've decided to stay in town this weekend. I need some space, time to myself.'

There was the briefest of pauses whilst David quickly mentally re-arranged his weekend plans. Golf with Bob this afternoon could easily be postponed. Annabel would just have to accept that an important business deal required his attention so dinner this evening would not be possible after all. This was too good a chance to miss. Polly intrigued him; he wanted more of her, and here she was offering herself. He quickly made up his mind.

'Clever girl' he said warmly 'but would you be able to spare a little of your space for me?'

She hesitated for only a moment.

'Yes, yes of course, lovely, when? What shall we do?'

He knew perfectly well what they would do, but he replied,

'I've got an old fisherman's cottage, right on the shore at Burnmouth. I'd love you to see it and it's going to be sunny today so it would be a perfect time. I'll pick you up around 12 o'clock.'

She thought quickly. Polly didn't want her friend and neighbour Caroline to see her going off in David's Porsche.

'No, no I'll come round to you. I can park easily enough outside. Polly could picture him smiling a touch sardonically.

'Whatever you say, Pollyanna. See you at noon.' He had gone.

As soon as she had replaced the phone, doubts started to flood her mind.

What the hell did she think she was doing? Think of the children, think of Richard. If only he'd insisted on staying with her in Edinburgh. Without the twins they would have had time for themselves. Time to talk to each other, to go out for lunch, to make love without being hurried or, as was frequently the case, just too tired to make love at all. But no. He obviously thought she was being unreasonable and he could hardly wait to leave for Whitewalls.

Sometimes she felt it was as if the Douglas's were his family and not hers. Then she thought - what about her mother? Rosie was clever, so capable, and so always right. She would be horrified if she knew what Polly had done and was about to do again. Well, she was 33 and quite old enough to make her own decisions, to know her own mind, to live her own life. And that was exactly what she was going to do.

She felt a rush of excitement and anticipation. What should she wear? A fisherman's cottage he'd said. Trousers and a loose tunic would be alright. Lace underwear? Polly thought she had a lacey black set, somewhere. Usually she wore M & S white cotton but today was different. She was going to meet her lover. Dismissing any lingering doubts she left the kitchen and ran upstairs to get ready.

Whitewalls

'Granny, why were you so cross this morning? Was it something I did, or John did, or was it mummy? You're hardly **ever** cross.'

Minty had thought hard about asking this question ever since breakfast that morning. Now she and Rosie were driving along in the Ford estate car which was the family's runabout on their way towards Selkirk and Pathhead Tower where Betty lived alone except for the Emperor who was the father of Empress, Rosie's Pekinese dog. Rosie smiled lovingly at her serious little granddaughter.

'No of course not, it was just Granny getting all fussed and bothered. Mummy was working last night and she's a bit tired so she didn't want to come today. I had hoped she was coming with you and me to see Great Grannie Betty. I'm sorry if I upset you. Can we forget all that and just have a happy visit?'

Minty was a forgiving child and understood that disappointment could make you cross. Besides, she loved Great Grannie's funny old house with just one room on each floor. It was like a fairy castle and there was always something interesting to do there, either inside or out of doors in the funny old walled garden with its swing on the oak tree and little wooden house in the far corner.

'Yes Granny and you're not cross now. little bit. Anyway, I love Great Grannie's. Will I be able to paint today do you think?' Rosie smiled. Minty was a delight as a granddaughter. She was orderly, sweet natured and altogether a very satisfying child to be with. Not like her mother, was Rosie's uncharitable thought.

'I expect so. You can do that whilst we have a good natter in the kitchen then we'll all have lunch together.'

They travelled in quiet harmony along the almost deserted country road with the car windows half open to let in the soft spring air and Classic FM playing quietly on the car radio.

The journey was soon over. Rosie drew up on the semi-circle of gravel in front of the oak door set low in the curved front wall of the ground floor of the grey stone Pele tower.

Before either Rosie or Minty could get out of the car, Betty rushed towards them, arms outstretched.

'Darlings, how lovely to see you? But where is Polly? I've pictures for her to take back to Edinburgh for framing and I want her to do some nibbles for me for my Bridge evening next week.' Without pausing for an answer she opened the door again and Emperor, strolled out in a dignified manner as befitted his advancing years.

Minty loved the little dog and immediately wrapped him in a tight embrace, which he suffered with as much patience as he could.

Rosie eventually managed to say,

'Well Polly's still in Edinburgh. She was working yesterday evening and decided to stay in Edinburgh and have what she calls "some space" so she's not coming until tomorrow.' Betty arched her eyebrows and seeing Minty looking questioningly, by common consent they dropped the topic and went through the front door and into the tower, with Minty and Emperor following closely.

The door opened straight into the tiny panelled hall with an open archway into the old-fashioned kitchen beyond. Masses of late daffodils were displayed in a huge copper vase set on the carved chest which also served as a hall table and repository for keys, dog leads, letters waiting to be taken to the post, pruning secateurs and gardening gloves, just discarded.

'Would you like to come into the kitchen for juice, Minty?' Betty asked.

'Yes please, Great Grannie, then can I go up to the studio and do some drawing and painting?'

89

'Of course you may, Darling. In fact, take some juice up with you and then Granny and I can have a good natter whilst we organise lunch.' Betty was still unsure about telling Rosie of the legal complication that had been brought about by Alistair's sudden interest in Whitewalls after all these years.

Soon Minty was at the top of the Tower in the attic room. It had windows on all sides which enabled the light to flood in, making it a perfect place for Betty to paint her colourful and very lush paintings as well as work at the tapestry and exquisite embroidery she also produced.

To Minty it was a place of delight, beauty and mystery. It was tidy enough to be inviting but with lots of low level cupboards crammed with lengths of fabric, hats, clothes of all ages, old dolls and ostrich feathers and boxes of old costume jewellery. There were so many possibilities for creating and making all kinds of things.

There was a trestle table with paints, brushes and pencils neatly set out on the top. A small easel, bought specially for Minty's use, was placed by one of the windows with her proper artist's smock made for her by Betty, hanging from one corner of the easel.

What should she do today, Minty wondered? She still felt a little bit anxious about her Mummy and although Granny and Great Grannie had tried to pretend nothing was wrong it felt all funny, somehow. Giving herself a little shake Minty pulled open the nearest cupboard and found an old-fashioned toy monkey sitting amongst a pile of brightly coloured pieces of silk and satin. She pulled the monkey out and sat it on top of the low cupboard on a piece of bright red satin.

Yes, that's what she would do; make a picture of a happy little monkey. It would be a present for Mummy and was bound to cheer her up; maybe make her laugh. She would draw his outline first then colour him with her Caran D'Ache chalks. Feeling happier and humming a little tune to herself Minty set to work.

Over mugs of peppermint tea in the kitchen Rosie and Betty had been discussing the vexing situation that had arisen because of Roddy's seemingly quixotic wish to leave his property and business to Richard. Betty had decided, for now, not to say

anything to Rosie about Alistair.

'The maddening thing is' concluded Rosie 'so far I haven't

even been able to speak to Polly about it. She hasn't come down

from Edinburgh this morning and wouldn't even speak to me on

the 'phone.' Even to her own ears Rosie sounded petulant and

unreasonable.

Betty looked at her daughter quizzically before replying.

She knew Rosie loved order and harmony to permeate everything

in her life. That much she admitted. What Rosie was less willing

to face if, indeed, she was aware of it, was the fact that if anything

got in the way, she was not simply irritated but capable of being

highly manipulative until she got what she wanted.

'Try not to worry too much. I know Polly is your

cherished daughter and you want everything to go so well for her,

but she's also a grown woman, with a husband and children of her

own. You simply can't go on wanting to solve all her problems

for her as if she were still at school!' Rosie knew she meant

well, but being spoken to by her mother like this made it worse not better. It sounded as if she thought Rosie was a child to be

humoured.

Tears pricked Rosie's eyes and her bottom lip trembled.

She replied defiantly,

'Of course I know Polly is grown up but that doesn't stop

me wanting the best for her, and for Richard and the twins, and

for Charles too just as I always believed you did for me.' She

sounded very hurt. She was very hurt. Betty got up and gave

Rosie an affectionate hug.

'Darling, you were born sensible, I never had a moment's

worry about you and it looks as if Minty is the same, but Polly

has inherited some of mine and your father's wildness of spirit.

'Anyway,' she continued,' why not wait until you see Polly then

you can find out for yourself at first hand how she feels.'

'You're right' Rosie conceded, a little stiffly and she did

not respond to her mother's affectionate overture.

'Now, can I help with lunch?' She could not bear to go on

with the conversation any longer.

'I've made a quiche and salad and I thought we'd have some early new potatoes from the garden. They're just about ready. In fact why don't you take a trug and see what you can get. They'll still be tiny but I love the taste, don't you?'

"Oh dear," Betty thought "she may seem calm on the surface but she does fret and she does like her own way!"

Rosie was dispatched to the small vegetable garden outside the kitchen and given a few minutes to compose herself. As her Granny went out into the garden Minty reappeared in the kitchen carefully carrying a sheet of cartridge paper and her empty glass.

'Look Great Grannie, I'm really pleased with this,' she said seriously, putting the picture of the little monkey down on the kitchen table.

She had captured its slightly mournful expression, with a hint of merriment in the eyes and the little scarlet jacket and the silk on which she arranged him gave a jaunty air to the simple but lively picture. Betty thought – "It has a touch of magic about it. This was done with a lot of love."

'It's for mummy,' she explained 'she's very tired and I thought it would cheer her up.'

'Minty, it's really very good. I'm sure she will love it. Why don't I get it framed with my pictures? Granny is taking them to Edinburgh for me. Then it will be a really good surprise present and mummy can put it up on the wall?'

'Oh, can us. I'd like that and I am sure mummy would as well.'

Rosie returned with her haul of tiny new potatoes, feeling more relaxed.

'What a lovely picture, Minty.' It really was very good. She was again filled with a surge of love for her granddaughter.

'And Great Grannie is going to have him framed for me to give to mummy as a present to cheer her up.' Rosie's eyes were bright but she just smiled and said

'What a good idea. Now how about lunch? I, for one am hungry.'

East Lothian

Polly had been very quiet during the 30 mile journey through the lush countryside of East Lothian, south east of Edinburgh, and across to the coast road. David had been delighted to see her but apart from a brief kiss on her cheek and the lightest of touches as he helped her into the low-slung Porsche they had been oddly shy with each other.

Soft, classical music was playing on the car's CD stereo system and Polly visibly relaxed as they sped through the golfing Mecca of Gullane and the lovely old village of Direleton with its ruined castle and famous Open Arms hotel and restaurant. She did not ask where they were going. However, she tingled now with excitement. 'Happy?' David enquired. She smiled at him.

'Yes, yes, though I can't quite believe I'm doing this.' His tone was gentle and tender as he replied,

'Pollyanna, with me you never have to do anything, and I mean anything, that you don't want to do. I'm really looking forward to showing you my hideaway. We'll have lunch, a walk on the beach and then, we'll see what happens.'

Polly felt a delicious shuddering feeling of excitement, expectation, and anticipation. She placed her hand gently on his taut, firm thigh and said,

'Oh, why not. I need a little more excitement in my life and you're the right man at the right time!' David simply smiled.

Soon they had reached the county boundary with Berwickshire. David turned the car off the main road, which rose, above the cliffs and drove down a narrow twisting track leading to the sea. Then to Polly's surprise the powerful car slid through a small dark tunnel on to a perfect, tiny hidden cove.

In front of them was a sturdy single storey cottage covered in white-painted harling, which sparkled in the sunshine. There was a powerboat secured at the side of the cottage and a paved area was next to it for the car. Polly gasped.

'David, it's lovely. It really is a secret cottage. You would never know it was here would you?'

'Romantic enough for you, Pollyanna?' he asked.

'Oh yes, yes.' She turned and kissed him hard on the lips. Briefly he returned her kiss then said.

'Come on, let's unpack the car and open up the cottage. I'll show you everything.'

David unlocked the solid oak door, which led into the open living space to let Polly go in front of him.

'Oh, David this is lovely 'she exclaimed. The walls were simply painted white with small seascapes painted in oils arranged on them. The floor was covered in deep blue sisal and the wood-burning stove was situated in the centre of the room. There were windows to the south and the north so the interior was flooded with a clear bright light. Two large squashy sofas, covered in blue and red checked fabric, provided comfortable seating. An oak table placed under the north window served as a desk. Bookshelves lined the walls and the curtains were made of dark blue mattress ticking lined with white linen.

A narrow galley kitchen with blonde wood and stainless steel fittings took up one wall of the room. The staircase of natural wood, fashioned like a ship's ladder climbed invitingly before disappearing on to a small landing with a porthole window looking out to sea.

She half-turned towards him. David immediately dropped the picnic basket, which he had carried from the car on to the small dining table and fiercely took Polly into his arms. Feeling an urgent and immediate need for him she wound her arms around David's neck and kissed him, hard. He needed no further encouragement.

'I think, Pollyanna,' he said softly but insistently 'that lunch and everything else can wait whilst I show you the bedroom.'

Leading her up the steep staircase with its white rope bannister and into the bedroom he flung open the small window, letting in the sounds and smells of the sea. With the minimum of preliminaries he pushed her onto the bed, piled high with white linen pillows and covered by a goose down duvet.

As he undressed her he laughed, triumphantly.

'Well, well, Miss Pollyanna. What's this? Black lace, very sexy, quite delicious in fact, but I think we'll take it off.'

Polly could find, and needed no words. Her need of him
was compelling. It was overwhelming and filled her entire being.

Years later she would have complete recall of that
afternoon. The intensive, savage lovemaking; the sea breeze
coming through the open window; the smell of their mingled
sweat and passion and the sheer joy of giving herself completely,
lustfully and without reserve to a man she barely knew but who
she felt she had known for ever. Every sound, every sense was
heightened. Climax followed climax. She cried out as they
roared away on a racing tide that neither of them even pretended
to try and control. Their cries mingled with those of the wheeling
seagulls on the beach outside. She was totally happy.

Chapter 4

Whitewalls

John was feeling pleased with himself. He had caught his first trout in Grandpa's Trout Pool. Taking Grandpa's advice he had used a juicy worm as bait and it had done the trick. The fish was big enough to be cooked. He was going to ask Granny or Mummy if she turned up, to cook it for his supper.

The morning had been fun. For a start there had been no women around making a fuss. Even so this weekend felt funny. His father had disappeared in the night - and John was far from sure that he **really** had gone home. If that were true why hadn't Mummy come back with him? It made him feel a bit achey and anxious. Catching his fish though, kind of made up for it.

'Come on John stop day dreaming' said Richard. 'Let's walk back to the house, clean your fish and put it in the fridge.' Then Grandpa and I are going to make lunch and you can help us. What shall we have?'

Well, that at least was easy.

'Sausages and baked beans, please. That's my very favourite food, except for fish of course,' he added sturdily, if not entirely truthfully. So with that decided, the three generations of Douglas males made their way to the kitchen.

The trout was quickly cleaned and put on a plate, covered in cling film and left in the fridge for later.

Soon the sausages were sizzling in a big pan on the Aga and John was given the job of stirring the pan full of baked beans.

Richard's mind was racing. Should he go back to Edinburgh to try to talk to Polly again? Or would it be better to give her some space? Then he felt angry. Roddy meant so well but seemed unaware of the problems his generosity was causing. It was even beginning to threaten Richard's marriage. He was aware of his father-in-law speaking to him.

'Hey, Richard, come back. I said would you like to go pigeon shooting in the bottom wood this afternoon? We can take the dogs with us and John can look after them and pick up for us. What do you say?'

Mentally, Richard shook himself.

'Sorry, yes, yes that would be great' he replied rejecting the idea of going back to Edinburgh to confront Polly again. He would have to choose the right time. Perhaps he should take her out for dinner? On the other hand if there was going to be a scene it would be better to be in private.

'At least if that is what you'd like to do, John?' Richard turned to his son who was looking at him anxiously.

'Yes, Dad if that's what you'd like to do as well.' Then all in a rush, John added

'I would like to see Mummy, though. It doesn't feel right that we're all here and she's on her own in Edinburgh. I hope she's not lonely.'

Jamie thought he had better take a hand in the conversation. He smiled at his grandson, and ruffled John's fair hair affectionately.

'Sometimes, John, it's best to leave women to their own devices. You'll see her again tomorrow so let's attack this lunch then we can get back outside.'

Cheered by the comforting food, surreptitiously feeding Pod and Pixie with little bits of sausages under the table and feeling quite manly John soon cheered up.

Pathhead

Rosie and Minty were driving back to Whitewalls. It had been a happy visit for Minty and she was particularly pleased with her drawing of the monkey. She hoped it would make Mummy happy.

Now she had shared with her mother her fears and concerns about Polly and Richard, Rosie felt more settled in her mind. She hadn't realised quite how much she still expected to be involved in Polly's life decisions. What she had fondly believed was a loving mother's interest could, she now saw, be interpreted as interference, even a direct attempt to control Polly, her feelings, her emotions, her career, and her life!

All at once, it was important to see Polly and try to tell her this. She thought rapidly. What excuse could she find for going to Edinburgh, right now? Yes, of course, the pictures, which had to be framed. Antonio, the framer used by both Betty and Jamie, lived above the shop in Edinburgh's New Town and he wouldn't mind a bit having a visit from her on a Saturday afternoon, especially if it meant business and a mild flirtation with Rosie. She knew he admired her.

Then they could call casually at Murrayfield Gardens and hopefully see Polly. Rosie thought she could have a chat and take her back with them to Whitewalls for the rest of the weekend. Or perhaps it would be better to telephone Polly first?

'Minty' she asked 'would you like to take your monkey picture right now to Antonio to be framed then we can go and see if Mummy wants to come back with us?'

'Yes what a good idea. Maybe Antonio could even frame it right away and then I don't need to wait before I give it to her.'

'That's settled then. We'll call home on the mobile and tell the men what we're doing.'

Rosie had been a reluctant convert to the benefits of a mobile phone and she still found it something of a novelty. She carefully pulled in to the next lay-by, took the phone out of her capacious bag and dialled her daughter's number.

There was no reply and the answering machine was not switched on.

'Bother', said Rosie your mummy must have popped out to do some shopping and forgotten to put on the answerphone. Let's still go to Edinburgh and after we've been to Antonio's we'll go and see her.'

'Alright, Granny, but please don't be cross again, will you?' It was very important that Granny didn't get cross and make her feel all achey and upset. Rosie smiled at the anxious little face looking up at her.

'Of course not. Now I'll just telephone Grandpapa and tell him about our plans.'

This time she got a recorded message of Jamie's voice asking the caller to please phone later. It was, in truth, something of a relief, as she didn't really want to have to justify herself to Jamie, so she just said

'Minty and I are on our way to Edinburgh to take some of my mother's pictures to Antonio to be framed. One of Minty's too, of a monkey, for Polly. Oh, and we might call in at Murrayfield Gardens, byeee.' That done they were once again on their way

It was a very pleasant late spring afternoon and the drive to Edinburgh was easily accomplished. Rosie did not really care for driving in the city but calmed by talking with her mother, Minty's presence and the fact that she was *doing* something instead of awaiting events gave her a purposeful feeling. The fact that, once again, she was interfering in Polly's life and overturning a decision made very forcibly by her daughter did not even occur to her.

Antonio d'Ambrosio - his real name - lived in a tiny mews house at the western edge of Edinburgh's Georgian New Town. He lived with his long-term partner in a chaotic and colourful flat above his workshop, which he had made from the garage that would normally have occupied the ground floor. He had come from Italy as a small boy with his parents and was now part of the thriving Scottish/Italian community.

Rosie managed to park the car and with Minty jumping up and down excitedly at her heels she rang the doorbell and spoke into the entry phone.

'Antonio, hello, it's Rosie Douglas. I'm sorry to disturb you I've brought some of my mother's paintings to be framed.'

'It is no disturbance, it is a great delight' replied Antonio in a warm caressing Italian voice which was so perfectly genuine it might have been a parody.

'Please come upstairs. Leave your paintings on the table in the 'all way and I will see to them later.'

The door swung open and the two went inside. Minty scampered excitedly up the steep metal spiral staircase. Rosie put down the paintings on the gilded hall table and followed rather more sedately. She always felt that there was something slightly risqué about visiting Antonio. He had a way of making her feel very attractive and desirable.

Antonio's sitting room was a warm, untidy place with pictures covering almost the whole surface of every wall. Low sofas with bright kelim rugs flung over them added to the colourful comfort. Roberto, the African grey parrot, sat contentedly on his perch near the window and squawked excitedly, "Ecce, bonjour, good morning, pretty, pretty girl" as Rosie and Minty were swept into the room by Antonio with another of his 'larger than life' embraces.

In fact, Antonio despite being gay and settled with his partner of over twenty years, George, had always felt a tendresse for Rosie with her tall, elegant looks, warm smile and sweet personality. He wished that Jamie would paint a nude of his wife and give it to him to frame! This was unlikely as Jamie Douglas's talents were painting exquisitely executed watercolours of Border scenes. Antonio secretly thought these a little dull. Lady Betty's paintings on the other hand were modern, strong, vibrant and highly contemporary coming from the easel of such an elderly artist. He liked them very much.

'Mr Antonio' asked Minty, politely and solemnly 'do you think you might have a frame that would fit my monkey picture I've just done for my mummy?' Antonio smiled, ruffled her hair and said

'Just one momento little lady. Let us give your beautiful Grandmama a glass of wine or some espresso then we will see what can be found.'

Rosie smiled warmly. She liked Antonio and adored his harmless flirtation, although something had made her careful never to mention it to Jamie. She feared, somehow, that he would not have been amused. Because she was driving Rosie opted for espresso and Antonio quickly made this in his smart Italian machine in the tiny galley kitchen just off the sitting room. Minty happily settled for lemon squash and quickly unrolled her monkey picture.

Do you like it, Antonio? She asked anxiously, 'Please say you do! 'He smiled broadly at the solemn little girl.

It is beautiful Araminta, and yes in a momento we will find a pretty little frame for it. It is a beautiful present for your lovely mama and it will make her and you very happy. Come, let us spend no more time, we will find it now.'

Rosie was enjoying her coffee and relaxing in the comfort of one of the cream squashy sofas. She trusted Antonio completely and readily waved them off to find the picture frame in the downstairs workshop.

The afternoon was warm and Rosie felt a little sleepy. She put down her coffee cup on one of the marble tables; settled back into a cushion for a moment, then fell sound asleep.

After what seemed like a few seconds she was awakened by Minty gently shaking her shoulder.

'Wake up Granny; it's time to go and give my picture to Mummy.'

'I wasn't asleep,' cried Rosie, 'just resting my eyes.'

Antonio was just behind Minty.

'Dear lady, I think you have regrettably to leave, Miss Araminta is determined to give her beautiful monkey picture to her Mama.' Antonio had found a pretty gilt frame for the lively study of the monkey and the finished result was very attractive.

Rosie yawned and rather reluctantly pulled herself up from the soft depths of the sofa. She clasped both of Antonio's outstretched hands in hers. He drew her into a bear hug before kissing her enthusiastically three times.

'Good-bye my dear, dear lady Rose. Promise you will come back to see me very soon. Your mother's paintings will be ready next Friday. Collect them yourself if you can.'

Minty was becoming more and more impatient and said,

'Oh come on Granny. I want to go. I need to go now.'

With that they were soon on their way downstairs and out into the street still accompanied by the extravagantly-gestured Italian.

Rosie didn't really like driving in Edinburgh these days.

Ever since the Council had made Princes Street one-way the

New Town traffic had increased enormously. So she cut

through the back streets and mews until she came to Moray

Place.

'Look, Granny. There's mummy's car, parked over there.'

Minty cried. 'I wonder where she is.'

Startled, Rosie slowed down to look thus attracting

angry horn tooting from the man following far too closely

for comfort in his BMW sports car. Flustered she drove on,

not sure whether or not Minty had made a mistake. She

hadn't done.

I know,' said Rosie 'let's still go to your house and

see if mummy's there. If she is perhaps we can persuade

her to come back to Whitewalls with us this afternoon.

That might not have been hers; there are so many 4 wheel

drive vehicles in Edinburgh now.'

They pulled up outside the well-kept stone terraced

house that Richard and Polly had made into such a warm

and welcoming family home. Today it looked deserted and somehow forlorn.

Minty jumped out of the car and raced up the narrow paved path to the front door and eagerly rang the bell. She so wanted to see mummy and to give her the picture. Rosie locked the car and followed more slowly. The ringing bell simply echoed in the empty house. No-one came to the door. Minty looked very crestfallen.

'Shall we wait, just a bit?' she asked.

'I don't think so,' replied Rosie, troubled by the whiteness of Minty's face and the slight tremble at the corner of her mouth. Damn Polly, she thought savagely. Why did she always have to put herself first? She was obviously out shopping in town or having coffee and gossiping with a girl friend. 'I really must talk to her and try to put a stop to this selfishness', she thought.

'I'll tell you what we'll do. Let's go back to Whitewalls and we'll get chocolate ice creams in Peebles on the way.'

'That will be lovely Granny' replied Minty trying to sound enthusiastic, 'but I do hope that mummy is alright.' Minty felt that she wanted to cry, though she did not know why.

So, thought Rosie a little grimly, so do I. Impulsively she scribbled a short note on a scrap of paper and put it through the letterbox. Then they left.

Edinburgh

As the Porsche sped effortlessly back to Edinburgh Polly lay back in the soft leather seat and stretched luxuriously. She was sated with love-making, sea air, wine and the picnic of smoked salmon sandwiches, ripe brie and grapes which they had eventually eaten outside on the little deck in front of the cottage.

David had wanted her to stay overnight with him at the beach cottage, but summoning up a small atom of common-sense Polly had refused the tempting offer.

'David, there's nothing I'd like better but I daren't. I must be home at some point this evening in case the family 'phones.' She couldn't bring herself to say, 'in case

Richard phones.' He didn't argue. He simply said smilingly

'whatever you say' and teased and cuddled her as together

they packed up the picnic things which didn't take long. A

last lingering kiss and they had soon been on their way.

As they neared Edinburgh David asked lightly,

'Will you at least let me take you out for dinner

this evening, Pollyanna?' She would love to do that, but did

she dare? Filled with her new-found recklessness she

responded.

'David, that would be lovely, but where could we

go that we wouldn't bump into anyone we know?'

'Leave that to me, my darling. I know the exact

place.'

'Where? Do tell me.'

'No, it will be a surprise and very discreet.' With

that she had to be satisfied. David drove up to her vehicle still

parked in Moray Place. Was it only 6 hours ago? And she hadn't even got a parking ticket. It seemed like forever. Polly felt that she had known David all her life.

He knew his feelings were becoming dangerously involved. This was a new situation for him. In some circles in and around Edinburgh he had a reputation of brief sexual relationships after which the girls or women were quickly dropped.

'I will come and collect you in about two hours. Eight o'clock alright?' Polly then felt a little afraid.

'It would be better if I got a taxi and met you.' David paused - it might be better to be a little discreet at this stage. There was no point in inviting the complication of being seen by nosy neighbours.

'Maybe you're right. Meet me at the Witchery restaurant by the Castle at 8.30, get a taxi I'll be waiting.' Then, careless of who saw them he kissed her warmly and still heady with passion she returned his kiss before climbing into the Rav for the short trip to Murrayfield Gardens and her family home.

Polly drove into the Gardens just after her mother and Minty had gone. Letting herself into the empty house she failed to see the scrap of paper with the scribbled message and went straight into the kitchen the make herself a cup of tea. She still tingled with heady excitement. Why shouldn't she have a little fling? What possible harm could it do? Just a dinner in a restaurant that she and Richard had never visited. Then, maybe just one more wonderful sensual experience with David before she took herself back into the real world. Also it would be a kind of revenge. If her family thought that she was flighty, well she would prove them right; even though they would never find out. She had better ring Whitewalls though. That would stop anyone calling her whilst she was out.

She dialled the familiar number and it rang for a long time. A wave of doubt assailed her as she pictured the big, yet cosy kitchen, the slightly shabby yet comfortable sitting room and the lovely gardens. She asked herself, was she putting more at risk than she could possibly gain for carrying on the relationship with David. Polly wished she knew.

A breathless Richard answered the call eventually and his voice broke into her reverie.

'Hello, Whitewalls' he sounded very proprietary.

'Richard, it's me!' She felt a pang of guilt. Richard, after all, had done nothing wrong. It wasn't as if any of this was planned. Things were just getting more and more complicated. She felt both excited and out of control; like a different person, almost.

'Oh, love. Are you alright? We're all missing you. John caught a trout in the pool and wants to have it cooked for supper. Minty's gone to Edinburgh with your mother to the picture framer, Antonio, or something like that. She's apparently got a surprise for you. Shall I come in and collect you? It's not late and then we could all have supper together. You and I could go and talk to your grandfather....' That was a mistake. Polly felt herself going cooler and answered,

'No, Richard. I'm fine. Just tired (that much was true). I need a little time on my own. Maybe I'll drive down tomorrow for lunch.'

'Do you want to speak to John? 'Before she could answer her excited little son's voice came on the telephone.

'Mum, it was brilliant fishing. I caught a trout and we're going to cook it for supper. Grand papa's out with the dogs and Minty and Granny aren't back yet so it's just Dad and me. We're going off to check on the ponies. I wish you were here too. When are you coming?' John was thinking to himself "Mummy must come, mummy must come!"

Before she could stop herself, Polly had made a commitment to go to Whitewalls in time for the traditional Sunday lunch, which was so much a part of Rosie's weekend.

'So, I'll see you all tomorrow, be good for Dad. Give everyone love and a kiss from me. Good-bye.' She hung up to avoid having to speak again to Richard. For his part he looked at his small son who was jumping up and down chanting.

'Mum's coming tomorrow, Mum's coming tomorrow.' He felt a surge of anger followed quickly by a barely recognised feeling of fear. He wanted to speak to Polly again, but he wasn't going to beg. Best to leave her be. At least she'd agreed to join the family tomorrow.

Polly wondered what to wear to go out to dinner. Her usual family life and cooking jobs did not require a glamorous wardrobe and she knew that the Witchery was one of Edinburgh's smartest restaurants, although she had never been there.

Riffling through her wardrobe she came across a deep turquoise blue short shift dress. It had been an impulse buy from the elegant up-market Jane Davidson's fashion salon at the famous half price sale but somehow she had never found the right occasion to wear it. Yes, perfect, with black strappy sandals and her good pearls.

Her heart still hammering with fear and excitement Polly decided to take a long aromatherapy bath. Relaxed by this, she dressed in her chosen outfit and decided that the effect was both glamorous and flattering. With renewed confidence she flung a light pashmina shawl over her shoulders and went downstairs to the waiting taxi.

The street was quiet and she was sure no one saw her as she left.

David had been busy. He had telephoned his old friend James Thomson and reserved a discreetly placed table for dinner in the magical Secret Garden restaurant at the Witchery close by Edinburgh Castle. It had a wall of glass doors and a terrace planted with foliage plants of clipped box, bay and hostas as well as ornamental laurels and a large multi-stemmed white birch.

In spite of being offered a "salon privee" in the turret David felt that they could risk the candlelit Secret Garden. Besides he was unsure if Polly was yet ready to spend an entire night with him. He didn't want to alarm or pressurise her. David knew how to wait. He had had a lot of practice. When he had decided to reinvent himself and get away from his sordid family roots he had made a long and careful study of how the middle and upper classes behaved. Shrewdly he had decided not to try and be a lawyer or accountant but instead used his artistic talents to carve a niche in the still acceptable world of interior design. Thus he knew most of the upmarket restaurant and hotel proprietors not only in Edinburgh but also in other desirable locations in Scotland. It was all a long way from his now totally obliterated roots.

He was there before Polly. David had organised a single long-stemmed pale pink rose to be placed for her on their table with a bottle of Mumm champagne cooling in the ice bucket. It might be clichéd but perfect for the romantic dinner that he had planned. He wondered fleetingly what his single mother, Marie, who had struggled to bring him up alone on one of Edinburgh's less salubrious Council estates would think if she could see him now. David had no idea what had happened to her. She could be dead from her drug habit for all he knew. He was alone in the world, without commitments and that was how he wanted things to stay. Until now.

James Thomson, the owner, greeted Polly as she arrived, putting her at ease with his elegant courtly manner.

'You must be David's guest,' he said as he escorted her through the courtyard still lit by the silvery spring north light and into the Secret Garden where David was waiting.

'How did you know?' asked Polly curiously. Flattered by the attention.

'He told me you were beautiful.' James replied. 'The rest was easy.'

David rose to greet her, smiling broadly.

'Thanks, James' he said, "this is wonderful. My lovely friend and I have a lot to talk about so we really appreciate the privacy. James smilingly opened and poured the champagne.

'I'll come back in a little while when you're ready to order. In the meantime, do enjoy the champagne.' With that he discreetly withdrew.

'You look stunning,' said David softly.

She laughed. 'Thank you'. She was happy.

'Don't be so surprised" she added teasingly ' I don't *live* in chef's whites and jeans, you know.'

'In fact, you scrub up wonderfully' he replied in the same light vein.

'Now, serious business, what would you like to eat?'

Polly was ravenous but equally would have eaten anything, or nothing. In the end they decided on the simplest of food, seared King Scallops to start, followed by rare fillet steaks. The decision to continue drinking champagne with their meal was easily reached.

They were wonderfully relaxed in each other's company and talked easily about David's business and golf. He promised to give her lessons. David talked to her about the hotels where he had designed the interiors, exotic locations abroad that he had visited, though she had not. Polly felt confident enough to be light-hearted about her family and the many traditions begun at Whitewalls and continued into her own married life.

All the while, though, there was a strong undercurrent of desire between them. By 11 o'clock they were ready to leave.

A taxi was quickly organised and they stepped outside the old restaurant into the blue night. As the taxi drew up David asked,

'Will you come home with me?' He was pretty

sure that she would agree.

Impulsively Polly replied,

'No, you with me.' I want you to be there, in my life, in

my bed, if only for tonight.'

'Are you sure?' he asked thinking this was an exciting

development.

'Yes, yes, I'm very sure.'

In what seemed only minutes they were on the other side of

the city and the taxi pulled up in Murrayfield.

This was the defining moment. David paid the driver and

they stood close together at the gate.

'Well, Pollyanna, are we going inside?' he asked.

He felt the timing was perfect. There was no husband,

children or other family to occupy her mind and thoughts.

Also he was curious to be with her in her own home. With

hardly a pause she replied

'Yes, yes I told you. That's what I want.'

Once inside the house Polly ignored the winking light of the answering machine and led David into the kitchen switching on the concealed lighting as she did so. He looked around and gently teased her.

'Very country living Pollyanna, very nice, tasteful.' It was very much as he had expected and not really his style, though he recognized that she had tried to recreate her own childhood home, whether consciously or not.

'Coffee?' she asked, feeling a little awkward now that her lover was here, in her own family kitchen.

'You' he replied. That was the end of the conversation and coffee was forgotten.

Not very long after that as she cried out in an ecstasy of passion, unbidden and most unwelcome a mental picture of her twins came into her mind - Minty so neat and solemn, John with his clothes untidy and his bright little face full of eagerness for life and questions about it. She faltered only momentarily as David rose beneath her, pulled her down again into him and was then carried away in a tide of unashamed abandon.

The telephone rang, unanswered, and ignored. The answering machine clicked on. Rosie didn't leave a message but felt a chill in the cosy warmth of her sitting room. She couldn't shake off a vague but deep feeling of unease. Mentally giving herself a shake she called to Empress for a last walk in the garden before they joined Jamie and turned in for the night.

The Haute Savoie

France

Madeleine was not happy. On the surface her plans were working out well. Although Sir Alistair was 30 years her senior he was still very good looking in a patrician way, with luxuriant silver hair, worn a little too long and a lithe figure that still radiated energy and purpose. Her considerable sexual needs were augmented elsewhere although Alistair was surprisingly sexually active.

She had made sure that they were legally married and that she was Lady Bruce by right, which made her also, she believed. Chatelaine of Chateau Belle Haute. Alistair had told her that he had purchased the Chateau and accompanying vineyard from the Leseure family. In fact, he was only a tenant on a favourable lease, which included the proviso that the vineyard was managed and that the château bottled wine was produced to the same high standards on which the Leseure's had built a formidable reputation. They had returned to the south of France because Michelle Leseure's health problems demanded an all-year round softer climate than that of the haute Savoie, where although the summers were long and hot, winters could be very cold, wet and snowy.

Alistair and Madeleine had met in the Rialto Casino in Nice. She had been a croupier, still glamorous but mature enough to have sufficient experience to be trusted by management and to be able to judge the clients. Alistair had been staying, as was increasingly his habit, with friends who had a house in Nice with a very nice motor boat to go with it. The Kerr-Perkins liked Alistair. He was witty, urbane, Scottish and slightly mysterious. He flirted elegantly with Susan Kerr-Perkins and drank whisky late into the night with her husband Andrew, saving them both from the tedium of having to spend evenings together trying to find something to talk about. Alistair gave the impression of being a man of means, but this was very far from the truth. Whilst he had retained a sizeable fortune following his divorce from Betty all those years ago, losses at Lloyds as well as some investments that had not yet paid off, meant that at the beginning of 2007 he was financially in pretty dire straits.

It had been a stroke of luck that the Leseure's' had wanted a good tenant to take over running the vineyard and to live and look after the chateau. Madeleine had been determined to marry him but he hadn't fought very hard against the idea. He knew that he was getting older and he thought, cynically, a younger wife would be an insurance against a lonely old age.

'Darling' said Madeleine over their breakfast of croissants and strong coffee on a fine late spring morning,' When shall we go to Scotland to your lovely house in the Borders?' He frowned. Now he regretted ever having told her anything about his former life. In particular he regretted getting carried away and telling her about Whitewalls and giving her the impression that he still owned the house and land.

'My dearest, we can't leave the vineyard right now. It is too difficult to get away for long enough to make it a worthwhile trip.'

'Pouf' she replied, 'Hubert and Michel can manage the work in the vineyard and Hortense will look after the chateau.' Alistair would not change his mind.

'Perhaps in the summer, my darling' he said, kissing her hand in the extravagant manner he knew she enjoyed. 'In the meantime we have to make quite sure the shoots growing on the old wood are carefully taken off, then the grass needs to be dealt with and the branches tied into place. This does all require very careful supervision. Hubert needs me to be here to give direction and support him.'

'Cherie, Hubert has been here for years. He can do all of that. You only pretend to be in charge, as you well know.'

He had to placate her, quickly.

'Darling we can't get away for long enough now. But if you are bored, why don't we take the TGV from Chambery and have a couple of days in Paris? We could stay with Lionel and Lucy Chambers. I have a standing invitation and I am sure that they would like you.'

He crossed his fingers as he said this, because he was far from that this would be the case but it was worth a try. She pouted, which was not particularly attractive with her mature features but he could see that she liked the idea.

'M'mm, maybe.' But could we not stay in a nice hotel? Why must we stay with your stuffy friends?'

Unable to bring himself to tell the truth, that he couldn't afford it, Alistair kissed his wife warmly, and said,

'It's much more fun to stay with friends, besides, I   want to show you off!'

Somewhat mollified by this statement she briefly hugged him and said,

'Well, I must go and look at my wardrobe. I am not sure that I have suitable clothes for Paris. Though it might be more fun to wait until we are there before I do any serious shopping.'

He breathed a sigh of relief and vowed to ensure that she was far too busy in Paris to have time for clothes shopping.

"That was tricky" Alistair admitted to himself but he thought, on balance "you handled that pretty well, old boy. Still need to pursue old Christian in Edinburgh for a spot of legal advice. Maybe he could get Whitewalls back for me, somehow?"

Throughout his long and colourful life, including during his marriage to Betty, Alistair had always operated on the basis that something, or someone, would turn up to get him out of sticky corners. So far, something, or someone, had always done so.

Still he waited until Madeleine had left in the Renault Clio run-about to go to Chambery, just in case she could find any clothes there that would be remotely suitable for Paris, before he picked up the phone.

When he had finished talking to his Edinburgh lawyer he put down the phone with a very pleased expression on his face! It seemed that there was just a possibility that certain matters had been overlooked in that long-ago settlement following his divorce from Betty. Even better, the errors may have been down to Betty's own lawyer.

Madeleine turned up the radio as she sped down the mountain road with its hairpin bends and stunning views. She paid scant attention to the spectacular scenery. Madeleine had other things on her mind. Not only did the prospect of a trip to Paris cheer her even, even though they would be staying with dreary friends of Alistair's, but she was also going to meet Michel in Chambery. Alistair thought that she gone shopping but she had an altogether more exciting activity in mind.

Chapter 5

London

Charles whistled happily as he bounded along the narrow mews street behind the Godolphin Theatre. He wasn't sure that he really understood the play in which he had just watched Maggie perform for the fourth time. There seemed to be a lot of standing or sitting and lying around doing what his Army background would dismiss as "navel gazing". In fact, he thought it was positively bad for people to keep delving in to their pasts. After all, he reasoned, you can never change anything once it's happened; you just have to get on with it. Still he didn't have anything like that to contend with right now and he had more pressing matters on his mind. He was not an imaginative man, rather straightforward and engaging in his dealings with others. Yet he had real determination when necessary. This was one of the reasons he was successful and popular in his army career.

Charles supposed that he was a bit of a stick-in-the mud but life didn't seem that complicated to him. He had enjoyed a trouble free boyhood in the Borders of Scotland growing up in the family home at Whitewalls on the Tweed and attending Fettes School in Edinburgh as a weekly boarder. His decision to make a career in the Army had been reached very easily. He had been an enthusiastic participant in the Officers' Training Corps at the Fettes and had done well. Also, his grandfather had been a solider and there was something satisfying about continuing a family tradition.

He had met Maggie quite by chance at a huge cocktail party given by his Colonel. She had arrived with someone else and left with Charles. In the following three months he had become absolutely besotted by her.

In fact, he intended to ask her to marry him. Once she'd agreed, he planned to take her to Whitewalls to meet his family. He was sure that they would love her. Charles didn't give any thought as to whether or not she would love them. Everyone loved his family. They especially loved his mother, Rosie, and he was sure she would approve of Maggie.

Maggie was feeling drained after her performance and really was dying to get back to her tiny mews home, have some warm milk with honey and hot buttered toast before going to bed. This was not an easy play and required a great deal of effort from her, leaving her feeling very tired. But Charles was coming to take her to Umberto's for supper and had said to her earlier that day on the phone that he had something very special to discuss with her.

Charles hand closed round the small green velvet box in his pocket as he entered the tiny cramped and starkly lit dressing room. He kissed Maggie and hugged her tightly.

'Come on Maggie. I'm taking you out to Umberto's for supper, hurry up and get ready will you?' He was used to giving orders and thought nothing of treating her a little like a junior officer. She gave him a big wide smile, her green eyes lighting up with tenderness at his sheer exuberance and energy coupled with rather endearing bossiness. Soon they were seated opposite each other in the small, softly lit restaurant sipping champagne.

'This is a celebration' Charles had explained when Maggie had shown surprise at the sight of the bottle chilling in its ice bucket with a white napkin folded round the neck. Umberto himself had opened the bottle and taken their order for a plate of antipasti to share, followed by spaghetti Carabonara and a simple green salad. Energised by the champagne Maggie felt happy to be with her handsome Army officer.

Maggie was not quite sure why she loved him, or, indeed, even if she did love Charles. It wasn't that he was particularly handsome, although his pleasing features and dark hair were very attractive. Certainly he was intelligent, though not brilliant and neither was he wealthy – unlike some of her previous boyfriends.

She loved the way his dark hair persisted in sticking up at the front despite his best efforts at slicking it down with Trumper's hair oil. He had soft brown eyes and the loveliest smile as his mouth turned up at the corners. Charles was handsome in a wholesome and unaffected fashion. The Army had not diminished his boyish enthusiasm for life. Indeed, he was very popular with his fellow-officers and men for that very reason.

'I want you to come to Scotland with me to meet my folks.' Charles announced as they forked up the appetising spaghetti.

'Oh Charles, when? The play has another month to run and I really can't get away until June at the earliest' she replied, not sure whether or not she really wanted to get so deeply involved yet. She knew that he was serious about her; even loved her. But did she really want the level of commitment it seemed he was seeking? Maggie's career was taking off and his Army commission still had three years to run. Ideally, she thought, it would be better to wait a while. Then again, really good, genuine and sexy men were pretty thin on the ground. She didn't want to lose him. With that thought in her mind Maggie had resolved to let the relationship develop. Besides he was a very good lover. He was both passionate and considerate. This again was one of his great attractions.

'Perfect' he replied. 'I'll give Ma a call and we'll have a long weekend. I think you'll get on fine with my parents and you'll meet Polly and Richard as well as Minty and John, the twins, to say nothing of Granny Betty. Then there's my grandfather, Roddy - he's not married to Granny Betty, she's divorced and my other grandfather lives in France. Grandfather Roddy's wife, my grandmother Lorna died ages ago.

'Stop, stop' she replied laughingly, 'you're making me dizzy but yes, yes I'd like that.'

His hand once more closed on the box. Should he give it to her now? What if she turned him down? That would be awful and so public, too, even though the restaurant was now almost empty. After refilling their coffee cups Umberto and his staff were bustling about with the kind of activities used by tactful restauranteurs to hint to lingering clients that they wanted to go home. Perhaps he should wait, go a little more slowly. She'd agreed to go to Scotland. Maybe he could propose to her there. It was only a couple of months away.

They decided to walk the short distance to Maggie's house. The cool spring night air revived them both and Maggie felt the now familiar tingle of sexual excitement as he put his arm around he shoulders. They paused only long enough to open the front door, which was midnight blue and flanked on either side by two bay trees in tubs, which were painted black and white.

In the tiny upstairs sitting room, Maggie drew the heavy cream curtains, and switched on the gold coloured lamps on either side of the fireplace. She threw her lavender pashmina wrap over the back of one of the two toffee coloured leather sofas and flung herself into its squashy depths, holding her arms out to Charles as she did so. She was filled with a surge of sexual energy. She couldn't wait. A delighted Charles joyfully responded to this highly charged mood.

Afterwards, wearing white towelling dressing gowns and sipping glasses of fine brandy from wafer thin balloon glasses Charles decided to take the plunge.

'Maggie, darling'

'Yes, Tiger.'

'I love you.' She responded happily

'I love you, too.'

'Will you marry me?' There he'd done it, he thought, actually said the words, proposed to Maggie.

She sat up realising he was serious.

'Darling, darling Charles. It's too soon. We haven't really known each other long enough. There are our careers to think about, my next job, the film, and your promotion...'

He stilled her voice with a gentle and loving kiss.

'But do you love me?' he asked anxiously.

They were now both serious, sitting side-by-side still but looking rather solemnly at each other.

'Yes, I love you, Charles, but could you please give me a little more time to give you an answer?'

He was momentarily very disappointed. Then his natural optimism reasserted itself. Of course she needed more time. He didn't know her family although he knew that both her parents had died in a car accident. Indeed he had not even met any of her friends. She hadn't met his parents. She didn't know Scotland. Charles had been brought up in the tradition, which believed families were important. He had a set of beliefs that meant people did not simply exist as individual human beings, but as part of a clan. You didn't live your life in isolation from your roots. Charles did not think all this with any degree of consciousness. It was just bred into his bones. This was how life was meant to be lived.

'Will you give me an answer when we are in Scotland?' He gently stroked her face. Her eyes filled with happy tears. If she turned him down now he would be hurt, but she would be in danger of losing someone who was becoming more and more essential to her very being.

'Yes, Charles, yes I will.' With that he had to be content. Later, sleeping in his arms she cried out,

'Please, please, no.' but she didn't wake and he held her close to him in the dark with the sounds of London, which never seems to sleep, seeping in through the heavy blinds and curtains, the distant rumble of traffic, even on a Sunday morning, and later the chattering of starlings at first light. Then Charles, too, slept.

Sunday dawned. It was a lovely spring morning. There was hardly any breeze and the sun shone down, weakly but it was welcome for all that. The traffic noise, too, had quietened and there was a peaceful air around the mews.

Maggie was awake first, and gingerly pulling herself into a seated position leaned back against the pillows with their white linen embroidered pillow cases 'inherited' from her French grandmother who had also bought for her the elegant bureau desk which was at the far side of the small bedroom.

Maggie's grandmother was a woman ahead of her time and determined to ensure that her granddaughter had sufficient independence not to have to rely on either a man or a job, and had a house of her own to give her the extra security that comes with owning property. This had become even more important after the sudden death of her parents, who had not been wealthy. In some ways Maggie had still not come to terms with the savage car crash that had robbed her of both her parents, long before their reasonably 'appointed time'. The gift of her own house had provided, and continued to provide some much-needed security.

She slid out of bed and stretched luxuriously. A whole day off. She loved acting but it drained her and the present play with its small cast was more demanding than most. Also she was playing the part of a woman some ten years older than she was which called for a good deal of thought and forceful projection on stage. Now, though, she had a day to herself to enjoy with Charles. He was sleeping still. One sun tanned well-muscled arm was flung across the pile of pillows and he was wearing a positively beatific expression on his face.

Quietly she went downstairs to the kitchen that had been made from the original garage. It was fitted with very modern granite-topped units, an expensive wooden block floor and bright yellow blinds at the window concealing the view of the brick wall outside but letting in the light, too. She put two croissants into the small oven to warm, started to percolate the Blue Mountain coffee which they both loved and poured two large glasses of fresh orange juice from the glass jug kept in the 'fridge.

Maggie was no cook and the smart 'fridge was almost empty but she did enjoy the best quality in everything - whether food and drink, clothes or men.

She loaded the warm croissants, unsalted butter, apricot jam, juice and coffee on to a tray and climbed the stairs back to the bedroom.

Charles was now awake, sitting up in bed and looking very pleased with himself. He had decided that Maggie's plea for time before she gave an answer to his proposal meant that she would probably say yes at the end of the day. Also it gave both of them more time to find out about the other areas of each other's lives. He was sure that his family would immediately welcome Maggie and warm to her lively, outgoing personality. Particularly he was certain that Rosie would love her. Charles truly valued his mother's opinion. As for Maggie's family, he knew both her parents had been tragically killed in a car accident. Her grandparents who lived in Yorkshire were really her only close family. He wanted very much to meet them and convince them that he was right for Maggie.

His musings stopped as the subject of them came through the door, carrying a laden breakfast tray. Oblivious of his nakedness he jumped out of bed and seized the tray, putting it on the small pale grey sofa at the foot of the bed, took her in his arms and gave her an enthusiastic hug and kiss. She responded briefly and warmly before pushing him laughingly away.

'You taste of toothpaste.' she said 'Come and have breakfast.'

Later, whilst Charles was out buying the Sunday papers Maggie had a long soak in a lavender-scented bath and thought about his proposal of marriage. She did love him and found him very exciting sexually but it really was too soon to tie herself down. Apart from anything else Maggie was quite sure that she was not cut out to be an Army wife. All the petty regulations and snobbish protocols would drive her scatty. She really believed she had acting talent and it was almost her duty to pursue this.

Also, what about her career? This evening, though she hadn't yet told Charles, they had been invited to a drinks party at the home of Roland Mackintosh, the film producer. He would be involved with her first film due to be shot at High Wynch Park in the Cotswolds. Maggie had a small, but important role in it that would hopefully lead on to greater things. She had worked hard to achieve some measure of success in her acting career that she could not envisage giving it all up to be an Army wife, no matter how much she loved Charles. But that was for the future and today was for living in the moment.

After a leisurely day of reading the Sunday papers, eating scrambled egg and smoked salmon for lunch, swiftly followed by more lovemaking they decided a walk along the Thames would be the very thing to blow away any cobwebs in advance of the drinks party at Roland's flat which, now she had told him about it, Charles was dreading. Confident and affable in familiar surroundings, whether at home in Scotland or in the camaraderie of the Army barracks he was much more shy when it came to meeting and mixing with people who had very different life styles to his own.

But Maggie was so excited about the party and people who would be there he knew he would make a supreme effort to exert his charm on them for her sake.

Later after yet more lovemaking they shared a somewhat cramped bath in the tiny mirrored bathroom.

'M'mm, pity we have to go to Roland's party' Maggie murmured as Charles gently soaped her shoulders."

'Yes, let's not go, let's stay here and make love instead.' he replied. Maggie   smiled but she was determined.

'I have to be there. Roland's is going to introduce me to Piers Romayne who, hopefully, will be directing me in "Country Pursuits." In fact, she was quite shocked that he could even consider for a moment not going to the party. Then, how could he really understand the importance of networking and of being seen in the acting business?

They left the house at 6 o'clock by taxi to cover the short distance to Roland's fashionable loft apartment. Maggie was wearing a slender pale green linen shift dress with an amber necklace and earrings given to her by Charles. She looked stunning.

It was already a noisy party by the time they arrived. Maggie immediately assumed her luvvy personality and dived in to the smartly dressed throng. She was soon deep in animated conversation with a snake-hipped saturnine looking man with a deep suntan and a wearing a pale pink linen shirt with immaculate chinos. His brown leather Gucci loafers were so highly polished that they gleamed. Charles disliked him on sight.

Charles moved away but he was too late. Maggie called to him.

'Darling, Charles come and meet Piers Romayne, he's going to be directing 'Country Pursuits' and there's almost certainly a part for me in it. It's going to be filmed on location at a place in Gloucestershire called High Wynch Park.'

At this Charles did a double take. Ignoring Romayne's proffered hand he said with genuine surprise,

'That's my Uncle Hugh's place. This must be his latest business venture - hiring it for making films. What a coincidence.'

'Maggie' drawled Romayne 'you simply *must introduce* me properly to this gorgeous hunky man.' Relief. He was clearly gay, thought Charles. No threat at all. It was a stupid name, made up no doubt, he thought. So he gave the other man a bone-crushing handshake and said heartily,

'Good to meet you. So you're bringing my lovely girl to the big screen. Splendid.'

Maggie looked startled. Even to his own ears Charles sounded totally false. In a more normal tone of voice, he added,

'Let me get us some drinks.' He quickly found his way back to the bar at the end of the large open space which was rapidly filling up with exotic-looking creatures of both sexes.

Just as Charles decided that he really had had enough, did not want another drink and was trying to signal to Maggie they should leave, he spotted a tall, flamboyant figure at the far side of the now very crowded room. Hugh had the same tightly curled hair as his sister, Rosie, but where her features were fine, even delicate, his were florid and fleshy. There was no mistaking the family resemblance, though. As brother and sister they were not especially close. Rosie loved Hugh but found his wife, Virginia, pretentious and difficult. As well, the distance separating the Scottish Border and Gloucestershire meant that they did not meet very often. In the early days Rosie had really made an effort to get to know Virginia well and to make a relationship with her sister-in-law but as time had passed she had more or less given up. This was particularly so as Virginia was very self-centered and all of the contact seemed to have been from Rosie towards her with little coming back in return.

Charles was fond of his uncle who always seemed to have some new business idea on the go and was rarely downhearted for long even when, as was usual, the fortune to be made never materialised. Letting out High Wynch Park, a grand Cotswold stone pile encompassing both Elizabethan and much later Victorian embellishments, to film companies was clearly the latest one. Spotting Charles, Hugh elbowed his way towards his nephew.

'Good God old boy. What are you doing here, wouldn't have thought you'd be involved with the film industry. Aren't they all nancy boys? I wouldn't have thought that's your style,' he boomed as he reached Charles's side. At the same moment Maggie, having caught

Charles's previous signal that he wanted to leave appeared in front of them. Warmly shaking Hugh's outstretched hand Charles put his arm round Maggie's shoulder.

'Uncle Hugh is Maggie. She's a very special girl and a talented actress. In fact, she is going to be in the film that's being made at your place.'

'Well, I'll be damned' exclaimed Hugh and immediately turned his attention and his well-mannered charm on Maggie.

'My dear' he murmured dramatically lowering his voice 'you are so beautiful, how did my nephew capture you?' She laughed,

'Charles and I met at an Army cocktail party and just decided we rather liked each other.'

'She's coming to Scotland in July to meet the folks, but you've stolen a march already. If this film comes off you may find me a frequent visitor to High Wynch during filming.'

'Delighted dear boy. Now must dash, meeting your Aunt Virginia for an early dinner and I'll get my head in my hands if I'm late. Keep in touch.' With that, after kissing Maggie and shaking hands with Charles he powered his way to the door and was gone. Long ago Hugh had adopted a very hearty "Hail fellow well met" persona to cover his basic shyness and feelings of inferiority that his formidable parents, Sir Alistair and Lady Betty had unwittingly instilled in to him. Even Rosie, his sister, was frighteningly competent. As for his wife, Virginia, he sometimes wondered why the hell he had married her, except that she reminded him of a pretty young matron at his prep school.

After saying a swift goodbye and thanks for a lovely party to Romayne, Charles and Maggie quickly followed.

Blinking as they left the dimly lit apartment they emerged into the evening sunshine

'Food?' enquired Charles.

'Oh yes, let's go to Ping Ho's for Dim Sum.' They both loved the Chinese custom of eating little dishes, accompanied by cups of fragrant Chinese tea served in small, delicately transparent cups.

Ping Ho's had become a favourite haunt and was in easy walking distance so they were soon seated with an almost exclusively Chinese clientele using their chop sticks to eat the delicate and flavoursome morsels, Schu Mai, little pork dumplings, tiny succulent ribs, spring rolls and delicious King Prawns with intensely spiced dips.

'What an amazing coincidence your uncle being at Romayne's party' said Maggie, pausing between mouthfuls for a moment.

'Hugh's always got some new business ploy on the go. I don't know why he didn't think of this earlier. Perhaps he didn't believe there would be enough money in it. But maybe the time is right now. What do you think, Maggie?'

'Mmm,' Maggie mused. You could be right.
There's been a lot going on in the British film industry
recently, using all kinds of settings. I mean, Alnwick Castle
was used for part of the Harry Potter films and Manderston
in Berwickshire is always being used for filming, as well as
Batscombe Park. So I think it is a great idea."

'Anyway, I hope you get the part so I'll be able to
come and stay over when you're on location' he added
enthusiastically.

'That will be lovely,' she said vaguely, not really
wanting the distraction of Charles around when she was
making her first film. He was so thrilled at the prospect
though, that she did not want to dampen his enthusiasm.

Eventually they were both full, Charles paid the
bill and they left arm in arm to stroll back to the cosy mews
house and a night of lovemaking.

Later that evening after Maggie had gone to sleep
Charles telephoned his mother. He knew that Rosie and
Jamie did not go to bed early and though it was almost

eleven o'clock he thought they would still be up. Besides he

couldn't wait to tell them the good news about Maggie and

the summer visit.

Chapter 6

Whitewalls

Rosie put the phone down in the kitchen. She glanced at the clock. It was just after 11 30 in the evening. Speaking to Charles always left her feeling good. They did not see nearly enough of him now he was in the Army. Still she was very proud of him and knew that both Jamie and his grandfather, Roddy, shared this feeling. A tiny frown creased her unlined forehead as she thought of the row brewing over Roddy's will but she resolutely pushed away the thought.

Rosie smiled to herself, for what seemed to be the first time since breakfast. Richard had finally managed to speak to Polly. He had not spoken about the content of the conversation but he had clearly been displeased that Polly was staying in Edinburgh for the day and not coming to lunch after all. The children had been very disappointed and upset. It had been a fretful day.

John had appeared to be more accepting of the fact that his mother would not be joining them. After riding his pony he had happily gone over to Roddy's to help in the stables. Minty, however, was very quiet and whilst Rosie was preparing the traditional Sunday lunch she sat quietly at the kitchen table trying to draw a picture of Dundee, slumbering and snoring in his usual manner in the basket in front of the Aga.

'Granny, have I done something to upset Mummy? I really wanted to see her and to give her the monkey picture. I was *sure* she would come today.' Rose turned her attention away from cutting carrots into neat batons and gave Minty a fierce hug.

'No, Minty, Mummy is just very tired and is having a rest at home. You'll be going back with Daddy this evening' she had added 'and you can give Mummy the picture then. I know she'll love it.'

With that reassurance Minty had cheered up and decided to take Pod and Pixie out into the garden and walk to the wicket gate to meet her father and brother who were due back from the stables with the big dogs.

Soon after lunch Jamie had disappeared into his studio, ostensibly to paint, but also for a snooze.

Unable to settle even to gardening, Rosie had gathered up Tweed and Heather, leaving an indignant Empress to languish in the sitting room and taken the lively Labradors for a good long walk along the river bank. This had restored some of her natural optimism and left her pleasantly, physically tired. As she had walked and enjoyed the clear Spring air, she had pushed to the back of her mind the deep unease she felt about Polly and Richard, which, she knew went far deeper than the latest spat over Roddy's Will.

It had, for once, been with a sense of relief she had waved the family off at three o'clock and had gone to her bedroom, taking Empress with her for an unusual rest away from everyone and everything. To her surprise, she had slept for over an hour and had woken up feeling more relaxed. After a refreshing cup of tea she had fed the dogs and cat and gone into her garden to do some weeding and to pick a tiny bunch of late primroses for her dressing table.

Eventually, Jamie had reappeared and they followed their usual Sunday evening pursuits of reading the Sunday paper supplements and listening to classical music, Beethoven was a firm favourite. What Rosie would have liked to do this evening was to have discussed what she labelled 'the Polly situation' with her husband. Jamie, though, had been in one of his quiet, reflective moods so she had resisted.

After Charles' phone call he smiled at her across the room.

'That's cheered you up, how is Charles?'

'Well he had some very interesting news. He's got a new girl friend and I think it could be serious. She's an actress called Maggie. He says she has red hair and green eyes and she's very beautiful and lively. He met her at a Regimental cocktail party and you'll never guess...'

'Probably not' Jamie responded drily 'so why don't you tell me?'

'Well, two things. First of all, amazing really, they met Hugh at a party in London and she, that is Maggie, is going to be in a film that's being shot at High Wynch Park. Then he wants to bring her here in July to meet us all, so I think it really is serious.'

Jamie got up from his wing chair and crossing the room, gave his wife a hug.

'Well, this probably calls for a celebration. Let's have a cognac.' Rosie did not often drink brandy but it sounded like a very good idea.

Half an hour later she was nodding off to sleep, so Jamie packed her off upstairs saying that he would take the dogs out for a few minutes and then lock the house.

By now the light had gone but the milky darkness was punctuated by a pale moon, which cast a peaceful, slightly surreal glow over the quiet garden.

"Everything will work out" he thought to himself, things usually did, in the end.

Jamie did not brood on events as a rule. But the current unrest amongst his closest family was troubling him. He did, in fact, agree with Roddy's decision to make Richard his heir. However, he now realised that, far from bringing them closer together this decision had driven a wedge between his daughter and her husband.

Still, there was nothing he could, or wanted to do about it right now except to give Rosie such comfort and support that he was able to offer. So he walked the Labradors briefly in the garden, settled them for the night and went off to see if he could help Rosie to relax.

Edinburgh

Richard sat by the dying fire in the sitting room. It had a handsome Victorian mantelpiece, covered with family photographs and invitations to drinks parties and Private Views from Edinburgh's many art galleries. The room was both elegant and comfortable. He was nursing the remains of a glass of Glenmorangie whisky. Polly had already gone to bed, saying that she wanted to have an aromatherapy bath and an early night. He really didn't know how to cope with her at present. Everything he said, and did, seemed not only to be wrong but did not appear to touch her at all. He felt as if he was living with a polite stranger.

As soon as they had arrived home Minty had unpacked her things and ran to Polly with the little framed picture of the monkey she had created with skill as well as love and enthusiasm at Grannie Betty's. Polly had been genuinely touched, and impressed. She had hugged Minty tightly whilst loudly praising the picture which had temporary but prominent pride of place on the mantelpiece. She had said 'We will put him there so we can all enjoy him whilst we decide where he's going on the wall.'

John had chattered away to his mother, about riding, about helping Great Grandpa Roddy at the stables and, best of all, catching his *first-ever trout in Grandpa's pool.*

By contrast, conversation between Polly and Richard had been stilted. It was polite, as if between two distant acquaintances. Polly felt guilt and resentment in equal measure. She was fully aware that almost all the fault was hers and that Richard did not deserve her to be unfaithful to him nor to be so ungracious about her grandfather's will.

'Did you enjoy a peaceful time, Polly?' He had asked.

'Yes, thanks. I seem to have been so busy lately. It was good to do nothing much' she said, not looking at Richard in case her eyes gave her away. Nothing much, only a weekend of all-consuming passion but also of warmth and closeness with David. Laughter and lightness had accompanied their lovemaking. It had at once felt so very right and natural. She knew that she sounded artificial and awkward but this seemed right now to be her only defence.

'How was your weekend, Richard?' She usually called him 'Darling'. How strange it sounded - Richard.

'I missed you, your parents missed you and, of course, the children missed you.'

Guilt caused her to respond more sharply than she had intended.

'For heaven's sake, Richard. We *always* spend all our spare time together, either as a couple or as a family. I simply wanted some time to myself, *some time for me, time to think!'* she cried. He looked so crestfallen even more guilt was added to the mix of her turbulent emotions. He was silent. He felt hurt. There was feeling of remoteness and coldness about Polly that sent a shiver down his spine. Then he had been angry.

'Well, if you don't care about upsetting me, what about the children? Minty and John were both very upset. Minty was especially upset after she went to all that trouble to do the monkey drawing for you. She thinks that she has done something wrong, something to upset you.'

Polly sighed heavily. Guilt was making her angry.

'Richard, I take off one weekend, away from my family, probably the first ever, is that so wrong?' Even as she spoke the words she felt traitorous. He didn't deserve this deceit.

Softhearted as ever, he took her in his arms. She felt stiff, unnatural. He lifted her face towards his and kissed her gently on the lips. He loved her *so much*. Confused and sad she tried hard not to pull away. She briefly hugged her husband, but he felt like a stranger.

'Darling,' she forced herself to say 'let's talk about it tomorrow. We're both tired and need a good sleep.'

'I'll take out the dogs then' said Richard. She was grateful for his tacit agreement and replied, 'Great, I'll just go up and check that the children have everything ready for morning.'

Edinburgh - Moray Place

The sun streamed through the heavy white curtains of David's bedroom as Polly arched yet again before letting out a primeval cry and gripping David tightly with her legs round his waist

He smiled and looked down at her with a mixture of tenderness and something very close to triumph.

'Did you enjoy that, Pollyanna?' he asked, silkily.

She stretched luxuriously and smiled with a brilliance that gave her face a wonderful, youthful and joyous appearance. Then she glanced at the clock on the glass beside table and sat up with a start!

'Oh, hell, David darling, *I must go.* I've got to collect Minty from school and take her to ballet. I'm running out of time.'

He held her and looking deeply into her bright blue yes, relented, kissed her and let her go.

He propped himself up on the pile of pillows and watched Polly as she dressed. Because she had spent the morning rushing around taking children to school, then going to David's flat to cook for a business lunch she was wearing her normal uniform of a short black skirt and white shirt. After the lunch guests had gone David had led her immediately, and wordlessly, to the bedroom. She had gone willingly.

Ever since the weekend when she had broken new ground and refused to go to Whitewalls, refused to obey her mother and her husband Polly had felt a new daring and feeling of freedom.

Inevitably, as Richard had maintained his slightly puzzled air of coolness towards her and projected an unspoken, yet critical view of her, Polly had increasingly, secretly moved closer and closer to David. He made her feel glamorous, sexually charged and fulfilled.

After a brief visit to the bathroom, and a final hug, she was gone, running downstairs to her car parked just out of sight around the corner.

David lit a cigarette, inhaled deeply and smiled to himself. Things were going well; very well, in fact. Far from Polly simply being an easy conquest, as he had originally believed, David now found himself developing increasingly strong feelings for her.

Polly ran to her vehicle. She saw that she had got a parking ticket and briefly swore under her breath before yanking it off the windscreen and putting it in her pocket.

The traffic was building up and she seemed to move from one slowly moving line to the next. Every traffic light between the West End of the city and Roseburn where the school was situated was at red. She sat at one of these anxiously drumming her fingers on the steering wheel. Polly could still feel the warm sensation created by David's lovemaking and the smell of him lingered on her skin.

Abruptly she was awakened from her reverie by the hooting of a car horn immediately behind her as the lights changed to green. She accelerated; she was nearly there.

As Polly swung the Rav round the corner of the steep hill leading to the school, she had to stop suddenly, stamping on the brakes. Immediately in front of the school was an ambulance, its lights flashing, a police car and a small knot of people standing in a huddle round a small, still form lying on the ground. A school Panama hat was lying on the road and the little girl's pale golden pigtails were ominously stained crimson.

Her stomach lurched sickeningly. It was Minty! Instinctively grabbing her handbag she leapt from the car and ran towards the scene. A young policeman standing at the edge of the group tried to hold her back.

'Sorry, madam, there's been an accident. A child has been knocked down. The ambulance has just arrived.' Polly pulled at his arm.

'You don't understand, that's my daughter, that's Minty who's been hurt.'

After that events moved in a blur, which at times seemed fast, and at others in the slowest of slow motion.

'Let the lady through' commanded the young policeman with a note of authority in his voice, 'it's her wee girl that's hurt.'

Polly sank to her knees on the road next to Minty who was unconscious and alarmingly still. As well as the blood seeping from her head wound, her right leg was sticking out at a ghastly looking angle.

'Someone do something,' she cried.

The young paramedics - one male and one female, were already unloading the stretcher, bring out a terrifying-looking clamp for Minty's head and coping efficiently as their training had taught them to do. They handled Polly's daughter with gentleness and a concern, which was both tender and professional. Soon she was in the ambulance. Polly crouched beside Minty, holding her cold little hand, calling her name over and over again.

In spite of the strenuous efforts of the paramedics Minty remained unconscious as they rushed towards the Accident and

Emergency Department of the Children's' Hospital. Mercifully the bleeding from the head wound had abated and Sam, one of the paramedics, said to Polly

'That's a good sign, try not to worry. They're waiting for us and Minty will be taken in as soon as we arrive.'

The ambulance driver, Carla, cut a swathe through the traffic with the blue light flashing and the siren blaring. It all seemed so unreal. Polly smiled, weakly, unable to speak. Oh God, Minty was going to die and it was all her fault. If she hadn't been late leaving David not, significantly, "if she hadn't stayed with David after lunch" none of this would have happened. True to Sam's word no time at all was lost and as soon as they arrived and a medical team was waiting for them. Minty was gently lifted on to a trolley and whisked away from Polly. She was left to give the details of Minty's doctor and to try and explain what had happened. A young nurse then led her to a quiet room.

'I want to be with my daughter' Polly cried.

'The doctors are working on her right now' explained the nurse whose badge said that she was "Staff Nurse Sally Mitchell".

'We'll take you to her as soon as possible. She's in very good hands. Now can I telephone anyone for you, your husband, and family?'

'I've got my mobile,' replied Polly. She needed Richard, she needed her husband, and she needed her mother!

'I'm sorry,' replied Sally 'you can't use it inside the hospital, because mobile phones can interfere with equipment. Why don't you give me your husband's number and I will telephone him? Then I'll get you a nice cup of tea.'

"A cup of tea," thought Polly "and my daughter could be dead - because it's my fault, because of me, because of David I was late." She said this only to herself and, as if in a trance, gave the nurse Richard's office number. Nurse Sally patted her shoulder, smiled brightly and left.

'I won't be long, dear, try not to worry.'

The next few hours passed in a blur of activity. At times she was aware of people talking to her. A kind doctor, Dr Masrif, held her hand and explained that the head wound was less serious than it had looked. Minty was still unconscious but that was not uncommon in cases of blows to the head. The staff were very hopeful she would come round. No, he couldn't say when that would happen.

Richard had appeared shortly after the nurse's call, white-faced, but strong. He held Polly closely as, together, they were taken to a small side room in the Children's Medical ward. Then they sat facing each other across the small, still form of their daughter who was wired up to monitors and an oxygen machine.

'I'm so sorry, Richard,' She said in an anguished voice 'it was all my fault.'

'Shush, how could it have been your fault? Minty apparently dashed out straight in front of the car that hit her. You weren't even there, darling, how could it have been your fault?' She insisted:

'But it was my fault. I was late collecting her.'

'Darling, I'm sure you couldn't help that.' Her eyes filled with tears. Richard was being so kind, so understanding, and so supportive. For a moment she wanted to tell him the truth, to confess everything. But even in her distressed state, something held her back and she remained silent.

Later, Polly was not sure when, as minutes lengthened into hours, her mother and father arrived. Richard slipped out of the small room to leave Polly with her upset, but composed parents. His parents, Moira and Stephen also arrived, shocked but quiet. They hugged Polly awkwardly; they were not demonstrative people. Moira wept briefly on Richard's shoulder.

'Don't worry, Richard' she said, trying to sound as if she was confident 'I'm sure it will be alright. Children are very resilient.' He was too choked up to reply. His parents stayed with Richard whilst Rosie and Jamie went with Polly to sit with Minty.

'Oh, Mum, Dad' cried Polly quietly 'what's going to happen? I was late. I should have been there, and then this might not have happened'

Rosie's heart hurt with the pain of her daughter's pain.

'The doctors think that she will come round, and soon,' said Jamie comfortingly.

'Dr Masrif had a word with your Mum and me as we came in. Minty is badly concussed, but she is young and strong. The head wound is more superficial than it looked at first. Her leg's broken but that will mend as well. He's talking to Moira and Stephen and giving them the full picture too.'

'But what if she dies, what if the doctors are wrong, what if she never wakes up. Oh, God, what are we going to do?'

Jamie held his shaking daughter with the utmost tenderness.

'We must all put our faith in the doctors and in God. Minty is a beautiful young girl, with all her life before her. I'm sure she will recover. He prayed he was right. Why don't you slip out for a few minutes with Richard? Your mother and I will stay here and Moira and Stephen can come in too, we don't want to leave them out in any way.'

At that point Nurse Sally reappeared and Polly was persuaded to join Richard for yet another cup of tea in the Parents' Room. It was very quiet, with just another young couple sitting as close together as the plastic chairs allowed, holding hands and waiting anxiously for news of their sick baby.

'Where's John?' asked Polly concerned for her other child 'he'll be so worried.'

'Darling, he doesn't yet know anything has happened. Remember he had gone to Harry Macdonald's after school and I phoned Karen. He's going to sleep over and we'll tell him in the morning when we know more about what's going on and how Minty is recovering.'

Some time later Rosie and Jamie left to spend what was left of the night at the house in Murrayfield. Richard and Polly resumed their bedside vigil. As the night went on they dozed intermittently. Doctors and nurses came in and out, checking on Minty. Clearly they were tired themselves but patient, kind and reassuring.

Then, just as the first tentative fingers of the dawn light filtered through the window blind, Minty stirred. Briefly, she opened her eyes.

'Mummy, Daddy, where am I? My head hurts, my leg hurts.' She then sighed, clasped her mother's hand and lapsed into what seemed to be an unconscious state again.

Richard rang the bell and the young Registrar who had taken over from Dr Masrif came quickly into the room. After being told what had happened he asked Polly and Richard to leave so that he could examine Minty. Soon they were called back. Dr Taylor was smiling. He put his arms round both their shoulders and said,

'She is sleeping naturally. We'll have to do more tests before I can be sure, but there's every chance she'll make a full recovery. Minty will be fine, you'll see.'

They both wept then. Reluctantly they agreed to the suggestion that they should go home for a few hours, rest and return later in the morning.

'If there's any change at all, we'll get you back immediately, but Sally will be with her all the time and we'll be monitoring her every second.'

Little was said as they sped back through the deserted streets of the city. The sky was a pale silvery blue, the air felt clean and fresh it was going to be a sunny day.

Chapter 7

High Wynch Park

Virginia, Rosie's sister-in-law sipped her Lapsong Suchong tea sitting up in bed. She leaned back against the stack of white lace-covered pillows and looked round her bedroom, in the early morning sunshine, with some satisfaction.

The house, High Wynch Park, was very old, reputed to be late Elizabethan. The walls were not straight but their pale lemon colour wash, crisscrossed by oak supports and beams complemented the oak four poster bed. The striking yellow and pink flowered chintz curtains framed the mullioned windows very satisfactorily. The fabric design was the wrong period, but the effect was good, she thought,

Really it was so much *nicer* having her bedroom to herself since she had persuaded Hughie to move into one of the more imposing spare bedrooms and make it in to his dressing room where he now normally slept.

'You see, Hughie' she had reasoned 'you know I sleep so badly but I don't want to disturb you by putting on my reading light during the night. Yet that is the only way I can get back to sleep again.' They both knew that this was really her way of saying that she didn't particularly want to have sex with him any more.

At first Hugh had been somewhat glum at being turned out of the marital bedroom.

'All very well, old girl' he had protested 'but what about, you know, rumpy pumpy?' She cringed at the public school terminology.

Virginia had summoned up the least glacial smile that she could manage and said archly and entirely untruthfully,

'But darling, Hughie, this means that when we both want to, well, make love, we will have a sort of special assignation.' With that he had had to be content, though it must be said the special assignations proved to be infrequent. Hughie had, however, sought and found satisfaction elsewhere. As far as he could see, his jolly mistress had no bad effect on his marriage. Indeed, it was quite the opposite.

Virginia turned on her bedside radio. It was tuned to Classic FM which she found so soothing. Looking at her pale blue leather diary she saw what she thought of as Hughie's bohemian contacts, the film makers, were coming to lunch and to look at the house and grounds with a view to hiring them to shoot a film there. She sighed and frowned briefly.

This was a new venture of Hughie's. He was always starting things she later had to take over and run efficiently. The Plant Nursery was one, the garden restaurant was another. Still, this latest venture might be more fun and they did need the money. Also Hughie had said something about meeting his nephew, Charles, at a drinks party in London and his girlfriend who might be appearing in the film.

When she and Hughie had first met he had seemed so dashing. He was still handsome in a florid kind of way but she did rather wonder if she had been too quick to accept his proposal of marriage and give him all the benefits of her well-endowed Family Trust, including High Wynch Park. Anyway, it was probably too late to do anything about it now. Virginia was very good at what she called "getting on with things."

She had better start getting up and organising everything. Languidly she sauntered to her connecting bathroom and ran a deep bath with plenty of Floris bath essence. Virginia had been born into the wrong age. If she had been a very grand Edwardian lady with plenty of servants she would have been a very happy woman. As it was, genteel poverty seemed to be her lot, with a lovely house and land but a casual laid back husband who always expected something to turn up to solve the latest financial crisis. Annoyingly in a way, something usually did.

Later that morning, Virginia went into the pretty dining room. The table setting looked elegant with antique white lace mats, crystal glasses and a pretty arrangement of spring flowers. This showed the polished Georgian mahogany dining table to good effect. She mused that attending finishing school in Switzerland had taught her, among other valuable lessons the art of creating an elegant impression. The lunch for Romayne, the film director, and Anthony Goodsman, his financial backer was important.

The cash flow situation was not good and the bank was pressing Hughie to reduce the overdraft. If there really was money to be made by hiring our High Wynch to the filmmakers that would, she told herself "be a very good thing." It might, too, she pondered bring some excitement into her life. She fantasized about getting a cameo part in whatever film was being made. Why not? She knew that she had kept her glamorous blonde looks and slender figure. Life had become boring recently. She was always worrying about money, or the lack of it, and she had long since stopped fancying Hughie as a sexual partner except on very rare occasions but had not, so far, looked for a substitute.

Virginia had met Hughie at a riotous weekend party in the Scottish borders when she was in her early twenties. She had been very attracted to his bouncy, lively, personality and love of fun. If she was honest – which was not very often – Virginia had also thought Hugh was wealthy in his own right. True, he had a modest income from a Trust established by his grandfather and some capital from his mother, Lady Betty from her divorce settlement but most of that had gone into High Wynch Park and the remainder had hardly grown enough over the years to support their extravagant lifestyle. It was certainly not enough now.

Because Rosie, Hugh's sister, had passionately wanted to stay at Whitewalls he had sold out his interest to his brother-in-law Jamie at an early stage. This had enabled him to buy High Wynch Park with, in turn, financial help from Virginia's family trusts.

What she had not realised, until it was too late was the income needed to support them both, educate their two selfish children and satisfy Virginia's social ambitions in up market Gloucestershire was not provided in sufficient quantity by Hugh's various money making ideas which usually turned out to be the opposite. High Wynch was a beautiful old house but even keeping it wind and water tight, never mind the expensive soft furnishings, the new kitchen and the elaborate gardens was a constant struggle.

Virginia could not afford to pay both a cook and a cleaner so her Cordon Bleu cookery course came in to its own when there was entertaining to do. Now she had her lovely new kitchen Virginia enjoyed cooking for guests though on a day-to-day basis she was not really interested in the kind of stodge Hugh enjoyed.

Today she had made a terrine of crab and prawns with a lemon dressing to be followed by tiny racks of spring lamb with lyonnaise potatoes and petits pois. She knew how much men liked puddings so she made a wicked sticky toffee pudding to follow, to be served with thick, clotted cream.

She wanted to make a favorable impression on her guests, so Virginia had dressed with particular care for the lunch party. Her slender legs showed off her immaculately pressed cream chinos, topped with a crisp white shirt from Helmut Lang and cinched together with a pale tan Hermes belt. On her elegant feet she wore pale tan pumps from J P Todd and the effect was completed with a simple long gold chain and gold knot earrings. Her freshly washed long blonde hair was held in place with the velvet hair band that she had never managed to discard from her heady days as a 'Sloane Ranger'. She knew that she looked like the classic English Rose, even if the bloom were now a little faded.

Hugh came in to the dining room as she was admiring her reflection in the pretty gold-framed antique mirror over the Georgian sideboard.

'You look good enough to eat,' he cried as he clumsily grabbed her from behind and tried to plant a wet kiss on her averted lips.

'Oh, Hughie, don't mess me up, our guests will be here in ten minutes and we need to create a good impression.' That sort of attention was the last thing she needed right now.

Crestfallen, he wandered off to the adjoining drawing room to make sure that the ice bucket was full, there were sliced lemons and the bottle of gin was at the ready. Hugh prided himself on pouring good, stiff drinks. None of your miserable pub measures were served at High Wynch Park. Consequently, the drinks bill was huge and guests regularly passed out at parties. Hugh though was genuinely considered to be a good, generous chap by their numerous friends and acquaintance and invitations to their parties were eagerly sought and accepted. In turn they, too, enjoyed a busy social life.

The front door bell rang and Virginia said,

'Hughie go and answer the door will you? If it's our guests bring them straight in here please, and then we can have a relaxing drink before lunch."

As always, reacting positively to the thought of a stiff drink, Hugh did as he was told. Virginia took another swift, admiring look at herself in the mirror and prepared to switch on her dazzling charm.

Her first reaction on meeting Piers Romayne was one of disappointment. He was very good-looking, but also clearly gay. Anthony Goodsman, on the other hand, was quite a different matter. He was stockily built, with dark brown hair, carefully slicked down with what she immediately recognized by the scent, was Trumper's Essence of Lime cream. Anthony had deep blue, searching eyes, a full, sensuous mouth and a warm, firm dry handshake. He was wearing a beautifully cut navy blue blazer with a brightly coloured silk handkerchief stuffed with artless casualness into the breast pocket. His shirt was deep blue which emphasized the colour of his eyes. He wore a smart silk tie and impeccable chinos with brown, highly polished Gucci loafers to complete the elegant, careless look that could only be achieved with work and serious money.

'Virginia' he said in a deep, sexy voice with just the hint of a Scottish accent 'How very kind of you to ask us to lunch. What a delightful house you have.'

Anthony was bogus. He had been born in the Gorbals area of Glasgow. The tenement houses had long since been pulled down and people rehoused in the new town of Livingston 25 miles away towards Edinburgh. Over the years he had carefully, almost too carefully, created a façade of gentility support by the creation of an extremely high level of personal wealth created through his various wheeling and dealing activities from which he always seemed to make a great deal of money. None of this, of course, was apparent until much later. Then it was too late.

Somewhere, in the pit of Virginia's very flat stomach there was a churning of what she was startled to find was the strong tug of primitive, immediate sexual attraction. This was something she had not experienced for many years in her marriage to Hugh.

In the brief pause that followed the introductions Hugh came to the rescue by asking affably,

'Now chaps, what's your poison, gin and tonic alright?'

Anthony quickly accepted. Piers asked for a spritzer, which meant that Virginia had to go to the kitchen to bring a bottle of chilled Sancerre from the fridge.

She was quite relieved to leave the room briefly to compose herself. Really, how ridiculous. She knew nothing about Anthony Goodsman yet here she was, fluttering inside like a teenager. It was a long time, a very long time since she had felt so immediately affected on meeting a man. Quickly she composed herself and told Sally, who was supervising lunch, they would be ready to eat in about twenty minutes.

When she returned with the wine Hugh and Anthony were already enjoying man-sized gin and tonics and with the business of sorting out Piers' spritzer, offering salted almonds and olives the conversation turned to the purpose of the visit.

It was soon apparent that Anthony called the shots. Piers waxed lyrical about the house and grounds whilst Angus quickly brought up the question of costs.

Before the discussion became too detailed, Virginia charmingly insisted they went along to the dining room. As she did so, she said archly

'We must eat before my little attempts at cooking are completely ruined.'

Anthony gave her a quizzical look as if to say "don't be silly, I can tell how competent you are" but the three men did as they were told.

The lunch went well. The food was a great success and Hugh had provided a very acceptable Merlot to accompany it, which Anthony, in particular, had clearly enjoyed...

They had coffee in the drawing room and the discussion continued in a very positive vein. At around three o'clock Anthony looked at his watch and said,

'We are definitely interested in High Wynch Park as a location for both outside and inside sets. So I wonder, Virginia, before we go, if you could perhaps show us round the house and grounds?'

Before she could reply Piers made a great show of looking at his Patek Philippe watch and said,

'I wonder if we should split up and Hugh can show me the grounds whilst Virginia takes Anthony round the house'.

Fleetingly, it crossed Virginia's mind that this might have been prearranged between the two of them. Surely not? But how intriguing if it were.

Anthony and Piers stayed until late afternoon. Apart from the lightest of touches to her arm and shoulder as Virginia gave him a tour of the house, Anthony was very polite and seemed to be genuinely interested in its history, the few remaining good paintings and the possibilities it held for filming.

M'mm, slightly disappointing, thought Virginia, though she was sure that she had not imagined the small, sexual frisson between them earlier. There was plenty of time, she could wait. After all she thought, sex is such a messy business but a little flirting is always good. Hugh had, to his surprise, got on rather well with Piers. Normally he hated being in the company of what he called "woofters". Piers had enthused about the gardens, in which Hugh took great pride, and said that could "visualise" romantic scenes being played on the sweeping lawns with their ancient oak tress and on, and around the large lake.

It was left to Anthony, just before the two of them left to say,

'Thank you so much, Hugh, for all the time you've spent with us today. We need to go away and work out our budgets but we will get back to you quickly.'

'Please, old boy' beamed a still mildly squiffy Hugh, 'come back whenever you wish', he added, graciously.

Finally, Anthony turned to Virginia. He shook hands with her, holding her cool and slender hand in his warm, but dry, clasp for slightly longer than necessary.

'Thank you for a lovely lunch, Virginia' he said in his low, quiet voice with its slightly Scottish accent. You've been very kind, and I look forward to returning your hospitality.' He thought to himself "I also wouldn't mind a little fling with you Mrs Ice Cool. Make her wait, though."

She flashed him her very best smile, mentally making a note to ensure that Hughie would be otherwise occupied if, and when the invitation came.

Later that evening, Hugh and Virginia were sitting together in the drawing room in an atmosphere of harmony enjoying a glass of cognac and discussing the events of the day. At times like these Virginia felt, almost, happy.

'Thanks for producing such a super spread for lunch. You really charmed Piers and Anthony. They were very impressed. I really think that this could be the start of something pretty big.' Hugh felt very pleased with himself. It looked as if this was going to be the money-maker that had proved so elusive in the past.

For once, Virginia could identify with her husband's enthusiasm. This project promised to be a great deal more glamorous than the last one. Though, come to think of it, growing organic fruit and vegetables was hardly calculated to set the pulses racing; film-making was quite a different matter.

So it was that Virginia, feeling relaxed and positively excited about the filmmaking project, and, in particular, Anthony Goodsman did not protest when Hugh followed her upstairs to bed.

'Squelchy' he said, hoarsely 'can I, er, come and visit this evening? Please?'

To her brandy-fuelled gaze, he looked quite sweet, so she responded,

'Oh, why not, Bouncy' she said, regretting the words as soon as she had spoken them.

'Give me a few minutes.' He thought that he had better have a quick shower in honour of the occasion. That was soon accomplished and he hastily wrapped a towel round his plump middle and made for Virginia's bedroom as speedily as he could.

Hoping that he might go into his own room and stay there, Virginia paid a quick visit to her own, pristine bathroom, sprayed herself all over with Chanel No 5 and popped smartly into bed.

The door opened with a flourish and a naked and very aroused. Hugh burst into the room. Virginia wanted to laugh, he looked so absurd. But showing a rare tact she managed to contain her mirth. The brandy had helped.

It was soon over. He was too ready, and she was too indifferent to want to prolong the lovemaking, if you could call it that. As Hugh's brief moment of triumphal entry took place, though, she thought fleetingly, "Oh hell, I've stopped taking the pill!" Surely at 46 she could not become pregnant again?

London

It was Sunday afternoon and, once again, Maggie and Charles had spent a most satisfactory morning. They had enjoyed the usual leisurely breakfast of fresh orange juice and warm croissants both preceded and followed by some very energetic, passionate lovemaking. They were still lounging in dressing gowns – smart navy blue velour in Charles' case and a pale green satin for Maggie.

'Maggie' said Charles, casually.

'How would you like to go to High Wynch Park for the weekend after your play finishes?'

'Why would I want to go there?' asked Maggie. It was not like Charles to be mysterious. He was one of the most open men she had ever met.

'Well, now' teased Charles, feeling very pleased with himself,' about your film Country Pursuits. Uncle Hughie phoned this morning whilst you were in the bath.'

'Stop talking in riddles, what has the film got to do with our going to High what's it called? Don't be a tease, come to the point!' Sometimes his boyishness exasperated her.

'Well he's just heard from Piers Romayne and that's a daft name if ever there was one, I'll bet he's really called Fred Brown. Anyway he has confirmed they are going to do location shooting at High Wynch Park and he and Virginia thought we might like to go and stay so you can look around the place.

Her reaction was all he could have wished. Flinging her arms tightly round his neck, Maggie hugged Charles and said,

'Darling, you clever, clever man. Of course we must go. What about in 3 weeks' time? 'Meditations' will end the Saturday before and I'll have a chance to confirm with Piers that he wants me.'

'I don't know about Piers Romayne wanting you. I know that I want you, now; back to bed or here?' It was here.

Chapter 8
High Wynch Park and Yorkshire

Hugh and Virginia waved Charles and Maggie off on their journey north with genuine exhortations to 'come again soon.' Maggie you must not even *think* of staying anywhere except in the house for the film. And Charles, please come and join us whenever you can.'

It had been a happy weekend. Hugh always appreciated a pretty face and a good figure. Maggie had both. Virginia had not expected to like Charles' "actressy girlfriend" but her own impending involvement in the glamorous world of film, to saying nothing of meeting Anthony Goodsman, made her to try and find out as much as she could about the whole subject in general and Piers and Anthony in particular.

She knew that Piers was gay, but equally that Anthony most certainly was not. Virginia discovered that he had never married but was known to enjoy the company of beautiful women and, over the years, to have conducted a number of discreet affaires. He was also very rich. Anthony was just the kind of man that she was looking for. Virginia was a vain and silly woman but she did possess the sort of icy attraction that appealed to men like Anthony.

It had, therefore, been very fortunate that whilst Charles and Maggie were weekend guests Anthony, too, had put in an appearance for Sunday lunch at Virginia's invitation. He had been visiting his mother who lived in a retirement home at Moreton in Marsh nearby and had been more than happy to revisit High Wynch Park.

Anthony was a worldly man who enjoyed the fine things in life, including highly discreet though short-lived affairs with sensuous and willing married women. He had flirted a little with Maggie but not enough to cause anything more than the merest flicker of jealousy from Virginia.

All these sexual undercurrents had completely eluded Hugh and Charles. In the uncomplicated manner so typical of their breeding and class they had simply enjoyed the good food and wine that seemed to be in ample supply, despite the financial problems that Hugh had confided to his nephew the day before.

Even the nonchalant way in which Hugh had passed on this information made it seem of no account. Like Mr Micawber, he knew that something would turn up. So far something had always come along to rescue him from penury. But he didn't want Charlie blabbing to his mother. Rosie was a good sort but if she really knew his parlous financial state she would want to do something about it. She had always made him feel a bit inadequate with her perfectly organized life. With luck this film business would sort things out for good.

But now Charles and Maggie were on their way north to visit Maggie's grandparents who lived in Yorkshire, before Charles rejoined his regiment and Maggie started rehearsals for the film, Country Pursuits.

Yorkshire

Charles drove the silver-grey Golf cabriolet northwards. The roof was down and the spring sunshine warmed their faces. The wind ruffled Maggie's hair into shiny, marmalade-coloured streams. Charles sang tunelessly, under his breath,

"Got myself a walking, talking, sleeping Living Doll!"
He was so happy.

Maggie just sat back, turned her face to the blue sky and relaxed. The noise of the car made conversation impossible. She was glad about that.

There was a lot to consider. She was very attracted to Charles. He was sexy, kind and made her laugh. On the other hand, he was intense and very serious; too serious maybe.

Still, Grandmama and Gramps were such good judges of people. Perhaps she would simply let events take their course and see what they thought of Charles. She had promised him an answer to his proposal of marriage after she had visited his family in Scotland. The planned visit was still a few weeks away. So there was plenty of time to see how events turned out. It was just the timing that was wrong.

Maggie was tired after the play and wanted to be on her absolutely best form for the film. Her part in it was small, but significant. It could certainly lead to better and bigger things, of that she had no doubt.

The roads were free from major hold-ups and after stopping for a quick pub lunch en route, by four o'clock they had left the motorway and were driving down the country road, which led to Middlewick Hall.

Suddenly Maggie cried,

"Turn left, just here!" The turning was into a gravel driveway, with no sign of a house.

"Just keep going, darling," she said. "We're nearly there!" Her tiredness went and she experienced the warm feeling that always came when she was going to see her grandparents.

After the final bend in the twisting, narrow drive, Charles had his first glimpse of Middlewick Hall. It was a lovely low, sprawling house, built of Yorkshire stone, which glowed in the afternoon sun. It looked very grand, but at the same time welcoming. He hoped to God that the old people wouldn't be too difficult. They were bound to want to give him a good grilling about his prospects, his career, what he could offer Maggie and so on.

As the car crunched to a halt on the well-raked gravel, which swept up to the stone pillars flanking an old oak open door, a cacophony of barking dogs, composed of assorted shapes, breeds and sizes rushed out and down the steps to greet Charles and Maggie.

Charles was just sorting out the fact that there were two golden Labradors, a whippet and a pair of Norfolk terriers when a stunningly beautiful woman ran lightly down the steps and cried:

"Maggie, my darling; here at last. I was beginning to think you had eloped! Is this the lovely Charles we've heard so much about?" 'My God,' he thought, so much for the ancient grandmother. It couldn't be, could it?

He found himself being hugged warmly, and kissed elegantly on both cheeks. Florette was tall, whippet slender with startling blonde hair cut into a beautiful smooth bob. She was dripping with pearls. She wore pale blue jeans with a pink gingham shirt and matching-coloured cashmere sweater. This was knotted round her neck like a scarf and the total effect was immensely elegant. At four o'clock in the afternoon Charles was amazed to see her face was beautifully made up and clouds of Guerlain's Champs Elysee perfume drifted round her. He didn't know what to think!

Maggie grinned broadly, and said:

'Charles, meet my grandmother.'

'Pouf' replied Florette 'she is such a tease. Tiens, grandmother indeed. You must call me Florette. I am much too young to be called grandmother'. He later discovered she was 75 years old.

Almost unnoticed, coming more slowly down the curving stone steps was a tall, distinguished-looking man. To Charles, he was reassuringly dressed in a very old, beautifully cut tweed suit. With it he wore a checked shirt, which was blue and yellow and looked very expensive. Over the shirt he wore an immaculate yellow cashmere slipover. At once Charles felt on firmer ground. This man looked more like his own grandfather, Roddy. His other grandfather, Alistair, he had not seen since he was a small boy. He was never talked about in the family and Charles had no idea why he suddenly thought of him. There was definitely some mystery but his parents had always changed the subject whenever he asked about it.

A black and white spaniel, stiff with age, was at his heels. Like his master, Brack, was a little aloof from the general melee that had greeted Charles and Maggie's arrival.

Maggie threw her arms around her grandfather and hugged him tightly. She loved him dearly.

'Gramps, it's so lovely to see you and to be here. This is Charles.'

He shook hands with Maggie's grandfather. It was a firm, slightly dry hand that clasped his with a strength belying his slightly frail appearance.

'Nigel Hardcastle, welcome to Middlewick Hall. It's good to meet you Charles. Now if can get these women and dogs calmed down let's go inside so you can relax from your journey.'

Charles grinned; this was the kind of guy that he understood. All at once he was homesick for the familiarity of his Scottish Borders home and his family. He had not been back for many months.

He wanted to marry Maggie, leave the Army, set up a rural business – something to do with agriculture perhaps, or wine even – and to have lots of children.

'I'll leave Florette to show you to your rooms and we'll meet again later for drinks. I need to go and see my keeper, but I wanted to be here to welcome you' Nigel said. With a wave that was half-salute he disappeared through an old oak door just off the hallway.

'Oh, you'll see plenty of Nigel later' said Florette firmly, 'now just leave everything and we'll have tea in the library.'

Obediently they followed. It was a lovely room, with a lavishly moulded ceiling. Oak bookshelves covered three walls from floor to ceiling. Stone-framed mullioned windows opened on to a terrace, filled with tubs of late spring flowers.

'What a wonderful room!' Charles exclaimed. Clearly this spontaneous comment pleased Florette.

'I'm glad you like it. We use it all the time. It's lovely in summer and very cosy in winter with the fire lit.' she responded.

'Oh Flossie' cried Maggie, throwing herself down on to one of the chintz-covered sofas, 'it is so good to see you and Gramps. How is everything? How's business? Are you selling lots of cashmere?'

Florette laughed. 'One question at a time, ma Cherie. I will ring for tea.' Turning to Charles she said, 'I imagine that even though you are a Scotsman, Charles, you will still enjoy an English afternoon tea?' Charles grinned,

'Of course,' he replied 'we still do this at home, too. In fact, it's one of my favourite things'. He joined Maggie on the sofa, stretched out his long legs and relaxed.

The door opened and a small, motherly figure came into the room, practically buckling under the weight of a heavily laden tea tray.

Charles leapt to his feet to try and take the tray but Joan, the Hardcastle's housekeeper, was determined not to relinquish it.

'Thank you very much, sir, but I will manage very well.' She plonked the tray down on to the walnut sofa table.

'Thanks so much, Joan' said Florette, graciously. Thinking to herself that this was all so out of date, but Nigel insisted that there should be no change as far as Joan was concerned. So the tradition of afternoon tea has continued.

'There's hot buttered crumpets, so don't let them get cold' said Joan, firmly, but with a sweet smile.

'Joan, this is Charles, Maggie's friend.' said Florette. Charles shook the diminutive, elderly lady warmly by the hand and said, winningly.

'How very nice to meet you and I love hot buttered crumpets'.

Joan looked him up and down appraisingly, and then nodded with what seemed to be approval. "Not enough nice young men around these days," she thought but this one will do.

'Very pleased to meet you I'm sure. I like a young man who appreciates his food.' She said, 'Dinner will be at 8 o'clock.' She was gone. Florette sighed a little.

'Dear Joan was with Nigel's family for years before I came on to the scene. Really she should retire but I am not brave enough to suggest it and Nigel would rather die first! So we all get along as best we can. Also she is a very good cook.'

Over tea, which he thoroughly enjoyed, Charles relaxed further. He had recovered from the initial shock of finding that Maggie's granny was the exact opposite of the cosy stereotype he had expected. He was looking forward to getting to know her better and, even more importantly, to getting her on his side. Charles was determined to marry Maggie and he knew if Florette approved she was much more likely to accept his proposal.

Come to think of it, he wasn't sure what his image of her had been. Certainly it was not the elegant, attractive and youthful looking woman sitting opposite to him in her beautiful drawing room.

After tea, Florette showed them to their rooms. These were on the first floor overlooking the garden with its view of the rolling Yorkshire dales.

'You see, you have to share a bathroom,' Florette said, smiling. 'There is a door from each bedroom. Very comme il faut!' Charles was searching for a suitable response but Maggie squeezed his hand warningly. She kissed Florette and said,

'Oh Flossie, I am sure that we shall work out some suitable signals to make sure we don't both want the bathroom at the same time!' Florette laughed. Maggie took this as a sign of initial approval.

Each room had a high double bed with walnut head and footboards. The beds were piled high with cushions and pillows on old, beautifully made patchwork quilts. There was a soft pale blue cashmere throw folded at the bottom of each bed. As well, there was a sofa and armchair in each room and a walnut dressing table with matching wardrobe and chest of drawers. The wardrobes had softly tinted old oval mirrors in the doors, reflecting the elegance and comfort of the bedrooms.

The overall effect was welcoming. Charles pulled Maggie into his arms and kissed her with passion and enthusiasm. Maggie returned his kisses with great urgency.

'Come to bed, now!' he commanded. She laughed and gently pushed him away.

'Not now, darling, later. Flossie has given us these bedrooms fully expecting us to spend the night together but even her very French attitude doesn't stretch to sex before dinner. Come on, let's go for a walk and track down Gramps; that should cool your ardour until later.'

As always, she got her own way and shortly they were walking across the courtyard to the rear of the house and into the Estate office. Here they found Nigel, sitting in front of a computer screen, looking, to Charles' eyes mildly incongruous in his immaculate tweeds and yellow cashmere pullover. He was every inch the country gentleman, whilst using the latest technology to look at comparative crop yields. Nigel was a gentle man but a very self-assured one. He had no need to be loud or to make a fuss about anything. His quiet authority meant he usually got his own way, whatever the issue.

Nigel rose from the desk and came to greet them. 'Hello you two. This gives me the perfect excuse to switch off this wretched machine and take you for a tour around, Charles, if that's what you would like. Are you coming, too, darling?' he asked Maggie.

'I think, after all, I'll go and find Flossie and we'll have a girlie chat!'   This would be a great opportunity for Gramps to get to know Charles. Giving Charles no chance to try and persuade to go with him for moral support, she lightly kissed each of them on the cheek and sped off to track down her grandmother and get her first impressions of Charles.

Nigel clapped his hand companionably on Charles' shoulder and said,

'Come on; let's leave the women to pull us to pieces. I'll show you round the place. I've some new wheat trials in the south field I'd like to tell you about.'

What a really nice guy, thought Charles as they set off, accompanied by assorted dogs, to look at the farm.

Maggie found Florette in her bedroom, lying on the velvet covered pale green chaise longue at the foot of her white covered bed. A CD of a Mozart concerto played softly in the background and Florette's eyes were covered with circles of damp cotton wool. She was wearing a plain fine cashmere wrap in a soft shade of ivory. When she heard Maggie come into the room, Florette sat up gracefully, took the pads off her eyes and smiled brilliantly at her granddaughter.

'Ma Cherie, you look beautiful, as always, but a little tired perhaps? Your Charles, he is too demanding peut etre?'

'Flossie' replied Maggie in tones of mock-outrage, 'yes but not just in that way!' She was so lucky to have such a modern-minded Grandmother; it almost made up for losing her own mother, though not completely. She pushed the pain of that away, hurriedly.

Florette patted the chaise longue.

'Come on, Cherie, sit down and tell me everything!' Maggie found it so easy to confide in her grandmother.

'Well, I do love Charles; he's handsome, sexy and kind. He absolutely adores me; we're really good together in every way, every way, but.........'

Florette remained silent and smiled encouragingly. Maggie continued,

'He wants to marry me; settle down, bury me away in Scotland and give me lots of babies.'

She looked so horrified at this latter notion and Florette placed her arm around Maggie's shoulder, lightly hugged her and said;

'Well, Cherie, I think you have answered your own question. You love your Charles, yes, but not enough to marry him and bear his children. At least not now, maybe not ever.'

Maggie felt great relief at her grandmother's clear understanding of exactly how she felt. The next feeling was one of panic.

'But what am I going to do?' she cried.

'What do you want to do?' Florette countered.

'I don't want to give him up. But I don't want to be tied down either.' replied Maggie, after a brief pause.

'Then,' said Florette 'that is precisely what you shall do. Enjoy each other; be your charming sexy self and tell your lovely Charles he must wait for your answer.'

It seemed so simple. She could have the best of both worlds. Charles would wait and if he wouldn't, he didn't love her enough.

'That's exactly what I am going to do. Now, Flossie, having disturbed your beauty routine I am going to and find Gramps and Charles. Then you must show me your new designs.' She jumped gracefully to her feet, deposited a light, affectionate kiss on Florette's smooth cheek and humming lightly under her breath "It's amore!" she set off to find the men.

As it happened, Maggie missed them completely. Charles had found himself warming to Nigel Hardcastle and after inspecting various fields he happily accepted Nigel's invitation to join him in the Black Bull for a pint of beer.

The beer was good. Nigel introduced Charles to a couple of local farmers as 'Charles Douglas, my granddaughter Maggie's friend.'

The conversation was easy. They spoke of The Labour Government's complete ignorance of the countryside; the far reaching effects of a hunting ban on so many families who

218

depend upon the hunt for their livelihoods and, inevitably, the parlous state of farming with costs rising all the time.

They met for drinks in the library before dinner. Florette was dressed in black cashmere trousers with a cream cashmere cowl-neck sweater that showed off her slender figure. Nigel had merely changed his tie. Charlie felt reasonably smart in his cords and checked shirt whilst Maggie was a vision dressed in a similar fashion to her grandmother but with a dark emerald green sweater in which Charles thought she looked good enough to eat.

'It's just us for supper', Florette announced 'so we'll be able to have a good family gossip.'

Charles wasn't sure he liked the sound of that, but after a couple of Nigel's stiff whiskies he relaxed and the rest of the evening passed in a pleasant glow. He opened up to Nigel and Florette about his family, Whitewalls and his grandparents and particularly about Rosie. Nigel asked appropriate, but not intrusive questions about Charles's Army career.

Maggie sparkled. Her chat with her grandmother and the plan to postpone the decision on giving Charles an answer to his proposal had given her the feeling of a weight removed from her shoulders. She did love Charles but there was life to be lived before settling down to marriage and all that would entail. They ate a beautifully cooked and presented meal of hot smoked salmon mousse, rare, thin slices of beef fillet, with dark wine-infused gravy and tiny fresh vegetables. There was a crème brulee for pudding and finally some good Wensleydale cheese.

Coffee was waiting for them in the library after dinner.

Charles enjoyed his after dinner brandy then about 11 o'clock said,

'I'm really bushed, does anyone mind if I turn in for the night?'

Florette simply smiled knowingly and said.

'Of course not, Charles, dear, off you go.'

Maggie just smiled. She would not be far behind.

'Thanks for a lovely evening' he said. Nigel shook his hand warmly. Nigel really meant what he said. Charles seemed a decent sort of fellow and would be a calming influence on his granddaughter. So it was with real sincerity that Nigel replied.

'It's been good to meet you. Don't rush away too soon tomorrow.'

Florette kissed him warmly on both cheeks and gave him a hug. Like Nigel she had taken to Charles though she still felt it was far too soon for Maggie to 'settle down'. Indeed one of the reasons she had given her the mews house was precisely so she would have more choices in the way she decided to live her life.

'So delightful, dear Charles.' Then dismissing him she said,

'Now off you go. There is plenty of hot water if you want a bath.'

Shortly after that Nigel said that he would take the dogs out for a last walk and Florette turned to Maggie.

'I see your dilemma, ma Cherie. He really is very sweet, but you are right to make him wait. Now shoo, and have a lovely night!'

'Thanks for everything, Flossie.' She hugged her grandmother and ran upstairs with a light step to join a more than

221

eager Charles in the deep bath filled with a herbal essence. Later

she lay contentedly in his arms in the soft, double bed and fell

asleep as the moonlight shed its silvery light through the open

window. A hunting owl hooted and disappeared into the country

sounds of the night.

Chapter 9

Scotland

'Mummy, I am so, so fed up with this stupid leg. It aches all the time. I wish I could go back to school. I'm bored!' It was so unlike Minty to whine but the accident had affected her very badly and with it she had lost much of her quiet confidence.

During the six weeks since it had happened Minty had made some slow but fairly steady progress in general, except her broken leg was taking time to heal and it was likely she would need to be in plaster for a while longer. There had been no question of her going back to school for the rest of the summer term. Her teachers had sent simple tasks home for Minty to complete when she felt well enough. She was a conscientious little girl and had been trying her best to keep up. A stream of her small friends came in after school most days and tried to cheer her up. Minty was popular and Polly was grateful for the diversion provided by the young visitors.

Richard was exceptionally busy in his office and seemed very distant. He and Polly were politely co-existing and both of them had pushed personal issues to the backs of their minds. During those first awful days since Minty had been knocked down outside school, they had stopped talking very much except about the mundane trivia of daily living and caring for Minty. John, too, was quieter than usual. He was very fond of his twin sister and had been deeply upset at what had happened to her. It didn't do for a tough boy to show feelings but he really hoped she would get better soon. All this stuff made his head sore.

Polly had continued to see David, despite a huge wave of stricken conscience that had, at first, engulfed her. Whichever way she rationalized it, Polly felt the cause of the dreadful accident had been the fact that if she had not been in bed with David for so long, or, indeed, at all, that afternoon she would not have been late in collecting Minty from school and Minty would not have dashed into the road and been so badly hurt.

Yet she couldn't give him up. When she was with David she was so sexually aroused, so intensely, immediately, urgently filled with a powerful sense of herself as a desirable woman. No, she wouldn't give him up. She would just be more careful.

Polly dragged herself back from her reverie. It was no use thinking about what might, or might not have been. She had to deal with the here and now. It was difficult to keep the business going, apart from the work that David gave her and she was disappointed that her mother had not been more willing to leave Whitewalls on a regular basis to look after Minty in Edinburgh. Richard's mother, Moira, did her best but seemed so much older and absorbed in her own social life of coffee mornings, bridge parties and "good works".

Rosie, though she didn't say so outright to Polly, felt if her daughter had really been concentrating on her family rather than the cooking business then maybe she would not have been late in collecting Minty from school that day. It was unlike Rosie to be so judgmental and it was an indication of her deep concern about Polly and Richard's marriage and Minty's welfare, she was taking this view. For although Rosie was a progressive-thinking and modern woman in many ways, she had a deeply held view that families were more important than any other single thing in life. Her own early experiences when she was damaged by the turbulence of her parents' marriage and messy divorce had made her determined to be the perfect wife and mother and to raise the perfect family. This was a major blind spot in her thinking but was, nevertheless, an ideal to which she clung determinedly.

Later that afternoon, Caroline McLeod, who was a good friend of Polly from their school days at St George's, had agreed to look after Minty for an hour or so. This was ostensibly so that Polly could have a "business meeting" with David. Only a white lie, she comforted herself as she rushed round to Moray Place and stolen passion.

Their need for each other was, if anything, more intense than ever and they wasted no time with talking. Afterwards, lying luxuriously in the large bed, with their legs comfortably entwined following a particularly intense sexual experience, David felt a dangerously tender concern for Polly. What had begun, at least for him, as a simple sexual encounter was now occupying far too much space in his agile mind; indeed in his whole life.

David had set out deliberately to make money, to discard his appalling upbringing in a tough and dangerous Edinburgh Council housing scheme. Until now he had given no real or lasting commitment to any woman. Now, here he was, against his better judgement and his established lifestyle, not only wanting to deepen his relationship with this middle-class girl from Murrayfield but also caring what happened to her young daughter.

Polly was exhausted. She had briefly drifted into post-lovemaking sleep with her head of blonde curls resting trustingly on David's bare chest. Then she woke up from her light sleep and sat up. From being quite shy and timid at the start of their relationship, Polly was now very relaxed to be naked with David and increasingly revelled in it. Now, in the way of all married lovers she looked frantically at her watch.

'Oh my God, David. Look at the time. I told Caroline I would be back by four and its quarter to already!' For once he didn't try to delay her but said,

'Pollyanna, darling, let's try to plan at least a couple of days away together. Even if it is just down to the cottage on the beach.

We can really be alone and sleep all night together. I would love to wake up in the morning and find you there next to me. I know, why can't your parents have Minty to stay for a week or two? You could farm John out to his friends and the saintly Richard could surely manage without you for a few days."

She would love to say "yes" Did she dare, she asked herself?

'David, I don't know. I'll have to see. Minty is certainly getting very fed up in Edinburgh and not able to get out unless I take her. I'm surprised that Mum hasn't offered, in fact. Now I really must get dressed and go!'

'Alright my Pollyanna. But I've had another idea. Lucy Jamieson has some little Siamese kittens ready for homes right now. Why don't I get one for Minty? It would be something special, just for her. I know you're all great horse and dog lovers, but Siamese kittens are really pretty and get on well with people and other animals.'

Tears pricked Polly's eyes. This was a kind and thoughtful side of David that made him even more attractive in her eyes, and one she had so far only glimpsed.

'I really think Minty would absolutely adore that. How kind of you.' She meant it, too. It was a truly thoughtful idea.

'We'll go up to Fife next week and collect one. She can take it away with her to the Borders, he asserted confidently.'

'Now I really do have to go,' said Polly. She had hastily pulled on her new lacey, glamorous underwear and her black skirt and white shirt whilst they had been talking.

'Must fly.' She kissed him warmly and, as so often before, she dashed out of the cool and beautiful bedroom, down the stone staircase and back to the mundanities of her troubled life in Murrayfield Gardens.

David waited until she had gone and picked up the phone to call Lucy in Elie about acquiring a chocolate point Siamese kitten for Minty.

When Polly drew up outside her house, she panicked to see that Caroline's car had gone. Quickly she ran up the garden path.

The front door was unlocked and, with her heart pounding, she ran into the house.

Her mother was sitting with Minty at the kitchen table. They were both writing in notebooks. Minty's face lit up when her mother came dashing in.

'Mummy, I'm writing a story. Caroline had to go but luckily Granny arrived just in time, so we're fine.'

"Thank God for Caroline" Polly thought. They had been at school together and whilst Caroline had gone to Oxford University and now had a high-powered job in the Scottish Executive as a senior Civil servant advising the Government on economic matters. Caroline had never married. She and Polly had remained close friends. Caroline managed to be both glamorous and caring, which contributed greatly to the fact that she had a large circle of friends from many different backgrounds and interests. Where Polly was tall, slim and blonde Caroline was smaller, more curvy and dark haired. She dressed smartly in clothes from Jaeger and Missoni, and had created her own special style with beautiful leather handbags from Italy and modern unusual jewellery.

Rosie forced herself to smile.

'Hello, darling. You look flushed. What on earth have you been doing?' Polly managed to give Rosie a quick hug. "If only you knew" Polly thought guiltily.

'Oh, lunch ran on and there was such a lot of clearing up to do!' she said, trying to sound casual but succeeding in sounding careless.

Rosie was trying hard not to be reproachful but couldn't disguise a hint of asperity in her voice.

'It's just as well that I decided to come in then Polly. Caroline just couldn't wait any longer. As it is, she was here for at least an hour longer than she had agreed.'

Minty broke in, not liking the achey feeling that was developing. 'Mummy, in a minute I'll read you my story. It's about Benjy, the little monkey that I painted for you.' Polly felt remorseful and hugged her stoical little daughter very tightly. She must be mad to put her family at risk.

'How's your leg, sweetheart? Is it a bit less sore?'

There was a loud crashing noise. Before Minty could answer, John burst into the kitchen. His tie was somewhere behind his left ear, his socks were wrinkled round his ankles and there was a large muddy streak across one cheek.

'Hi, Granny, hello Mints, guess what mum, I scored a try at rugby this afternoon and James McBride said that he thinks I'll get into the team. And James McBride should know, he's the captain.' At last here was something that would make them all notice him again.

'That's wonderful.' Polly managed to say, followed by 'Go and wash your hands then you can have some milk and gingerbread.'

'Polly,' said Rosie, 'I've had an idea. I was in town having lunch with Miriam Smith and we went to the Gallery of Modern Art. You know there were children playing outside in the gardens and I just thought, that's what Minty needs, being out in the fresh air I mean. Why don't you all, and I mean all, come down at the weekend. Get Minty's teacher to send some school work and between us at Whitewalls we'll make sure that she's happy and has plenty of things to do. Pod and Pixie could come too, of course. She can stay on with us when you come back to Edinburgh.'

'Oh please say yes, Mum,' cried Minty 'I'm sure I would get better faster at Whitewalls.' Her pale face lit up at the thought of going to where she was always happy and where there weren't any funny feelings about her parents to bother her.

Polly felt relief and guilt combined. Here was a way out that would allow everyone to be more relaxed and let her see more of David.

'Thanks Mum. I'm sure that it would be lovely for Minty and a big help to me, too!' Again, Rosie felt irritated. What was the matter with Polly? She sounded so stilted and so selfish, immediately thinking of herself.

'It's Minty your father and I are thinking about. Good country air and feeding up are just what she needs. I'm sure your father would like her company in the studio. He's painting a lot right now for his Exhibition in Edinburgh and Minty could do some painting with him.' Rosie was determined to make it clear, without actually saying so how selfish she thought Polly was being in this trying situation.

By now John had eaten two large pieces of buttered gingerbread and drunk a huge glass of milk, leaving a white moustache on his top lip. Maybe he could get a new Harry Potter book out of this. Along with millions of other children, the fictional Harry had become his hero. Indeed Richard and Polly truly believed John wouldn't have bothered with reading at all without Harry as his role model. However, he was a wise little boy and intended to choose his moment before asking.

Richard arrived, looking tired and strained. He hugged Minty and John but avoided looking directly at his wife. He smiled at Rosie,

'How are you mother-in-law? It's really good to see you. Sorry I haven't been down to Whitewalls much recently.'

Rosie returned his smile. She was very fond of her gentle son-in-law and this gave her the perfect opportunity to press home her plan. After she had explained it Richard said gratefully,

'You're so kind, Rosie, as long as you're sure it won't all be too much. And are you sure about Pixie and Pod?' 'Quite sure' replied Rosie firmly, 'and of course it won't be too much trouble. Anyway, Molly is happy to come in for more hours so Minty and I can make a plan.'

'Will I have to do lots of school work, Daddy?' asked Minty, anxiously.

For the first time in many weeks Richard and Polly smiled at each other with real affection. The anxious little face of their daughter briefly united them in love for her.

'Don't worry about a thing, darling girl' said Richard. 'Mummy will sort everything out with school, and we'll all come down at the weekends, won't we?' He looked appealingly at Polly for support and she responded with a relieved smile. There were enough distractions at weekends at Whitewalls. Maybe, too, it was time to talk to her grandfather, Roddy. Perhaps she could get him to change his mind about his will, if she played her cards carefully. She felt rather better.

'Right' said Rosie, decisively 'that's settled. You'll all come down to Whitewalls on Friday evening until Sunday. Minty will stay on and we'll all have a good time. Now I must go. We're going to Tim and Anne's for supper this evening and tomorrow I have a meeting about the garden opening with Alison Murray from the Children's Hospice movement. I'm beginning to wish I hadn't said I would do this.' She didn't mean it, of course, being public spirited was an integral part of Rosie's character.

Polly was relieved. She and her mother seemed at last to be communicating again in a reasonably amicable way. She wished, though Rosie would stop treating her like a young girl and realise she had grown into a woman with her own needs, desires and the ability to manage her own life and, particularly, her marriage.

Still it was with a lifting of her spirits she said to Minty and John,

'Shall we get a Harry Potter video to watch this evening and a takeaway pizza?'

'Oh yes, please, Mum' the twins chorused together.

Rosie looked horrified at the thought of the takeaway pizza but sensibly said nothing. She hugged and kissed her grandchildren, daughter and son-in-law and left them to play happy families.

Whitewalls

Rosie was humming under her breath – "Smoke Gets In your Eyes" for no particular reason. She felt happier, more settled in herself. Molly was glad to hear it. Since wee Minty's accident and the change to the established routine of weekend visits from the whole family that could be *relied on* Mrs D. had not been her usual cheery and serene self.

Molly reckoned, to her way of thinking, all this bother could be traced back to when Polly had started all that cookery business nonsense. It wasn't as if they really needed the money, she thought. Richard was an Edinburgh lawyer and surely made enough for them all. No, Molly had decided, she would need to put Polly right on a few things before matters got quite out of hand. Her place, Molly believed was at home, looking after her husband and the bairns. Well *someone needed to speak plainly to Miss Polly and get her to see just what was important in life.*

Molly felt better when she had made up her mind to talk to Polly, though she didn't think she would mention it to Mrs D. until afterwards. It might be seen to be overstepping the mark; especially as she was a bit touchy right now!

Rosie came into the kitchen where Molly was emptying the dishwasher and said,

'Oh. Molly do you think that you could do an extra hour or so every day? We've decided Minty is going to come here for a few weeks until her plaster comes off. She's getting schoolwork to do and I'll need to spend some time helping her with that. Then I've got all the gardening to do to get everything ready for the opening. It's only two months away and that's not long. Plus Mr D. has announced that he is having an art exhibition in Edinburgh so we're going to be busy!' but she smiled as she spoke. Her world was settling around her again.

'Now that is good news, Mrs D. The wee one will get better much faster with some country air, to say nothing of some good fresh food! Of course I'll help out. The money will come in useful too.'

'The whole family is coming down at the weekend. They're bringing Pixie and Pod as usual but then they'll stay here too.' This was less good news; dratted wee beasties, yapping and getting under her feet, Molly thought. Still it would be a small price to pay to get Minty better and, just as important, Mrs D. settled again. Mr D. seemed alright, but then he had an altogether more placid nature. He never let things get him down!

On the whole, Molly concluded, it would all be for the best. In this positive mood she clattered upstairs to get the bedrooms ready for the impending weekend.

Edinburgh

David was feeling very pleased with himself as he drove back south over the Forth Road Bridge to Edinburgh. Beside him in a closed wicker cat basket a tiny chocolate point Siamese kitten mewed anxiously.

'Alright, little one. You are going to have a very happy time, I promise!' God, he was going soft in the head, where was the cool, sophisticated interior designer now? Lucy had been astonished when he wanted to buy a kitten. She knew that he would not consider for a moment spoiling the perfection of either his apartment or the beach cottage with an animal of any kind.

'Whoever she is, you must be badly smitten,' she had said rather sharply to David when he had arrived to collect this special present.

Lucy was, to tell the truth, piqued. It was the first time that she could remember when David hadn't even attempted to get her into bed – not even for a "quickie". She had no idea who David was seeing now. According to the smart set in Edinburgh, which she joined from time to time, David had some mysterious blonde girl friend, who none of them was allowed to meet. He made plans to see people, and then just abruptly dropped them. They all guessed, correctly, that the blonde was married.

He looked at his Rolex watch, with the diamond encircled dial. It was half past four. Should he take the cat straight round to Murrayfield? He knew Polly would be there with the children and it would suit him to hand over the gift in person to Minty. On the other hand, he didn't particularly want to run into Richard, or did he? David was curious about the man he increasingly regarded as his rival. He'd recently tried to get Polly to talk about Richard but she had seemed very reluctant to do so.

Deep down, David envied the upper middle classes. This was particularly true of the Edinburgh establishment with its heavy predominance of lawyers, bankers and stockbrokers who sent their children to private schools and who served on important committees, like the Edinburgh International Festival, the Arts Council and the Merchant Company. Their country-based counterparts tended to belong to the anachronistic "royal bodyguards".

These were the Royal Company of Archers, who owned an exquisite Georgian Hall on the south side of the city and whose principal function was to provide a guard of honour at the annual Royal Garden Parties held at Holyroodhouse where the Queen and other members of the Royal family stay when they are in

Edinburgh. They also held an annual archery competition that always seemed to be won by some crusty old country gentleman.

It was deemed to be a high honour to be invited to join this august body. There were no lady Archers yet. Similarly the High Constables were the "townie" equivalent. They wore elaborate dark blue uniforms and black top hats. They carried silver batons, with which to protect their Royal charges. Recently they had admitted two women, but females were not encouraged. The Archers wore bottle green uniforms with berets topped by an enormous eagle feather. Opinion was evenly divided as to whether they looked very foolish or very grand and there was never any question of admitting females.

The Merchant Company of the City of Edinburgh, and its members were equally the subject of envy or scorn but had gone up the social scale immensely since HRH The Princess Royal had become the Master. They, too, had been obliged to allow women into the membership. The Company owned and administered some of the city's private schools, though not St George's which, again in Edinburgh's stratified society was considered to be more exclusive. Part of David yearned to be one of the chosen ones but another, and perhaps deeper part of him despised it all.

He decided. He would deliver the kitten in person as an important client of Polly's business, showing concern for her little girl following that nasty car accident. "Surely," he lied to himself, "there could be no harm in that."

Unusually, there was a parking place right at the door and he neatly maneuvered the Porsche into it. He retrieved the mewing kitten in its little basket and bounded up the garden path to the green front door before he could change his mind or, unusually for him, lose his nerve.

David rang the doorbell. A prettily flushed Polly who was both delighted and, at the same time terrified to see him opened the door quickly.

'David' she exclaimed 'what on *earth* are you doing here?'

He smiled warmly at her. She looked pleased.

'Aren't you going to ask me in, Polly? I've brought the kitten for Minty; he's beautiful.'

Poly then saw the basket and exclaimed,

'Oh, you are a darling.' She made up her mind. "What possible harm could there be in asking him to come in for a few minutes?" Although they were going to Whitewalls later Richard wasn't likely to come home just yet from the office. Surely no-one could object to her best 'client' bringing a present for Minty – could they?"

Suddenly she didn't care.

Taking the basket from him she said,

'Of course, come in.'

Polly led the way through the hall to her slightly untidy kitchen. Minty was sitting on a small sofa, tucked into the alcove below the cuckoo clock. Her crutches were propped up at the end of the sofa and she was busy scribbling in a notebook. John was sitting at the kitchen table, scowling over his homework. Minty, who rather liked David, smiled at him, which lit up her pale face. She was, he thought, heartbreakingly fragile and he thought "this was how Polly must have looked when she was small'. He felt very moved.

'Hello, kids,' David said rather too heartily.

''Lo' replied John and turned back to his arithmetic. He didn't particularly like David, although he didn't know why.

'What's in the basket, David?' asked Minty. The kitten project had been kept a complete secret. For obvious reasons Polly hadn't told Richard. She reckoned that if he was presented with a fait accompli and Minty's certain delight in the kitten, they would get away with it.

David smiled again at Minty. She really was rather sweet.

'It's a present for you. Do you want to open the basket?' She could hardly wait.

'Oh, please. Can you put it down next to me?'

He did so and the mewing sounds became louder as she opened the top of the basket and with infinite tenderness and care lifted out the small, beautiful chocolate point Siamese kitten. Minty gasped with delight as David very gently picked up the tiny creature, mewing and wriggling and laid it on her lap.

'Oh, thank you, David, thank you so much.' She cried and spontaneously lifted her cheek for him to kiss, which he did with a gentleness that surprised him and brought a lump to Polly's throat.

'I just thought that he would cheer you up a bit' David said, a little gruffly.

This tender mood was broken by a loud "yeuch" from John who had been watching this little scene, with narrowed eyes, in silence. "I do not like David" he said to himself. "Dunno why, but I don't".

'Well' he said, 'it's a ratty little cat. Pixie and Pod will kill it and eat it!'

'John!' exclaimed Polly in horrified tones as Minty's eyes filled up with tears.

'How can you say such a horrid thing?'

Luckily, although he knew nothing really about children David did know that you shouldn't give a present to one child in front of another unless you had something up your sleeve to make things more equal.

From the pocket of his dogtooth check jacket he extracted a wrapped paperback copy of a Harry Potter book. He hoped John hadn't read it.

'John' he said firmly, 'I'm sure that Pixie and Pod will love the kitten and it will help Minty to get better more quickly; cheer her up.'

John considered. His twin sister had been miserable for ages now and couldn't really be in his gang with a broken leg. In fact, the gang only consisted of the two of them, which had severely curtailed all adventurous activities since the accident.

'I brought this for you." David saw the more mollified expression on John's face and pressed home his advantage.

'I hope that you haven't got this one," he said handing over the book.

'Your mum told me that Harry Potter was your favourite and this book has just come out.'

John took the book with a studied air of indifference.

'Thanks,' he said for he was a well brought up little boy 'I haven't read this one.'

David and Polly looked at each other. They both smiled and then, irrationally, they were both afraid.

Before anyone could speak again the kitchen door opened. Richard came into the room. There was silence as he took in the scene before him. Then Polly rushed in with

'Hello, darling, you're early, we didn't expect you yet.'

'Evidently' said Richard drily, then turning to David, 'and you are?" Polly was about to introduce them when Minty said,

'Oh, Daddy, this is David, he's Mummy's friend and he's brought me this beautiful Siamese kitten. Look the kitten loves me already.'

The men looked at each other with barely disguised hostility whilst Polly blushing attempted to retrieve the situation.

'Richard, this is David MacLean. He's one of my best clients and he's been very concerned about Minty and so he's just arrived with this adorable little creature to cheer her up!'

Even to her that sounded improbable, even false. Would Richard take it at face value?

248

The two men shook hands briefly; each tried to outdo the other in the firm handshake stakes that are so much a feature of primeval male rivalry. Richard was icily polite.

'Very good of you, old chap, but you must let me pay you for it.'

A small smile played around David's lips as he answered, equally politely.

'Wouldn't dream of it, old boy, please think nothing of it.' He couldn't believe that he had actually called another man 'old boy'.

Luckily at this moment the kitten took centre stage, decided to do what kittens do and peed on Minty. John found this hysterically funny and whilst Polly flew to mop up the kitten and Minty, Richard said

'Now you really must excuse us, David isn't it? We're all going down to my in-law's place in the Borders this evening and Polly has a lot still to do to get everything ready.' That made it as clear as he could, without actually throwing David out that this was his territory and this was his family.

Hearty goodbyes followed. Polly attempted to sound cool and David nonchalant. He said to Minty,

'Do enjoy your new little friend' and to John

'Could you come out to the car with me do you think? I've got a litter tray and some kitten food. You could be in charge of carrying them in.'

'Can do,' replied John, being cool like his hero, Harry Potter. The two of them retreated from the kitchen. Polly poured small saucer of milk for the kitten and Richard turned to speak to her.

'Are we going to Whitewalls as planned this evening? We're expected and I suppose the cat will have to go too though I would have thought your mother had enough to do without another animal to be looked after.'

Minty's smile would have melted the sternest heart and her father loved her dearly. So he smiled, dropped a kiss on top of her head and said more gently,

'That's a most generous present, Minty. You must think of a suitable name for him.'

'Oh, Daddy, I just have. He's going to be called Chocolate Buttons, and we'll call him Buttons for short.'

Over Minty's head Richard gave Polly a look that could easily have been a warning. She turned away.

After that Polly and Richard were fully occupied with the preparations for going en masse to Whitewalls. Richard and Rosie had both been most insistent that Polly committed herself to staying the whole weekend. She had not dared to object; telling herself that with Minty safely settled at Whitewalls she and David could go back to their stolen afternoons together. Maybe even more than before.

By the time Richard's Volvo estate car was loaded with rather more luggage than usual for a family weekend at Whitewalls and Buttons had been fed then introduced to a highly excited Pixie and Pod, Polly felt quite exhausted.

Richard simply refused to think about the motives of the suave, dark haired and handsome man who seemed to be so at ease with his family that, without any prior discussion having taken place, he could produce an expensive pedigree kitten as a present for Minty. But some deep primeval sense of invasion of his family was not far from the surface as Richard drove them out of Edinburgh on to the Peebles road.

Buttons cried piteously throughout the journey, which started Pixie and Pod yapping in sympathy. John decided to be rude about his sister's kitten and reduced Minty to tears by talking about her "little rat cat".

Polly was conscious of a headache developing and of feeling generally trapped and very fed up with her life.

Richard remained silent, apart from occasional remonstrations to his children.

'Will you two please stop arguing and Minty try to ignore the kitten. He's probably frightened and will need some time before he's settled down. And John, please remember that Minty has had a horrible time and needs to be encouraged, not upset!'

John fell silent. His father was so rarely cross and almost never raised his voice. Just now, though, he had sounded exactly like Mr Brown from school so he must mean it.

'Sorry Dad, sorry Mints' he said gruffly. Minty smiled sweetly. She was loved her twin brother and she had a very forgiving nature. Polly remained silent, lost in her own thoughts.

'Polly, come back,' said Richard with a touch of asperity in his voice. 'I said, does your mother know about the kitten?'

'No, no' she replied hastily, 'but I'm sure she won't mind.'

Indeed, Rosie was so pleased to have all Polly's family together under her roof she didn't mind at all.

Jamie and Rosie were both a the front door to meet them and in spite of the undoubted undercurrents simmering between them both, Richard and Polly relaxed enough to ensure that the evening passed well enough.

Buttons was a bold little creature once he was allowed out of his basket. He calmly walked over to Dundee, who was sprawled as usual by the Aga and licked him bravely on the nose. At first Dundee affected to be outraged by this interloper but mewing enticingly now, Buttons was permitted to settle, albeit tentatively, next to the comforting ginger bulk of the older cat. They made an enchanting sight.

Before a family supper round the kitchen table Jamie and Richard took the twins off to inspect the ponies. Butterball and Snowball had been getting fat and frisky through lack of exercise. Rosie had borrowed a wheelchair from the Red Cross. John was put in charge of wheeling the chair in which Minty sat, very composed, neatly stowing her crutches at one side.

As Rosie and Polly watched the party go through the kitchen garden, accompanied by the black Labradors, Tweed and Heather, Empress and the excited Norfolk terriers, Pod and Pixie a lump came into both women's throats. Rosie hugged Polly. Polly's eyes were bright with tears but she just said,

'Thanks, Mum. Shall I help with supper? I could do the table and make a salad?'

Rosie sensed this was not the time for a parental lecture of any kind so she simply agreed. Mother and daughter worked companionably enough together to produce a simple meal of fresh roasted chicken with new potatoes and salad to be followed by a

huge home-made apple pie with cream, and ice cream for a treat.

Later, after the noisy return of Richard, Jamie and the twins,

they all took their places at the table. Rosie looked round her

busy kitchen, with Polly and family apparently now in harmony

and allowed herself a moment of maternal satisfaction.

When Richard joined Polly in their bedroom she was

already in bed, apparently asleep. The room was Polly's

childhood one and whilst it had been redecorated and a

comfortable double bed installed to replace the brass-railed single

one it was still a girl's room with two of her father's watercolours

of the River Tweed on the walls as well as her 6th Year school

photograph from St George's.

He had shared a companionable short stroll with Jamie and

the dogs before turning in. The two quiet men had always liked

each other and there was no need for much conversation.

However, Jamie knew Richard was troubled and said to him,

'Don't worry, Richard, things have a way of working out if

we let them. You've all had a pretty rough time over the last few weeks and it's been a great strain all-round.' He had slapped his hand warmly on Richard's shoulder and that was all. It had been enough, though, to make the younger man feel he was not alone.

Richard had always felt slightly uncomfortable making love to Polly in "her" bedroom but his need for her now was urgent. When he joined her in bed he took her in his arms and kissed her with much more passion than usual. So even Polly, using avoidance tactics couldn't still feign sleep. She tolerated the kiss then said,

'Oh, Richard, not now, I'm too damned tired. Go to sleep, please!'

He stroked her breasts through the rather prim nightdress she tended to wear when staying at Whitewalls. He really did want her. But she pushed him away and turned over on her side.

'Darling, what's wrong? Polly, tell me. You've seemed so different since Minty's accident. You've been withdrawn, remote. No-one is blaming you, if that's what you think!'

She turned towards Richard and gave him a perfunctory hug to shut him up.

'Please try to understand,' she said, attempting to sound sleepy rather than irritable.

'It's still been a hell of a time. I'm worried about Minty and I've been trying to keep everything going, including my business.'

'Damn your business' he said roughly 'I earn enough for our needs!'

It was not in Richard's nature to force himself on Polly, however great his need for her. So he kissed her again and had to be satisfied for now. Soon Polly was really asleep but Richard lay awake for some time beside her, looking at the starlit sky through the open curtains and wishing with all his heart that everything could be alright again between them. Eventually he, too, slept.

Buttons had crept out of his basked and wriggled himself in beside Minty. He was neatly curled up with his tiny chocolate and cream coloured head resting contentedly on the pillow.

Pixie and Pod had been banished to the kitchen with Tweed and Heather. John had staged a mild protest to Rosie.

'Granny, it's not fair, they always sleep with us in their basket ...' but seeing quite a cross expression on his grandmother's normally happy face, he had decided not to pursue the matter. He contented himself with a muttered...

''Cos of that little rat cat I s'ppose' before stomping off for his bath.

Later still, Rosie, quietly opening the door, looked in at her sleeping grandchildren. A lump came into her throat as she saw the neat little figure of Minty, lying tidily as usual in the bed, with the equally neat and composed kitten sleeping peacefully next to her, curled into a little brown and cream comma.

John, as ever, was under the untidy heap of duvet, pillow and the teddy bear, which he still refused to discard, also hanging perilously out of the bed!

Giving herself a mental shake, she knew she was happy that at least she had them all safely tucked under her wing at Whitewalls tonight and Charles, too, would soon be home, Rosie went to join her darling Jamie in what the actress, Mrs Patrick

Campbell, had memorably described as the "deep, deep peace of the double bed".

Saturday passed in the usual hurly burly of activity that characterized family weekends at Whitewalls.

Minty was unable to be very active but John was prevailed upon to push her in the borrowed wheelchair to the stables, where two very frisky ponies were kicking and squealing in adjoining boxes. They were too used to being out in the field when not being ridden by the twins to appreciate the comfort of deep straw beds and nets filled with fresh hay.

John had secretly pretended to himself that he was one of Queen Boudiccea's trusty soldiers pushing his temporarily injured queen in a small chariot to inspect her magnificent steeds. This nearly made up for the embarrassment of pushing the chair.

After they had fed the ponies carrots, John saddled up Butterball, with some help from Richard, who then took over wheelchair duties whilst John took the pony out for some exercise, promising rashly also to ride Snowball later on.

With his hard hat firmly plonked on to his head, John (aka Harry Potter in his secret life) went off on his next big adventure, riding alone.

Rosie recruited Polly to help with the garden. So the two women hoed and weeded in a pleasant and relaxed fashion. It was a mild spring day with a gentle breeze and high white clouds in the blue sky allowing plenty of sunshine to warm them at their task.

Rosie thought that she would broach the subject of the state of Polly and Richard's marriage. That was a mistake.

As soon as her mother asked in a carefully "casual" voice,

'Is everything alright between you and Richard, Polly?' Polly tightened her mouth and stiffened. She countered with another question.

'And why should it not be alright?' she asked with more than a touch of asperity in her voice.

Rosie, treading warily, said,

'Well, with Roddy's surprise announcement about leaving everything to Richard, Minty's accident which has been a great worry to all of us, much more for you two, of course, and there seems to be such a strained atmosphere between you both ....' Her voice unusually tapered off. Polly looked angry and her reply readily confirmed her feelings.

'Mum, please don't pry. Don't speak to me as if I were still a child. I'm not. I am a married woman, a mother of two children and run my own, successful business! Yes, things have been difficult, but everyone goes through bad times as well as good. I don't want to discuss Richard and Grandpa – it's between them, nothing to do with me any more. Charles might feel upset, too, but that's for him to sort out, not me and certainly not you!'

Rosie looked at Polly in amazement. Rarely had she seen her so angry or vehement. She paused, before replying. Polly looked defiant. Rosie put her arm round her daughter's shoulder. Polly stiffened.

'I didn't mean to pry, just to help. I thought you might just like to have a chat about things.'

Polly shook her head.

'That's the trouble. You always mean to help. You're so bloody perfect; you and Dad, perfect people, perfect lives, perfect harmony, perfect marriage. How can anyone measure up to that in reality?' There, she had said what she had been thinking for so long. She didn't feel good about hurting her mother but Polly thought "it's time she let go".

Leaving Rosie looked bewildered, and feeling hurt; she turned on her heel and went away into the house.

The two women avoided each other as far as possible, for the remainder of the weekend. Jamie spent some time with Minty in his studio where she had her own area set up, complete with a table at just the right height, and her drawing pad and Caran d'ache colour sticks neatly set out beside it.

Richard spent much of the weekend with Roddy at the Stud and John happily tagged along. He liked being with his Dad, his Great-Grandpa and the horses.

On Sunday afternoon, Polly, Richard and John returned to Edinburgh to begin another week. They left Minty behind. She was composed, as ever, happy to be with her loving grandparents, as well as her kitten.

Chapter 10

Edinburgh

Richard dropped John off at Edinburgh Academy at quarter past eight on Monday morning following the family weekend at Whitewalls. John leaped out of the car, keen to get on with his day. He had really enjoyed his weekend and he had loads of stuff to tell his friends, including leading out the new foal who was very, very strong and Great Grandpapa had said that John handled her very steadily, very well. That had made him feel really proud.

'Bye Dad, going to Henry's after school, so remind Mum not to collect me.'

With that he was swallowed up in a crowd of boys, similarly clad in the distinctive dark blue blazer, blue and white striped tie and grey flannel shorts. Even at this early hour John's tie was already round the back of his neck, one sock was at half mast and his pale blue shirt tail hung out at the back of his shorts.

Richard smiled as he watched his sturdy son, so full of life and confidence; disappear among the melee through the school gates. He sighed. If only his life were as uncomplicated at John's seemed to be. Everything had seemed fine until Polly had this idea of the cooking business and whilst he was immensely flattered at Roddy's generosity it had driven a wedge between them. Then there was something about David MacLean that he really did not trust. Oh well, better put that all out of his mind, there was a lot to do at work.

He turned up the volume of his CD of Beethoven's 6th symphony and drove on to the underground car park of McGregor, McLeod and Ross, the long established Edinburgh law firm where he had worked for the last ten years. Richard knew that he was very close to being made a partner, but was it what he really, really wanted? In many ways he was happiest in the country; staying with his in-laws, whom he loved, and whose way of life seemed infinitely attractive and settled. He was so happy when spending time with Roddy and horses, feeling free. He been flattered and moved by Roddy's revelation that, after his death, Home Farm and the Stud would be left to him. Really he couldn't understand why Polly was so upset about it all, they were married and shared everything, didn't they?

Fiona, the very pretty and equally bright personal assistant who Richard shared with Henry McLeod's father, Robert, was not yet in the office and Robert was going straight to Court that morning. Richard and Robert had been at Edinburgh Academy together and had remained friends through university. Their early years together at McGregor, McLeod and Ross had progressed harmoniously without too much in the way of competition or rivalry between them. It was an uncomplicated friendship but deep and solid for all that.

However, their wives were not close friends. Polly and Karen got on well enough but apart from their joint interests with the children, particularly with Henry and John being best friends, they rarely saw each other on non-school related occasions or office functions.

Robert was a very laid back, yet conventional man. His family had all been 'in the law' and his choice of career had been natural with no agonising or doubt involved.

Richard, on the other hand, had largely followed what his parents had expected him to do, despite some fairly serious doubts about it being the right path.

Stephen, Richard's father was a manager at one of the large insurance companies that are so much a feature of Edinburgh's financial scene but had wanted, and expected, that all the sacrifices he and Richard's mother, Moira, had made to pay for the Academy and to support Richard through what his mother insisted on calling 'uni' would amply be repaid by their only son entering the Edinburgh establishment. They saw themselves as basking in his reflected glory as he became a High Constable or even a Royal Archer.

Richard sat at his desk, ran his hands through his soft mousy brown short hair and let out a huge sigh. His boyish looks and lean frame gave him a very youthful appearance, which Polly had once found so attractive. In general, people liked and trusted him. His seniors in the firm noted and approved of this and he was being seriously considered for the promotion that would be the next step in his, so far, unspectacular though sound career.

The door opened and Fiona whirled into the room. She was petite, bouncy girl with short, shiny dark hair'; worn in a short bob. She had a wonderful smile and a sunny disposition. Almost without exception people warmed to her. As usual she was wearing her uniform of closely fitting black trousers and white shirt topped with a scarlet jacket cut like an Army officer's mess jacket.

'Hi Richard, lovely morning, hope you had a great weekend. Mike and I went paragliding in Perth, it was just sensational! You should try it – cheer you up a bit.'

He hadn't been aware of looking unhappy, but the events of the past few weeks had been a strain and he realised that he must have seemed somewhat down in spirits, particularly to the bright and carefree Fiona. Oh, if only Polly could regain some of her bounce and cheerfulness and leave behind all the brooding and dark moods. At a deep level he was afraid of losing her.

With an effort, he smiled.

'Thanks, Fi, but I think that I have enough excitement in my life right now. Any chance of a cup of coffee, please?'

'Of course, Richard, and I've brought in some wicked chocolate biscuits.'

The telephone rang. Fiona answered it, moving smartly from fun and frothy mode to cool efficiency. She might like to give the impression of frivolity but in truth she was highly efficient. Really she wanted a career in the media, but the lawyers' office would do for now and was great for meeting people.

'Yes, Mr Johnston. You want Richard to have lunch with you today in the Alba Club? He's right here; would you like to speak to him?'

She arched her pretty eyebrows and handed him the telephone.

'Good morning, Richard' said Hamish Johnston, McLure's Senior Partner. He spoke in a formal, even old-fashioned way, as befitted the Senior Partner of a prestigious Edinburgh law firm.

'Sorry about the short notice but if you can manage to organise your day to have lunch with me at the Alba Club at one o'clock I'd be grateful.' Both men knew that Hamish Johnston was simply being polite. A request to lunch with the Senior Partner was a summons, not an option.

'Thanks, Hamish' responded Richard alertly, 'I'd like that, very much.'

He wanted to know what this was all about but wisely did not ask. Hamish was one of the old school of Edinburgh lawyers and a senior and well-respected figure of the Edinburgh establishment, too. He did not issue commands to lunch at the Alba Club lightly.

'I will see you in the Bar at one o'clock' Hamish said and rang off.

Fiona grinned, 'That sounds important' she said, and 'good job I brought the choccy biscuits you'd better have two, to give you extra energy.'

Richard cheered up. He knew Hamish didn't ask people to lunch at the exclusive Alba Club for no good reason. Richard was aware he had kept his work going at the high standard expected at McLures in spite of Minty's accident and the strained atmosphere at home. Maybe there would be some good news.

The morning passed swiftly and uneventfully. At a quarter to one Richard left the office, went downstairs and out into Queen Street into the bright spring sunshine. He walked purposefully up the steep hill of Hanover Street, across George Street with its elegant and expensive shops and downhill again to where the Royal Scottish Academy sat, in its classical splendour, at the foot of the Mound on the south side of Princes Street.

The building where the Alba Club is housed discreetly is situated in a dreadful-looking 1960's building. Inside, however, all is dark wood and hushed voices as befits an old-established gentleman's club. Originally the committee had frowned upon the practice of business lunches. But as more and more former "gentlemen" who had made up the earlier membership engaged in professional and business lunches and dinners, a blind eye had been turned to the practice. Women were still not permitted to be full members.

Richard felt excited at the prospect of lunch with Hamish. All at once working in the law seemed a very satisfying career. After all, he reflected Whitewalls and all that it represented was

271

there for him at weekends and holidays so perhaps, after all, he had the best of both worlds.

The Steward indicated that Mr Johnston had just arrived and was waiting for Richard in the Bar.

Hamish Johnston was quiet, shrewd man. His chalk-striped business suit was exquisitely tailored and he was wearing a pale blue shirt and discreet, but expensive dark silk tie. He liked Richard, and felt he would make a good Junior Partner in the firm. Hamish was shrewd enough to know that Richard, though very competent, still had doubts about his career. What Hamish was about to tell him would surely dispel any such uncertainties? Richard, he mused, was a pleasant and presentable young man with a solid marriage. His family background was pretty ordinary, but sound. It had, of course, done him no harm to marry into the Douglas family. Amazingly these things mattered even now in the 21st century. Edinburgh, whilst being a vibrant capital city, still retained a deeply conservative 'establishment.'

Hamish shook Richard warmly by the hand.

'Hello, Richard, good of you to come.' As if he had any choice, Richard thought.

'Gin and tonic?' his host enquired.

'Oh, thanks; just a small one, please' Richard replied. He didn't normally drink at lunchtime but it would be unwise to refuse.

Hamish clapped his hand on Richard's shoulder

'Relax, Richard. I simply thought it would be good for us to have a quiet lunch together and a chat about your future.'

Richard grinned and, as bidden, tried to relax.

Over the very Scottish lunch of soup, followed by steak and kidney pudding and cheese, washed down by a decent bottle of claret, the conversation ranged easily.

The topics were safe; golf, horses, a shared interest as Richard now discovered, living in the city versus living in the country and so on.

Over coffee Hamish suddenly gave Richard a very direct look and said.

'Grace and I, as you know, were so sorry to hear about Minty's accident.' They had sent flowers to Polly and a wonderfully illustrated copy of The Wind in the Willows for Minty, adding the inevitable Potter book for John.

'I hope,' Hamish continued, 'she's still making good progress?'

"Well there have been a few setbacks so she's now down at Whitewalls with the in-laws and St Georges are setting work for her so she doesn't get left behind."

Their coffee cups were refilled and the dining room was, by now practically empty.

'Richard, my partners and I have been talking about the future direction of the firm and the need to bring younger blood more closely into the management of the business. All law practices these days have to be businesslike or they don't survive. We've identified a need for another Junior Partner, maybe two. So, we would like to offer you the opportunity to take a share in the practice.'

Richard opened his mouth to speak but Hamish lifted his hand to show he had not yet finished.

'I realise finding the necessary capital might not be totally convenient for you right now but we are prepared to help you and you will also be paid pretty much as you are at present but with a share of profits, too.'

Now Richard did respond.'

'Hamish, what can I say? I think it would be a wonderful opportunity. Thank you very much for thinking of me for a partnership. I'm sure Polly will be just as pleased.'

'What I want you to do before you respond formally are to speak to Peter Crawford who is, as you know, the financial brains in the practice. He will go over that side of things with you and then you can talk it over with Polly and come back to me with your decision.'

Richard smiled broadly now.

'I'm pretty sure that the answer will be yes.' He felt flattered and pleased.

Hamish smiled and signalled he wanted to sign the bill. The lunch was over.

His step was springy as Richard strode back along Princes Street up Hanover Street and along George Street to the office. He decided to take Polly out to dinner and give her the good news. Why not? John was going to Harry's after school anyway and he could probably easily stay overnight. The Witchery – that would impress her. He would push the boat out and maybe get their currently non-existent sex life back on track.

He had promised Hamish he would not discuss the proposed promotion with anyone in the office until decisions had been reached by both parties. Even so it was difficult not to say anything to Robert, who arrived back from Court not long after Richard's return from the prolonged Alba Club lunch. Richard was, in fact, then very tempted to drop a hint but, fortunately, his natural caution prevailed. Anyway Robert was pretty pleased with himself. He had won his case in the Sheriff Court and was more than happy to expound on how well he had defended his client and seen off the Procurator Fiscal.

'How about a drink after work to celebrate?' he asked Richard.

'Thanks. It will need to be quick one though. I'm taking Polly out to dinner this evening. It's meant to be a surprise, cheer her up a bit. Will it be okay, do you think, for John to stay overnight at your house after rugby? ' Robert replied at once, 'Sure, no trouble. I'll give Karen a call and they can pick up some things on the way home from school. Is Polly working this afternoon?'

Richard grimaced. 'I'm afraid so, for that fellow David, something, or other. These smooth interior designer types never seem to do anything except ponce around and have lunches.' He had felt uneasy about David, ever since the cat incident but he pushed it to the back of his mind. After all these arty men were always a bit bent.

'Consider it settled, Richard. I'll see you in the bar of the George at 5 30. I must go and tell William about my success.' William Harper was the Court Partner and not easy to impress so any opportunity had to be taken whilst a case was still 'hot news'.

Richard tried to reach Polly on both the house and mobile numbers, but in each case the answering services clicked in. So he had to leave brief messages saying that he was taking her out to dinner and that he had organised that John would stay over at Henry's house.

Polly and David's 'stolen afternoons of passion' ought now to have taken on a more urgent quality or begun to pall. Neither was the case. Despite a little worrying voice that reminded her of the inherent dangers in what she was doing, putting her marriage and children at risk, Polly was still drawn to David like a moth to a lighted candle. David, for his part, found what had begun as simply a sexual adventure was becoming more and more important to him. The truth was he was falling deeply in love for the first time in his life.

Neither really knew what to do. Both were uncharacteristically afraid. So they continued to meet whenever and wherever they could, increasingly taking risks, going out together for lunch at the Café St Honore and Fishers in the City, dreading but almost wanting to be seen together.

When Polly switched her mobile back on and the message bleeper sounded she looked quickly and said,

'Oh God, I wonder what's brought this on.' By now she was dressed and David, who was lounging on the black leather sofa in his immaculate dressing gown, looked concerned.

'What is it, darling?' he asked

'It's Richard. Says he has something important to tell me. He wants to take me out to dinner this evening. Do you think that he knows about us? What will we do?' she cried.

Hiding his own feeling of anxiety, David got up and hugged Polly gently.

'No, Pollyanna, I'm sure it's nothing to worry about. Maybe he is having a fit of conscience for neglecting you! That's all it will be, you'll see.'

She still looked troubled.

'I'd better go, there just may be something else going on.'

They kissed passionately. He didn't, for once, tease her or try to make her stay longer.

Later, dashing into the house, Polly saw the red light on the answering machine was flashing and, mindful of what had happened before when she had been with David and Richard had tried to reach her, she picked up the message.

It was from Richard. The same message as on the mobile answering service. There were butterflies in her stomach? What could it be? Had he found out about David? Anyway he would hardly want to take her out to dinner, would he, if that were the case?

Polly made herself a cup of tea and went upstairs to have a long relaxing shower then she supposed she should find something fairly smart to wear.

She was still swathed in her bath towel with a towel turban on her head when she heard Richard come in. He bounded quickly up the stairs and into their bedroom.

'Hello, darling' he said very cheerfully, kissing her on the back of her neck. Momentarily she stiffened; this was a David embrace. Richard didn't notice though and followed it up with a deep kiss on her mouth.

Deliberately smiling warmly at her husband, Polly made a big effort and said,

'Darling, what's all this about? Do tell!'

Richard responded happily,

'No, Polly, you'll have to wait. Wear something glamorous. We're going to the Witchery. "No! That was *their place* – David's and hers." But she couldn't say anything.

By this time Richard, whistling to show how pleased he was with himself, had stripped off and gone to have a shower. After drying her hair Polly put on a simple black sheath dress, some makeup and added her pearls. They had been Richard's wedding gift to her almost ten years ago. That seemed like another life.

In order to avoid any further intimacy, she called out,

'Richard, I'll see you downstairs.' If he heard her above the shower and his tuneless rendering of Cliff Richard's song 'Congratulations' which he was belting out with great vigour, he didn't answer.

Polly found it very strange to be having dinner at the Witchery with Richard. When she looked back to the first evening when she had shared dinner and the excitement of the start of their affair with David she still experienced a powerful feeling of excitement. Oddly, they hadn't been back there, preferring to keep that first magic evening locked away in their memories. She had a moment's anxiety when James Thomson, the urbane owner of The Witchery greeted them and said,

'Mr and Mrs Graham, how lovely to see you. You both look so well. The champagne is on ice waiting for you, would you like to go directly to your table?' With true suave professionalism there was absolutely no indication from James that he had seen Polly there with an altogether different man.

In the end, Polly relaxed. Over the excellent meal, Richard's enthusiasm about the proposed partnership and his clear delight in having been singled out by Hamish, she was reminded of the boyish charm and enthusiasm that had attracted her to him so much in the first place. Over the coffee and brandy, taking her hands in his Richard asked, 'So, darling, shall we go for it?'

She softened. 'If it is what you really want, and we can afford it, why not?"

They returned home by taxi sitting closely together.

With the house to themselves that night and the effects of the champagne and brandy relaxing them both, they made love in a very satisfying way that had been absent for so long. And if Polly closed her eyes at the moment of climax and saw David's dark and mocking face above her, it made no difference to Richard's pleasure and supreme satisfaction. As he drifted contentedly to sleep, he reflected this had been the best day in his life for a long, long time.

Chapter 11

Whitewalls

At Whitewalls Rosie was trying to turn her attention again to her garden. Apart from the previous weekend working in it with Polly, she felt she had neglected the garden recently, especially since Minty's accident.

She was troubled by her granddaughter's slow progress with walking and felt Minty was spending too much time being wheeled about in her chair. But what could she do to help matters? Rosie was not good at letting things take their course. She was forever pushing and pulling to move things along.

'I don't want to fall, or hurt my leg again, Granny' Minty explained when Rosie had gently raised the subject with her.

Jamie had been so good with Minty, too. He had encouraged her to draw and paint in her own corner of the studio. As well, he had taken her over to Roddy and together they had gently lifted her on to Snowball and supported her whilst the pony, quiet for once as if sensing his usual boisterous style was not wanted, walked on a leading rein through the fields and pathways down to the river bank. Roddy, seeing this had felt very touched. Indeed he had felt a sharp pain in the region of his heart, which he dismissed as mere sentiment.

'I want to take Minty to North Berwick for a few days.' Rosie told Jamie. In fact, it wasn't exactly unplanned. She had been wracking her brains to come up with something to distract Minty, and herself for that matter.

'What on earth for? And where?' he answered fairly mildly. Why couldn't Rosie just "be" for a change? She was forever poking and prodding at life these days.

'Hasn't she got everything she needs here? And why North Berwick, anyway?' he asked thinking at the same time that any such excursion would be bound adversely to affect the smooth running of his household. Rosie answered him in a firm voice,

'She's become too dependent, particularly on the wheelchair; everything here is too familiar and I think we need to get her into a different environment for a while. Joan Mackeson's cottage is available next week. It's right on the seafront and we could go straight on to the beach. In fact, Joan suggested it when we were chatting on the phone yesterday. So I've slept on it and I think it's a good idea.' If Rosie were completely honest, the thought of getting right away from all her pressing problems and never ending tasks was very attractive, even without the undoubted benefits there would be for Minty.

'Well, if it's such a good idea, why can't Polly take her? And what about John? He's been very good and cheerful but he seems to be getting more and more left out of things.' Jamie rarely felt exasperated with his wife but things were getting seriously out of hand and he might have to, somehow, put his foot down. He hated that thought.

Rosie sighed heavily. Why was Jamie suddenly being awkward? In all their serene years of marriage together he had rarely questioned either her judgement or her actions. Still she tried to sound patient and calm.

'Look, Polly's preoccupied with work and she still feels guilty about the accident. John is happy in school and with his friends. It wouldn't be right to take him out now. Besides it really is Minty who needs building up and cheering up; me, too, for that matter. Some bracing sea air might be just the thing. Molly will take over here and we'll be back before you know we're even gone. Anyway, haven't you got paintings to finish for your Exhibition as well as running the farm?'

Jamie hugged his wife tightly. He felt remorseful. Rosie was so kind; always thinking of others. It was a novel idea, and indeed a worrying one that she might express some weakness or need of her own.

'Poor love, you are looking a bit peaky, not yourself at all, and no wonder,' he said noticing that she did, indeed, look washed out. He went on,

'Actually it might be a good idea to get Minty away from here for a while and perhaps you could relax a bit, too!'

Rosie gave him one of her special wide smiles. He pulled her gently to him, kissed her equally tenderly and said,

'As always, you have my blessing. I'll take Minty to the studio this morning. She's working on something important to her. Also, I'll sound her out about North Berwick. It's important to know if she would like to go there.'

Rosie smiled gratefully and went back to her lists in her usual efficient manner. She was pleased with Jamie's support and more happily went off to start organising what they were going to take with them to the seaside.

Jamie was thoughtful as he went off to retrieve Minty and her chair to go to the studio. The relaxed, easy tenor of his life had been disturbed. Whilst he was a sensitive man in many ways, particularly through his art, he did like an ordered and calm existence, which is what he normally enjoyed.

Minty's face lit up when he called to her from the kitchen garden where she was sitting on a rug on the grass playing with Buttons, who, though growing a little was still tiny and neat, like his owner. The wheelchair was parked nearby.

'Time for some art work Minty. But we'll leave the chair behind and your kitten as well. It's not far to the studio and you can hang on to my arm.'

She looked doubtful, scared even. "Oh no," she thought. "I can't do this. I'm not strong enough. I might fall and hurt myself again."

'Come on, Minty' he urged.

'What if I fall over?' she asked in a trembly voice.

'Then I shall pick you up. Easy, but you won't fall, I promise.' He wished he were as sure as he sounded.

'Well, I'll try but I must bring Buttons, will you carry him for me?' Minty was not so weak that she was above trying a little gentle guile on her kind grandfather.

Seeing that was the only way to get his granddaughter's agreement Jamie concurred. He didn't really like cats; in truth he was more used to shooting them to protect the game that he reared, which he then went on to shoot, seeing nothing incongruous about that in his countryman's rulebook. Still he was determined to get Minty moving without crutches.

Slowly, nervously and hanging on grimly to his arm Minty walked with him to the studio whilst Buttons clung to his shoulder.

'But how am I going to get back?' she asked, anxiously once they had arrived and she was safely ensconced in her own little area by the north-facing window.

Jamie felt a stab of guilt. Poor child. She'd been through such an ordeal and, somehow, through it lost her confidence. He hadn't really been paying close enough attention, thinking his quiet little granddaughter would shake off the setback and be back to normal quickly.

Jamie put his arm round Minty's slender shoulder and hugged her.

'Come on, Minty, love. The worst is over. You'll soon be as good as new.'

He was rewarded with a heart-breaking smile that reminded him so much of his Rosie.

Rosie, having resolved the issue of borrowing Joan Mackeson's beach cottage felt much more cheerful. Briefly she thought of trying to take along a friend of Minty, too, but swiftly rejected the idea. Her plan was to get Minty away, enjoy some bracing sea air, which would help to rebuild her confidence and prepare for a return to normal life. The leg plaster was due to be removed in three weeks' time and more progress urgently needed to be made so she was ready for that. Besides she was looking forward to spending time alone with her granddaughter and away from her own hectic life.

In the end, it was all arranged with the minimum of fuss. Richard and Polly were consulted, but whilst they were unsure of the value of the proposed seaside trip for Minty, both knew better than to cross Rosie, or question her reasons when she was clearly determined on the plan.

Jamie, for his part, was rather looking forward to a few days 'bothying' as he put it. Though being left to the ministrations of Molly, who given even half a chance, would spoil him completely with all his favourite meals would be no hardship at all!

So two days later a now excited Minty and a more light-hearted Rosie were packed and on their way to North Berwick. As well as the necessary clothes and provisions, fishing nets and buckets and spades they were accompanied by Empress and

Buttons who had forged a very sweet friendship – probably as they were both small and recognized at some primeval level that together they were a bulwark against the bounding Labradors and yapping Norfolk terriers. At the last minute Pixie and Pod were added to the party.

North Berwick is a bustling seaside town, some 20 miles south east of Edinburgh and, as the name suggests, north of the Border town of Berwick. Apart from the local authority finally closing the increasingly decrepit, unheated outdoor swimming pool – in the teeth of vociferous local opposition – it had changed remarkably little since the 1960's. Even the High Street remained relatively intact, with a Woolworths and real shops, including greengrocers and bakeries. These co-existed happily with art galleries and old-fashioned newsagents that also sold buckets and spades and little fishing nets for children.

Joan Mackeson's tiny cottage was huddled just off Forth Street, almost right on to the beach. It had a tiny garden and, even more importantly, a private parking space at the side.

Minty had been very quiet during the journey through Peebles, to the outskirts of Edinburgh, round the City bypass and on to the coast road. They travelled through Aberlady, Gullane and finally reached North Berwick.

Empress and Buttons had spent the journey snuggled together in their spacious double carrying basket, and even the terriers had quietened down with just an occasional yap to remind Rosie and Minty they were there.

As Rosie finally turned into the space beside Beach Cottage though, Minty's face lit up and she said,

'Oh Granny, look, it's lovely like a little doll's house and you can see the beach, it's right there!'

Rosie let out a huge sigh of relief. Her instincts, she knew, had been right and she immediately experienced a lightening of spirit. Slowly, carefully, but with increasing confidence with every step Minty went into the tiny hallway and through to the sitting room.

'Granny, come and look, it's like being right on the beach, we're nearly in the sea.'

Rosie knew the cottage well but had purposely not told Minty very much about it, hoping its delightful situation on the beach and quirkiness of the cottage would give the immediate impression of a fun and secret place. It was with the feeling of a great weight being lifted from her shoulders that Rosie heard the hint of animation and excitement in Minty's voice.

The floor was of old oak planks, polished by many feet through the passage of time and whilst the cream and blue rugs might be a bit of a hazard for Minty's crutches and need to be uplifted, they looked warm and welcoming; as did the two squashy sofas, one right under the curved window, both upholstered in a blue and cream checked fabric. The shelves on the wall adjoining the window were crammed full of old books. There were Dornford Yates and John Buchan tales for the grown ups and everything that Arthur Ransome had written, including the perennial favourite 'Swallows and Amazons' as well as an impressive shelf of Enid Blyton stories so the needs of children were also well met.

There was a gate-leg table with a rush-seat chair at either side, against the wall right next to the tiny kitchen, which contained everything you could possibly need for making meals whilst on holiday.

Luckily the bathroom was on the ground floor, as well as a pretty blue and white painted bedroom with two single beds, complete with thick white cotton bedspreads from Portugal. On the walls were little oil paintings of fishing boats and children playing on the beach.

A narrow, steep wooden staircase led upstairs to two other small bedrooms. Minty limped towards it. She smiled at her grandmother and said,

'I'd love to explore up there, but we can save that for next time when my leg is working properly.' Minty felt a new courage and warmth running through her.

'Of course, we can. Do you mind sharing your bedroom down here with me, darling? Or I could go upstairs with Empress if you and Buttons would rather be on your own with Pod and

Pixie.' Rosie asked. She was keen that Minty made the decisions as that, too, would be good for her confidence.

'No, no, it will be such fun. We can pretend to be friends away on an adventure.' Minty was feeling braver, but not so brave that she wasn't still a little afraid of falling if she had to get up in the middle of the night.

For what seemed like the first time in a long time she was smiling and there was a hint of colour in her cheeks.

'Right,' said Rosie 'time for action. We'll open the windows, as it's such a nice day. You keep Buttons and the dogs safely in here and get them used to the place and I'll bring everything in from the car. We'll have some tea and then go on an exploring expedition.'

Left to her own devices, with Buttons careering round the room, jumping over the sofas watched by a disdainful Empress, and positively encouraged by Pixie and Pod Minty got herself over to the Enid Blyton books, by hanging on to the furniture. She was at last able to take possession of a Famous Five book to read and savour later on. Whilst Enid Blyton was long out of date in the modern world of children's reading her books were exactly right for a rather scared young girl who was still in a very jumpy frame of mind.

Afterwards, Rosie looked back at these few golden June days, spent with Minty in North Berwick as healing, calming and fun. The weather was kind, sunny and warm but with, for once, gentle breezes blowing pleasantly across the sand and providing just enough ozone to invigorate both of them.

From the first cosy evening with hot and tasty fish and chips from the nearby café, eaten by both of them with great gusto, through gentle promenades along the High Street, a visit to the Seabird Centre and little trips to Dirleton and Tantallon to see the castles, Rosie and Minty achieved an easy harmony, which never again left them. Years later, when Minty was happily married with a daughter of her own she always recalled that special few days with her grandmother as one of the best times of her life.

Minty's walking ability improved in leaps and bounds and whilst the ungainly leg plaster meant that she was unable to paddle in the shallow beach-side sea water, she derived great amusement from watching her Granny kick off her sneakers and hold up her cotton skirt until a wave, rather larger than the rest, gave the hem a very thorough wetting. They both laughed when this happened and Rosie was pleased at Minty's almost uncontrollable giggles.

After an early, simple supper evenings were spent playing card games, doing jigsaws or reading before a tired, but increasingly happy Minty went to bed in the little white bed under the window with the blue sprigged floral curtains only softening, not completely blotting out the early summer north light.

She slept easily and deeply, with Buttons curled up beside her on the bed and the little Norfolk terriers shared a basket at the foot. Rosie, too, enjoyed some of her deepest and most dreamless sleep in a very long time.

Five days later when they were packed and ready to leave, Minty gave Rosie a beautiful little picture of the harbour with tiny pictures of the animals dotted about and two figures holding hands – a Granny and a granddaughter. There were no crutches. It was a charming picture and painted with such love.

Rosie felt a great lump in her throat. 'It's for you to remind you, for ever Granny, about this time we've had together. I feel just about well again and not funny and uncomfortable in my head, as well as my leg being so much better. So I wanted to say thank you.' Rosie couldn't speak. She just hugged Minty, kissed her on the top of her head and smiled. Finding her voice at last she said,

'Thank you Minty, I will get Antonio to frame this and keep it beside me for ever.' She did.

Whitewalls

Despite his mild fears of feeling neglected, Jamie, too, thrived during the brief separation from Rosie. He still got up early, dispatched his farming duties pretty smartly then spent the days finishing work for his forthcoming exhibition in Edinburgh's prestigious New Town Gallery.

His style was gentle but, at the same time, his depiction of the scenes of Border countryside that he loved so much showed a timeless perspective so those viewing the works could imagine themselves in the landscape and feel they really were there.

Hamish McLucas, who ran the highly successful New Town Gallery, situated in the 'art gallery cluster' around the upper end of Dundas Street in the New Town had already staged exhibitions of Jamie's work. They always sold very well and the next one was he was certain would be just as good as those that had gone before. The day before Rosie and Minty were due to return from North Berwick, Jamie had arranged to have lunch at the Arts Club in Rutland Square. He drove into Edinburgh, parked his car in the Castle Terrace car park and enjoyed the ten minute stroll from there to the Club. As well as artists and dealers the Arts Club was also a popular haunt of advocates and other members of the legal profession. The food was simple, almost homely, but it suited both men well.

'Have you ever thought of giving up the farming to paint full-time?' Hamish enquired. Jamie had, indeed, thought about it but too much depended on his being able to continue farming, at least as long as his father was still alive.

'Can't really afford to do that, much as I am tempted sometimes' Jamie replied.

'You really are very saleable, you know. But if that's your decision then I shall just carry on doing the very best that I can for you on the current basis.' Jamie reflected that this meant that he retained the best of both of his worlds, the land and painting. He was a fortunate man.

That settled, they concluded their business amicably enough. Jamie was conscious that he had to drive back to the Borders so declined the offer of a brandy from his host and offered Hamish a lift back to Dundas Street. 'Well, it's a bit out of your way, but I'll be lazy and say yes anyway. Come in and look at the latest Annabelle Traquair's pictures; I think they are the best that she has done.' Hamish was a charming, old-fashioned type of Art Dealer. He was not greedy and represented his artists well without taking too great a cut from the sales. In the Edinburgh Art world he was well respected and, equally important, almost universally liked.

301

After a brief visit to the New Town Gallery which, in fact, reassured Jamie his own work was at least equal to the standard of a number of paintings displaying the all-important red dot, denoting that they had been sold, Jamie said goodbye to Hamish and went back into Dundas Street. Seeing a traffic warden briskly approaching his old Mercedes, parked on a single yellow line, he jumped in smartly and turned on the engine.

He was just about to pull out when a sleek black Porsche came down the hill at some speed. There was a dark haired man at the wheel and a pretty, curly-haired blonde woman in the passenger seat. They eyes met briefly. She put her hand to her mouth and turned her head away. It was Polly.

Jamie would not have thought too much about it had it not been for his brief glimpse of the guilty expression on his daughter's face. There was probably a simple and innocent enough explanation but he was sure that she had seen him. Why had she not at least waved?

He drove off in a very thoughtful and rather troubled frame of mind.

'That was my Dad, David, he saw us. I'm sure of it!' Polly said.

David just laughed, reached over and kissed her behind her right ear.

"Relax, Pollyanna. We were hardly seen in a compromising position. I'm a client, what could be wrong with my driving you home?' They soon reached his flat in Moray Place.

'Coming in?' he asked silkily, 'or has seeing Daddy scared you off?' He was teasing but there was a touch of mockery and malice in his voice.

She turned in the seat, took his face in her hands and warmly kissed him on the mouth. Polly was damned if either her father, or her lover were going to make up her mind for her. So she replied with more than a touch of bravado,

'What are we waiting for?' then added. 'I suppose you're right. But it would have looked more convincing if we had stopped and I'd introduced you!'

David drew up outside the apartment and turned Polly's face towards him. He very deliberately and passionately kissed her on the lips not giving a damn if there was anyway to see them

together.

Chapter 12

High Wynch Park

Virginia was in her element. From initially pouring scorn on Hugh's idea of making money by renting out the house and grounds to film maker, Piers Romayne, she was now convinced it had all been entirely her own idea. After all, it was a glamorous world and one that suited her very well indeed.

She had even wheedled a harassed Romayne into giving her a small part in the film. It was only as a sophisticated guest at a stuffy country drinks party. Still, she got to dress up in a little black dress (her own naturally), wear enormous pearls which looked like fakes but were, in fact, family heirlooms and make silly conversation. She proved to be a natural performer. In fact, though he had no intention yet of telling her Romayne thought Virginia could have a very satisfactory small career playing aristocratic bitchy types.

At first Hugh was very doubtful about this turn of events. However, years of conditioning himself to Virginia's strong personality meant that any objection he could think of was rapidly demolished. As usual, he gave in without a struggle.

He did, though, decline Piers' offer to include him in the cocktail party scene.

'No thanks, old boy. Grateful for the offer but not my style. Leave all that kind of thing to Ginny.'

Unknown to Virginia, Anthony Goodsman had agreed to take part in that scene in the film. It was so unlike him Piers could hardly believe his ears when Anthony agreed to the not very serious suggestion that he should take part.

'Do you know?' he had said, 'I think that I might rather enjoy that.' Anthony had seen the Extras sheet with Virginia's name on it and thought this might be a good way of providing an opportunity to progress his intended sexual conquest of the cool blonde. For some time now Virginia had been playing very hard to get. He had an instinct, however, which told him she could be persuaded into an affair with him. Like most men, the more she feigned indifference the more interested he became.

Anthony had never married. He had enjoyed a number of satisfying, but unemotional relationships with a series of glamorous career women whom he had met in the course of building up his financial empire. Thus he always had a good-looking woman to accompany him to the many Receptions and Dinners to which he was invited. This also meant that there were no questions asked by anyone regarding his sexuality.

Hugh had not realised the extent of the upheaval that takes place when a private home, however spacious it is – and High Wynch Park was very large – is turned into a film set. He more and more frequently disappeared to a small, rose covered cottage in the village of Lower Compton some ten miles away where his mistress of many years standing, Angela Prescott lived. Sometimes, he reflected, it was very useful to be considered to be a bit of a fool!

Virginia, who was more street-wise than her husband had insisted only the Director, Piers, the principal stars and Maggie, who counted as family, could stay in the house. The rest of the cast were either put up in local hotels or guest houses, with the more up-market ones, in Virginia's opinion anyway, staying with friends of hers as paying guests. They, in turn, found it all 'frightfully exciting' and it was the hot topic at the regular round of dinner parties.

The grounds of High Wynch Park were also home to a number of caravans, mobile loos and caterers. Whilst the outbuildings, including a large disused garage had been fully taken over both for sets and for storing of props and costumes, the overall effect on Hugh's gardening activities was quite minimal though he was equally able to use it as an excuse for putting things off. In fact, he found it quite a relief to be able to say, whatever the issue

'Oh dear, we'll have to leave that until this dratted filming is over.'

High Wynch was only one of the locations for the filming of Country Pursuits. The plot was one of sex in politics, intrigue in high places with a couple of murders thrown in to bring some action and excitement to what would otherwise be only a comedy of class and manners.

Piers believed there was an untapped, largely middle-class audience for films that were glamorous, with lovely and sophisticated settings, together with titillating, though never vulgar, sex. The success of such films as 'Gosford Park' further reinforced this view and there was already a great deal of interest from major film distributors.

Caroline de Montford, a glamorous actress who, despite her professional name was a product of RADA, born in North London and really called Tracey Jones, was the female lead. She played the wife of the politician, who was having a tempestuous affair with the wife of a prominent member of the main opposition Party. Maggie played the part of the glamorous young woman who was head over heels in love with Simon Bradfield, the Minister who was unable to resist her, and who she decided to blackmail, with dramatic consequences.

Ralph Tremaine played Simon Bradfield. His dark good looks and perfect profile rivalled those of better-known actor, Hugh Grant. He did, however, cost much less.

At the heart of the plot – such as it was – was the attempted assassination of a Government minister and the implication in it of Simon Bradfield. This was a highly improbable scenario but provided the script with enough intrigue, twists and turns to balance the glamour and froth of the Westminster scenes, dinners at the Ritz and beauty treatments at Harrods and the apparent elegance and luxury of the well-heeled country life on the other!

Maggie was involved in both strands of the plot and was enjoying herself hugely. Charles was taking the opportunity of coming down to High Wynch Park to stay whenever he could. He was still pursuing her with relentless cheerfulness. She found, in fact, that she rather enjoyed this attention and noticed that the other female actors were envious of her handsome soldier boyfriend.

'It's wonderful you being here and I'm so proud of you.' he said over and over again. Maggie found him so attractive in bed that she couldn't bring herself to push him away. She did, though, try to explain that almost all her energies had to go into her acting and this was her big chance.

'Charles, darling, it is lovely to have you here too,' she said when they were lying luxuriating in a languid, warm and relaxed atmosphere following a particularly passionate encounter in the pretty bedroom Virginia had allocated to Maggie in the East wing.

'But you mustn't mind if I seem a bit distracted. This is my big chance and nothing, and no-one, not even you, must be allowed to get in the way.' But blind to all except her magnetism and his own urgent need, right then, to kiss the nape of her neck and start deeply and slowly to make love to Maggie again he smothered her protests with kisses and pushed her back against the piled-up pillows.

Virginia had invited Anthony to stay for the weekend following their brief appearance together in the scene. Neither of them had realised that filming can be a very boring and drawn out process, often with hours of filming before the producer is satisfied even with short scenes.

If Virginia had not been involved in the film Anthony would have pulled out after the first tedious session. However, he was pretty determined to make a conquest and so he stuck it out.

They managed to sit closely together on the same sofa in the scene, and no-one was any the wiser about their intentions. In fact at this point, neither Anthony nor Virginia was really certain how it would turn out or what, if anything, would develop. Each of them wanted a relationship but only on their own terms.

'Hughie's going away fishing for the weekend and I really hate being on my own,'

Virginia said to him during one of the interminable breaks. As a chat up line it didn't amount to much but it gave Anthony the message he was seeking. He moved in quickly.

'Perhaps you would come out to dinner with me this weekend, then? Would that help you to be less lonely?' he asked as they finally finished the scene where the suspicions of the politician's wife, Miranda, were first aroused. This was where she was supposed to see the intimate way her husband, Simon

Bradfield, had looked at Felicity, played by Maggie and the attention was really focused on them.

'I have to go up to London for a couple of days' he added 'but I could easily return on Saturday. I should hate you to be lonely without Hughie.'

She flashed him her most engaging smile.

'What a lovely idea! Why don't you come up on Saturday and stay over? Most people will have gone and we can probably have a really nice quiet time. I might even manage to cook dinner for you,' she added archly.

He simply smiled, squeezed her hand and said silkily.

'I will really look forward to that. I will bring champagne.' To himself he said

"You haven't lost your touch, old boy. This one is really ripe for picking underneath that Grace Kelly, icy exterior."

Virginia could not understand quite why she felt so excited and aroused at the idea of seducing, or being seduced by Anthony. Normally she did not care about sex and thought it all overrated and messy.

The truth was she was bored with Hughie; her children had left home but she did not want to believe the rest of her 'prime', as she liked to think of it to herself, would be spent in the same manner as recent years. She was bored. Attractive women, in their mid forties are often ready for an affair if only to prove that they are still sexually desirable. Virginia was not looking for commitment from Anthony but for excitement and confirmation she was still an attractive woman.

Maggie and Charles decided to go up to London on the Saturday morning and spend a weekend on their own together at Maggie's mews house.

'We can order food to be delivered from Partridge's and stay in bed all day if we want to do' she said. She felt a welling up of warmth and affection, mixed with desire towards her handsome lover.

'That sounds like perfection to me' he responded. 'I'm sick of sharing you with all these other people. I want you to myself for a while, out of bed as well as in it.'

Maggie was returning for more filming the following week so they quickly tossed some essentials into an overnight bag and by ten o'clock on Saturday morning Virginia was waving them off as they left in Charles' sports car. Charles could hardly wait to get her to himself, whilst Maggie was looking forward rather more to some peace and quiet after her hectic schedule.

Hughie had left early to go on a fishing trip with an old school friend, Peter Palmer, and Virginia had given him a very special, and mildly guilty, hug and kiss as he left, saying,

'Keep warm and dry darling. I know it's Spring but I don't want you catching pneumonia.' As well he might, Hugh looked somewhat startled at this unusual, and not even very appropriate remark.

Still he soon put any such thoughts out of his mind. He was looking forward to some very good fishing and a few drams afterwards in a very comfy and congenial riverside pub where he and Peter had been going for years. He would also call in and see Angela on his way back. With any luck he could arrange to stay overnight with his immensely comforting lover who ran a hairdressing salon.

Anthony was due to arrive in the afternoon, so Virginia had plenty of time to prepare. She decided it would be best to appear to be very cool; casual yet sophisticated; a woman of the world. The truth was she did not really know how she felt. She was more excited about seeing Anthony alone than she would admit to herself. Indeed she was experiencing some extremely sexy thoughts that had absolutely nothing to do with her apparently devoted husband and everything to do with the man whom she hoped was about to become her lover.

The house was very quiet after all the activity of recent weeks and she had given Sally Johnson, the cleaner, the whole weekend off. Singing to herself Virginia found some beautiful white linen sheets and pillowcases and meticulously made up the bed in her room with them. If that was where she and Anthony finished up, all well and good. If not, there was nothing lost.

Virginia decided that the food would be simple but delicious. She planned to do some fresh and juicy king prawns with a tangy sauce to begin and a simple casserole of chicken cooked with white wine and mushrooms, served with wild rice to follow. Tiny pots of bitter chocolate and a big piece of ripe Brie cheese with grapes would round off the meal. Anthony had promised to bring the wine but she put a bottle of Tattinger champagne to chill in the fridge to get them "in the mood", whatever the mood turned out to be.

Anthony was humming to himself as he drove towards Badminton and the delights of High Wynch Park. He was enjoying the delectable prospect of the seduction of Virginia after, he hoped, an excellent dinner with enough wine to release her inhibitions, but not so much that she would not give herself willingly and with enthusiasm.

London

Charles and Maggie were both looking forward to some time together, just the two of them. Maggie was tired after filming. Although she had enjoyed it all, she was now keen to be alone with Charles in the privacy of the mews house.

For his part, Charles was determined further to persuade her at least to agree a date to visit his family in Scotland and, hopefully, to get her to agree to becoming formally engaged.

As soon as they had unpacked Maggie decided that a long luxurious bath full of Floris Stephanotis bath essence would be the perfect preparation for an intimate afternoon and evening. It would be one that would concentrate on sensual pleasures.

Charles willingly popped along to Partridges where he bought champagne, some delicious-looking pate, a ready roasted chicken and salad. He added some crusty bread, unsalted butter and a hunk of cheddar cheese. As an afterthought, he also bought two bars of Green's organic dark chocolate and a bottle of fine brandy.

He whistled happily as he made his way back to the house and Maggie. After stowing the supplies in the tiny kitchen he ran lightly upstairs.

Maggie was just out of her bath and swathed in a huge white bath sheet. They enjoyed a long, lingering kiss before Charles went to shower. By the time he had finished Maggie was already in the bedroom with the curtains drawn against the afternoon light. She had put on a silky long slip of cream satin and her red hair, still damp from the bath curled over her bare shoulders. Maggie looked good enough to eat.

Throwing his own towel down on to the floor Charles took Maggie in his arms and made love to her in a highly passionate, loving and totally satisfactory fashion.

Later, before they dressed to have their picnic dinner he renewed his appeal to Maggie at least to make a firm promise to go with him to visit his parents in Scotland. Basking in afterglow she readily agreed and, for the first time, he felt sure of her. Maggie loved Charles; of that, at least, she was quite certain.

Right now the prospect of spending her life with him was a very sweet one.

Charles wasted no time in telephoning Rosie to give her the good news.

'I know you'll love her, Ma, she really is the sweetest, loveliest girl and she wants to come home with me and to meet you and Dad and Polly and everyone.'

Rosie was delighted. She knew that, of course, you shouldn't love one child more than another but she had always felt so close to her son and couldn't wait to meet Maggie. He had always been the sweetest-natured boy. As a young child he had been very loving and affectionate with an endearing habit of winding his arms around her neck and saying,

'Mummy, I love you.'

'I so want to meet Maggie, darling' she said to Charles during their telephone conversation. 'She sounds very glamorous so I hope that we are not too old-fashioned and boring for her.'

Charles laughed delightedly.

'Of course not, Ma, she's lovely and very down to earth. Anyway, I've got to go, Maggie's cooking dinner,' he said without a blush. Maggie deliciously naked very far from cooking was stroking him in a most arousing way. They would eat later from the goodies that Charles had bought from the Partridges, which required no cooking of any kind.

He quickly put down the phone and reached for her yet again.

High Wynch Park

The evening was going well. Anthony had arrived early. He had brought with him a fine Sauvignon blanc and a small bouquet of exquisite creamy rosebuds with a hint of palest pink on the petal tips. Virginia had chosen her clothes with great care. She decided on grey silky palazzo pants with soft gold coloured lining. With them she wore a simple cream silk tee shirt and a light jacket in the same material as the trousers. Her jewellery was simple, pearl and gold earrings and a pearl and gold chain around her neck. She had thought briefly about removing her wedding ring but decided that would be too obvious.

They had enjoyed dinner, which she had served at a small round table in the drawing room. After dinner, which had been preceded by champagne, they had enjoyed a glass of brandy, in thin old balloon glasses, sitting on the terrace overlooking the rose garden, which looked lovely in the gathering dusk.

Anthony casually draped his arm across her shoulder and Virginia leaned luxuriously into his body. Correctly interpreting this as the signal to go further, he pulled her gently to her feet lifted her face towards his and kissed her deeply and slowly in a highly pleasurable way. Not long after that first kiss she led him upstairs to her bedroom. The bed was most invitingly turned down, the heavy curtains drawn across the mullioned window and the two bedside lamps cast a gently rosy light across the king size bed, with its white linen sheets and soft downy pillows.

Chapter 13

Selkirk

Betty was having dinner with the Colonel. John Prendergast had persuaded her to join him for a meal at Holly House in Stitcholme. His housekeeper, Jean MacLean, had left an excellent homemade chicken and ham pie to serve hot with tiny new potatoes, peas and carrots. To follow she had provided a simple dish of early strawberries, homemade shortbread and clotted cream. Betty had a taken a piece of Dunsyre Blue cheese, a heart of celery and some home-made oatcakes.

When they had finished eating, John sighed in a satisfied way and sat back in his chair. 'It is so good to have company for dinner, Betty' he said 'As you know Beatrice and I kept to ourselves, with notable exceptions like you, and it can get a bit lonely since she died. Though I have my garden, which is a great joy, especially now the evenings are getting so light. I didn't finish the grass until about nine o'clock yesterday. Anyway, it is lovely that you are here but we can have a talk about this troublesome business. Let's go into the Conservatory for our coffee.'

When they were settled in the old basket chairs, with comfy cushions John offered her a brandy.

'Best not dear' Betty replied, 'I have to drive home and the police are not as tolerant as they used to be. 'You could always stay over, in the spare room naturally!' was his reply.

Then she became more serious. 'John what can we do about this horrible muddle over the divorce settlement?'

John smiled sympathetically and placed his large square hand over Betty's tiny one and gently squeezed it. He smiled affectionately and went on 'From all that you've told me and I also checked with my own lawyers, not giving your name, of course, it does look as if there is potentially a real problem. Have you any idea why Alistair is raising all these questions now after all this time?'

Betty replied, 'The only thing I can think of is that his new wife has been told some story about the Scottish estate that he is still pretending to own and as usual, he is short of money. John, you could help me by coming with me to see Andrew Ramsay at McArdles in Edinburgh on Tuesday. I have an appointment with him and he is going to go over the legalities of this whole business and the claims Alistair seems to be making. I know I am pretty independent but it would be such a comfort to have you by my side.'

John didn't hesitate. Patting her shoulder affectionately he said,

'Of course, my dear. I'll get Bill to drive us and we'll have lunch at Fishers in the City afterwards for a treat. I'm sure everything will be sorted out.'

Betty stood up and so did the Colonel. Standing on tiptoes she kissed his cheek gently.

'Oh, John, you are such a good man. That will make the whole horrid business much more bearable. Now, I must go. I've had a lovely evening but it's way past my bedtime and Emperor will have to have a walk, too.'

'Well, if you're sure you won't stay I'll see you to your car. Please telephone me the minute you are safely in that tower of yours!' Betty's feisty manner returned as she felt an enormous sense of relief in not having to face the problem alone.

'Don't fuss, for heaven's sake. I drive myself all over the place, all the time.' With that, John found her brightly coloured padded jacket, with its hectic design of brightly coloured jungle animals and vegetation printed all over it, helped her to put it on and insisted on escorting her out into the soft night, helping her into the shooting brake and standing at the gate watching her remarkably speedy "get away" and standing, watching until her tail lights were out of sight.

He was sorry about her trouble, of course, but delighted she had not only accepted his help but had asked him for it. He called to Bluff, his arthritic spaniel and together they took a brief stately walk round the newly cut lawn before turning in.

Betty, too, felt much better about everything as she abandoned her Morris in front of the Tower and she let herself in. An indignant Emperor rushed out of his basket by the kitchen range to greet her. They took the briefest of walks before she, too, closed her house for the night and climbed the steep stairs to the top of her little castle. Perhaps surprisingly she soon floated into a deep and dreamless sleep. Let Alistair do his worst. She had taken him on before, and won.

Whitewalls

Jamie had to get up to go to the bathroom yet again. He had first noticed this urgent need to have a pee during the night when Rosie had been away with Minty in North Berwick but it was getting worse. He prided himself on never having a day's illness in his life and thought most things mended themselves, given time. Therefore, he had not mentioned the problem to Rosie on her return but he realised she was bound to notice something was wrong.

Rosie usually slept deeply but even she realised Jamie kept getting in and out of bed several times each night. She resolved to tackle him about his increasingly frequent nocturnal trips to the loo.

She chose to ask him about it over breakfast. Jamie felt irritated and yet relieved when Rosie said to him,

'Darling, when did you last see Dr Morris?' Nevertheless he replied a little sharply.

'Why on earth would I want to do that?' thinking, "so she has noticed."

'Because,' replied Rosie calmly, 'I can't help noticing how often you are getting up in the night to pee. It may be just a chill, but I really think that you should have it checked out at the surgery.' She didn't say outright, but she was filled with a feeling of foreboding. Jamie was just at the age when prostate cancer, or the possibility of it, needed at the very least to be ruled out.

Trying to sound unconcerned, all Jamie would say was,

'Alright, if it goes on happening I'll pop in and see Graham Morris. He wants to discuss buying a new gun before next season anyway.' Rosie was sharp in her reply,

'Don't be difficult, you can talk to him any time about a gun. I meant go to the surgery and get yourself checked out properly. I'll even come with you if you want me to do that.'

God, that was the last thing that he wanted. "Don't nag," she said to herself and only remarked as lightly as she was able to manage,

'Please, Jamie. I would be much happier if you would at least make an appointment at the surgery soon.' She felt, somehow, that this was very important if only to eliminate anything nasty.

'If it will make you happy, then of course I will.' He hugged her tightly as they both got up from the table to start their busy days. With that she had to be satisfied. For once Jamie's usual calm was ruffled and before he could change his mind he rang the surgery in Peebles and made an appointment for that morning. Graham Morris's last morning appointment had been cancelled so he found himself agreeing to take it so that there was no time to think further and change his mind.

Village doctor's waiting rooms are not the easiest places in which to sit when it is perfectly possible that you are going to be given some potentially serious news by your GP. These were Jamie's thoughts as he tried to remain detached from the assorted groups of local people with coughs and colds who were sitting, sniffling in the waiting room.

However, he did not have to wait too long before he was called in to see his old friend, Graham.

'Sit down and tell me what I can do for you Jamie.'

Graham Morris asked.

The two men were good friends but managed to separate their friendship from the professional relationship of doctor and patient.

'Well,' Jamie started hesitantly. 'I seem to be having problems with my waterworks.'

'H'm, what sort of problems? Do you have to get up in the night, for example? Or do you feel a stinging pain; is there any sign of blood?'

Jamie replied after a short pause,

'Really no pain or anything else you mention. Though I have to get up in the night, at least two or three times to have a pee.'

'Well, first thing is to have a look and see if there is any abnormal swelling in the area. Then I'll take some blood and we will see if we can eliminate anything that might be causing a problem.' Graham said calmly and professionally.

Jamie felt a sudden dread. Surely there could not be anything seriously wrong with him. Could there?

The physical examination was swift and painless enough. Equally the blood sample was taken with the minimum of discomfort and a few minutes later he was leaving the surgery with an injunction not to worry. Graham said he would phone with the results in about a week.

He got back in the car to drive home but did not want to face Rosie and her kindly and undoubtedly loving questions yet. He needed some time alone. So he left the Jeep parked at the bottom of the Hill field. He climbed the fence and walked up the hill towards the point where for years he had gone to think things over, if there was something on his mind that troubled him.

This time, however, he felt a chill, as if someone, somewhere was trying to tell him something. Jamie was not prone to introspection or to pessimism and as he took in the beautiful view down to the riverbank, where he had spent so many hours fishing happily his mind was soothed and his heartbeat slowed down. Just a precaution after all. Good to have things checked out. He had always been healthy and was secretly proud of his fitness and his ability to take life as it came.

'Is that you darling?' called Rosie as Jamie went into the kitchen. He braced himself for her questions and put a cheerful expression on his face. He gained a reprieve. Then Jamie remembered, Rosie was going out.

'It's nearly time for me to go to my Garden opening meeting and then I need to go to Edinburgh to collect some plants from Dobbies. So I've left lunch for you. There's some ham and pea soup and a quiche in the fridge.'

'Thanks'; he said 'don't you want to know how I got on at the surgery?'

She kissed him hard on the lips, and then looked lovingly into this face.

'Of course I do. But I'm trying not to bombard you with questions that you probably can't event answer yet!'

He put both his hands on her shoulders and smiled at Rosie. It was a moment of complete understanding. Then he spoke.

'Graham couldn't find anything obvious but he's taken a blood sample and he'll ring me when he gets the results. It's probably nothing, maybe an infection. So let's not worry about it. I'll go and see Dad, and then I've got to check the sheep in the top field. I might do some painting this afternoon. Anyway, don't you fret about it, off you go.'

'There's just us this evening' replied Rosie, a little reassured, 'and we'll have a very special dinner. I'll get some fillet steaks from Forsyths in Peebles. I miss having Minty around but it's much better for her now to be back in Edinburgh with Polly, Richard, John and all her friends. Oh, I nearly forgot to tell you, she's going back to school, just part-time to begin with. I really think that the turning point was our visit to North

Berwick. She really seemed to get some of her old confidence back.'

Jamie replied, reflecting, not for the first time what a lucky man he was to be married to such a caring wife.

'You were right about that, too. Now please go or you'll be late and blame me! Where's the meeting?'

'It's at Anne Elgin's at Eddleston so that's on my way to Edinburgh. With that she departed, leaving a thoughtful Jamie who decided to have a strong cup of coffee before he did anything else.

Rosie was tired again. She reflected as she drove along the narrow road then through Peebles to Anne Elgin's house that the once even tenor of her life had been jolted far too much recently. The row with Polly over Roddy's will had upset her more than she was prepared to admit. Then there was Minty's accident, which Rosie privately thought would never have happened if Polly had not been late in collecting her from school. On top of all that, her normally ebullient mother appeared to have something on her mind that she was, unusually, not prepared to share even with Rosie.

She gave herself a mental shake and turned the radio volume up. Classic FM was always soothing. The music was a little unchallenging but soothing was what was needed right now. The Garden opening needed some urgent attention. Anne Elgin was going to be a great help and was very experienced in these matters. She and her husband Tim had long been opening their beautiful garden for charitable causes. They had both offered not only practical advice but also, even better, help with arrangements before and on the day itself.

In a way Rosie felt overwhelmed at the thought of having to organise everything but in another way it was a welcome distraction from everything else that had seemed to dominate her life recently.

The sun was shining as Rosie drew in to the imposing white-pillared driveway of Moorfoot, the elegant yet pretty and comfortable home of her friends. The garden was springing into life. Although the sweeps of daffodils were finishing, there were still tulips in clumps just starting to show their colours and bluebells under the trees, which were coming in to leaf rapidly. She wound down the car window and breathed the fresh spring air with a mounting feeling of optimism and well- being that had seemed absent from her life for too long.

Meanwhile, Jamie had taken Tweed and Heather along the road to the Lodge to have a chat with his father about the farm. As he walked up the familiar track to the house Jamie reflected that somehow with all the other family dramas taking place, he had neglected his father recently. Roddy was so undemanding and apparently self-contained, it was easy to forget he might be lonely or unwell. Although Jamie felt he and Rosie had a close relationship with Roddy he now wondered what this amounted to in terms of help and support. His father had been a widower for so long that Jamie could scarcely remember Lorna, his mother except with distant and happy memories. After her death Roddy had retreated into himself as far as any display of emotion was concerned and, relieved in a way at this, Jamie had accepted this was his father's way of dealing with the profound loss that he had undoubtedly felt.

Jamie went into the Lodge through the back lobby with its miscellany of boots, waxed jackets and tweed caps, which were arranged in his father's typically ordered fashion. He pushed open the kitchen door and called out,

'Hello, Dad, it's just me!' There was no reply but he knew that his father would not be far away. The kettle hissed gently on the old cream Rayburn stove that had been there for as long as Jamie could remember. Roddy was probably down at the stables. Jamie was just about to leave the house to find his father when he heard a noise from the adjoining room which had long since stopped being a dining room and was now known as the 'office'.

Roddy was sitting at the oak desk reading through what looked like a legal document. He looked up and smiled at his son. Jamie was shocked. How old his father looked. They all took it for granted that Roddy would go on for ever, but he was an old man after all. No, it didn't bear thinking about right now.

'Hello, son, to what do I owe the honour of the visit?' asked Roddy and smiled, which at once lightened his face and Jamie's moment of disquiet passed.

'Just thought I would look in and see how you were. Nothing special really. Rosie has gone off to a meeting about the Garden opening then into Edinburgh so I thought we might have a look at the sheep in the top field and then you could have lunch with me back at Whitewalls. What do you say?' Jamie asked, hoping his father would agree.

Making a visible effort to stand up from the desk Roddy replied,

'Thanks, Jamie that would be good. I have been sitting at this damned desk for far too long this morning and you know that I would always rather be outside if I can.'

'Are you feeling alright?' Jamie asked, anxious again.

'Just the odd twinge, which is only to be expected at my age' his father replied, with another smile 'now let's go.' Leaving the copy of his will on the desk Roddy put on his old tweed jacket and the two men went off to inspect the sheep before

338

making their way, via the stables to Whitewalls for a beer and a companionable lunch.

Chapter 14

High Wynch Park

Virginia stared at old Doctor Brennan in horrified amazement.

'But it is simply not possible,' she cried 'there must be some ghastly mistake. I just do not believe it.'

The Doctor, who knew Virginia and her family very well smiled in a kindly, almost sorrowful fashion.

'Virginia," he said in his best avuncular voice 'It is true, you are around two months pregnant.'

She felt absolutely awful. It was bad enough if what Doctor Brennan had told her was true but it was worse than that. She was not sure whether the father was Anthony or Hughie. The one night that she had let Hughie into her bed and her body during the last few months had been so near to her "night of passion", not yet repeated, with Anthony; it could be either of them.

340

Tom Brennan knew nothing of what was going through his patient's mind, although he fully understood her sense of shock. Her two existing children were grown up and off her hands. She was 46 years old, not impossibly late to have another child, however. Though he doubted whether she had the right temperament to cope with this.

He patted Virginia on the arm in an avuncular manner and said, soothingly

'We need to make absolutely certain but I think the blood tests will confirm the diagnosis. You will need time to tell Hugh and to decide what you are going to do.'

Virginia spoke again,

'What do you mean, what are we going to do? I can't possibly have another child at my age. No, no, a termination is the only possible way out.'

The old doctor smiled reassuringly and said,

'Let's not take a hasty decision, my dear. This has been a great shock to you. Your hormones are all over the place and I don't think you should take any immediate decision. If, as I hope, you do decide to continue with the pregnancy there is every reason to suppose you can have a perfectly healthy baby. In my experience a late child can bring a good deal of happiness and, as well, certainly would keep you young.'

Virginia visibly shuddered. But she pulled herself together somehow and managed to leave the surgery without crying, saying,

'Well, I'll think about it, talk it over with Hugh and come back to you, as if the unwanted pregnancy were some sort of business proposition!'

'Don't leave it too long' he answered and let her go.

She drove home in a turmoil. Her worst fears had been confirmed. But what could she do?

"Keep calm" she told herself, "think, and think carefully." Her first instinct was uncharacteristic of her. "I'll wait, do nothing today, and say nothing yet."

Luckily Hughie was full of excitement of his own. Piers Romayne had been so delighted with High Wynch Park as a location setting for Country Pursuits he wanted to use the house and garden extensively in a costume drama. It would be a very lavish production, with a much larger budget.

'So my darling' he said excitedly – as if she had been listening intently –'I really think that this will put High Wynch on the map and make us a lot of money.'

She fought to sound light and pleased,

'That's wonderful news. But let's see it all in writing before we celebrate too much!' He preened himself thinking "she's pleased, she really is pleased." He could not help but hope this was the beginning of a new start for his marriage as well as for his financial situation.

For her part, Virginia felt thankful there was a distraction that meant Hughie was interested only in the prospect of making his fortune at last and would hopefully not notice when she withdrew to try and decide what to do.

Then it came to her. She would telephone Anthony and get him to meet her in Cirencester or Broadway so she could break the news to him. She fantasised he might be delighted and want to take her away to start a new life. Deep down, though, she knew this was highly unlikely.

It occurred to her the easiest course of all would be to go back to Dr Brennan and ask him to make the arrangements for a termination. Yet despite her feelings of acute anxiety she felt a certain excitement and the opportunity for a kind of fresh start, whatever happened.

It took quite a lot of nerve, even for Virginia, but she telephoned Anthony and arranged to meet him for lunch in Broadway at the famous Lygon Arms Hotel. He had not sounded too enthusiastic but was intrigued enough to agree. He was having second thoughts about continuing a relationship with Virginia. Part of her sexual attraction had been Virginia's apparently icy and aloof manner but really, he thought, that was just a façade and there wasn't a great deal of triumph in breaking it down any further. Besides, if Piers was going to use the house and grounds a lot he didn't want to put complications in the way of good business.

There was a brittle atmosphere as Virginia attempted to flirt with Anthony and to be alluring, even suggestive, over lunch. But by the time they had reached the coffee and he was pointedly looking at his watch she simply had to say something.

'Anthony, darling' she began. He frowned but said nothing. She tried again.

'I honestly thought that we had been so careful, but it seems that we weren't careful enough'

His manner suddenly changed from urbane and aloof to something much more mean.

'What the hell are you trying to say, Virginia? Because if it is what I think it is, you don't catch me so easily. It's the oldest game in the book.'

She felt wounded and then afraid. Next she decided to fight.

'What I am trying to tell you Anthony is that when I allowed you to seduce me, I thought you wanted a relationship not simply a sexual encounter, though it seems that I might have been wrong about that. Still I have to tell you I am pregnant!'

There was a short silence. Then he said,

'And what makes you think that I am the father, even supposing that you have managed to conceive at your age? What about the saintly Hughie? He is your husband after all. So don't think for one minute that you are going to palm this off on me. If he doesn't want it and you don't want it, just get rid of it. It's easy enough, especially given your age.'

She felt hurt, anger and disgust. What had she ever seen in this man? No wonder he had never been married. He was a horrible, arrogant user of women. She felt cheap and used. She decided to cut short the painful occasion.

'Clearly,' she said in the haughtiest voice that she could muster 'I was very mistaken about you! However, I have no doubt your generosity will run to paying for lunch. I must go. Goodbye Anthony. I hope never to see you again.'

He merely smiled sardonically; half rose from his seat and gave a last parting shot,

'Goodbye my dear. I think the cost of lunch will just about cover it.'

Angrily, she marched out of the restaurant and drove home to decide what to do. Like Scarlett O'Hara in "Gone with the Wind" she decided to "wait until tomorrow" to come up with her plan.

Looking back later she was amazed how easy it had all been. Once he had recovered from the initial shock of her announcement that she was pregnant and had already seen Dr Brennan, Hughie had been wonderful.

'Vee, how terrific, a wonderful surprise, a little one to keep us young and be with us in our old age!' His pink face was wreathed in smiles. He ran his hands through his blonde curly hair and then gave her a huge, rather painful hug. She had baulked a bit at that; it wasn't like him to be so flowery.

'But how on earth, when? It must have been that night after the filming, how superb but we must wrap you in cotton wool and really look after you now sweetheart. This whole filming lark has brought a lot of luck with it, first the money now this!'

She couldn't help smiling, perhaps this would really all be for the best.

'We must ring Alexander and Roberta,' said Hugh 'they will be surprised but once they get over the shock I'm sure they'll be pleased.'

Virginia was very far from sure that they would be pleased. In fact, she thought, they would be horrified. She was right; they were.

They met at Roberta's miniscule flat in London, just off Wilton Street, to discuss what she called 'the situation'.

She worked in advertising and was considered, not least by herself, to be the most creative member of the family. Although Virginia was fond of saying,

'Roberta gets her talent from me you know. I really could be an interior designer if only I had time!'

Roberta was a rather plain girl with a horsey face and a stridently confident manner that did not sit easily with her artistic credentials but she was a bright young woman and, like her father, Hugh, knew a great deal more than she ever allowed people to discover. Alexander, on the other hand was a sweet-natured young man with a gentle manner bordering on diffidence. In fact, he was rather clever and his keen eye and shy manner had turned out to be great assets at the Fine Arts Auction Company, where he had worked since coming down from Cambridge. Thanks to a generous Trust Fund set up for both of them by Virginia's father the two of them were financially independent and able to afford smart, albeit small flats in the Knightsbridge area and a life style that was not totally dependent upon their earnings. To say they were 'spoilt' was simply to say they had choices not open to all of their generation, although shared by many of their immediate circles.

They had always got on well together, partly because during their early years when money had been plentiful and nannies were employed to look after them before they went off to boarding school they had not seen very much of their parents. They had been very sheltered but, at the same time, lived a life that was detached from their father and mother's everyday activities. Their shrewd grandfather had ensured that the Trust Funds could not be plundered by either parent, so even during the difficult years Hugh and Virginia had not had access to their children's capital, even though they had used the income to pay school fees.

In fact it was money that was concerning the two of them most after hearing the news that they were, entirely unexpectedly and, they thought obscenely to have a brother or sister.

'I didn't even imagine for one minute that they still did it!' said Roberta with a shudder.

'Please, let's not even go there' said Alex. Then he continued 'but let's go down at the weekend, both of us and find out just what they intend doing about it. Mummy says they have decided the have the sprog but maybe you can talk some sense into her.'

Roberta was extremely doubtful if she, or anyone else, could persuade Virginia to any course of action she did not want to follow.

'Well, I'll try, but you know Mummy. Once she's decided on something she never changes her mind. What we must do, though, is make sure that it doesn't affect our Trust Funds though I suppose it will have to come into the Inheritance eventually."

Brought up in the financially secure, as they saw it, world of the Trust Fund cushioning them they saw nothing wrong or even incongruous in discussing their future brother or sister in these venal terms.

'Right, well we'll see what we can do?' Alex said, 'Now, Sis, how about going out for a spot of dinner. I'm fairly flush just now so I'll pay. Italian or Chinese?'

They decided on Italian and sauntered off feeling pleased with themselves to the small local restaurant run by the Trevetti family with delicious food at considerably less than the usual London prices.

Whitewalls

After the turbulent events of recent months Rosie decided she wanted to spend a whole day in her garden. After breakfast she announced to Molly, who was roaring around with the vacuum cleaner and Jamie who was going to visit his father, about whom he was beginning to feel rather concerned, before going off to spend a day on farming pursuits there would be no lunch today and everyone would have to fend for themselves.

'I'll just take a couple of baps and a flask with me then,' said Jamie, amiably enough. In truth he was quite pleased not to have to come back for lunch. Rosie's meals were always good but sometimes the ritual of lunch round the kitchen table on a working day seemed to take up a lot of time and he had a lot to do. Still he was a bit surprised when Rosie, although smiling when she said it, replied,

'Well make them yourself, will you? There are plenty of rolls and ham and tomatoes in the fridge. I think there's some ginger cake left as well. Why not have that, too?' They were the kind of questions that don't require answers and before Rosie disappeared, dressed for serious gardening she said to Molly,

'Molly, help yourself to coffee won't you. I've got a flask and a sandwich. If anyone wants me urgently you'll find me in the rose garden. I want to do some weeding before Harry comes tomorrow to cut the grass.'

What was wrong with them all these days? Molly asked herself. All this rushing around and routine being upset. Molly thrived on routine and Rosie never usually had to ask her to do specific tasks, they were all well-established so she was a bit put out at Rosie's parting shot,

'Oh, and Molly, I think we should make a start on clearing out the blue bedroom ready for Charles coming up. At least his girlfriend can have that and he will have to make do with the old dressing room.' Molly sniffed,

'Well Mrs D, thanks for telling me I'm sure. When is this all happening?' She got a very unsatisfactory answer,

'Oh, I don't know exactly but very soon and we want to have everything ready. Just start sorting out all the boxes we put in there. Some things will have to go back to the attic and see if the curtains need washing. They probably will do.' And with that she had gone.

Jamie smiled placatingly at Molly,

'It's been a difficult time Molly for all of us and I think Mrs D needs what I believe is now called "some of her own space".

You know we think of you as one of the family and I am sure she doesn't want to upset you. Perhaps we all get a bit stuck in routine and it's good to have a change sometimes.'

Molly liked Mr D. He was a real gentleman and knew exactly how to treat you. He wasn't over-familiar but made you feel appreciated. You knew where you were with him.

'Oh, I know' she replied 'the world's a very different place these days, women out working leaving their bairns for other women to look after and it's all rush, rush even here in the country and all these terrorists around, I don't know what the world's coming to.'

Despite the fact that there was little likelihood of terrorists attacking the douce countryside of the Scottish Borders she was troubled by this modern age and felt happiest in the world of farming, changing seasons, the big house and her own cosy cottage. She didn't say any of this, judging for once the Douglas's had troubles of their own to contend with so contented herself with a heavy sigh and one of her bon mots

'Aye the world is surely going towards hell and damnation in spite of all we can do.' With that she bustled off to complete her work as planned, before tackling the blue bedroom. She didn't really mind doing extra and was looking forward to meeting Charles' actress girlfriend. Of the two Douglas "children" it was Charles that she preferred. He was a lovely boy in her eyes and she thought it very fitting he should be following his grandfather into a military career – as long as he didn't have to go to any of these foreign places and get blown up.

For his part Jamie had a wonderful mental picture of Molly in full combat gear setting out in a tank to take on the Iraqis and anyone else who got in her way.

Rosie went into the gardens with a great feeling of release. It seemed forever since she had spent a whole day working in the peace of the place that she loved best in the entire world. She was sensibly dressed in corduroy trousers, a check shirt with sleeves that could be rolled up or down as required and sturdy brown leather ankle boots that would withstand anything the garden cared to throw at her. Whether she was wrestling with weeds, greenfly or black spot on the roses Rosie always found that she could focus and concentrate better in the garden than anywhere else in her world.

Over the many years that she had been in charge of the garden at Whitewalls Rosie had, almost single-handedly done a great deal of work in planning and planting. The garden was large running to over five acres but she had made it manageable. At the heart of it was her beloved walled rose garden.

In the centre parterre was a statue of Eros she had found in a scrap yard outside Edinburgh many years ago. It was perfect for the location and had only needed minimal cleaning to give it a weathered and classical appearance. The garden was laid out in individual beds, edged with trimly cut box. There were Silver Jubilee, Lily Marlene, Prima Ballerina and Glen Fiddich varieties and included the strong yellow, Grandpa Dixon which had been included even though it had no scent. Rosie did not like mixed beds and her sense of order showed in the planting.

Before Rosie tackled the weeding she decided to begin in the glasshouse which was built against the south-facing wall of the garden and separated from it by flagstone paths leading to shallow steps. Whilst it was a headache looking after the Victorian conservatory, where previous generations had grown peaches and even grapes Rosie loved it dearly and was loathe to let it go even when Jamie grumbled mildly about the cost of keeping it wind and water tight as well as replacing glass panes. There were geraniums, pelargonium, pots of lilies and hydrangeas as well as campanula and hostas in pots getting ready to replace any in the herbaceous border that had not survived the winter. It was a warm day and as she worked in her garden Rosie enjoyed the feeling of the sun on her back and the soft clear air on her hands and face. Soon the heavy weight of care she felt had been on her shoulders for these last weeks began to lift. Life seemed possible again – optimistic even. She would not allow herself even to *think* about the possibility of something being seriously wrong with Jamie. Her family had surely had more than its fair share of problems recently. It was just as well she was unable to look ahead at what was in store.

Edinburgh

For once both Polly and Richard were home together after breakfast. John had been taken off to school by Henry's Mum, Karen, and Minty was now sufficiently recovered to join her school run again and had also been picked up. So they sat companionably enough opening the post, which was pretty heavy that morning and having a cup of coffee.

Richard picked up a letter addressed to both of them. He read it quickly then said,

'I wonder what on earth this is all about! Mind you with all the fuss being made over Minty I am not really surprised.'

'What are you talking about?' asked Polly mildly. She had been feeling less nervy recently and her relationship with Richard, whilst not especially close had settled to a little more than the politeness that had featured in the aftermath of the accident.

'Here, read this. The Head of Junior School wants us to go and see him about John's lack of progress and general attitude this term. I knew you should have paid more attention to him. He's bound to have been feeling left out.'

She was immediately on the defensive again.

'That is hardly my fault' she cried. Though secretly, in her heart she knew that it was indirectly or directly because of her that Minty had been knocked down and with everything that followed, John had been pushed into second place.

'Let me see the letter,' she demanded, taking it from his hand. She was sick of feeling guilty about everything. After reading the letter quickly, she composed herself and said,

'Well let's not read too much into this. We can go and see the Head and his form master and maybe think up a treat for him that doesn't involve Minty.'

Richard felt some sympathy for Polly. His career was on the rise, she had gone through a very bad time over Minty's accident, blaming herself for heaven's sake perhaps they should get John sorted out then the two of them go away somewhere for a long weekend. He wanted to recapture some of the closeness and fun that they had enjoyed earlier in their marriage. In a way this wretched business over Roddy's will had not helped, he saw that in spite of all his reassurances Polly had felt slighted and pushed aside. Richard was still not sure why Roddy had willed everything to him but short of outright refusal of Polly's grandfather's generosity he could not think what to do. He was very fond of Roddy and had initially felt very honoured when told of the bequest. In fact, he knew that running the stud, small though it was, and training a couple of racehorses was really now too hard a task for Roddy's decreasing energy. Richard felt he should talk to Jamie and Rosie about this but hesitated to burden them any further with more worries.

'You look miles away, Richard.' There was a touch of asperity in Polly's voice, 'I said shall I telephone the Academy and make an appointment for both of us?'

'Sorry,' he replied, bringing himself back to the current situation 'please. But could you check my diary with Fiona first I'm going to be pretty busy myself over the next few weeks and we don't want to let John down, do we? Now, I must dash, there's a Partners' meeting this morning.'

With that and a quick kiss on Polly's cheek he left the house in a thoughtful mood to start his working day.

Polly's mobile phone rang. It was David. For a moment she was tempted not to pick up the call but she did. Yes, she could get away and yes they could go down to the cottage for lunch but she must absolutely be back by four o'clock. There must simply be no danger at all of a repeat of being late to collect Minty.

'Can't wait, darling' he said in his carefully cultivated husky tones 'wear some sexy knickers for me to take off.' For a reason she could not explain to herself Polly felt irritated. What did he think she was, just someone to have fun in bed with? Perhaps but wasn't that what she wanted too? No long term commitment, no interference with her family, no future?

Chapter 15

Haute Savoie

Sir Alistair was humming tunelessly to himself. On the French

desk in the drawing room of the Chateau lay an important letter

from Edinburgh. It appeared his wily lawyer might be on to

something. Quite apart from pleasing Madeleine, who was

becoming less important as his boredom levels with her rose, the

prospect of perhaps being able to regain Whitewalls was a very

attractive one indeed.

The trip to Paris had gone well, he reflected, and apart from

trying to discourage Madeleine from spending money that he

could ill-afford he had enjoyed himself. Now was the time to

make an investment in his future, by travelling to Scotland and

becoming once again the owner of Whitewalls.

Should he take Madeleine with him? He would rather not

be accompanied by his flighty and unpredictable wife but short of

having a bust up with her, Alistair could not really think how he

could get out of it. The matter was decided as he was on the telephone to the travel agent in Chambery;   Madeleine came into the room.

'There you are Cherie, what are you doing?' She had not managed to read the letter but was determined to find out what it contained. It must be something important.

'Just arranging a trip to Scotland for us' he replied 'it's about time you saw where I come from.'

'And the house?' she enquired 'we will stay there.' He thought quickly,

'That may be a little difficult, darling, family tenants you know, but we will see what can be done.' He thought to himself – if I turn up at the house my own daughter is hardly likely to turn us away, especially if I say we are just visiting and it was so long since I had seen her and the family. So he hurried on,

'Too complicated to explain, my dear, but the house is occupied by family so I am sure we will be made very welcome.' Even to his ears that sounded highly unlikely. In order to divert her attention he said,

'I have to go and talk to Hubert about looking after things whilst we are away, then I need to get organised for the trip. I'm certain you will like Scotland though the country isn't very smart and you will need to take some casual clothes.' He thought that mentioning clothes would divert Madeleine.

"He's hiding something" thought Madeleine and I will find out just what that is but I will go along with the story for now.

Whitewalls

Rosie came off the phone and ran to find Jamie. He was in the studio painting, getting ready for his forthcoming Exhibition.

'Whatever's the matter? Where's the fire?' he asked as she burst breathlessly into the building banging the door behind her.

'It's my father. He wants to pay us a visit and bring his French tart with him!' Now she had Jamie's full attention. She hadn't seen her father for years and only heard about his marriage to Madeleine fairly recently. In fact she was so firmly devoted to her mother she could not even contemplate having her father and his wife to stay in what had originally been Betty and Alistair's

364

home. Yet she had not been able, on the spur of the moment, to think of a reason to refuse.

'When are they proposing to come?' asked Jamie, practical as ever.

'In about ten days' time, she said. What Mummy's going to think I have no idea but I suppose I can't keep it from her?'

Jamie came across from his easel and put his arms comfortingly around his wife,

'Of course you can't, but it is all so long ago I don't think Betty will care two hoots one way or another!' Privately Rosie thought that her mother would care very much but didn't say so. Jamie continued in the same emollient vein,

'Maybe he just wants to see us all, for us to meet his new wife, and see his grandchildren and great grandchildren. After all he's never even met Richard, let along Minty and John. Let's not get too agitated about it.'

Realising that she wasn't going to arouse much in the way of indignation on Jamie's part Rosie went back to the house to telephone her mother.

As Rosie had predicted Betty was not at all pleased at the prospect of her ex-husband's visit with his new French wife but even now could not bring herself to tell Rosie exactly why she was not only angry, but also afraid. Instead, she deflected the conversation by suggesting she and Rosie took a trip to Edinburgh, collected some paintings from Antonio, had a little lunch in Harvey Nicols and maybe looked in at Murrayfield after that just to see how things were progressing there. After a moment's thought, Rosie agreed to the plan. Whilst she had masses to do, it would be good to get away on the spur of the moment and there was already soup and quiche ready for lunch. Perhaps Jamie and his father could have a picnic lunch together for once.

As always Rosie felt better once she had decided upon her 'plan' and went back to tell Jamie that he was on his own for much of the day.

Roddy was trying to ignore a painful left arm and a feeling of great tiredness that had recently come over him. He felt cold, he felt old. To cheer himself up he decided to check up on the horses that were in the stables though he did not feel up to going into the low fields where most of them were turned out. If Richard came down later he could do that or Jack, the groom-cum general yardman would make sure they were all right.

The stables, like the Lodge were old, rather shabby but immaculately tidy and ordered. These days not all the loose boxes were full but there were enough horses, including the ones at livery, to ensure the familiar and well-loved scene of sunshine on cobble stones and at the sound of his approach equine heads peering enquiringly over the open half doors.

Princess whickered a greeting as he went towards her box. The foal was growing fast and after some fuss and squealing had been moved to her own box next to her mother. Soon her still furry-looking face was looking out at him. Roddy went first into Princess's box, which smelled sweetly of straw and hay. Many breeders and trainers now used wood shavings or, in his opinion worse, rubber flooring in the boxes. He prided himself that his horses were all very well fed and their "hunter beds" of deep straw were the best that could be provided. Princess looked well.

He thought he might put her back in training next year. She could have one last season over hurdles. If not he might try her on the flat at Musselburgh. Kelso and Perth were both long-established course specializing in National Hunt races, over hurdles and fences. Musselburgh Racecourse, near Edinburgh staged racing both on the flat and over obstacles, as did the course at Ayr on the west coast so there was a good enough choice of tracks without travelling out of Scotland.

Jack was in the yard, just finishing off the morning chores. He was one of the old school and treated the Major with great respect, touching his cap and saying,

'Good morning, Major, what a fine day it is. The horses are fairly enjoying being out and I thought to take Princess and the foal out for a breath of air and a peck of grass this afternoon, just to the paddock. I think it's about time. Would you be agreeable to that?'

Roddy thought how lucky he was to have Jack, as in spite of Richard's undoubted enthusiasm and growing knowledge he knew if he were on his own he would have had to give up the

Stud business long ago. He felt the sun on his back and knew he was a fortunate man.

'Good idea, Jack' he replied 'what's more I'll come with you. I'm going up to the house for a bite of lunch with Jamie but I'll be back by half past two so why don't we go then?'

So it was agreed and Roddy continued his walk, with his lurcher, Tess, at his heels towards Whitewalls and a 'bachelor' lunch with his son, with whom he always felt very comfortable.

When Roddy arrived at Whitewalls, Jamie was finishing opening the mail that had arrived late that morning. There was a brown envelope from the Borders General Hospital. It appeared that his PSA levels – whatever they were – had come out as abnormally high in the tests sent to the hospital by Graham and an appointment had been made for him to see a consultant, Mr Williams, the following Tuesday.

'Hello, Dad' he looked up as his father came in after wiping his feet carefully on the doormat. 'Come away in. I don't know about you but I could use a stiff gin and tonic!'

Roddy was surprised. It was not that Jamie did not enjoy a drink but he was rarely heard saying that he *needed one.* Jamie continued,

'I've just had a piece of disturbing news. I need to go and see a chap at the Borders General next week, something wrong with my waterworks. Not unexpected. Just a shock. Come through into the sitting room and we'll have a drink before lunch.'

Roddy put his arm briefly round his son's shoulders and said, slowly,

'Well let's not imagine the worst, you've always been healthy but it's as well to investigate things. What's the trouble?"

'Come on and I'll tell you over a drink.' replied Jamie, grateful his father was there to share the news.

Roddy was calm as ever, but he thought to himself "this should be happening to an old man like me, not to Jamie with so much of life still in front of him!" All he said was,

'Does Rosie know?' He knew how much Jamie relied on the strength of his wife.

The reply surprised him.

'No, it's only just arrived. She knows that I went to see Graham to be checked out but that is all she knows and I don't think I will say anything until I've been to the hospital. I don't want her to worry unless I have to do and she has been through such a lot in recently She's just getting back to normal again and now we've got her bloody father and his French piece coming, to say nothing of the garden opening, Polly and her dramas and Charles bringing his girlfriend for a general inspection!'

Roddy kept his counsel and they both enjoyed the unaccustomed gin and tonic before sharing the lunch of soup and home made quiche Rosie had left for them. By tacit consent neither mentioned again the worry of the impending hospital appointment and instead talked of safe, neutral things – the farm, the fishery, and the horses and whether or not Jack needed more help in the stables.

Rosie drove towards her mother's house in a reflective and disturbed frame of mind. Just when she thought life was settling down again into the well-loved pattern of family life she had nurtured carefully, another threat had appeared on the horizon. It had been so long since Rosie had any proper contact with her father he was, in her mind, a stranger. He was never talked about and her mother had not mentioned his name for many years. How on earth was Betty going to react to him coming back so unexpectedly into their lives? Even worse, how was Rosie going to explain that she had agreed to let him and his wife stay at Whitewalls?

Betty was ready for the trip to Edinburgh when Rosie drew up at the front door of the Tower and seemed cheerful enough as they set off through the Borders towards Edinburgh and their rare lunch in the city.

'Ma, I am truly sorry about being bounced into letting Daddy and, what is she called, Madeleine, I think, come to stay. I was so surprised I found myself agreeing before thinking about it!'

Betty wondered if this was the time to tell Rosie about the legal battle that lay ahead. Probably not, she thought to herself "keep your own counsel for now", unless the opportunity arose over lunch when the two of them were together in neutral surroundings. So she replied as casually as she could,

'Oh, darling, don't worry. He could always charm the birds off the trees. I guess that was one of things that attracted me so much to him in the first place! A lot of water has gone under all our bridges and he is your father, after all.'

Rosie was pleasantly surprised at this seemingly quite casual acceptance of something she had dreaded explaining and her mother's reaction was a relief.

During the journey the chat turned to gardening and the garden opening, to Charles and his girlfriend Maggie who was at last coming to stay.

'I wonder what she'll be like,' Rosie mused 'I don't really know any actresses. I hope that she won't find us dull and pedestrian.' Betty felt a real rush of warmth towards her loving and so capable daughter who had the warmest heart and was almost totally lacking in conceit or self-interest.

'Darling with the kind of welcome I know you, and all of us, will give to her she can't fail to be relaxed and happy. Now where are we going to park the car for this Ladies Who Lunch treat at Harvey Nicks?'

'Well, St Andrew's Square will give us a couple of hours and that should be long enough provided that we can find a meter. As it's Tuesday maybe that won't be too difficult. Then we can collect your pictures from Antonio and go and pay a surprise visit to Murrayfield Gardens and see the children and Polly after school,' Rosie replied feeling happy and enthusiastic again.

They found a parking space easily enough and were soon seated in the spectacular Forth Floor restaurant at the top of the upmarket department store at a window table with wonderful views over Edinburgh and across the Firth of Forth to Fife.

Over a glass of white wine and a very acceptable lunch Betty decided to tell Rosie about Alistair's "out of the blue" claim that the divorce settlement had not been correctly registered and he intended to claim back possession of Whitewalls and the farm. Rosie was horrified.

'But Ma, he can't do that. He simply can't. It's years and years ago. What is your lawyer saying? What absolute cheek.

Well that settles it. There's no way he and his French tart are coming to stay at Whitewalls.' She paused for breath.

'Darling, it has all come as a great shock to me too. But the lawyers on both sides believe that his claim at least has to be investigated and this is happening. I didn't want to worry you with it because you've had so much to deal with in recent months but once you told me that your father was coming to stay I felt I had to confide in you.'

Rosie looked at her invincible mother whose bottom lip was trembling and who, for the first time Rosie could remember, looked old and vulnerable. Betty put her hand on Rosie's, visibly "pulled herself together" took a strong gulp of Pino Grigio and said brightly,

'But darling, he has never got the better of me in the past and I am quite determined your father is not going to win this battle. So I suggest you don't alert him to the fact that you know anything at all and we will "play it by ear". In the meantime, John Prendergast is helping me with seeing the lawyer and so on. Now before you say anything, John is very discreet and until we know what we're dealing with it's really better for you and Jamie, in fact for all of us, to keep this quiet and low key.'

Not for the first time Rosie was filled with admiration for her mother. A few minutes ago she had seemed momentarily crushed but equally quickly the spirit and the fight were back. Rosie could even feel a little sorry for her father.

After lunch and a brief look at the lovely, expensive merchandise in the flagship store, without buying as much as a pair of tights, Betty and Rosie went back to the car and set off to collect the latest batch of Betty's paintings from Antonio. For once they did not linger and after hugs and kisses from Antonio they made their way to Murrayfield to see for themselves how the land lay in Polly's household.

Rosie managed to hide her relief when she saw Polly's Rav parked outside the door, which was exactly where it should be mid-afternoon and Rosie profoundly hoped, just for once, Polly was not away cooking yet another business lunch but at home for the arrival back from school of Minty and John.

'I hope we won't be intruding.' Betty said with just a hint of anxiety.

'Ma, don't be silly, Polly will be delighted to see us. I thought about 'phoning but this way it's a surprise.' She added, silently to herself "and Polly will be off-guard and I might just begin to find out what's really going on because something is happening that isn't right."

Polly heard the doorbell just as she was in the kitchen in the middle of trying to find out why John's form master had asked to see Richard and Polly as a matter of urgency. Both children had just arrived back from school.

'Oh, damn," she said "who can that be?'

'Mummy, you swore' said Minty, primly. 'Why? I thought you told us it showed a lack of knowledge of English if people swore.'

Polly just gave her daughter a dirty look and said 'stay there both of you.'

By the time she reached the door her mother had already opened it and was ushering Betty inside.

'Hello, darling' said Rosie cheerfully, 'we were unexpectedly in town and thought that we would come and have a cup of tea with you all before we go home.'

Inwardly, Polly groaned. This was all she needed. But she rearranged her face into a semblance of welcome and said,

'Well, it's all a bit hectic but why don't you go into the sitting room and I'll send Minty through.'

But Betty was having none of that.

'Don't be silly we'll come into the kitchen. I love kitchens and yours is always so very nice.' With that she dashed off to the kitchen and was greeted with great delight by Minty. John took the opportunity to slope off up to his bedroom. He knew why Mr Brown wanted to see his parents. But really he had only been fighting back and what else was he expected to do?

'Great Grannie and Granny have you come to see me? Look I'm doing some special drawings and I'm getting my plaster off this week!' Both Betty and Rosie hugged Minty and privately thought she still looked rather peaky but then she had been through a great deal.

Polly was distracted. Earlier David had been at his most demanding. As well as a seemingly insatiable sexual appetite as far as she was concerned he now seemed to want to be involved with the rest of her life, too. It had all started with his gift of Buttons two months ago and it was getting too much for her. Richard was working longer hours now he had become a partner and Polly knew that she should give David up before they were well and truly found out. However, she made a big effort to be charming to her grandmother, civil to her mother and to produce some Earl Grey tea and home-made gingerbread. So they passed a short hour pleasantly enough even though there was an air of underlying tension.

Whilst Minty was being fussed over by Betty and Rosie Polly went upstairs to tackle John. She made the mistake of being cross with him before hearing his side of the story.

'John, what on earth has been going on at school? You used to get on so well with everyone and now Mr Brown has written to us saying that you have been bullying one of the other boys and Harry has been involved as well.'

'Oh you never listen to me' he shouted to his mother 'we haven't been bullying, we've just been protecting our gang. All you can think of these days is Minty, Minty, Minty and your cooking; nothing is any fun any more.' Immediately she felt sorry. John was such a good, solid little boy who had never complained over the difficult weeks since Minty's accident and had never been in trouble at school before. Life had been hard for him and she and Richard had been so wrapped up in themselves they had probably made their young son feel very much on the periphery of their lives.

She hugged John and though he struggled and pushed her away, he was really glad of the contact.

'Sorry, anyway' John said 'though we weren't doing nothing wrong. Well maybe a bit of fighting but nothing important. Old Brown just has it in for us. You go and tell him Mum, you tell him I am not a bully.' Polly looked at her rumpled little boy with a more understanding smile, 'Daddy and I will have a chat with you about it later so that you can explain to us what has been happening. Now come and see Great Grannie and

Granny before they go back to Peebles and you get ready for Cubs.'

Later, as they drove away the two women were quiet, each wrapped in her own thoughts, not only about their personal concerns but also about Polly and her children and how pressurised modern family life seemed to have become.

When they arrived at Stitcholme before Rosie could turn the car up the hill towards the Tower Betty said,

'Just drop me off at John's place please I want to talk to him before we go off to see the lawyer on Friday. He is so sensible and keeps me calm about it all.' After doing as she was as her mother asked, Rosie drove on to Whitewalls in a very reflective mood.

As she let herself in and went straight to the kitchen Rosie thanked God, not for the first time, for the stability and comfort of her home and the haven from the world it represented. To her surprise Jamie was sitting at the kitchen table with a mug of what looked like instant coffee and a rather serious expression on his face pretending, she thought, to read the Scotsman newspaper.

He jumped up at once, enveloped her in a bear hug and gave her an enormous kiss on the lips then held her close to him.

'Darling,' she cried 'steady on, I've only been to Edinburgh for an afternoon, not to Africa for six months.' But she hugged him back and looked very directly at him.

'Can't I give my lovely wife a hug and kiss if I want to do?' he asked. Whilst he had decided not to tell Rosie about the hospital appointment Jamie was scared and suddenly his resolve weakened.

'Sit down, darling' he said, 'I have something to tell you.'

Chapter 16

High Wynch Park

The atmosphere over dinner in the kitchen at High Wynch Park had been barely cordial. Alexander and Roberta had not troubled to hide their horror, even contempt towards their parents and their decision that Virginia would ahead with her pregnancy. Now she had stopped being sick all the time Virginia had started to bloom.

To her amazement she felt wonderful and looked glowing. Hughie was like a dog with three, never mind two tails and to their grown-up children the parents were altogether too damn smug.

The telephone went and Roberta picked up the receiver on the oak kitchen dresser. 'Yup' she said 'I'll just get him, hang on Aunty Rosie.' She passed the telephone over to her father and lit up a cigarette. This was too much for Virginia.

'Roberta, I know that you don't think I should be having this baby but at least don't smoke in front of me, or anywhere in the house except your bedroom for that matter. Your father and I have decided that your little sister, or brother, is going to have the best start in life we can manage and my inhaling your cigarette smoke would be so damaging both for baby and me!' Slightly to her own surprise, Virginia realised that she meant every word and

383

just at that moment she felt the small fluttering of the first movement of her unborn child."

'Hughie, Hughie get off the phone, come here, the baby's moved, quickly come and feel!'

'Bye, Rosie, got to dash, baby just moved, apparently. I'll call you back later but what a cheek the old boy has.' He put the phone back and went across to his wife, feeling a surge of male pride and obediently put his hand on her swelling stomach, though to be honest he couldn't feel a thing.

'Old girl, how absolutely wonderful, shouldn't you be lying down with your feet up or something?'

'This is all too much for me,' Alex announced 'coming Bobby?' he asked his sister, 'let's go and have a game of billiards and leave these two love birds to do the baby thing.'

Roberta made a face but got up from the table and had the grace to say,

'Sorry, Ma, leave the dishes Alex and I will do them later. Sorry about the smoking as well.' Rather to her own surprise Roberta began to feel better about what she had previously thought of as "this whole disgusting business". It might even be fun to have a little one around.

Once Virginia and Hughie were cosily ensconced in the Den she said to him,

'Now what did your saintly sister Rosie want? It's not often we hear from her. It must be all of four years since we last saw them and then we had to go to Scotland.'

'Well, darling, we may have to go again. My father is about to turn up from France, complete with his French Tart, wife number three! I think they could do with a bit of moral support and Rosie has suggested we go up for the Garden Opening and apparently Charles and Maggie are invited, too.'

'Well, that might be fun,' Virginia mused 'especially as I've stopped throwing up. In fact, I'm feeling rather well right now.'

Not for the first time Hughie marvelled at the vast improvement in temper that Virginia's pregnancy had brought with it.

'Well, I'll ring her later and say we'll go.' So that was easily settled.

Yorkshire

Florette was feeling particularly summery and at peace with the world. The weather had been sunny for days, the garden was well under control, as was Nigel and the business was doing almost unexpectedly well with pretty summer flowery shirts and tiny pastel cashmere camisoles.

Maggie and Charles were about to pay a short weekend visit and Joan was busy in the kitchen cooking all kinds of treats for them to enjoy. Florette was still unsure as to whether or not Charles was the right man for her granddaughter, but equally she was wise enough not to try and influence Maggie one way or another. It would be interesting to see how their relationship had progressed over the months since the filming of Country Pursuits and all the excitements that had produced.

Niggling away in the background was the fact that Charles just might be posted to Iraq or Afghanistan but by tacit agreement nobody had actually raised the subject. Nigel and Florette had discussed it and whilst they both agreed that the decision to go to war against Sadam Hussein had been controversial, the British Army had to play its part and that might have a direct effect on Maggie, as well as Charles. They both agreed the subject would not be mentioned by either of them over the weekend and were determined that Charles and Maggie should have a relaxing time in the beautiful Yorkshire dales.

In spite of the background to the visit, Florette was looking forward so much to seeing Maggie and also Charles, of whom she was becoming increasingly fond the more she saw of him. Particularly, she was very heartened by his absolute love for Maggie and his devotion to her. Also Nigel liked him and felt he would be a good, steadying influence on his step-granddaughter. So the visit began with high hopes from them all.

The atmosphere over dinner had been relaxed and Florette was impressed by the way in which Maggie seemed to be taking Charles rather more seriously than before and the easy manner between them spoke of a relationship which was growing in depth and commitment.

'Maggie is coming to Scotland with me at the end of the month,' Charles confided when they were sitting outside on the terrace as the light faded, enjoying a glass of Nigel's best brandy.

'Yes, I have been practising my reels and shopping for a kilt and a bonnet' Maggie said light-heartedly. 'Seriously, though, I have heard so much about the family and Whitewalls from Charles I feel I know everyone already. It sounds a great way of life and I can quite see why he loves going home as often he can.'

Unusually, Maggie did not have another acting role lined up for the next few weeks so the plan was for Charles to get some leave. They intended to go to France for a short holiday and return in time for the family gathering in Scotland.

Later, in their bedroom Charles and Maggie were having a serious talk. After the first weekend Florette had abandoned the pretence of separate rooms and they now openly shared what had always been Maggie's room with its high, comfortable bed, with a mullioned window overlooking the gardens and furnished in the understated "country house" style that was her grandmother's hallmark.

'So there is just a possibility I might be sent to Iraq or even to Afghanistan. Right now everything is changing on a daily basis and whilst it wouldn't be my choice of a posting I will have to go if we are called upon.' For almost the first time in their relationship Maggie felt afraid for Charles. Yes, she knew he was a regular soldier but had not given much thought to what that might mean in a war situation.

'Oh, I do hope not!' she cried 'you read such awful stories about what's happening in Iraq and Afghanistan, people getting injured and even killed every day.!' He saw his moment.

'That's why I would love us to get officially engaged and then the whole world will know we love each other and intend to make our lives together.' Maggie's eyes filled with tears and she flung herself, albeit a little theatrically into Charles's arms.

'It means so much to you and to me too. You know I love you. I just felt I needed more time but, oh I can't bear to think about you being sent to that horrible, horrible war or anywhere else dangerous but I do understand that you might have to go if you're needed. So yes, yes I will become engaged to you. When shall we tell people? Shall we tell Florette and Nigel this weekend? I would love to do that.' Once Maggie made up her mind about something, immediate action was required.

Laughing with delight at that moment Charles would have agreed to anything. He wasted no time in leaping out of bed and from the corner of his suitcase triumphantly brought out the dark green velvet box. He pulled Maggie into an upright position and then went down on one knee beside her. Suddenly it was all serious. "Help" thought Maggie 'Am I really, really ready for this?'

Romantically Charles took her hand, went down on one knee and asked,

'Maggie, darling, will you marry me and stay with me for ever?'

At that moment she knew; she knew she loved him with all her heart and without hesitation answered,

'Darling, yes of course I will.'

The ring fitted perfectly and the square cut emerald, flanked by two fine diamonds was perfect for Maggie's colouring. It looked as if it had been designed precisely with her in mind.

'And now, Mrs Douglas-to-be, shall we have another practice run whilst I have my wicked way with you?'

Maggie needed no persuasion.

Haute Savoie

Alistair was sitting at his desk trying to work out if he could manage to go to Scotland without Madeleine. She came into the room with a decided sparkle in her eye and a number of expensive-looking carrier bags.

"Cherie, you will never guess what I managed to find in Chambery! There is this new shop selling things from Scotland and I have bought some very chic trousers in a lovely tartan and also a most delicious cashmere sweater for our trip!"

Inwardly he groaned. Firstly they could not afford any extravagance until he had got his hands back on Whitewalls and secondly he could just imagine Rosie's reaction at her young stepmother turning up dressed in tartan. "Oh what the hell" he thought, "let's just go and I'll think of a way of keeping Madeleine's mouth shut until we're sure of what's happening." Mentally he gave in. If he won the legal battle then Madeleine would share in new-found prosperity and if he lost …… well she could make up her mind to stay with him or to go and, truth be told, he was getting bored with her so this could well decide the outcome of a marriage that he had not really been passionate about, except for its sexual content, from the very beginning.

Madeleine was not stupid. She was fully aware for his own reasons Alistair was not totally relaxed about taking her with him to Scotland. Also she knew that their marriage had been one more of convenience for each of them than a great love match. It had suited her very well to get out of the rather seedy life she had been living as a croupier and assume at least a mantle of respectability. On Alistair's part for a man of his age he was remarkably virile and sex on a regular basis was important to him. Without his feelings being particularly engaged, he and Madeleine enjoyed the kind of sexual relationship that men, many years his junior, only dreamed about. But in his heart of hearts Alistair was beginning to feel his age and part of him longed for the settled way of life in Scotland that, in hindsight, he realised he had so thoughtlessly tossed aside.

He didn't really care whether or not Madeleine came with him to Scotland. He thought his family would dislike her – as he was beginning to do himself – but equally there was a part of him that would be very proud to show off his much younger, and undeniably attractive wife.

So he just smiled at Madeleine and said 'I have booked the plane tickets and spoken to Rosie so we will be organised to go at the end of the month. The gardens are going to be open to the public for charity and you'll get the chance to meets lots of people.'

"That will keep her quiet" he thought to himself.

"It sounds very, very boring but I will play along with him until I see just what I can get" she thought.

And so the plans were made and Madeleine decided to "reward" her husband with a very loving siesta after a rather good lunch of pate, salad and cheese accompanied by an excellent chateau-bottled red wine.

"Altogether very satisfactory," thought Alistair afterwards. "Life in the old dog yet" he told himself.

"That should keep him happy" Madeleine told herself, "well worth a fake orgasm" to get her closer to achieving her ambitions.

Whitewalls

Roddy had decided to enter Border Prince for a two mile hurdle race at Perth racecourse. The racecourse was over the Forth Road Bridge and around 35 miles north of Edinburgh. It would be good for his dam, Princess's future reputation as a brood mare to have another win to her name from one of her foals.

He felt more cheerful and less tired, though he was still concerned about what was happening over at Whitewalls. Roddy had always deeply disapproved of the philandering Sir Alistair and considered it "good riddance to bad rubbish" when he had finally gone to live abroad, leaving Betty, of whom he was very fond, to build a new and independent life for herself. He really could not understand why Rosie was allowing him to come and stay, with his French wife as well. It simply confirmed the total lack of sensitivity he felt was an integral part of the other man's personality.

However, Roddy decided to concentrate on more important things and picked up the phone to speak to Richard about his plan to run Border Prince. 'Roddy, I think that is a great idea' was Richard's enthusiastic response. 'We'll have to get him back into full training though to make sure he's fit.' Roddy was heartened by Richard's reaction and they resolved to decide on the training plan the following weekend.

Rosie was once again compiling lists. She still bitterly regretted saying her father and Madeleine could stay. She had forgotten how persuasive he could be. Also relations between Rosie and Polly had still not recovered completely and part of the trouble was that Polly had categorically refused to talk about anything relating to Roddy's will, as well as the fact she was continuing to work, despite Richard's new position as junior partner in the law firm. In the middle of all this John was still under a cloud at school and Minty, whilst recovering well physically from the car accident was still diffident and, at times, withdrawn.

She wished Polly was being more helpful but didn't really know what else she could do. Maybe she could ask her to have Alistair and Madeleine for a few nights in Edinburgh to share the burden and perhaps Polly could somehow get to know her other grandfather. She glanced at her watch. It was lunchtime but there was a chance that Polly would, for once, be at home and it was worth a try before Roddy and Jamie came in to eat.

Polly was having a somewhat tense lunch with David in a small, discreet Italian restaurant in Edinburgh, called Il Castello. It was owned and run by Giuseppe, a small, fine-boned sensual Italian who had started there as a chef many years ago and who now owned the business. Giuseppe could always recognise a fellow-traveller when he saw one. He knew David though not very well, through a succession of beautiful women but had not seen this attractive blonde girlfriend before. She, Giuseppe thought, was a class act – sexy but aloof. Polly was just the kind of woman he admired! He positioned himself where he could hear something of their conversation, or rather argument. It was a familiar story, but with a twist. Usually the woman was trying to persuade the man to leave his wife, not the other way round.

David thought, "I can't believe I'm doing this but I can't go on with this hole in the corner stuff. She's got to leave him". Aloud, he said

'Pollyanna when are you going to make up your mind to be with me all the time? Tell Richard, I'm sure he must know that something is going on, especially if you don't have sex any more!' That, of course, was a lie. Giuseppe knew it was a lie. It was what everyone said in the throes of an affaire that was getting out of hand. He then saw a change of tactics.

David leaned across the table and looked deeply into Polly's eyes.

'Darling girl,' he said seriously ' I am tired of this half existence, snatching hours here and there, you always being nervous about being seen by someone you know, or who knows you. I'll willingly take on John and Minty and your family will come round once they see how happy I'll make you.'

Polly did not want to continue such an important conversation in public. So she simply smiled at David and said,

'David this isn't the right place to talk, let's go back to your flat and see if we can decide what to do next.' Whilst Polly did not want to let him go, she was far from sure that she could give up everything else in her life for David.

David signalled to Giuseppe that he wanted the bill.

'Of course,' he answered professionally 'I trust everything was to your satisfaction?'

He thought to himself "though I think that you are going to find it difficult, my friend, to persuade her to leave her husband. She is too comfortable. Be wise and be satisfied with what you have!" Naturally he showed nothing of this worldly wisdom to David and smilingly said goodbye as David and Polly left.

Chapter 17

Whitewalls

Peace had returned to Whitewalls. Jamie was busily painting in the Studio, getting ready for his Exhibition. Molly was crashing around the house in her inimitable style, preparing for the visitors. Rosie had taken refuge in her garden and was busy weeding and making notes of the gaps in the herbaceous borders. She saw there was deadheading to be done and made a note of that too. It was Friday morning and Rosie was looking forward to the weekend and seeing Polly, Richard and the twins again.

The sun was shining with the promise of summer that can so often deceive in the lowlands of Scotland but there was a fresh breeze with a cleansing feel to it. She looked at her watch. It was noon and time to go in and prepare a salad for lunch to follow the vegetable soup she had already made. That would be her first task before she went along to persuade Jamie away from his easel. It was warm enough to eat outside and maybe they would enjoy a glass of white wine. There was lightness in her step as she left her gardening tools in the greenhouse and returned to the kitchen.

Though, of course, nothing is ever really how it seems. One of the reasons that Jamie had retreated to the studio was that he was exceedingly worried about the hospital appointment and tests to be done the following Tuesday. He had still not told Rosie, but his resolve was weakening. They had never had secrets from each other and it came to him that he could not really face this without his wife at his side. Ever-meticulous he cleaned his brushes and set them neatly back in their places before going off to find Rosie to tell her the truth and ask her to go with him to the General Hospital.

Equally Rosie was still troubled. Try as she might to concentrate solely in the moment on her gardening, there was a great deal on her mind. Although on the surface things seemed to be going better for everyone she felt unease in the core of her being. Apart from anything else Jamie had clammed up about his visit to the doctor and would only refer in the vaguest of terms to 'more tests'. It really wasn't good enough, she decided. Over lunch they were going to talk about it and everything else as well. She felt better. Action always suited Rosie better than introspection and putting her trowels and secateurs in the trug, along with the notebook she made her way back to the house.

Once they were sitting at the old teak table outside the kitchen in their usual places, facing each other over bowls of Rosie's vegetable soup they both started to speak at once.

'Rosie' Jamie began "I haven't been completely open with you …' simultaneously she said

'Jamie I've been worried about you, we've never had any secrets until now but I feel so strongly there's something you're not telling me about these tests.'

There, she thought, it's out in the open. Jamie felt only relief. Lunch forgotten, he reached over and took his wife's hand,

'Darling girl' he said 'after all you've been through recently, with worries about Polly and Roddy, Minty's accident, John's problems at school, and your father suddenly reappearing, I thought you had more than enough to worry about without getting upset about something that may turn out not to have existed at all.'

Did that mean, she wondered, all was well? No.

'The truth is, and I have so wanted to tell you, I have to go to see the Consultant at the General Hospital next Tuesday. It seems there is a problem with my prostate though I think it's been found early enough to be treatable.'

In a moment they were in each other's arms, hugging closely and both close to tears. Rosie gave herself a big mental shake. She knew where she was now. She would be supportive, do what had to be done, that was her role and one that Rosie knew she was good at fulfilling. Jamie felt a huge sense of relief. It had been so hard keeping the secret from Rosie and he knew without her help and support it would be almost impossible for him to get through whatever was to come.

London

Maggie was feeling restless. She loved the London mews house for the haven it provided when she was busy working either on the stage or, as recently, filming. But she was not really a domestic animal and the novelty of playing house, even with Charles getting away to spend time with her whenever he could, soon palled.

She was still harbouring a little doubt about agreeing to become engaged to Charles but she did love him and he had been so persuasive. Perhaps after their trip to Scotland to meet the family she would be more sure and able to envisage the life they would have together once they were married. However, she intended to have a reasonably long engagement so they had time to plan and for her career to develop in the way that she wanted, which was most definitely towards films.

When she heard about Virginia's pregnancy she had been absolutely astounded and even more surprised at the decision to have the baby. Maggie could not imagine having children yet although, she mused, some time in the future with Charles she could see it happening. In the meantime she had started to look forward to going to Scotland and had received a very warm and friendly letter from Rosie, Charles' mother, who sounded kind and welcoming. Rosie had told her there would be quite a gathering of family and it would be great to meet them all after hearing so much from Charles. Clearly the Douglas family had a very strong sense of who they were and a great loyalty to each other. This was quite outside her own experience as an only child with parents who had been very wrapped up in each other and their own lives. This had been one of the reasons that whilst she had been very sad when they were killed in the tragic car crash she had always felt even closer to Florette and Nigel than to her mother and father.

"Yes" she thought "on balance she was sure she not only loved Charles but also she wanted to spend her life with him and become part of the family that had nourished him and made him into the kind and loving man that she had fallen for months earlier." She picked up her mobile and scrolled down to his number.

'Darling, just a quick call. Have you got the date yet for our visit to Scotland? I really can't wait to meet them all and tell everyone we are officially engaged.' Charles, who had been in the middle of a meeting, was very startled. His Commanding Officer frowned across the desk and Charlie cursed himself for having left on his mobile phone. So he just said quickly,

'I will be in touch with you as soon as we have a confirmed date. Thanks for calling, goodbye.' And hung up. For a moment Maggie was cross, then commonsense prevailed and she realised he probably wasn't alone. 'Right' she thought, I'll go and do some retail therapy in Harvey Nicks. That idea cheered her up and she quickly got her things together and ran lightly downstairs to start her shopping expedition.

Whitewalls

Rosie and Jamie sat very quietly, very close together as they waited for the Consultant to come back into the room. Mr Williams was a young man, or at least they both thought separately that he was a young man. Hopefully, though, he knew what he was talking about.

As he came through the door they looked up expectantly and hopefully, but he looked grave. Peter Williams sat down behind his desk and opened the buff folder.

'Well, I expect you are anxious to know what we've found.'

"That has to be the understatement of the year," thought Jamie but it was left to Rosie to ask.

'Yes, can you tell us please? We are obviously very worried.' The Consultant produced a boyish smile and continued,

'It could be worse. It could, in fact, be much worse. There is an indication that the enlargement could be malignant but fortunately it is of a type and stage that can be treated with a fairly new procedure developed in America which involves planting Radon seeds at the site of the prostate gland. They will work on the tumour and destroy it without causing any of the usual side effects of surgery. We need to do this as soon as possible and once the seeds have arrived – they need to be specially ordered – I'll arrange for you to come in. Ideally we can do this as day surgery but you may have to stay in overnight depending on how you come through the procedure and how your blood pressure reacts. Now have you any questions?'

"Dear God," thought, Rosie "he's talking about something that might be terminal as if it were removing an ingrowing toenail." For once she was bereft of words. Jamie looked at her, then said,

'Yes, what chances are there of completely curing it?'
Peter Williams was glad his patient had asked a very
straightforward question.

'Because of where it is and the size and shape of the
tumour, they are very good indeed provided the disease hasn't
spread. Of course there is always a risk attached to any procedure
carried out under anaesthetic but problems are rare.' He turned to
Rosie and looked enquiringly, hoping that she would not say
anything, but she did.

'Mr Williams,' she began, and then felt tearful 'we have
been happily married for a very long time and I couldn't bear it if
….' She started crying and he gently pushed the box of tissues,
kept ready on his desk for such a purpose, towards her. Jamie
took her hand; she mopped her tears, blew her nose noisily and
said,

'I'm sorry, usually I can cope with anything but this is so
unexpected, so new to us.'

Peter Williams gave her the benefit of the understanding
smile he had so successfully cultivated and looking briefly at his
watch, concluded,

'Please try not to worry, we've caught this at a very early
stage and I am very confident your husband will be as right as
rain.' They both found the cliché comforting and soon walked
out of his office, arm in arm, to the car with lighter steps.

They completed the journey home almost in silence. There
was a great deal to think about. Recently life had been

complicated by other family matters, other family members whose needs had taken precedence. Now they were faced with a new problem. This was a new situation. Both of them had enjoyed tremendously good health all of their lives. situation. Being faced with a potentially fatal condition was something both Jamie and Rosie had not been prepared for and they had no mechanisms to deal with this stark reminder of their own mortality. Like many prosperous, middle-aged and contented couples they had supposed they would live for ever.

As Jamie drove into the familiar drive leading to Whitewalls Rosie put her hand gently on his arm. Deliberately making her voice light she said,

'Let's go and have a drink and talk. I don't think we should tell the children anything yet. Polly and Richard have their own issues, Charles is so full of excitement about getting engaged and ….' At that her voice faltered. He turned to her and smiled; he was back with her.

'We will talk about it, but not worry about it. Come on the dogs will be dying to be let out and I am sure you have a list of things as long as your arm to do so let's get on with living.'

"So this was how it was to be," she thought, "probably for the best." Rosie gave Jamie one of her most brilliant smiles and said,

'We'll beat this together. I'm quite sure.'

Arm in arm they went together into Whitewalls.

Haute Savoie

At last Madeleine was ready to leave. She had packed carefully. Although when required she could appear to be either silly or glamorous, or both, Madeleine was a very shrewd woman. For a while now she had suspected that Alistair had lied to her about his financial status. Certainly she would never have married him if she had not thought he was wealthy. He had misled her. She calculated if this mystery over property and land in Scotland was solved in his favour then she would stay with him. If not she would only remain until something, or someone, turned up to enable her to have the lifestyle she craved. Certainly she did not want to alienate Alistair's family – at least not until she found out the truth about the mystery of who really owned the house and the land in the Scottish Borders.

They were flying from Lyons to London and then on to Edinburgh where, apparently, Alistair's granddaughter called Polly (a stupid name that belonged to a bird in her opinion) would meet them. They would stay with her for a couple of days and she would then drive them on to Peeblesshire. Hubert had been prevailed upon to drive them to the airport in Alistair's car, in exchange for having the use of it in their absence so they set off in some comfort to begin what was to prove an eventful visit.

Edinburgh

Polly was in a bad mood as she drove out to the airport to meet the Grandfather she had last seen when she was a little girl.

From what she had heard about him and his behaviour she was not looking forward to meeting him again though, trying to be fair, she supposed he had his side of the story, too. Still, with all the other complications in her life right now, between Richard's partnership in the firm, having had to borrow money to buy his share then David becoming ever more demanding and the children needing more and more of her attention she felt pulled in all directions. She had not been happy when her mother had asked her to meet Grandfather Alistair and his wife and to have them to stay for a couple of days.

After much discussion Jamie and Rosie had decided not to tell the rest of the family about his cancer. But maybe that had not been a good idea. The Douglas's had always been unusually close as a family and to Rosie it had not seemed right to withhold the news from them. Jamie had, however, been adamant.

'They will only worry and I don't think we should tell them until the day before I go into hospital and that's still two weeks away.'

Polly sensed something was wrong with her parents. Her mother seemed distracted and whilst her father was, on the surface, his usual calm and gentle self the easy smile and ready laughter that had been part of her life for so long seemed almost to have vanished. Still, the more immediate problem was only a few minutes away. Polly gave herself a mental shake as she pulled into the airport car park and found a space not too far away from the Arrivals Hall.

Polly spotted her grandfather first before she saw the tall, blonde woman wearing a beautifully cut navy blazer, tight jeans and tee shirt which clung to her undoubtedly shapely figure. The look was completed by an elegantly knotted silk scarf in shades of red, white and blue. "Very British" thought Polly rather nastily. Then she saw Alistair. She was shocked at how like her mother he was – or rather how much Rosie looked like her grandfather. He was tall, quite spare with white curly hair, a pronounced sun tan and the same brilliant sapphire blue eyes as her mother. Totally unexpectedly she felt a surge of recognition and dashed forward to hug Alistair. It was no exaggeration to say that in a very special way at that moment they "fell in love".

'I hope this is alright, you're coming to stay with Richard and me and the children in town for a couple of days whilst they get everything organised at Whitewalls.' Polly said as they went about the business of wheeling the luggage to the car and general chat about the journey, amazement at how easy it had all been and other non-consequential remarks were exchanged.

Madeleine was very used to summing people up instantly and thought to herself, "this is very interesting, there may be something happening here I can turn to my, to our advantage!" Alistair had been totally unprepared for this meeting with the granddaughter that he had last seen as a baby and for whom he now felt the most tremendous tug of emotional recognition. He had thought he was prepared for all that was to happen but he had not prepared for this.

Polly kept up a lively chatter during the drive from the airport into Edinburgh and the affluent suburb of Murrayfield.

'Richard has just become a partner of the law practice' she said 'so that means a lot more hard work and investment in the future but he has done really well to get so far at his age.' Slightly to her own surprise she discovered she really meant it.

Madeleine was tired of being ignored and said,

'You 'ave two children I believe, Polly. What are their ages?' Polly was surprised Alistair had not even told his wife that John and Minty were twins but replied in a civil tone,

'Didn't Grandad tell you? They're twins and they are almost eight years old. They are really looking forward to meeting both of you!' She couldn't believe how nice she was being to Madeleine and Alistair. She must be going mad. But then who was to say all the bad stories she had heard about her grandfather were true? And if they were true why were her parents even contemplating having them to stay?

Richard was bringing the children home from school so there was a little time before they arrived. Alistair decided on a charm offensive.

'My dear girl' he said putting his arm around Polly's shoulders and hugging her lightly under the baleful gaze of Madeleine 'it is so good of you to meet us and have us to stay in your charming house until the weekend.' She found herself returning his warmth.

'Well, it has been a long time since we heard of you and Mum has been under quite a lot of strain recently with one thing and another, including looking after Minty when she broke her leg badly after being knocked down by a car outside school. Anyway, you will meet them all soon enough. Why don't I show you both to your room and then we can have some tea whilst we wait for Richard to bring home the children.'

Madeleine thought the guest bedroom was comfortable enough, though not nearly as grand as she had envisaged. More or less innocently she asked Polly when being shown the ensuite bathroom,

'Tell me, my dear; is this another of dear Alistair's properties?' Now Polly was genuinely puzzled,

'No, of course not, this belongs to Richard and me, just as Whitewalls belongs to Mum and Dad. In fact, I don't think Grandfather has any property in Scotland any more. I wonder what gave you that idea.' Madeleine's suspicions were increasing but, wisely, she decided to laugh it off."

'Oh, my dear, I have no idea really what Alistair owns, or doesn't for that matter.' There the matter was left.

Richard, meeting Polly's legendary grandfather for the first time was not impressed. He though Alistair was altogether too smooth and plausible, particularly considering all the history of deceit and deception. Also Richard was deeply suspicious of the motives of the older man wondering why he had chosen this particular time to come back into the lives of his family.

However, Richard was polite to him and his sharp and shiny wife, with whom he could find absolutely nothing in common. Thankfully, John and Minty behaved with real charm and listened with apparently genuine interest to their great-grandfather's unlikely stories of escapades and heroic deeds.

Alistair went to visit his lawyer and came back with a pleased expression on his face. Largely to please her grandfather Polly had taken Madeleine shopping in George Street and to Edinburgh's exclusive boutique, Jane Davidson, where she had bought a beautifully cut Louis Feraud jacket and to Harvey Nichols where they had a surprisingly good time looking at the expensive clothes but only purchased items from the delicatessen after sharing a "girlie" lunch in the Forth Floor restaurant. It was part of Madeleine's plan to get Polly on her side. She had seen how taken with Alistair the younger girl had been and, equally, Alistair had paid Polly extravagant compliments about her house and her wonderful cooking – a little too generous in Madeleine's opinion but no matter, it seemed important to cultivate her.

In spite of this surface congeniality Polly was relieved when her parents arrived two days later to collect the visitors. Richard had not been happy having them to stay, although they had taken the whole family out for supper at La Venezia, a charming Italian Restaurant and Pizzeria in Hanover Street, which John had described as "cool". Richard had managed to disguise his dislike of Alistair and his venal wife and resolved to get to the bottom of exactly what the older man was hoping to gain out of this visit. He was soon to know.

Chapter 18

Whitewalls – The Stables

Roddy was a contented man. Preparations for Border Prince's race were going well. He had retained his Training Permit over the years although the number of horses he ran was small. The Douglas name was still very well respected in racing circles and since starting his small yard at Whitewalls Lodge he had notched up some memorable successes.

As well as the home-bred horses Roddy's good "eye" for conformation and an encyclopaedic knowledge of bloodstock lines had enabled him to buy horses formerly run on the flat at very reasonable cost and transform them into the jumping animals he loved.

In his mind Roddy knew the time was approaching when he needed to make a decision about continuing with the training yard or giving it up. He had hoped perhaps Richard's undoubted interest in and skill with horses would have made him want to become involved more fully. But commonsense had dictated that Richard was a young man, with a wife and children and a way to make in the world with school fees to pay and a lifestyle to maintain. Nevertheless he knew that Richard was genuinely interested in the stables and would do everything he could to carry on the traditions Roddy had established. If he was honest to himself, this knowledge had been part of the reason he decided to make Richard his heir. At least when he was gone, Roddy believed, something of the old life at Whitewalls Lodge would continue.

This particular Saturday morning he was delighted to see Richard coming up the path to the kitchen door in readiness for going to the stables and getting Border Prince ready to go on to the gallops. With him would be Archie, who wasn't strictly speaking in training but in his time the old grey had been a fast runner and a good jumper and made an ideal training partner for the younger, less strong gelding. The gallops, which led up the hill behind the Lodge House were constructed from old tyres bound with vast quantities of Vaseline to stop them from freezing in the winter and were ideal for building the stamina necessary for jumping horses to acquire if they were to win races.

'Hello, Major' called Richard, who had always used Roddy's courtesy Army title finding it easier than calling him Roddy. 'How's the Prince today? Do you want me to ride him or shall I take Archie and Jack can get up on the star?'

Jack joined them in the yard and said,

'If it's all the same to you Guvnor I'd be keen to get up on the Prince and see how he's come on since we put him into full work.' So it was agreed. Roddy decided he would drive himself up to the gallops in the old landrover, whilst Jack and Richard rode the horses up the hill to meet him.

Whitewalls

Madeleine was bored. She was sitting in splendid isolation in the drawing room at Whitewalls, listlessly flicking through a

Harpers & Queen magazine. Alistair had gone to Edinburgh for yet another meeting with his lawyer. Rosie had gone to visit her mother and as she had said, perfectly politely though in a very cool voice, to Madeleine it would not be appropriate to take Alistair's *latest wife* with her. Even Madeleine who was a stranger to sensitivity could understand that! She was beginning to think it had been a great mistake to come with Alistair. Without asking him outright which, for her own reasons, she did not want to do Madeleine was unsure about the extent of the 'legal issues' which was all Alistair would tell her, neither did she know for certain whether or not her husband actually owned any property of any kind in Scotland.

She rather liked the country house in a way but there wasn't much to do. In Edinburgh at least there were some fairly smart bars, shops and hotels but it seemed to Madeleine that Polly and her husband had rather dull lives. Had she known about Polly's double life, not unlike her own back in France, she would have been amazed. These people were so cool and undemonstrative, no wonder Alistair had wanted to leave Scotland at a pretty early age.

Alistair had hired a car as no one seemed very keen to lend him one and whilst he was spending money he really couldn't afford it gave him independence to go into Edinburgh to see the lawyers, who were at least hopeful of a result and to drive round his old stamping grounds, sometimes with Madeleine, who couldn't see the point of it all.

To alleviate her boredom and as she had the house to herself Madeleine decided to have a snoop around and see what she could find out. Unfortunately for her, Molly was upstairs doing some tidying up and muttering to herself about the "dreadful disruptions" and the nuisance old Sir Alistair was stirring up with Rosie and with Lady Betty.'

Just as Madeleine was examining the contents of Rosie's dressing table drawer Molly burst into the room like an avenging dervish,

'And what, Madam, are you doing in here may I ask?' she said feeling quite outraged at this Frenchie woman's behaviour, snooping around in Mrs D's bedroom for heaven's sake.

'Oh, I was just having a look around at the rest of the house, if you must know. I am family after all!' she said with an ill-judged attempt at being both light-hearted and patronising at the same time. Molly was more than ready for her,

'In polite society, which this is, we would never ever dream of prying into the hostess's personal property and I think you should leave this room at once.' Madeleine did feel guilty, but only at being found out she snappishly replied,

'Oh I am just leaving anyway but Sir Alistair will not be pleased when I tell him that the cleaning lady has been rude to his wife.' Molly sniffed meaningfully and stood at the bedroom door until Madeleine flounced out of the room.

The Pele Tower

Rosie and Betty were sitting companionably enough in the small, crowded kitchen of The Tower which took up almost all of the ground floor, with only a small cloakroom before the first of three flights of spiral stairs led to the sitting room, the bedroom and bathroom and, right at the top of the building, the Studio. Betty was coming to the end of the full story about Alistair, the claims that he was making on Whitewalls and the general disagreeable nature of the whole business. Rosie felt sick.

'But how can that possibly be right? Whitewalls was part of the divorce settlement. There is no way that my father can now claim it. What the hell does he think he is doing?'

Betty was being very brave and very strong. She looked at her daughter with great affection. Rosie had always been a tower of strength, to her, to the family and everyone who knew her. She was 'good old Rosie, you can always rely on her.'

'Rosie, you know I have never said very much about your father and his behaviour in the past. There didn't seem to be any point and as you know I believe in getting on with life, making the best of things. But this is not totally out of character. He has, I believe, run out of money and this seems to be a last-ditch attempt to get his hands on something valuable. I am really sorry that you have him under your roof, though hopefully it will not be for much longer and if you can, please don't let him know that we are on to him. John Prendergast is being a tower of strength to me and hopefully the Judge will agree that despite the

414

technicalities of the registration of the divorce settlement everything was done in good faith.' There was a small silence.

Rosie needed to confide in her mother about Jamie and the cancer.

'Ma, there's something else that I have been keeping from you; trying not to worry you but Jamie's got cancer! It's in his prostate and he is going to have treatment but I am so worried for him and, as you can imagine, he is being very brave.' Betty hugged her daughter, tightly.

'I would expect nothing less my darling. You made a very wise choice there when you decided to marry Jamie. I thought at the time you were both so young it may not have lasted but I was wrong. You've grown together and you will get through this as you have survived everything else.' After further discussion about Jamie's treatment and prognosis Betty decided that they had probably talked for long enough and said, 'Now I think that you had better get back to Whitewalls and try to carry on as if you think nothing is wrong.'

Rosie felt better. She took strength from her mother and believed she possibly could see this situation through, as well as be there for Jamie and his forthcoming ordeal. It would not be easy but life was not easy! Feeling more composed she hugged Betty warmly and set off to drive back to Whitewalls.

Once Rosie had gone Betty sank down exhausted into her favourite chair. She took a deep breath and picked up the telephone. The number she dialled was that of John Prendergast.

Once again she needed his quiet strength. Although she had coped for so many years on her own, fiercely independent and living a rich and full life, quite unbidden came the thought that at last it might be a great comfort to have a more personal relationship with a man in her life. One that would be mutually supporting and sustaining. Her affection for John Prendergast was very real and based on a mutual respect for each other, as well as upon years of friendship and shared values.

John was pleased but also concerned to receive Betty's telephone call.

'Why don't I come up to see you and we can go over all the papers again and make sure that we know what we are doing before the next meeting with the lawyers if that would help.'

Betty felt very relieved,

'Yes, John it would help a great deal and I really don't want to be on my own right now. Rosie has been and I have told her everything but she has so much to cope with I don't want to burden her any further. Also there's some worrying news about Jamie's health, which I'll explain when I see you.'

Whilst John felt very sorry for Betty he did muse that perhaps through her troubles he might eventually persuade her they could have some kind of future together in the years that please God, were left to them. It was lonely growing old alone and with no family apart from nieces and nephews, who lived in the south. His life was indeed a solitary one. So it was with a certain lightness of heart and step that he picked up his car keys, whistled for the dog and set off to give what help and comfort that he could.

Edinburgh

'Great Grandpapa has been telling me the most amazing stories about things he used to do at Whitewalls when he was a little boy.' John was very taken with this magical man with white hair and blue eyes and who must be very old but seemed to be such a lot of fun. In spite of her mother's views and knowing little or nothing about the current situation Polly, too, found her grandfather interesting. Everything he told them about became a story, an anecdote and an adventure. She could quite see why women were attracted to him. Richard did not share her views and as Jamie and Rosie had now confided in him about the real purpose of Alistair's visit he could scarcely bring himself to talk to Polly's grandfather and had been very relieved indeed when the couple left Edinburgh to go to Whitewalls. Minty had been rather frightened of Alistair who was quite unlike anyone she had ever met before in her rather sheltered life. Oddly, though, she had not minded Madeleine who she thought was very pretty and friendly as well in a grown-up kind of way. Madeleine had talked to her as if she were someone whose opinion counted about what to wear and whether or not she needed special clothes for the country. Minty had thought about this and said,

'Well we mostly wear things like jeans and our jodhpurs if we are going riding. Would you like to ride my pony? She's lovely, silvery grey and we call her Snowball. Actually she is quite small but so are you and as you're thin you wouldn't be too heavy for her?' For once in her rackety life Madeleine was touched and thought fleetingly of what she might have missed. She gave the solemn little girl a hug and said,

'Oh, Minty, you are very, very sweet but I 'ave never ridden an 'orse and I think that it is too late to begin this now. But promise you will look after me when at your Grandparents, I would like them to think that I am a nice person and take good care of your Great-grandfather!'

Minty had been pleased at this. It was not often that she was entrusted with special tasks. Everyone seemed to think that she needed to be fussed over since she had the accident. She had decided Madeleine was good news after all, even if her mother and father didn't think so and Minty resolved she would do everything to make sure that her darling Granny and Grandpapa knew what a truly nice lady had come into their family.

Whitewalls

Alistair had not been totally insensitive to the growing tensions as he and Madeleine stayed at Whitewalls. He was pleased with the way the legal case was shaping up and thought he could risk taking Madeleine away for a little while to stay with the Montgomeries in Perthshire. James and Catriona had been friends of his for many years and even after the acrimonious divorce from Betty they had remained in his "camp". They still lived in some style and comfort in the old family home outside

Blairgowrie although they spent part of each winter in South Africa to escape the harsh Scottish climate. Madeleine was behaving suspiciously well and was being particularly charming to Minty. He knew that Rosie did not like her and was only being pleasant to keep the peace. Secretly he was rather proud of his daughter and though not prone to regrets he wished that he could rebuild a relationship with her. But even he knew if he achieved what he hoped to gain by challenging the divorce settlement, Rosie's life could be in ruins and he did not allow himself to have feelings of warmth towards her. He liked Polly, though, and could see in her some of the restlessness that had been in his own blood for so long.

'Goodbye, have a lovely time, give our best wishes to the Montgomeries said Rosie as she and Jamie waved Alistair and Madeleine off giving them, as Rosie thought, some well-earned respite until they had to face Jamie's hospital treatment.

Chapter 19

Whitewalls

The date for Jamie's admission to the General Hospital for the radon therapy treatment that would hopefully cure the cancer in his prostate gland was coming ever nearer. Since they first discovered what needed to be done, however, neither Rosie nor Jamie had talked about it. It was as if they felt by not talking about it, somehow it would go away. Rationally, they knew this was not true but they were both afraid.

They each were profoundly glad Alistair and Madeleine were off their backs and away in Perthshire, Charles and Maggie seemed absolutely fine and, for once, there were no immediate worries about Polly and her family. Lady Betty was spending more time with John Prendergast and it seemed he was helping her a great deal.

'Do you know, darling,' Jamie said after breakfast four days before the hospital appointment 'I feel we have a little peace at last and I am going to the studio to paint and to sort out pictures for the Exhibition.' She gave him a loving hug and replied,

'In that case I am going to lose myself in the garden again. There's still lots to do and I now have some space to get on.'

With that they went off to pursue their respective interests, each strengthened by the love and support of the other.

Soon after they had left the kitchen the telephone rang. Molly was crashing about with the vacuum cleaner – from which, these days, she was rarely detached, the answer phone had not been turned on and she didn't hear the incessant ringing until just before it stopped.

Roddy put the phone down. Perhaps they were all busy and the pain in his chest and arm had gone now. It was probably something and nothing; a touch of cramp maybe. He hauled himself out of his red leather wing chair and went off to find his boots before going to the stables. The sun had begun to have a little strength in it and he felt a little warmth starting to touch his face. It had been a long winter and spring had been late in coming.

Still, preparations for Border Prince's race at the next Perth meeting were going ahead well and Roddy decided if he could get a win out of the horse then this would, indeed, be a fitting conclusion to his career as a National Hunt trainer. As he went out to the yard he reflected he was very blessed with his family in an age when families seemed to mean less than ever before and children were given so many material things but often so little love. He was particularly fond of his great-grandson, John, who seemed a sturdy rather old-fashioned little boy and who was showing a very satisfactory interest in the horses.

The Pele Tower

Betty was not keen on showers but had been persuaded to have one installed in the tiny bathroom which adjoined her bedroom. Though she would not admit it, even to herself let alone anyone else, it was these days rather easier to walk into a shower than to climb in and out of the deep cast iron bath she insisted on keeping. Whilst in the shower one evening after a hectic day of both painting and gardening and trying to keep her spirits up despite the knowledge that Alistair was trying to get Whitewalls back from the Douglas family she was soaping herself when she felt a lump in her right breast. At first she had thought she was imagining things. After all you acquired all kinds of odd lumps and bumps as you got older. She tried again, no there was a definite small swelling where there had been none before.

Whilst she would dearly have loved to have ignored the lump and hoped it would disappear of its own accord, Betty had never flinched from facing whatever was in front of her. As soon as the surgery was open she telephoned to make an urgent appointment to see Dr Macfarlane, who was a young female doctor for whom Betty had a great deal of time. On the very rare occasions that she required medical attention she had found Linda Macfarlane to be both sensible and direct. 'Oh why, oh why does everything bad have to happen at once?' she thought. She knew there was no answer. It was just all part of life.

The Stables

Jack was very pleased with Border Prince. The race was only a few weeks away and it looked as if the horse would be "spot on" to win. The Major would be delighted with him. Jack and Roddy had worked together for a long time; they shared a

422

special bond that was much more than employer and employee. Recently Jack had been a bit worried about the older man, sensing that all was not well, though if asked he could not have put his fears into words.

Richard, too, had been enjoying his closer involvement at the weekends with getting the horse ready. His own riding had become bolder and he could really see himself doing much more of this in the future. He thought it now seemed as if he potentially had the best of both worlds. Of course, Roddy would still be around for a long time to come but in future when his law career was even more firmly established Richard felt he could look forward to a life spent between the city and the countryside that he loved so much. Even Polly's remoteness and prickly attitude which he really failed to understand had seemed less obvious lately and Minty's accelerating recovery had also meant she was back at school and Polly could get on with developing her business. This reminded him; he needed to ask her if she wanted some help with her accounts. She was still doing a lot of work for David, who he did not care for at all. He had decided it was better, however, if he did not interfere.

Whitewalls

Jamie was dreading going into hospital even though it was to be only as a day patient. Rosie would drive there with him in the morning and collect him, all being well, later that day. The symptoms from his prostate were not getting any better and he had, so he thought, faced up to the fact that the procedure to implant the radon seeds that would, with luck, kill off the cancerous cells and shrink the tumour would not be too bad and Rosie and he would be able to put it all behind them and resume their orderly, gentle way of life.

They had decided to tell the rest of the family that he was just going into hospital for a day for tests. This had been Rosie's idea.

'Darling, there's no point in getting everyone worked up about this. It will be much better when we can tell them all is well again.' She had said this to him as much to reassure herself as any wish to protect her family's feelings. Whilst Jamie had really wanted to confide at least in his children he had gone along with her suggestion.

'Rosie, I would rather have talked at least to Polly and Charles. We're not a family that usually has these kinds of secrets and I don't think we should start now. Still as long as we tell them as soon as it's over I suppose there will be no harm done.'

So the matter was not really resolved but was not discussed until they were in the car early in the morning of the appointed day, making their way to the hospital and whatever fate had in store. Jamie was driving. In a vague way that made him feel he was still in control of the situation.

'How are you feeling?' Rosie asked to break the silence. She was feeling cold, although it was a beautiful sunny morning. What if something went wrong? There was always a risk with general anaesthetic. It might not be possible to do the treatment for some reason no-one had thought about. Jamie replied briefly.

'I'm fine, love. It will all soon be over and then we can get on with our lives. There are such a lot of good things going on. There's your garden opening, Charles' engagement, Roddy running Border Prince and your father can't stay for ever. Though I don't dislike him quite as much as I thought I would do.' This, of course, was before Jamie knew the full extent of Alistair's treachery. He continued, 'then young Minty is so much better and Richard's partnership is going well. We're lucky, Rosie, we have so much to be grateful for.'

So it was finally with some optimism, as well as a great deal of apprehension that Rosie left Jamie in what she hoped would be the more than capable hands of the hospital staff and drove thoughtfully home to await news.

The next few hours passed in a blur for Jamie. He was unaccustomed to hospitals and found it hard to surrender himself to the procedures necessary before he finally reached the operating theatre. However, everything was clearly explained to him and the attitude of all the staff was unfailingly optimistic and kind so the experience was not so much traumatic as troublesome and uncomfortable. Naturally he was anxious but drew on his reserves of faith and resilience and trusted the professionals to do what needed to be done.

London

Charles was looking very serious when Maggie arrived at the London house full of joie de vivre. She had been booked for a film to be produced in the autumn, with a much bigger part than her debut one in Country Pursuits. Maggie came in to the sitting room like a whirlwind, her cheeks flushed and eyes bright. He thought that she had never looked more desirable. His heart sank at the thought of the news that he was about to give to her. Even though it had been on the cards it was still going to be very difficult. Although Charles knew that all army personnel sign up to go to war if necessary, the reality of the posting to Iraq could not have happened at a worse time for his personal life. He had no idea how Maggie would take it. Really it had never been discussed.

'Hello, darling you're back early' called Charles from the top of the stairs. 'I've something to tell you.'

Whitewalls

Jamie seemed to have made a rapid recovery from the hospital experience although he was more tired than he would admit, even to himself. Rosie was careful not to appear to be fussing too much although, if she were honest, she was terrified there might be complications.

'I've got another appointment for the hospital to see Mr Williams' Jamie announced as they opened the morning post over breakfast two weeks' later. 'They say it's a routine follow-up so here's hoping it will be alright. Thank God that awful bruising has gone. That's one thing they didn't warn me about.' Rosie felt a rush of great affection for this man who had sustained her for so long and who she loved with all her heart. She could not have borne it if she had lost him. Not that there had been an immediate threat to Jamie's life but if the cancer had not been detected …. She didn't dare think about it.

'When is Border Prince running?' asked Rosie.

Jamie replied 'I'm not sure but soon. Why don't we go over and see Roddy and check with him. I think it will be at Perth.'

'We could all go along and make it a family occasion' Rosie said 'it would be great fun and we could take picnic. If it is a Saturday or Sunday meeting the children could come too. Even Polly might be interested in coming along. Deep inside Rosie felt weary. It was almost as if her bones were exhausted and she longed for a return to the tranquil ordered life of a few months ago when she had felt in control. There were going to be issues, too, as Jamie recovered from his operation. They had been warned he might become impotent. No! She firmly put that thought to the back of her mind as unworthy. Their very satisfying sex life had always been a cornerstone of the marriage and contributed greatly to their happiness together.

Jamie, too, was lost in his own thoughts. Recent events, not least the discovery of cancer had profoundly disturbed the even tenor of his life. Now where there had been certainty there were problems. He supposed it had all started when Roddy had decided to leave his estate to Richard. That seemed to have set off a chain of events that had caused more bother in a few weeks than over the many years of his life and marriage so far.

To her immense relief, her father and Madeleine had extended their stay in Perthshire and she had not told them about Jamie's operation. Apparently Madeleine was a big hit with the county set and Alistair was more than happy with his old friends and the plentiful supply of gin, whisky and reminiscences.

The legal business over the divorce settlement and the possibility that Whitewalls might, after all, belong to Alistair was a long shadow being cast over the lengthening days as spring gave way to early summer.

Madeleine was getting restless with country life saying, 'The countryside is all very well but darling there is so much of it and it is rather boring.' Alistair just smiled and flattered her by saying,

'But Madeleine everyone loves you here. You have really brightened up their lives and it won't be for much longer, I promise you.' Wisely she expressed herself content to stay on longer without further complaint. Alistair had still not told her what was happening with the lawyers but she had shrewdly worked out it had something to do with the ownership of Whitewalls and the farm and that had to satisfy her for the time being. For his part, Alistair was now beginning to feel very slightly conscience-stricken though he told himself he had no choice but to try and regain the properties. Even he realised he had received a much warmer welcome from his estranged family than he had any right to expect. There was too much at stake to behave other than in his usual entirely self-centred manner and he soon got rid of any twinges of conscience.

Edinburgh

Richard whistled as he parked the Range Rover in his designated space in the partners' car park at the office. This new arrangement was one of the perks of his promotion and he had to admit that among the extra responsibilities these small things felt good. Also he found that he was able now to speak out about improvements that might be made to the old-established firm's ways of communicating their services to clients as well as accounting electronically for the time each lawyer, or account manager, spent on clients' business.

At first he had been rather diffident in putting his ideas forward but encouraged by his guide and mentor, Hamish, he was now speaking with greater authority and being included increasingly in strategic planning which he found suited him very well indeed. There was still some strain in his relationship with Polly and the family problems which he realised could be serious. On the whole, though, he had the air of a man pretty well satisfied with his life.

His mobile phone rang. It was his mother-in-law.

'Hello Richard, how are you?' she enquired sweetly. He hoped nothing was wrong. It was unheard of for Rosie to call him on his mobile phone. Was it Polly, or the children? He felt anxious

'I'm fine;' he replied 'is there anything wrong? How is Jamie? It's not Polly or the children or Roddy?' he added.

She smiled to herself. Richard was so earnest and conscientious at times to the point of pessimism.

'No, not at all.' I apologise for ringing you at the office but I wanted to ask your advice about a plan I have." He found himself sighing then thought "this doesn't happen very often so it must be important."

'That's fine mother-in-law what do you have in mind?'

Rosie was encouraged by his patient interest and went on,

'Well we've all had a bad few months with Minty's accident and Jamie being ill and all this legal mess with my father so I thought we needed a really nice family occasion to cheer us all up! Anyway, you know Roddy is planning to run Border Prince at Perth races next month and I thought we should make a family party and take a picnic and just relax and enjoy ourselves but we'd keep it as a surprise and not tell Roddy until we actually arrive and surprise him! The race meeting is on a Saturday. What do you think?'

Richard was so relieved the plan entailed nothing more onerous than a family outing and readily agreed to ask Polly to do the catering.

'We'd love to come with the children; it sounds like a great idea.' he said cheerfully. Rosie was so clearly pleased

430

Richard was prepared to go along with her plan she felt a much-needed lift in her spirits. He picked up the phone again to ring Polly. There was no reply. Her mobile was switched off. Where was she?

Moray Place

Polly and David were having an argument. These seemed to be getting more frequent, particularly as David placed greater demands on Polly. The events of the past few weeks had made her feel fragile. She was finding it increasingly difficult to continue with the double life of her marriage and family and the still very strong attraction she felt towards David. He was pressing her to spend more time with him and he wanted to take her to Gleneagles Hotel for the weekend next month.

'But David, I can't. What on earth am I going to say to Richard and the children? I'm just going off for the weekend with my lover?' He frowned darkly.

'Now you're being silly. I am sure that if you really wanted to come there's an old girl friend around who could suddenly need you to go to London shopping with her,' he retorted.

Inwardly she groaned. If only she didn't find him so attractive, it would be so much easier to end this double life which was becoming increasingly exhausting. Yet she could not quite bring herself to give him up. He decided to give her an ultimatum of sorts.

'Well at least come down to the cottage and stay overnight. Otherwise I will think that you don't care for me any more,' he said silkily, 'you choose the date and I will fit in with it but it must be in the next four weeks. Ideally we should have a whole weekend starting from the Friday evening. At least we need Friday and Saturday nights.'

She replied with almost a note of fear in her voice, 'and if I can't, what then?'

'Well' he answered 'we would then need to bring everything out into the open, tell Richard and you would have to choose between us'

Now she was horrified.

'You can't mean it David. Richard would be devastated and my family would disown me!' she cried without pausing to think of the effect that her answer might have on David.

His face darkened. Beneath the urbane persona that he had carefully created for himself the boy from Muirhouse, raised by his drug-taking single mother with a father who he never knew he had learned to play tough and dirty from an early age. Yes, he was very attracted to Polly almost in spite of her solidly middle-class background but he didn't like to be crossed. In reality it was highly unlikely he would precipitate a crisis by making her choose between her traditional, privileged way of life to start a new life with him, estranged from her family. He did not understand why she was so influenced by them, "like the bloody

432

Waltons" he thought to himself – "perhaps it's time Miss Pollyanna was taught a lesson."

He pulled her to her feet and gripped her shoulders tightly.

'David, stop it. You're hurting me.' She cried.

'Oh, I thought you liked a little rough treatment Pollyanna. You've certainly not objected to some interesting positions in bed.' He retorted, angry but still curious to know her reaction.

She was shocked. Sexual adventure was one thing and David had awakened in her feelings and expression that she had not before experienced but this seemed more sinister, more threatening.

'David, please don't be like this. Of course I want to spend a whole night with you, wake up together in the morning, be a couple but it's so difficult for me to get away, you must know that. But I will try to come to the cottage with you, we can't risk a hotel like Gleneagles. I'll think of a reason and let you know very soon. Now I really must go.'

He was pleased with this reaction but wanted to keep her just a little scared of him.

'Not so fast my beautiful lover, time for a little session before you go and become the perfect wife and mother again.'

She did not need much persuading and indeed felt strangely aroused by this new, rougher side of David who had always seemed so sophisticated.

433

Later in the evening she found an opportunity to form a plan. Richard was in a particularly good mood and both children had done their homework without bickering and were tucked up in bed. Polly briefly reflected this was like "the old days" before David had come into her life. They were sitting at the kitchen table over a supper of poached salmon with home-made hollandaise sauce, tiny new potatoes and fresh asparagus with a particularly fine bottle of white wine when Richard remembered Rosie's call that morning.

'Darling,' he said for they were at least on the surface back to their old affectionate ways, 'I nearly forgot. Your mother 'phoned me this morning. No, don't panic' he added seeing her face become anxious, 'she's only had one of her plans. She must be feeling better too.'

She replied with relief, 'well what is it and does it involve us?'

'Yes, it involves all of us as well as Roddy, Jamie and Border Prince!'

Surely, she thought, Border Prince was a horse, what on earth had that to do with anything?

'Oh get to the point, Richard.' She said.

'Well' he replied feeling and looking rather pleased 'Roddy has entered Border Prince for a race next month at Perth. It's a Saturday meeting and the plan is that we all go up for the day with a picnic to witness what Roddy is pretty sure will be a triumph. I think I told you that he is planning to give up training

434

and to concentrate on the breeding side so this will be his last race as a Permit Holder. It would be a surprise for him. Your mother, of course, wants you to do the picnic!'

Her mind raced. Maybe this would be the opportunity to get away with David whilst everyone else was safely in Perth. She could invent a cooking weekend and make it appear quite natural. Perhaps a client in the west needed catering for a whole weekend. She would think of something. So she smiled at Richard.

'It sounds fun and making a picnic will be no trouble at all. Do we know if my grandfather and his wife will till be around then?' Richard wanted to confide in her about the legal battle instigated by Alistair but Rosie and Jamie had sworn him to secrecy, so he felt he had to respect their wishes.

'Not sure about old Alistair and Madeleine – if that's her name.' Of course he knew perfectly well that was her name but he felt somehow she was behind the old man's plotting and, therefore, to be despised so her name should be spoken as little as possible.

'Oh well, it won't make any difference from the catering point of view. What's the date?' she asked.

'Not certain, but I think it's the third Saturday in June' Richard replied. 'I'll find out for sure tomorrow'

After a long scented bath she later felt very drawn to her husband for the first time in a long time and rather to his surprise she initiated love-making to which he gladly responded. Polly was not experienced enough to realise that adultery often added a certain sexual spice to a marriage which was going through difficulties. But at the moment of Richard's climax the face she saw, dark with passion and desire was David.

Chapter 20
Yorkshire

Florette put down the telephone after receiving an anguished call from Maggie. Nigel looked at her in a concerned fashion over his gold half-moon reading glasses. They were sitting on the terrace enjoying a gin and tonic before lunch whilst Nigel caught up on that morning's Daily Telegraph.

'What's wrong my dear?' he enquired mildly 'you look as if you've had something of a shock.'

"That was Maggie, Charles has to be sent to Iraq or Afghanistan to the war; she is very upset and nothing can be done to stop it!" Nigel smiled indulgently at his wife. When she was upset she became very French and excited. He tried to calm her.

'Well, he is a soldier and that is what soldiers expect to do – serve their country.' Oh dear, that was not a great success.

''Ow does lovely Charles being sent to be blown up serve the country?' she demanded. He tried again.

'Charles is an officer, he will not be going alone and you cannot be sure that he is going to Baghdad or Afghanistan. I think his regiment is in the south of the country where things are easier.'

She got up with a 'pouf' and announced, 'I will go and ring Maggie again and tell them to come here for the weekend and you can find out all about it and I can comfort our dear grand-daughter.' Nigel smiled indulgently. He adored Florette but felt that she fussed rather over Maggie who was, after all, her step-granddaughter but thought perhaps this was because she had been unable to have children of her own. In any case he was very fond of Maggie and had really taken to Charles during the recent visits to Yorkshire and their trip to London to see Maggie's latest play. So he answered with a smile.

'Why not? Do them good to get up here for the weekend if they are free. But don't be too disappointed if they don't want to make the effort. It's a long drive and they have a lot to talk about together.'

When Florette came off the phone she smiled a little triumphantly.

'I spoke with both of them and they want to come. They will leave London very early in the morning and be here in the afternoon. Then you can explain to Maggie that it will be fine for Charles to be away with his regiment and he will come to no harm.' Nigel reflected he would be able to do no such thing, but there was no arguing with Florette in her present mood and whilst she bustled off to make arrangements he poured himself another gin and tonic.

London

After Maggie had spoken to her grandmother she was much calmer. When Charles had told her he was being posted to Iraq or Afghanistan she had panicked visualising all kinds of horrors from his being scarred by being shot at, to certain death by being bombed.

'Charles, are you sure that you don't mind our driving up to Yorkshire for a very quick visit. I am sure Nigel will be able to tell you helpful things and nothing ever seems quite as difficult when I have talked to Florette.'

Charles was grateful they were going to see Maggie's grandparents. Because he came from such a close-knit family himself he did not find it at all strange she should want to discuss this latest development with them. She knew, of course, it would make no difference to how she felt about Charles. Maggie loved him and, if anything, her love became more intense because of the cold chill that gripped her heart when he told her the news.

At least they were more relaxed and decided to have a quick dinner at Umberto's before an early night. The plan was to start their journey no later than six o'clock the next morning.

Later Umberto was to remember that very special evening. It was not that they ate anything different from their usual choices or even drank very much but they looked, he thought, as if a golden glow was surrounding them and they had eyes only for one another. It was as well they did not know what lay ahead. Umberto had second sight and he did not like what he saw. Sometimes, he reflected, God and the Virgin Mary could be very cruel.

The Stables

Roddy came off the phone to Weatherby's, the company which handles all the entries for horseracing throughout Britain, with a satisfied smile on his face. Jack was in the office at the time and was glad the old man looked so pleased?

'That it done, then?' he asked. Prince entered for his race at Perth is he?'

Roddy replied by clapping Jack on the shoulder and saying 'that's about it Jack, my last entry as a Permit holder.' Jack smiled. He was not so sure. What would the Major do without his horse racing? He soon had his answer.

'I'm going to concentrate on the breeding side and selling horses as I've always done but that will be the main business after this. I want Richard to learn more about that operation too so he can carry on once I've gone'. Jack was ready with his reply.

'That's all well and good Major and it won't be for a long time yet I'll be bound.' Roddy smiled at the old groom who had been with him for so long.

'I'll need you beside me more than ever, Jack; we'll go on working together if you're willing.' Jack smiled showing the gaps in his front teeth. He was mortally afraid of the dentists and never went near one.

'Try and stop me Guvnor he said.' He went off whistling through the gap in his teeth to check up on the stables.

High Wynch Park

Virginia was getting bigger and, much to her own and everyone else's surprise she was absolutely blooming during her "unwanted" pregnancy. Hughie had retained his initial enthusiasm once the pregnancy was confirmed and they had decided – or rather Virginia had decided they would go ahead and have the child. Even on the financial front things were going better, largely thanks to Piers Romayne who was setting what promised to be a blockbuster film at High Wynch Park.

Hughie had mentioned to Piers that Virginia was pregnant. Whilst Piers thought to himself "God how ghastly" what he actually said was, 'my dear boy how absolutely splendid. I must tell Anthony, he will be very pleased for you both.' Anthony, of course, was nothing of the kind. All he said, however, was 'How very charming, but aren't they rather old for that sort of thing?' Piers was briefly puzzled. He had thought Anthony had taken a shine to Virginia, which was why he had troubled to mention the pregnancy in the first place! It was not a matter that exercised Piers' mind for very long and he and Anthony were soon planning the finance for the new film.

'Well, darling, what do you think?' Hughie asked Virginia as she reclined on the sofa looking, she fondly believed, like an elegant version of Mother Earth.

'Sorry my love. What did you say? I was miles away.' "My God," she thought, "I am becoming more and more out of this world"

'I said Rosie is planning a big family weekend to take in Roddy's last race as a National Hunt trainer and Charles' engagement to Maggie, as well as her Garden opening. She has invited us to go up and stay.' "Well," Virginia thought "that might be amusing." She knew Rosie ran a very comfortable

443

home and she would be fussed over and looked after very well. She yawned and stretched with all the languor and grace of a large and self-satisfied pedigree cat.

'Do you know, I think I would enjoy that. Also isn't your father in Scotland with his latest wife? That could be fun, too! Do you think we should fly or take the car?'

He was so delighted Virginia had agreed, he would go along with anything she suggested.

'Let's fly and hire a car in Edinburgh. Alex can drive us to Heathrow or Stansted and we'll make it a bit of a holiday as well.' So it was agreed. Hughie even undertook to book the flights and car hire and went off whistling to look at the internet. Virginia decided it was time for her to relax and put her feet up with her latest Jilly Cooper novel. Now the ghastly sickness had stopped, she was almost enjoying her pregnancy and all the fuss she was getting. Part of her would not admit it, but she secretly hoped that the baby would be Anthony's, though she knew that he would never agree to a DNA test to decide one way or another. In the meantime it was really all turning out for the best.

Yorkshire

Florette found Nigel in the garden dead-heading some of the early roses and late perennials. He enjoyed gardening. He found it relaxed him and gave him a chance to think whilst being gainfully occupied. He adored his second wife, Florette, but she was, he reflected very "full on" and not the most restful person to be with. The news about Maggie's fiancé being posted to Iraq or Afghanistan had really jolted her and she did not know whether or not the engagement was now a good or bad idea. Nigel believed it really made little difference; but then he had been a professional soldier and took a more pragmatic view of conflict.

Florette had some news for him. In her hand she held a letter. It was from Rosie.

'Nigel, Charles's mother has kindly written to me and invited us both to Scotland for a long weekend next month. Charles and Maggie are going to announce their engagement, her garden is to be open to the public and, as well, Charles's grandfather's horse will be running in a big race at Perth racecourse. I should very much like to accept. Please say that you will come with me!'

Inwardly Nigel groaned. Like many men he hated to have his routines disturbed and was not keen to go and stay in someone else's house; particularly with people he had not met, however charming they might be. But he knew how important this would be for his wife so he smiled and said,

'Well I suppose if we have to do, it is perfectly possible!' Then he added, 'no more than three nights though. I can't be away for any longer than that!' Florette was well satisfied with his response.

Whitewalls

Rosie was feeling more cheerful than she had done for a long time. She loved nothing better than a big plan, unless it was a family gathering as part of the big plan. Charles had telephoned his father and told him about the posting to Afghanistan. Naturally they were both upset but as Jamie had sensibly pointed out that sort of thing did happen if you were a regular soldier.

'After all, Dad went right through the Second World War and came out more or less intact. So try not to worry.'

'I'll try,' she said, thinking "that's much easier said than done. My poor darling boy how can I bear it?" It was this news that had given her the initial idea for the family gathering and it had grown from there. She was a little surprised that Hughie and Virginia had so readily agreed to come but detected with her pregnancy Virginia had somehow become a much nicer person. Rosie always enjoyed seeing her brother on the all-too-rare occasions they were able to get together. Then she had the idea of asking Maggie's grandparents since they were the only family she had. It would be a hectic weekend with going to Perth Races and the garden opening but it would be the sort of time she relished with all her flock around her.

With her notebook in her hand she sat at the kitchen table and started to make her lists. Hughie and Virginia would clearly have to stay at Whitewalls in view of her sister-in-law's pregnant condition and they could have the guest suite with its own bathroom. Perhaps she could squeeze in Charles and Maggie, too. Though she would come back to that one. Of course she knew they slept together, but under her roof? Maybe not. What about Polly, Richard and the children? That was fairly easy. They could all stay together at the Stables Lodge and share in the excitement of getting the horse ready for his race. Sir Alistair and Madeleine could hopefully be persuaded to stay overnight with their long-suffering friends in Perthshire and only return to Whitewalls on the Sunday for the garden opening. Yes, that should all work. For the first time in ages Rosie felt, once again, in control of her life and her family. Oh, and perhaps Charles and Maggie could share his old room. This was the 21st century after all.

Edinburgh

David was making a plan. Whilst Polly had capitulated on the ultimatum to stay overnight with him at the cottage, this was not going to satisfy him for very long. He scarcely understood why Polly had become so important to him. David was a practiced womaniser and had a large number of attractive female conquests to his name. Compared to some of them Polly was neither the most beautiful nor the most interesting. For that matter, he reflected, in some ways she was quite ordinary. Polly, he thought, typified a certain type of middle-class young mother, attractive but not beautiful in the usual sense of the word, educated but not intellectual and sensual but not very experienced in sexual matters.

The more he thought about it, the more David wanted to prise Polly away from her smug middle-class existence and her dependency on and loyalty to her family. At some deep level he resented her for having had the kind of upbringing he really would have chosen for himself. This would have been a million miles away from the drug-crazed single mother living hand to mouth on a sink estate in the part of Edinburgh that Polly had probably never visited and maybe didn't even know existed, which had been his own childhood.

He planned to have wonderful, sensual time with her for two nights away from the comfort zone of Edinburgh and really to turn up the pressure on her to leave Richard and possibly her family behind. He was prepared to wait but not for too long.

The Pele Tower

Betty looked at the innocent-seeming white card sitting on her desk. She had an appointment to see Mr Carron, the breast cancer specialist at the General Hospital. It had arrived swiftly following her visit to the surgery where Dr Linda had tried to reassure her but had added,

'It's most probably nothing at all but I would prefer you to be seen quickly by Duncan Carron who is one of the best specialists in Scotland. He runs clinics at the General so there's no need for you to go to Edinburgh. As this lump has only just appeared we don't want to waste any time in getting it checked.'

Who was she to take with her? Normally, she would have turned to Rosie but her daughter was caught up in the plans for this great family gathering she was planning for next month and she did not have the kind of female friend who you could trust to keep quiet about something like this. She did not want to go alone.

She would ask John Prendergast! Being of an unconventional nature, Betty did not see anything particularly

450

incongruous in asking an elderly male ex-army Colonel to go with her to have this very female matter investigated. She knew, of course, he had feelings for her and maybe, just maybe she was tired of being an independent woman and living alone. She did know latterly when with John, she had felt somehow safe and less alone.

'Of course I will come with you, my dear' John said as they sat drinking coffee later that morning in his very neat and comfortable conservatory. He added, 'You know that you can call upon me for anything at all. In fact, I'm very glad you confided in me about the wretched business with Alistair and the legal wrangle and, as you know, I'm hopeful that will be resolved in your favour and soon. I know this is rather different but you can rely on me to be discreet.' She put her tiny hand on his large, capable one with yes, signs of his age showing with liver spots and creases but which, like the rest of him, was beautifully kept. She felt a surge of tenderness towards him. Perhaps she had been too distant for too long and for the first time in many years

451

admitted to herself that recently without him she would have felt very lonely indeed.

As she got up to leave she leaned over and kissed him warmly on the cheek.

'Dear John, you are such a comfort to me. I know I can rely on you utterly.' He helped her to her feet. He was moved more than he could say she looked so small and vulnerable beneath the bright clothes and even brighter manner.

'My dear, dear Betty what a lovely compliment. I shall cherish it. I'll come and pick you up in good time on Thursday. I will drive. It's not far and at this point you probably want to keep this quite private.' As he was of the same generation, he knew exactly how she felt. So it was all decided and she left with a heart less fearful and some feeling of optimism restored.

The hospital visit had not been nearly as terrifying an ordeal as Betty had secretly feared. She finally admitted to herself having John with her had made all the difference. The hospital staff had mistakenly thought that they were a couple and it had seemed easier not to correct the supposition. This had proved particularly comforting as the news did not look very good.

'We want you to come in for a small operation to remove this little lump and check that all is well' the consultant, Duncan Carron said. 'You are in amazingly good general health, particularly in view of your age.' At this Betty threw him a dirty look. She was proud of her energy and zest but then she realised that he was probably being kind. Mr Carron continued 'And it is wonderful that you have your husband here to look after you.'

'Oh, he's not my husband!' she cried 'we are just good friends'. That will shut him up about my age, she thought. It did. Still he smiled broadly, shook them both warmly by the hand and said, 'Please try not to worry; my secretary will telephone you with a date for you to come in as a day patient and we'll get you sorted out.'

This time Betty thought she would confide in Rosie and Jamie. After all what was the point of being part of a large, and mostly loving family if you could not share the difficult times as well as the joyful ones. After John had left her with strong entreaties to call him if she felt at all unwell or worried, she made herself a strong coffee and took it outside to sit on the weathered teak bench outside the kitchen door, with Emperor at her feet, to soak up some of the afternoon sunshine, which felt good seeping into her tired bones. As soon as she had finished her coffee she resolved to drive over to Whitewalls and tell them the news.

Edinburgh

Jamie began to feel so much better. Whilst he still had some dull aches and bruising from the operation to sort out his prostate gland he knew how fortunate he had been in that not only had it been caught early enough but also from the follow-up tests it seemed to have been effective. Neither he nor Rosie had yet broached the subject of impotence and, in fact, so much seemed to have been going on in the family, with Alistair and the legal challenge and getting his pictures ready for the forthcoming exhibition that lack of time as well as desire had put their sex life "on hold". He put these thoughts to the back of his mind as he drove to Edinburgh to see Hamish at the Gallery to finalise

454

arrangements for the Exhibition due to take place very soon and, hopefully, to take Polly out for lunch. It had been so long since he and his daughter had spent any time together without other members of the family being present and she had been on his mind recently. They had not even spoken recently about Roddy's will and the implications of Richard being made the heir. Jamie's own nature was so generous he had not felt even the smallest twinge of resentment about his father's decision but this was one of the things he had also not discussed with Polly.

Polly had offered to give him lunch at her home but when he telephoned her to make the arrangement Jamie had been adamant.

'No, darling. You cook all the time I am going to take you for a decent lunch. What about Fishers down at the Shore. You can usually park there and the food is really good. Plus it will give us a chance to have a good chat. I'll collect you from home around 12 30 and I'll book a table.' Polly could not think of a good reason not to meet her father for lunch, besides it was ages since they had been together outside the hurly burly of the family and her father never pushed her too hard either for answers or justifications for anything that she chose to do. Mind you she was not sure how forgiving he would be if he knew about David. Not very, she guessed. So she just said.

'Thanks Dad. I'll look forward to it.' She was, she then realised, very happy about spending some time with her father; just the two of them over lunch. Maybe she could talk to him about Richard and the children and most of all herself?

Chapter 21

Whitewalls

It had been Polly's idea for her mother and grandmother to spend a couple of days at Stobo Castle Health Spa to have some complete pampering and relaxation. In a rare moment of reflection and, indeed, gratitude to these two women who had done so much to influence and support her, even when she had not appreciated it, she thought this would be a real treat for both of them. She would pay for it all and accept no arguments or excuses about being busy! It was beginning to dawn on Polly she had become selfish and this seemed like a way of atoning. Perhaps, she reflected, it wasn't possible to "have it all". For the first time in many weeks, she realised her life was a good one, her husband was caring and faithful and she was surrounded by a loving family. She chose not to include her affaire with David in these reflections.

She telephoned Stephen Winyard, the delightful and urbane man whose late mother, Gaynor, had founded what had become one of the world's most exclusive, yet accessible health spas. The

Spa was in a 19 century castle further down the Tweed valley. It was patronised by the rich and famous as well as by many others just longing for the mixture of peace, luxury and pampering to be found there. He was delighted to help and promised Rosie and her mother would have a delightful room and the best therapists the Spa could provide. Also, Polly insisted on paying for the visit. So when she told her mother and grandmother they had to find two days in the next two weeks to go away and be pampered both older women could hardly demur and, indeed, for different reasons each was touched by Polly's kindness and generosity.

'Why on earth do you want to go there?' asked Jamie in genuine amazement when Rosie told him of the plan. 'After all it's only a few miles up the road from here. Can't you just go for a day?' He was thinking of his own comfort but also it seemed like a waste of money to him.

Rosie thought for a moment before answering. Then she said.

'Polly and I have not been getting on well recently. I thought she was being selfish and self-centered. Mum has become very worried about the legal challenges, things that she thought were settled long ago and she has just told me that she has found a lump in her breast that needs investigating. Now it is probably nothing but frankly this plan is a godsend. We will both appreciate it and come back all ironed out and pampered within an inch of our lives. So my love you will just have to thole it and look forward to next month and all the family celebrations.'

Jamie knew when he was defeated and said, 'Well I think it is terrific that Polly is thinking about you both this way and what's more I'll tell her when we have lunch together in Edinburgh this week.'

Edinburgh

Fishers is a bustling bistro with a proper bar and dining room right on the shore at the busy port of Leith on the north side of Edinburgh. Jamie had collected Polly from Murrayfield and they had driven together to Leith making casual conversation on the way. Then Polly said,

'We're a bit worried that Minty's leg is not quite right yet,' she confided. 'I haven't said anything to her but it is possible that she might need another operation to straighten it properly.' As she dropped this small bombshell Jamie managed to find a parking space near the front door and just turned, squeezed her hand and said,

'Something else to talk about over lunch!'

For what seemed the first time in a long time Polly felt relaxed and able to enjoy being in her father's company. They ate delicious mussels in white wine and garlic, the juices mopped up with crusty, fresh French bread, followed by Dover sole accompanied by glasses of crisp, dry white wine. The conversation was general until Jamie, slightly bracing himself for Polly's reaction, raised the subject of Roddy's will.

'I think,' he said carefully 'your grandfather sees you, Richard and the children as an entity. He has become really fond of Richard and wants to give him and you, of course, the option eventually of a different way of life if that is what you choose."

The way her father put it, the proposition of Roddy leaving the Stud and house to Richard in his will sounded entirely reasonable. The truth was the mad feelings of restlessness and lack of fulfillment that had originally led her to David had recently diminished and she had begun to appreciate again her husband, her family and the way of life to which she had been born.

'Oh, Dad I wish we'd had this talk before. It all sounds so reasonable the way that you say it. I know how pleased Richard was but I spoilt it for him because I suppose I felt resentful.' "How I wish I had not let this simmer on so long," she thought "I really have been a bad bitch." The conversation then turned to more general topics and the lunch ended with coffee and pleasant feelings of comfort with each other.

After lunch Jamie took Polly back to Murrayfield Gardens and went in with her briefly before leaving to return to Whitewalls. Whilst he was there Minty and John were both dropped off at home on school runs and he had the added bonus of seeing them. John dashed in as usual, clothes, hair and satchel all over the place with his school tie loosened and behind his ear and his socks around his ankles.

He threw his things down on the hall chair and said cheerfully,

'Hi Grandpapa, how's tricks?' He thought that sounded kind of cool. Jamie smiled and replied in similar vein,

'Tricks are just fine thanks John. Have you heard about our big weekend that we're planning for next month? You'll be able to help Jack get Border Prince ready for his race at Perth.'

'Wow, cool, thanks. Must go and change. I'm playing cricket with Henry and some of the others before tea.' Jamie smiled at Polly.

'Well he seems fine. How's my dear granddaughter?' he asked turning to Minty who was still quite slow in her movements.

She replied with a shy smile. 'I'm doing really well except I might need another little operation on my leg but I'm fine really and doing quite a lot of sketching still. Do you want to see?' Of course he did and she went gingerly upstairs to her room and came down a little later, still in her immaculate school uniform carrying a number of very clever pictures of Buttons. He felt a stinging in his eyes and so very proud as she showed him a series of five watercolours of the very pretty little cat in different and amusing poses.

Reluctantly refusing tea he left. As always there was a lot to do, including looking in at the gallery on his way back to the Borders and reporting progress to Hamish who was starting to fuss a little about the pictures for the Exhibition. So he gave Polly a big hug and kiss and said, on leaving

'You seem much happier Poll and more relaxed. Remember you can come and talk to me any time you like, about anything.' "If only I could," she thought "but I couldn't tell you about David." Still she felt greatly comforted and replied,

'Thanks Dad for that and for a lovely lunch. Give my love to Mum. Tell her I will ring her about the food for the big party.' Adding to herself "I really wish I was going to be there". But she was too afraid of what David might do if she let him down.

So Jamie set off in good heart, whistling as he drove through the afternoon traffic to the New Town. He knew that things would work out. They always did.

Stobo Castle Health Spa

Betty had not taken much persuading to go with Rosie to Stobo Castle Health Spa. She was tired and apprehensive but determined not to be pessimistic about her forthcoming breast cancer operation and desperately wanted life to return to some semblance of ease and pleasure. For her part Rosie was very touched by Polly's gesture and only regretted she was not joining them.

'Sorry Ma," Polly had said "it really is difficult for me to get away. Besides the two of you have been through the mill and you deserve some pampering.' Rosie replied,

'Well you know your Dad thinks it is quite ridiculous to go and stay when we live practically next door but it will be absolute bliss, I know. Thank you so much.'

Part of Polly really wanted to take off for 24 hours, leave everything and everyone in Edinburgh behind and join her mother and grandmother for some real luxury, lovely massages, great food and relaxation. Knowing she was going to have to deceive them all next month when the family party was due to take place, she realised it would have been hard to keep up a façade in front of the two most perceptive women she knew.

Stobo Castle Health had been taken over by the Army during the second world war, had fallen into decay and had been bought by the Murray Philipson family whose resources, however, were insufficient to restore it to anything like its former glory. In the early 1970s Gaynor Winyard who was then chairman of the Women's' League of Health and Beauty came up with the idea of buying the castle and transforming it into a haven of relaxation and beauty where clients could come and lose weight and, if they wished, to enjoy beauty treatments whilst soaking in the peace and splendour of the beautiful Peeblesshire countryside.

'I'm sure we are going to enjoy this' Rosie said as they crunched to a halt on the gravel directly in front of the imposing front door of the castle. She went on,

'It will be absolute bliss to do nothing except relax, eat food prepared by someone else and have a massage and a facial, as well as you all to myself.'

Betty felt a rush of affection towards her tall capable daughter who reminded her in many ways of her own father; strong, patient and immensely kind.

Stephen Winyard was there to meet them as they arrived in the Reception area just at the top of a short flight of steps guarded over by a suit of armour. Tall and handsome with a beard and kind eyes Stephen still took his inspiration from his late parents, especially his mother, Gaynor. Though he always readily acknowledged the support his father, Bob, had given to the enterprise.

After shaking them warmly by the hand he confided.

'We've had a very late cancellation so I have had you upgraded to the Cashmere Suite. I think you'll like it.' The two women smiled at each other. It was getting better by the minute.

Soon, escorted by Trish, the Spa Director who had been there since the venture started and who had a very warm manner, as well as Stephen. They were marveled at the sheer opulence and luxury of the aptly-named Cashmere Suite. Everything from wall coverings to curtains to luxury throws on the bottom of the cashmere enfolded double twin beds exuded style. Privately

Rosie thought that the Italian parquetry decorating the bed heads

was a little over the top but she loved the luxurious bath products

and gorgeous towels.

'Darling, come and look at this bath' cried Betty, oblivious

of Stephen and Trish standing smiling happily at their delight, 'I

couldn't possibly get in here, I'd never get out again. It's just as

well there's a shower, too.' The limestone oval bath was

absolutely immense and Rosie thought, briefly, how good it

would be to share it with Jamie.

'Ladies, we'll leave you to settle in then come to the Health

Spa once you are ready. You'll find Trish has fitted in a number

of lovely treatments for both of you.' Stephen said before

showing them how to work the matching plasma screens

discreetly embedded in the walnut panelling at the foot of each

bed. He added, 'Just call Reception if there is anything at all you

want and I will see you later at dinner.' With that he was gone.

After making sure they had everything they needed in the way of shampoos and lotions Trish quickly followed leaving mother and daughter on their own.

Betty giggled, feeling lighthearted for the first time for ages, 'He really is rather sweet isn't he? I knew Gaynor, his mother, of course though Bob was always in the background. She was very ahead of her time with diet, health and beauty retreats! Anyway I think that they would be proud of the way in which he has invested in all the improvements and really put this place on the map.'

'Mum, I absolutely agree but now I am going to change into this lovely white dressing gown and go up to the Spa. Are you coming?' Bring your swimming costume, too, and then we can go into the pool and the steam rooms.

'Try and stop me' was her mother's spirited reply. So they retraced their steps back up the stair to the newly-added conservatory style Reception area adjoining the Spa and treatment rooms next to the fabulous indoor swimming pool to find out what treats were in store. En route they looked in at the newly re-vamped shop and Rosie earmarked some luxurious products to buy at the end of the visit. Pauline, who had formerly been in charge of the Spa but who was now responsible for the running of the shop and all its lovely pampering stock assured them that they would have plenty of time to come and browse later. So they each decided to relax and enjoy the total experience and to try and put their various worries away at least for the duration of the visit.

They enjoyed their soothing massages straight away and returned to the suite to put on casual clothes to go for dinner in the smallest of the three dining rooms. They had been given a table for two and the conversation went easily between them on safe topics. After a most enjoyable dinner, with good, healthy food and the indulgence of a glass of wine each they wandered down to the famous Japanese Garden with its waterfalls, plants, bridges and gazeboes creating a timeless and gentle experience that soothed and calmed them. They sat for a while in the soft twilight looking at one of the whirling pools.

'Darling, I have something to tell you,' Betty said. 'Now I don't want you to worry. Everything is organised.' Rosie felt a chill pull at her heart. "What now," she thought? "What else is going to go wrong?" She took her mother's little hand in hers and held it tightly but she only said, as calmly as she could,

'Tell me, what is it? Not more problems created by my father?' The older woman replied gently and lovingly,

'Well darling, I have a little lump in my breast,' Rosie gasped and tried to speak but her mother stilled her, 'I've been to the hospital and a very nice consultant had a look and I have to go in for what they call a lumpectomy just to take it away before it can do any more damage. I wasn't going to tell you and I don't want it to spoil this lovely treat but somehow it is easier to talk about it in this tranquil place and it doesn't seem quite so daunting.' Rosie had marshalled her thoughts and asked,

'But when did you find out? Why didn't you tell me, I could have come to the hospital with you? How awful going on your own.' Betty squeezed her daughter's hand,

'I wasn't on my own, John Prendergast came with me. It was really quite funny because they assumed that we two old dears were married to each other! I was going to tell them that we were lovers but that would not be true and they might have been shocked.'

At this Rosie laughed, hugged her mother and said,

'You are incorrigible Ma, as well as very brave. And John too. I am so glad if I wasn't there he went with you. He is a dear, kind man.'

'Now don't you start getting any ideas' said Betty trying to be prim 'he is a friend and at present that is all he is.' The tension was broken, they laughed and then they got to their feet, deciding to return to their splendid suite, sample all the luxurious bath products and have a medicinal brandy.

Edinburgh

Polly was having her hair cut and highlighted at Raymond's salon in Morningside. She had gone to him since she had been a teenager and in the manner of many lovely male hairdressers he was something of a confidante as well as a skilful purveyor of dreams that represent the "perfect hair style" every woman wants.

'Well, Polly' Raymond enquired, using 'how is life treating you. Is the business going well, any more children planned?' The

471

last question might have been offensive from someone else but Raymond had flirted with her for years and she didn't mind. She smiled at him reflecting a bright and spirited face in the mirror,

She answered with a grin, 'hardly Raymond, I have quite enough with my two already and now Minty has recovered almost completely from the| awful car accident I intend to develop my own life to the full.'

'Good for you, he replied, now let's see if we can make you even more attractive than ever.' He concentrated on giving her a swinging bob that highlighted her fine features and she left an hour later feeling decidedly desirable. This was just as well as her next stop would be Moray Place and David. It was only two weeks now until the planned weekend away and she had still not told Richard, or for that matter her mother she would not be joining the big family outing but would, instead, be "working." The prospect of telling them filled her with horror for despite her new sophisticated hairdo and awakening sense of her own sexual power, in many ways Polly was still the young girl wanting her parents' and her husband's approval.

The Lodge

Roddy leaned over the white painted fence and watched, with great pride, Border Prince rolling around in the small paddock where he was enjoying some fresh grass and kicking his heels just for the fun of it. There was a more serious purpose though in putting the racehorse out for fresh air and grass. The race was two weeks away and Roddy believed it was important not to let his highly strung animal get too wound up. Hence he gave him plenty of variety on the gallops, in the fields and now in the paddock where he could see people and they could wander over and talk to him. He saw Rosie approaching with the Labradors and Empress who was panting as she tried to keep up with the bigger dogs.

'Hello, Roddy' she called out to him, the dogs running round her feet. 'How is it all going? He does look marvellous. Dogs will you calm down' she cried as she went over to lean on the fence next to her father-in-law. Do you think he has a real chance of winning?'

Roddy smiled broadly. 'Yes, as a matter of fact I do. He has a very good chance. Perth is a good galloping track and he is well handicapped for the race.' In some categories of racing, horses carry weight according to how well they have been running. So those winning more races have to carry a heavier load than others who have not been running so well. In theory this means all the horses should cross the winning line together. This doesn't happen very often in practice, though occasionally two or three horses may do just that.

Rosie had a reason for asking, of course. This was her surprise plan for the family gathering but she was beginning to realise that she could not in all fairness just spring it on Roddy on the day. It wouldn't be fair, and besides she wanted Polly, Richard and the twins to stay at the Lodge to make room for all the other guests, so she had decided to tell her father-in-law and make it sound as if it was all part of a plan to celebrate Charles' engagement to Maggie and the Garden opening as well as going to the races to see what Roddy was now determined would be the last race for which he had trained a horse.

The weather had been fine for some time but today the skies were cloudy with the promise of rain to come.

'I wish we could have some rain for the garden' Rosie said, Roddy replied in a similarly casual voice, 'I could do with it for Prince, too. He likes a bit of cut in the ground.'
This gave Rosie the opening that she needed.

'Well, I've decided it's time we had a family get together and hopefully put the past few months behind us. I've invited Maggie and Charles for that weekend to celebrate their engagement and her grandparents are coming too. Maggie's parents were killed in car crash years ago and she's an only child. She is particularly close to Florette, who's French and sounds lovely on the phone. Her grandfather is called Nigel, as I think I told you and he farms in Yorkshire so you two should have plenty to talk about.' Roddy smiled, thinking, "It's so funny but everyone thinks that because you are farmers you automatically have things in common". He supposed that it would be at least a starting point. Then he was aware that Rosie was still talking to him.

'We're going to be a bit short of space and I wondered if Polly, Richard and the twins could squash into the Lodge with you?' His heart sank a bit at this. Since Lorna's death he had got used to his own company and developed a somewhat Spartan way of living that nevertheless suited him. But he hadn't the heart to turn his daughter-in-law down and for the first time in a while she was full of enthusiasm and brightness about her plan.

'I'm sure we can work something out' he replied.

'We can all come up to Perth on the Saturday and watch Border Prince and his triumph. Polly is going to make a big picnic and, if we can all stand it I think my father and Madeleine will come.' He frowned at this last piece of information. He did not like Alistair Bruce but realised as ever, Rosie wanted her whole family united. So he kept his peace on the subject.

'Now Rosie, there are no guarantees with horseracing as you know, though I am hopeful he will win and it would be good to have you all there with me.' She beamed a smile as the first drops of rain began to fall,

'That's all settled then,' she announced 'we'll work out the details later. I'm going to take the dogs and dash back. I think this rain could be quite heavy.' With that and a quick hug and kiss she was gone.

The rain was heavy and the dry gardens soaked it up gratefully. It also meant that Jamie had the best reason in the world to go into his studio and make the final selection from his paintings to be shown at the Exhibition. He felt himself blessed; he was recovering well from the prostate cancer, his wonderful wife Rosie seemed to be coming back to her serene, efficient self and even the cloud on the horizon of his father-in-law's ridiculous legal attempt to reclaim Whitewalls did not seem to be getting anywhere. In this positive frame of mind Jamie whistled as he began looking through the Border scenes he had painted with a great deal of love, fortunately matched with equal skill.

Edinburgh

'Well, Sir Alistair, I have examined all the documentation carefully and it does appear the divorce settlement from Lady Betty was not properly registered. Therefore there is some reasonable doubt about the robustness in law of its provisions. Now quite obviously your intentions at the time of the settlement were reasonably clear but as you are now in a different situation the Courts might, and I only say might, and in view of the errors made most regrettably by Lady Betty's legal advisors at the time, permit us to reopen the matter.'

Alistair had always been a gambling man; another of his less attractive habits. So he thought for a moment then said to his solicitor who was looking at him thoughtfully over a pair of half-moon gold-rimmed glasses,

'Tell me, Christian, what do you think are the chances of winning any such case? Could it be 50/50 or better?' The lawyer who was experienced enough but did not know Alistair well paused before speaking, then he replied.

'Certainly no better than that. It is an unusual situation and whilst you could win on the technicality and leave your former wife to sue her lawyers it is extremely difficult to predict. You are both getting on in years, you daughter and her husband are well-established in the properties and your former wife, too, is elderly.'

Alistair rather bridled at even Betty being referred to as "elderly" but he could see where this was going. It would be a huge gamble; possibly the biggest one of his life. Quite uncharacteristically he decided he needed a little time to think this over.

'What would be the cost of taking it to court? Would you be willing to consider a no win no fee arrangement?' he asked.

Christian Hookley was a shrewd man and had already decided that the only reason his titled client was going to these lengths any was that he was extremely short of cash and, indeed, any assets of value. He paused, then said

'Well, it is not normally the way in which the practice works, as you probably know and I would have to consult my partners. Why don't I do that and Sir Alistair, you could take some time to think over the whole matter before we go any further.'

Alistair felt that was a great relief. He could play for time for a little longer and he could try to ingratiate himself with his daughter and her husband though even he was sensitive enough to recognise that Jamie couldn't stand the sight of him and that Rosie naturally sided with her mother. Still all was to play for. So he rose to his feet and graciously extended his hand for the lawyer to shake before making an elegant exit with the words,

'That really does sound very sensible. One would not want to put money into pursuing a court action not certain to succeed. Why don't we schedule another meeting for, say ten days time?'

This was agreed. Alistair was in a thoughtful mood as he set off back to Perthshire, his long-suffering friends and, of course, Madeleine. He could not stall matters for much longer and things would have to come to a head. It would be a gamble to go ahead without an agreement on fees. On the other hand he was a gambler at heart. On balance he would probably go ahead with the court case, whether or not Christian could swing an agreement.

London

In spite of the underlying concerns Charles and Maggie shared about his possible posting to Iraq or Afghanistan their relationship entered a new phase. As well as the excitement they shared in making love and enjoying a very physical way of expressing their feelings towards each other there was a depth and tenderness developing that gave an added dimension to the time they were able to spend together.

After a particularly loving and gentle Sunday they were relaxing with the Sunday papers strewn around the sitting room of the Mews House when Charles became very serious and took her in his arms.

'Darling Maggie, I'm so very, very happy you are going to marry me and that we're going to Scotland soon, together and I know that my family will love you so much.' She felt a lump in her throat and she became tearful. Charles was such a sweet man, so gentle and yet so strong. Yes, she really did love him and despite wanting to wait before they formally became engaged, the prospect of his posting overseas and the need for them to belong officially to each other had become not only attractive but also essential to her peace of mind.

'I'm really looking forward to going to Scotland next weekend and meeting your family. I feel I know them already. Still I'm kind of relieved too that the grandparents are coming to join us and give me some moral support. It was so kind of your mother to ask them and amazingly Grandad is coming as well as Florette. Normally he refuses any invitation unless he can get to his own bed at night. So she must have worked some magic charm on him.'

Charles replied with some pride, 'Mum's like that though, very persuasive I mean and I know she is going to love you to bits. Anyway, darling I've booked the flights and my sister Polly will meet us at Edinburgh and I think we'll hire a car for the rest of the weekend after we've been to her house and met Richard and the twins. They're a really good pair of kids and Minty has been incredibly brave over breaking her leg when she was knocked down by a car after school. John is well, John is a regular little boy I suppose. He's really sturdy and loves being down at Whitewalls, messing around with the horses and helping Dad and Grandad. Richard's kind of quiet, I suppose, but there's nothing to dislike about him either.'

Maggie did think to herself but did not say "The Perfect family. How the hell can I live up to them? It's all a bit Waltons and apple pie." The trouble was that Charles really believed all this and it was certainly not in her plan to disillusion him. So she smiled sweetly and suggested they went out to Umberto's as she didn't feel like cooking. In fact she had no aspirations of any kind to be a domestic goddess but what Charles did not know wouldn't hurt him at this stage in their lives.

High Wynch Park

Virginia thought she was getting larger by the day. She could scarcely see her once slender ankles any more. Perhaps this was just as well because they were swollen too. In fact, she was beginning to regret accepting Rosie's invitation to go to the family weekend but Hughie was being so sweet to her and so eager to go to Scotland that she hadn't really got the heart to let him down. The old Virginia would not have hesitated for a moment. The old Virginia would not, of course, have had a one-night fling nor become pregnant. But she had!

Roberta, who had just announced that she wanted to be called Bobby as it was more cool was home and for once was behaving well. The shock of her mother becoming pregnant had given her quite a jolt. Indeed, she had become to question for the first time the shallowness of her own life and the aimlessness of the endless round of London parties, smoking pot as well as cigarettes, fooling round with a job that did not truly engage either her attention or her intelligence.

They were sitting companionably enough at the kitchen table when she asked,

'Mum what does it feel like, I mean getting pregnant ......?'

Virginia found herself smiling 'do you mean at my age?' Her daughter had the grace to look a little abashed, 'Yes, I suppose so' she replied. Virginia reflected that she could not remember the last time that she and her daughter had shared an even remotely intimate conversation.

'Well, I won't pretend it wasn't a shock. After all your father and I had you and Alex when we were in our early twenties. Marriages go through, well, phases I suppose and after the first passionate can't get enough of each other part, things settle down until eventually the rest of your life takes over.' Roberta's curiosity was further aroused.

She asked, 'Did you think, you know, you might not keep the baby?' Her mother replied, 'You mean did I think about having an abortion? Well the answer is yes, I did think about it but then, somehow, it didn't seem right. Things are going better for us financially again and they do say that a late baby keeps you young.' Roberta brought the conversation to an end by reverting to her usual personality, saying

'Well mamma, it's probably a good thing as I can't see that I will ever want to have a sprog so this gets me off the hook. Anyway you're positively blooming, as they say, so I will love you and leave you, I'm going to Cirencester to meet the gang.' With that and an airy wave she was gone leaving Virginia to resolve that the new baby would be brought up really to appreciate his or her parents. Altogether, she reflected, things were turning out rather well.

Edinburgh

Polly knew they were taking a great risk. David had not been back to the house since he had delivered Buttons shortly after Minty came out of hospital. Richard knew she still did a lot of work for him though she had been careful to cultivate one or two more clients and was equally wary of mentioning David's name in case she inadvertently said something that might arouse his suspicions.

But as the weekend away drew closer so David had stepped up the pressure. He had insisted on visiting her at home in the afternoon when the children were still at school. Eventually she pushed him away and looked at her watch.

'David, get up and get dressed you really have to leave. The children will be home in about twenty minutes and you know how children talk and what on earth would they say if they saw you now!' He gave her a lazy smile,

'Probably why are you and David not wearing any clothes?' She laughed at that and threw a pillow at him and dashed off to have a quick shower. Just as she was shrugging into her jeans and white tee shirt and bustling David into the shower the doorbell rang.

'Damn, who can that be?' she asked, not expecting a reply as she ran downstairs.

She didn't recognise the silhouette outlined in the half glass of the frosted inner front door of the hall. But she opened the door. It was Alistair.

'Hello, my dear' he said with what he hoped was an engaging smile. 'I've just finished a meeting in town and thought I would pop in to see you before I go back to Perthshire. May I come in?'

She was flustered now; both cross and pleased at the same time.

'Oh, yes, of course do come into the drawing room.' Polly thought she sounded as like Mrs Bouquet asking some important official to come into her gracious abode. She hoped to God that David wouldn't come running downstairs in his bare feet and give the game away. But, of course, that is exactly what happened.

'David, back upstairs' she hissed. He looked startled and turned but at that moment Alistair emerged from the drawing room where he had been doing a recce of the paintings, all by Jamie and not to his taste. Aha, he thought, what have we here? Is my granddaughter, the saintly Rosie's little ewe lamb perhaps a chip off the old block, it's written all over their faces.

There being nothing else for it, David decided to brazen things out. He turned and extended his hand to Alistair, smiling winningly,

'Hello, Sir' he said warmly 'I'm David McLean, Polly does a lot of work for me and my business colleagues. She is a marvellous cook.'

Alistair thought "well, I certainly admire his cool" but he doesn't fool me for a minute. Then he decided to file the information away for future use and responding heartily and as if he hadn't noticed David's bare feet and shirt hanging out of his trousers.

'I'm Polly's grandfather. We live abroad at my chateau in the Haute Savoie so I have not been in Scotland for a long time.

It's good to meet you.' At that he gave David a very firm handshake then gave Polly a hug.

'Is this a bad time?' he asked 'only I didn't think that we would be in Perthshire for as long as this and just wanted the chance to say hello.' This exchange gave Polly time to collect herself and she smiled warmly and said,

'Why don't we go into the kitchen and have some tea. The children will be home soon Grandad and you might as well wait to see them. David you said that you were in a hurry to get to a meeting so I'll say goodbye now.' "Hell" she thought "that sounds pretty weak but the more I say, the worse it will get, so it will have to do." David took his cue and said goodbye but as he was leaving the house the door opened and John catapulted himself through it, followed by a rather more sedate Minty.

At the sight of his great- grandfather he beamed. He had been very impressed with some of the stories he had been told about the old man's adventures.

'Hi Great-Grandad how are things, are you staying for tea, are you going to Whitewalls? If you are I'll take you fishing. I'm good at catching trout.'

Alistair replied, pleased with this warm greeting, 'Well, I can stay for a little while as I have to go back to Perthshire but I would love to come fishing with you at Whitewalls as soon as I can. Did I tell you about the huge pike I caught in the River Tweed when I was a boy?' But we'll have to see.' He turned to Minty who hung back shyly.

'And how are you, Little Princess, recovered from your horrible accident I see and as pretty as ever.' David took the opportunity to leave, slinging his cream jacket casually round his shoulders as saying,

'Thanks, Polly, some good ideas there. I'll phone you tomorrow after I have spoken to my client in Argyll. This was to be the cover story for Polly's absence at the family weekend. With that he went, without a backward glance and Polly became caught up in the unexpected and not altogether welcome visit from her grandfather. For his part Alistair set his mind to charming his great-grandchildren and his granddaughter but when Richard arrived home he did not linger knowing Richard did not like him and also he thought Polly's husband knew rather a lot about the claim on Whitewalls.

'Goodbye my dears' he said in his rich fruity voice 'I'm looking forward to seeing you again very soon. I gather your mama has planned a special weekend for us all to enjoy. With that after hugging Polly, waving a languid hand in the direction of the children and a nod at Richard, Alistair departed.

Chapter 22

Whitewalls

Rosie was feeling satisfied with her life. Her plans for the big family weekend were shaping up nicely. Also, after what had seemed an interminable length of time, last night she and Jamie had been able to make love again. At times, they had both despaired and thought the warnings of possible impotence had been the truth. But, she reflected, life had shown them a great kindness and lying once more in his arms after a really satisfactory though gentle act of love her life had seem once again complete.

'Well, Mrs D, everything all done for the big visit?' asked Molly but the question was rhetorical. She did not expect an answer. When she was on form there was nobody like Mrs D for being organised. Hopefully all the nonsenses were over though she would give a lot to know why the old man, Sir Alistair, was still hanging around. He was up to something, of that she was quite certain.

'Yes, thanks Molly. You've done a great job with getting the bedrooms ready and I spoke to Richard about their staying at the Lodge with the Major so there will be enough room for Maggie's grandparents. They sound really nice and I am so looking forward to meeting them and Maggie. She sounds lovely and Charles is very much in love with her. Anyway, Richard thought the twins would love being at the Lodge It will be an adventure for them and I don't suppose Polly will mind too much.'

'No trouble at all Mrs D. I like to see everything going well.' Molly responded, adding silently to herself "and I hope that this is the end of all the troubles and we can get on with living."

The Lodge

Roddy was pleased with the way in which Border Prince was responding to the intensive training he was doing in preparation for the race at Perth. The horse was good tempered and easy to train but, nevertheless, had a keenness as well as a turn of speed that augured well. His jumping was pretty well perfect, bold but neat at the same time.

On his visits to the Lodge, Richard was becoming increasingly involved in the finer points of getting the horse race-ready and recognising when it was time to give Prince a rest and a change by turning him out into the field to have a good gallop and roll around.

'They gets sick of work if you give them too much, just like us I reckon', Jack said to Richard as they were leaning companionably on the fence watching Prince buck and rear and then have a very satisfactory roll in patch of dried mud.

'Jack, how long have you been with the Major?' Richard asked. He liked Jack for all his taciturn manner and reserve. Jack looked at young Richard. He was a good enough young man and he had a way with the horses you would never have guessed to look at him. Also he was fearful for the Major's health; he had seen the shadow and felt that it would not be long now. He was glad Richard was there.

'I can't rightly remember' Jack replied 'but when I came out of the Army, from the Veterinary Corps the Major said that there was a job for me and I've been here for, I suppose, about 20 years. Mind you, I'm glad you're in with us now. Major's not getting any younger and he thinks a lot of you.' Richard found there was a lump in his throat and replied, gruffly,

'Well it's mutual. I think a lot of him, too.' Then he added, 'Do you think this boy has had enough rolling around? If so I'll bring him in.'

'Aye, I reckon so; I'll give you a hand then I'll see to the others.' Jack replied in perfect harmony. It had settled him knowing that Richard would be carrying on if, and when, the Major retired or … no he wouldn't even think of that. Anyway, time to get on. They were all very pleased with the horse and it would be great if the Major could end his training career with a bit of a flourish. A win would be fantastic. He said as much to Richard, who replied that he couldn't agree more. So the two men turned to the immediate task of persuading a very lively, fired up racehorse he was to come in from the field where he had been quite happily larking around and get down to some serious work. Eventually they caught Prince and took him back to the stables for a wash down and grooming before going up on the gallops to fill his lungs with good, fresh air.

The Pele Tower

Loathe as she was to admit it, Betty was tired, in fact, she felt very tired. The consultant had been reassuring about the removal of the small lump in her left breast and it could be done as a day patient probably with local anaesthetic but she was worried. Also there was the legal challenge to the divorce settlement and that seemed to be possibly going to be referred to the High Court, which did not bode well. She was increasingly relying on John Prendergast.

'Betty, my dear, you know that you can rely on me completely to do whatever you wish, whether coming to hospital with you or helping to take care of you afterwards We've known each other for a long time and I'm very fond of you.' This was said when they were having coffee in her kitchen at the Tower where, if truth be told, she was feeling increasingly isolated.

'John, I know, and believe me I am very grateful. In fact, I don't know how I would have got through these last few weeks

497

without you, and that's the truth. Would you come with me to Perth for the race meeting? That way we could travel together and leave early if we get tired or have had enough.' He smiled warmly and took her hand in his and squeezed it very gently.

'Betty, of course I'll come with you. Even better we'll take a driver so that we can sit together in the back and pretend to be very grand! We could take some champagne with us for the journey. How does that sound?' She smiled with such sweetness that his heart felt warm.

'That sounds wonderful' she said. She meant it.

Murrayfield

Polly was in a quandary. She had still not told Richard she would not be taking part in the big family weekend Rosie had been planning with such keenness and expectation. Even whilst filling her freezer with miniature quiches, vol au vent and sausage rolls for the picnic, normal simple activities she usually found soothing, Polly could not relax as she tried to work out when to tell Richard she had to go away that weekend without precipitating a row. Perhaps she would build up to it by mentioning it casually over a family meal, when he could not quiz her too closely and also when she could point to how much preparation work she had done.

She had just finished making batch of chocolate muffins to freeze when she heard Richard coming home from the office. Minty was having piano lessons after school and John was playing football with Harry. So they would go and collect the children and she would propose a family supper together after that. Even better, they could all go for a pizza treat and she could tell them right there and then.

'Hello, darling', she called cheerfully as he let himself into the hall.

'Something smells good' he said 'what are you up to? Cooking for clients?' That would have been the moment to tell him but it passed.

'No, for the family picnic. I am going to freeze everything then it can all go in cool bags on the day. Now why don't we both go and collect the twins in ten minutes then all go out for a pizza. We haven't done that for ages.' Richard's heart sank a little. He had been looking forward to seeing the children, possibly helping with homework then a good whisky and soda before supper with Polly. However, it looked as if she had been cooking all afternoon and he didn't want to be churlish.

'Oh, all right then. Let's do that. I'll just go and change.'

It had been, reflected Richard a couple of hours later a very successful family outing. Whilst pizza was not his favourite food, the branch of the chain they visited in Queensferry Street was pretty up-market and frequented by residents of the New Town as well as younger professionals looking for a reasonable place to have a glass of wine or two and a little supper straight from work. Sometimes, he thought, it was good to throw routine out of the window.

John gave a small burp and Minty giggled. 'Mummy, Daddy John's made a rude noise' she said. 'Well I can't help it that was a really, really good pizza' John retorted. Richard smiled; it was good to hear a little banter between them, especially from Minty. Then Polly spoiled it all.

'I've something to tell you all. It's about the weekend Granny is planning. I know it will be lovely, going to Perth to watch Border Prince then having a big picnic and all going back to Whitewalls. Then there's the Garden opening on Sunday. But, the thing is, I won't be able to come with you!' Her family looked at her in stony silence. Their disapproval was palpable. It was John who spoke.

'Well, Mum, it seems to me you are being very selfish' - how grown-up he sounded she thought fleetingly. 'Everyone is so looking forward to seeing Border Prince run, we're to have a big picnic and then all be there on Sunday when the Garden is open to people' and, he added accusingly 'that's to raise money for poorly children.' Polly felt wretched. Then Minty spoke,

'Mummy, what's so important that you can't come and be with us?' "Well put" thought Richard. Polly felt even more wretched then said,

'Look probably here isn't the best place to explain, let's go home and I will tell you all about it.' "Another set of lies" she thought grimly.

It didn't get any better later on. After the twins had their bath and were in dressing gowns sitting with their parents and being allowed to watch a DVD of Wallace and Gromit, which was one of their favourites, Polly tried again.

'I am so sorry everyone. But I have a chance to get a new client who will make a big difference to my business. The snag is that they live over on the West coast and want me to cater for a big dinner party they are holding in their castle for some very important guests and I will have to stay over there on the Friday and probably Saturday nights. I will be back by the Sunday afternoon and catch part of Granny's garden opening.' Even to her ears it all sounded rather lame. The children just looked at her in silence and Richard said, stiffly,

'Well if that's your priority that's what you must do but I know everyone will be very disappointed, probably most of all Roddy. It will be his last race as a trainer.' "Yes, thought Polly miserably" and this will just confirm his low opinion of me!"

'Now' said Richard decisively 'you can watch the end of the DVD and then off to bed I think. It's a school day tomorrow.' They went quietly.

Later Richard said to her, rather sadly, 'Poll, what is this really all about? You can't still be angry over Roddy and the will. I thought we had talked through the whole thing and resolved it.'

Guilt made her reply defensively.

'Richard, how many times do I have to tell you? I am trying to build up a business and that has to come before a family picnic! David has given me this very good introduction, I've agreed to do it and I can't let the people down.' A coldness entered his voice.

'I might have known David McLean would come into the picture somewhere. Well, I am very disappointed, your mother will be furious and Roddy will be hurt, to say nothing of the children but if that's your decision that's it. Will you still manage to do the food for the picnic? And will you ring your mother and tell her?' She felt tearful but determined not to show it.

'Of course I will. How could I not?' she cried. There the matter was left. But Polly did not sleep well.

Whitewalls

To say Rosie was furious after she came off the telephone from Polly would not be an exaggeration. Jamie was in the sitting room with her and, therefore, in the direct line of fire.

'I just cannot believe how selfish Polly has become. She's known about the family weekend for quite a while now. What was to stop her from saying she is simply otherwise engaged? Instead of doing that she seems prepared to drop everything to go and cook for some family in the West who she doesn't even know!' Jamie sighed.

'Yes, love, I know. But really it's better if we don't interfere. I am sure Richard and everyone else will be just as disappointed as we are. But if she's made up her mind we shouldn't interfere. At least she is doing most of the food and if she can come over on Sunday to help with the garden opening that's at least something.' Rosie didn't really want to engage in another debate on the subject so simply said, completely changing the subject,

'Do you want to take the dogs out with me? I could do with some fresh air and a walk to clear my head.' He smiled, 'Yes, let's go down to the river and give them a good run. Jamie took his wife's hand as together they collected the dogs and went to seek the solace of fresh air and the river.

Moray Place

Polly tried to persuade David they should choose some other weekend than the one which clashed with her family events. She was unsuccessful. They were in bed, in the afternoon and she knew, as he knew, soon she would have to get up, get dressed and go to collect John from school.

'No, Poll, we have an agreement' David said in a dangerously silky tone of voice. 'We agreed you would come away for Friday and Saturday with me. Be firm with your family and I said, at least for now, I would not say anything to your husband.'

'And what happens after that?' she asked jumping out of bed and hunting for her lace thong.

'That, Pollyanna, remains to be seen and whether or not you've been very good!' Feeling panicky she thought "no that means whether or not I've been very naughty". The trouble was that she still found David very sexy and he made her feel really wonderful, passionate and special. He smiled warmly and said.

'Little darling don't make such a big thing of it. We're going away together, to the cottage we'll make love, walk on the beach, I'll cook for a change and we'll have some fabulous champagne and just for once you can untie your apron strings. Kiss?' She couldn't resist. Polly kissed him passionately, yanked on the rest of her clothes before he could pull her back into his arms and fled.

The Lodge

At last Roddy pronounced himself satisfied with the preparations for Border Prince's race and the plans for going to Perth were finalised. He thought he would go in the horse box with Jack, Richard would bring the children, Jamie and Rosie would transport Charles's fiancée and Maggie's grandparents who were staying for the long weekend. Hugh, with his pregnant wife, Virginia would drive in their hired car. He was sad Polly was not joining them, something about a cooking job but he wondered, deep down, if it did not have more to do with her being angry still about his will. He had tried more than once to explain but she had apparently made light of it, saying,

'Grandad, it is entirely up to you what you do with the property and anyway the situation won't arise for a long time '

Rosie was still cross about Polly but had been totally unable to get her daughter to change the plan she had concocted. At least Polly had been out with all the food destined for the picnic at Perth before racing. Also, she had managed to extract a promise that by Sunday afternoon Polly would be down to help with the teas for the Garden Opening.

Edinburgh

With all the other activities going on at Whitewalls and elsewhere Jamie's Exhibition had taken a back seat. However, preparations had been continuing, the pictures selected and hung

and the evening of the Private View had arrived. For once Polly
was not being relied upon to do the catering but she, Richard and
the children were all expected to be there. She had not mentioned
it to David and he had decided not to tell her he was on the
Gallery's invitation list and intended to be there. He wanted to
see how far he could push Polly and how well she could disguise
her feelings in front of her family.

There was a pleasing buzz in the gallery and at least half a
dozen red spots indicating sales had already been put on pictures
of the Borders countryside that were Jamie's speciality. The
sparkling Italian Prosecco was going down well and tiny canapés,
Polly thought weren't as good as hers, though in reality they were
delicious, were being eagerly consumed by the large group of
varied guests. Grannie Betty was there, escorted by John
Prendergast who had hired his driver to bring them in, refusing
the offer either to stay over at Murrayfield or to come with Jamie
and Rosie.

'Darlings,' she had said sweetly but firmly 'we probably
shan't stay for very long but John insisted on making the

arrangements and he is being so kind to me right now, I am happy to go along with him.' Whilst Rosie had felt a twinge of envy at, in some way as she saw it, being replaced by John Prendergast, she was really thankful there was one less individual for whom she felt personally responsible.

When David put in an appearance, the Douglas family was assembled as if in a tableau clustered around one of the bigger pictures that had just been sold to one of the prestigious Edinburgh banks. Rosie had never seen David before and her first thought was he was very good looking. Her second was why does Polly look so uneasy and why had Richard's mouth tightened as soon as he saw David coming towards them. Rosie did not want to recognise what she felt was in front of her. Something was not right here.

'Hello Polly, hello Richard, Minty, John.' David greeted them as if they were all good friends. Polly could feel herself blushing but managed to say,

'Oh, David, how nice of you to come along. Let me introduce you to my parents, this is Rosie, my Mama and the artist here is my Dad, Jamie.' They shook hands and the sticky moment passed. Jamie looked again at the handsome man in front of him and remembered where he had seen him before. He had been driving the Porsche with Polly in the front seat as Jamie had emerged from the Gallery a few weeks ago. Jamie sensed this man was bad news. However, he had shaken the outstretched hand and murmured, 'It's very good of you to come along, do have a look at the pictures and let me know if you have any questions about any of them.' David was quick to reply,

'As a matter of fact I would like to buy the large one over here. Was it was painted from your home in the Borders?' Jamie was in a bit of a quandary. Despite all his instincts telling him this man was bad news, he could hardly refuse to sell him a picture, particularly as it was the largest and most expensive in the show at £5,000. He replied, a little stiffly.

'Well, by all means come and have a closer look before you decide and I'll describe the location to you.' David smiled his foxy smile. This all suited his purpose very well indeed. Probably fortunately Hamish saw the exchange and realised for some reason Jamie, usually so placid, was a bit worked up and not altogether happy. He went over to the two men who had moved a little away from the others.

'Hello, I'm Hamish McLucas, gallery owner, how may I help?' he asked extending his hand to David who took it and returned a dry, firm handshake.

'Hi, David McLean. I'm an interior designer and Polly does work for me and my clients. I'm very taken with Jamie's landscape of the Tweed and I would like to buy it.'

Polly found that she was shaking, whether with fear or anger she was not sure. Deliberately she turned her back on David, leaving her father and Hamish to talk to him. She took Minty's hand saying,

'Now poppet come and see what a surprise Grandpapa has for us. You remember that lovely picture of the monkey that you did for me at Great Grannie's well, he's put it in the exhibition with an NFS label on it.' Minty's eyes lit up,

'Really, Mummy, where is it and what does NFS mean. Over here in the Reception area and NFS means "not for sale" because I am never, ever going to part with it, but it is your first exhibition.'

The sticky moment passed and David left without saying goodbye but having cornered Jamie into saying that he could go down to Whitewalls at some point to see where the picture, for which he happily paid £5,000, had been painted.

For his part David was very pleased with himself and none of them referred to the matter again that evening. Polly thought that Richard might have said something when they got home after supper and once the children were in bed. He did not.

Whitewalls

At last, after what had seemed forever to Rosie, the big weekend arrived. She had planned it like a military operation but had, perhaps surprisingly, shown little or no signs of stress whilst organising beds, meals, people to be met at the airport and marshalling her team of helpers for the garden opening.

For his part Jamie had, probably wisely, gone along with whatever tasks were allotted to him. The Art Exhibition was continuing and the pictures were selling well. He was still "kicking himself" at agreeing to David McLean's sly request to come down to Whitewalls to see where the picture he had bought was painted. However, Jamie had at least asserted himself sufficiently to say that it would not be at all convenient until after the weekend.

'This is such a delightful place, everything is so soft and relaxed, yet so pretty,' exclaimed Florette after being shown round Whitewalls by Rosie. She really appreciated the main guest room with its comfortable bed, chintz curtains and comfy sofa, gentle landscapes painted by Jamie on the walls and the modernised ensuite bathroom. Florette had feared they might not get anything nearly as attractive as this. Nigel really did not enjoy being away from Yorkshire one little bit but he had been making an effort and got on really well with Jamie, to the relief of both their wives.

Also, Nigel had visited Roddy at the Lodge and duly admired the absolutely on form Border Prince who was as ready for the race at Perth the following day as he would ever be. Again the two men had a shared appreciation of the Services and whilst privately were concerned about Charles's impending tour in Iraq told each other, and, therefore, themselves that it would be "bloody bad luck" if anything happened to him.

'Your family is so great' Maggie told Charles. 'I don't know how good I am at playing "happy families" but your mother and father have both made me feel so at home. I can see why you want to come back so often. There's something about this place that feels very special' she added. He gave her a huge hug and an enthusiastic kiss.

'How could they not love you?' was the response 'and they're so happy for us both. I know all these outings are a bit full on but at least this way you get it all over in one go. At Perth you'll even meet my wicked grandfather who, you'll have gathered is most definitely the "black sheep" of the family. I don't know how my grandmother is going to react to seeing him with wife number three! That reminds me, we're expected at The Tower for tea so we'd better get a move on. You'll just love her house – it's like something out of a fairy story.' She smiled happily at him and went indoors to brush her hair and put on a cardigan for in spite of the sunshine it was still cooler here than in the warm dampness of London.

Betty was looking forward to seeing Charles and Maggie and having a proper chat with them. Dinner the previous evening had been fun but hectic with all the introductions and it had been a relief when Nigel and Florette turned out to be such kind people. She had been quite amazed at the transformation her pregnancy had brought about in Virginia. She was particularly pleased about that as she had always felt Hughie did not assert himself nearly enough and, in fact, she had wondered whether or not the marriage would last. However, here it was, back on track with all the excitement of a new life to come and some more prosperity ahead for her son who had suffered his share of financial setbacks.

As they drove up the bumpy track to the Tower Maggie's eyes grew wider.

'I see what you mean. It's like a place in a children's story, Rapunzel maybe!' she exclaimed and they drew up outside the little oak door which was immediately flung open by Betty. Emperor shot out busily barking with excitement to welcome the visitors.

'Oh be quiet will you?' admonished Betty 'come inside both of you' she said reaching up to hug each of them in turn.

After an afternoon tea of sandwiches and home made fruit cake, supplied by Molly, baking not being Betty's forte in the kitchen Maggie asked if she could see the rest of the house.

'Of course you may. Why don't you go and see for yourself' Betty suggested 'and Charles you come and have a look

516

at the garden with me.' Maggie loved the Tower and for a few moments fantasized about she and Charles living there. This was immediately followed by the thought of how impractical that would be. Still, it was a happy thought and one she would share with Charles later.

On the drive back to Whitewalls he said 'Well you were a great hit with Grannie and she doesn't lavish praise easily.'

'I thought she was really sweet to me and what energy and life she has. How old is she?' Charles smiled and said

'It's supposed to be a closely guarded secret but she's actually 77. She did say to me she wants to leave The Tower to us in her will so I hope that you don't mind, I said "yes" and anyway I am sure she's good for another twenty years at least!'

'That would be wonderful. Our own Scottish retreat as well as our London Mews.' She replied, happily. In this relaxed frame of mind they drove back to Whitewalls and all the hurly burly of family fun awaiting them before the next day's big event at Perth Races and the Garden Opening on Sunday.

Burnmouth

In spite of her huge reservations about giving in to David's ultimatum to come away with him for a weekend or face the fact he would tell Richard about their affaire Polly was in a relaxed frame of mind as she and David sped towards the coast. It was a lovely day with the promise of real summer in the air at last. She had, in her mind, decided this would be the last time that she would submit to David's conditions for the relationship. Polly looked at his strong profile as he drove the car fast, but safely. He really was very good-looking but lately she had felt more than a little afraid of him.

'Happy Pollyanna?' he asked, savouring both his victory in getting her to come away with him and anticipating the next forty eight hours they would spend together. In reply she smiled and stroked his thigh provocatively. 'You'll just have to wait until we get there, but not for long afterwards.' As they went beneath the tunnel leading to the isolated fisherman's cottage with its own boat mooring she felt a surge of anticipation, resolved to give herself up to the experience and let the future take care of itself.

518

The Lodge

As he did his evening rounds in the stables Roddy reflected, once again, he was a fortunate man. Border Prince, race ready and gleaming with fitness whickered softly as Roddy entered his box and gave him a couple of carrots. He really looked a picture.

'Well old boy, win or lose tomorrow it will be my last race but I think you've still got some running in you.' The evenings were lengthening now and it was still light as he went across to the main house with Richard and the twins in the ancient landrover for an early family supper. Tomorrow would be a long day and Roddy had decided to go up to Perth in the horsebox with Jack, which meant a six o'clock start to get over the Forth Road bridge and up to Scone outside Perth where the racecourse was in an idyllic setting close to Scone Palace. If nothing else, it would be the quietest way to travel. He was getting a bit old for all the noise and bounciness of his great-grandchildren, much as he loved them and besides it would take the two of them to get Prince into and out of the box and settled at the Racecourse stables at the other end.

Whitewalls

Border Prince's race was not until three o'clock, so with the exception of Roddy who despite entreaties from the family to travel with them, stuck to his guns and left around 6 am with Jack and Border Prince safely loaded in the immaculate, though ancient horsebox, the various groups of family had a gentle start to the day.

After some discussion it had been decided three vehicles were necessary to transport everyone, the food and drink, travelling rugs and all the other paraphernalia Rosie deemed necessary for a "proper picnic". So Jamie and Rosie would take the twins along with Hughie and Virginia, using the hire car Charles and Maggie would take her grandparents and Betty and John Prendergast would be making their way separately with a driver. The plan was to meet in the car park for the picnic lunch and then make their way to the track for the all-important race. It was expected that Alistair and Madeleine would come with their Perthshire friends and if spotted would be invited to join the party

520

for a drink. 'After all,' Rosie said 'let's be fair, the Montgomeries have had to put up with the two of them for three weeks now.

The Tower

'This is really exciting.' Betty declared as John helped in into the back of the grand car that he had hired, complete with the driver, Percy, for the occasion.

'At the very least it makes a change from going to General Hospital and a welcome one at that' John replied in the clever way she thought he had recently acquired, of almost being able to read her thoughts.

'Let's just make up our minds to have a lovely day, shall we? The weather's fine, the forecast is good and I am determined we will both have a day to remember, whatever happens.' Not for the first time recently she realised how much fonder she was becoming of this gentle, courtly man and if, only if, she decided to spend more time with him, well was that the most awful prospect?

It was with great optimism and enthusiasm the clan set off to drive to Edinburgh, over the Forth Road Bridge and on to their destination. Richard still wished Polly had been with them but he had more than his hands full with the very excited twins and was also desperately keen for things to go well for Roddy and Border Prince.

Perth Racecourse

Rosie felt very pleased. Everything was going according to plan. The day was sunny with a light breeze. The picnic was great fun and thanks to Polly's preparations and some additions of fresh fruit, a ripe brie and a home-made fruit cake there was more than enough food for all. Not wanting to tempt fate Jamie said,

'Let's have wine or beer, and John and Minty can have some orange juice. We'll save the champagne for later.' Roddy tried to introduce a note of caution,

'Well, let's hope we have something to celebrate' he said. It was Betty who replied merrily – partly because she was enjoying her day so much and partly because of the extra glass of Sancerre that had gone down very easily – 'I vote we have champagne whatever happens Roddy, but we have every faith in you; the horse will win and John, if you would be so kind I intend to find a bookie and put £10 to win on him.' Off she tottered, slightly unsteadily holding fast to John's tweed-clad arm.

At last it was time to go into the parade ring along with the other owners and trainers. It was a large and jolly party and even Alistair and Madeleine entered into the spirit of the occasion. Jack led the horse round the parade ring. He was number 7 on the racecard with a total of 14 runners altogether over the two mile hurdle course.

Once the horses had gone down to the start the Douglas clan split into groups to find vantage points to watch the race. Richard took the very excited twins up the old stone steps to the stand from where owners and trainers were allowed to watch the races, Betty and John decided to watch from the comfort of the Owners and Trainers bar with Virginia and Hughie. She was enjoying herself more than she had imagined possible but Virginia was tiring a little and was glad to be sitting down in front of the big television screen. Jamie, Rosie, Alistair and Madeleine decided to stay by the running rail. Roddy and Jack disappeared to their own vantage point near the finishing line. Nigel, Florette, Charles and Maggie decided to join Richard and twins in the stand and shouted as loudly as anyone, urging Border Prince to run like the wind. There is a strange phenomenon about horse racing where the punters appear to believe that the horses can actually hear them and take encouragement from the yells of "come on my son", "come on Prince, you can do it" or whatever the horse is called. Maybe it is true.

It was a thrilling finish and the commentator's voice rose in volume as the 14 thoroughbred horses negotiated the brush hurdles at speed and when they came round the final bend at the to of the course he was calling out,

'It looks as if Red Cumin has the race sewn up but here comes Border Prince in hot pursuit, Likely Lad is joining in the battle, it's a fight to the finish, Border Prince clears the last hurdle in fine style and romps home with Red Cumin in second place, Likely Lad is a close third.'

From their different places, the clan rushed to the parade ring again to stand in the Winner's place in the unsaddling enclosure. Rosie brushed tears away and even Sir Alistair looked pleased. Madeleine tottering along in unsuitable high heels was sensible enough not to complain about the rough ground.

'We won, we won, we won' chanted the twins and Richard had a grin on his face that stretched from ear to ear. He would ring Polly on her mobile as soon as the result was finally confirmed after the jockeys had "weighed in". Betty and John proceeded at a more sedate pace to join the rest of the party and were pleased at the roar of applause as Roddy led in the victorious runner with Jack at the other side. It was a popular result with large numbers of race goers having enjoyed a flutter on the Whitewalls entry. Horses always seem to know when they have won and the big dark bay accepted the pats, the plaudits and cheers and even kisses as no less than his right. The racecourse photographer took lots of photographs of the happy family party.

Richard shook Roddy's hand and then, uncharacteristically, gave him a great hug saying

'Well done, what a marvellous training feat, what a great way to finish your training career – unless you change your mind!' Roddy smiled warmly,

'You played your part too, Richard. It's your victory too. No, I won't change my mind. This is my last race.' They proudly watched as Roddy who owned Border Prince as well as trained him went up to collect a handsome silver cup from congenial race course Chairman, David Whitaker, whose wife, Fiona had bred Lucius one-time winner of the Grand National and whose daughter, Lucy Normile was a trainer herself. This was the occasion for more photographs to be taken.

'Well done, that was a great training feat. I'm not sure that this is really going to be your last.' David said. Roddy just smiled and assured him this was, indeed, the case.

The whole clan was entertained to more champagne by the Racecourse hospitality team who seemed entirely to share their delight in Border Prince's victory. Only the drivers and children abstained. After her second glass Betty rather unsteadily put her little hand on John Prendergast's tweed-clad arm and announced royally,

'My dear John. I have had a wonderful day and am now ready to depart. After all we have supper this evening and the Garden Opening tomorrow. Shall we find the driver and go?' Amid smiles and hugs the couple made their stately way to the car park after collecting their winnings of over £100 each and left for home. It was not long before they were each "resting their eyes" snoozing gently and leaning against one another in the back of the limousine. They were happy.

Burnmouth

Polly was enjoying herself more than she had thought would be possible, given she had still been made to feel she was letting her family down by not being with them for what seemed, to everyone else, to be a momentous weekend. David was going out of his way to be gentle and tender; they were having fun. As well as passion there was pleasure. The walks along the beach, collecting unusual shells, an exhilarating trip in the boat with the waves crashing over them as the wind increased in speed and the simple but delicious meals that they rustled up together all made this a very special time. This was, of course, David's intention.

'Glad you came, Pollyanna?' he asked on Saturday afternoon as they sat outside on the deck warming their faces in the early summer sunshine. She linked her arm in his and smiled.

'Yes, very glad. Whatever happens I won't ever forget this lovely weekend together. Just you, me and the sea!' He did not pick her up on that. For now he was content to be in the moment.

'David, I have an idea. Let's go back to Edinburgh this evening. I want you to stay with me in my house; I want you with me all night, in my bed.' He smiled lazily,

'Darling, if that's what you want, that's what we'll do.' It was decided.

As part of her "getting away" Polly had switched off her mobile phone and left it in the bedroom so when Richard tried to call to tell her the news of Border Prince's win all he got was the anonymous-sounding answering service. Momentarily he was annoyed but left a brief message and concentrated on getting the still excited twins and everyone else rounded up and into the right transport for the journey home.

Whitewalls

It would be fair to say all of them, from John and Minty, to Betty and John Prendergast as well as Virginia and Hughie, Florette and Nigel and indeed everyone else, were tired at the conclusion of an exciting and thoroughly satisfying day. Then there was the additional excitement of the Garden Opening to look forward to the next day. So they all, except Alistair and Madeleine, made their way back to the Borders and to Whitewalls where the signs for the Opening had already been put up with neatly produced posters and directions for parking in the field next to the river. Rosie was tired but in a good way. Apart from the absence of Polly, the day had gone beautifully and what a thrill it had been that Border Prince had won the race. The twins were being allowed to stay up for early supper with the grown-ups so after checking on their ponies and promising them a ride in the morning before all the people came to see the garden. They quickly washed and then helped Granny to set the big table for the meal.

The Lodge

Roddy felt more inclined to put his feet up with a large whisky than go across for yet another family meal to Whitewalls, but Rosie had worked so hard and the plan was for an early supper so he had left Jack to do the horses, including the hero of the hour, Border Prince. He reluctantly pulled himself out of his chair and decided to walk the short distance.

True to her word supper was early and the twins who were dropping with exhaustion and excitement went to bed without too much fuss.

'Rosie, dear if you don't mind I'm going to go back with Richard and the children and we can all get an early night.' She looked at her father-in-law; she realised he was really tired and reminded herself, again, he was no longer a young man.

'We'll go in the car' Richard insisted 'save your legs and get these two settled. Then you and I can check on the horses and have a large whisky, which I think we've earned.' Jack had gone off duty, the horses were all fed and watered and Roddy and Richard went into Prince's box to make an extra fuss of him. There in the quiet and gathering dusk Richard experienced a momentary shiver as they stood stroking and horse and giving him a well-deserved carrot or two before making their way back into the Lodge.

The twins were already fast asleep. They had been too tired even to have more than a quick bath and it was not long before Roddy announced than he, too, was going to turn in. 'Goodnight, Richard sleep well. I hope those two rascals don't wake you up too early. I'll be up and about anyway but I'll try and keep them quiet. They can come to the yard with me.'

'Goodnight, Roddy and once again can I just say how grateful I am for putting such a lot of faith in me for the future. 'The reply was brief but sincere.

'Richard, I am quite sure everything will be safe in your hands and you'll find it all as rewarding as I have always done. But you might have to wait a while yet.'

Before going to bed Richard decided to try Polly's mobile once more but with the same result. There was no answer and he did not feel inclined to leave another message.

It was now a gentle, dark night with stars just emerging as Roddy took himself off to the stables again to have a few quiet moments with his favourite horse. The pain when it came was swift and savage; there was a huge bright light, after that, nothing.

In his flat in the stable yard Jack was finding it difficult to sleep after the excitement of the long day. The horse had done his very best for them all and seemed no worse for the experience. Major looked a bit done in though, Jack hoped he wasn't sickening for anything.

Around dawn Jack got tired of tossing and turning and decided just to get up and go down to the stables. He was aware of the noise of his boots on the cobbles in the stillness of the morning and something took him straight to Prince's box. He went inside and stood for a moment whilst his eyes got used to the gloom. Then he saw. Border Prince was lying in his straw bed. The horse's eyes were open and next to him, lying so very still with his arm across the prone animal was the Major. Jack

knew. He felt for a pulse. There was none. He took off his cap

and bobbed his head as a mark of respect, saluted and said

simply, 'Goodbye Major'. Then he steeled himself to go up to

the house and break the news.

Chapter 23

Whitewalls

As usual, Jamie was up early. He had gone down to the kitchen which, despite all the events of yesterday was pretty tidy with only a few serving dishes waiting to be put away, remaining on the worktop beside the sink. Heather and Tweed were dying to get out for their early morning walk, whilst Dundee merely opened one eye from the comfort of his basket, yawned and went straight back to sleep again.

As he opened the kitchen door he saw Jack, standing there with his cap in his hands.

'Oh, Sir, I dinnae ken how to tell you this. It's the Major, he, he's gone.'

'What do you mean, gone? Where has he gone?' Then Jamie realised what Jack was trying to tell him. The old groom cried now, tears coursing down his weather-beaten face.

'He's deid' Jack managed to say. Wordlessly, Jamie put his arms round the older man's shoulders and drew him into the warmth of the Whitewalls kitchen.

Without asking Jack, Jamie made two strong mugs of tea with plenty of sugar and poured in a tot of whisky into each of them.

"Have you sent for an ambulance? Who's with Dad now? Is it Richard?"

"I said, he's deid and I thought best to come straight here. The Major's in the stable, with Prince."

"Oh, God," thought Jamie, maybe there's still a chance.

'Come on Jack let's get straight over to the Lodge. There's maybe a chance he's just unconscious or in a deep sleep.' Jack knew differently but didn't argue.

They were soon in the stable and Jamie realised Jack was right. He felt the tears come into his eyes but knew he had to be strong.

'Let's put a blanket over him' he said, knowing there was no point. 'I'll go and phone the police and an ambulance. I think that's what I have to do. Then I'll wake Richard up and get him to take the children to our house and he'll have to tell Rosie.'

'Right you are sir'. Jack didn't see the need for conversation. 'I'll bide with him in the meantime' was all he said.

Rosie simply could not take it in. 'What about the children, have you told them Richard, were they there?' Richard took charge. He gave Rose a warm hug.

'Will you take John and Minty back to Whitewalls? When things are under control here I'll go to Edinburgh and collect Polly as soon as she comes back from the West. We'll obviously have to cancel the garden opening or maybe Tim and Anne Elgin could take over. I'll find out.' For once in her life Rosie was glad not to be in charge.

After making sure everyone knew what to do, the ambulance and doctor were on their way as well as the local police, John and Minty safely at Whitewalls Richard got into the car and drove back to Edinburgh.

He was pretty sure Polly said she would drive back from the West after dinner on the Saturday and be ready to leave for Whitewalls on Sunday morning. This way he would be able to break the news and take her back with him. As he drove the familiar road Richard's thoughts were in turmoil. Quite apart from the sadness and shock at Roddy's sudden death it began to dawn on him there would be, or could be, massive complications with Polly and the rest of the family if, indeed, he was to inherit the Stud and all that went with it.

He glanced at his watch as he drove through almost deserted streets of the west of Edinburgh towards his Murrayfield home. It was just before eight o'clock. He thought he would be in good time to catch Polly before she set off for Whitewalls. Richard had asked Rosie and Jamie not to phone her. The news needed to be broken by him.

Pulling up quickly outside the house Richard did not notice the Porsche car parked next to Polly's Rav. He ran quickly up the path, unlocked the front door and went into the house.

It was very quiet. Apart from a jacket thrown carelessly over the hall chair there were no signs of life. Polly was not in the kitchen. Quickly he ran upstairs. Maybe she had been so tired she was still asleep.

He opened the bedroom door. Polly screamed and he soon saw the reason for it. Not only was she naked in the bed but David McLean was in bed with her. Their limbs were wrapped round each. Hurriedly David grabbed the duvet and pulled it up over both of them.

Richard was furious. He yanked the duvet back and exposed his wife and her lover. David didn't wait to be hit. He leaped out of bed and grabbed his clothes.

'Get out, get out you bastard' Richard shouted. David didn't need to be told. Pulling his clothes on hastily he said,

'All right, I'm going, I'm going. I'll call you Polly, don't let him blame you or hurt you.'

Polly started to cry, deep sobs coming from the heart of her being. Richard threw her dressing gown at her as David made his escape.

'There's no easy way to tell you this, Polly. Early this morning your grandfather Roddy died. He was found by Jack in Border Prince's loose box. He was lying across the horse. I've been trying to get you on your mobile all weekend to tell you the horse won yesterday but I assumed you were in the west and out of signal. I was wrong, wasn't I? You've been with that scumbag all weekend, away from me, your family, your children. How could you have sex with him in our bed? God, you disgust me, Polly.'

She was scared. Polly had never seen Richard like this before. Quickly she ran into the bathroom, had the quickest of showers then scrambled into clean underwear, plain black trousers and a white shirt. She grabbed a cardigan and her handbag. All this time Richard had not spoken to her.

'Get in the car and I'll tell you what happened on the way.' Was all he said

The first part of the journey through the west of Edinburgh, which was just beginning to stir with people going to early communion services or out to buy Sunday papers, was done in silence.

Polly spoke first. 'Richard, please, I can explain. We got carried away ....'

'Don't you want to hear about your grandfather's death? Isn't that more important than your cheap little affaire?' She nodded, mutely.

'We all had a wonderful day at Perth Races yesterday, even without you. Everyone got on really well, including old Alistair and Madeleine. Then Border Prince won his race, which was really exciting. Then the twins and I went to stay at the Lodge, which you knew about. This morning Jack couldn't sleep so went to check on the horses and that's when he discovered Roddy's body. We got an ambulance and the police but there was nothing to be done.'

'The twins, do they know?' she asked tremulously.

'I thought it better to tell them and they're with your mother back at Whitewalls. Now when we get there we'll say nothing about this morning. I'll deal with that later. Everyone's in shock but the garden opening is going ahead with Tim and Anne Elphinstone taking over.'

After that they lapsed into silence again for the rest of the journey. Polly felt numb whilst Richard tried to concentrate on driving as quickly but as safely as he could.

All to soon it seemed to Polly they had gone up the drive and were pulling in to the circle in front of Whitewalls. Minty and John came running out to meet them.

'Mum, it's awful, Grandfather Roddy has died. Jack found him in the stable this morning.'

'He was with the Prince' Minty added solemnly 'so at least he wasn't on his own'. Then she burst into tears and threw herself at her mother. John did the same to Richard and they hugged their children. The awfulness of Polly and David being discovered in Edinburgh was, for the moment, put aside. Rosie then appeared.

'Come inside all of you. We'll have some coffee and I'll update you on what's happening. Minty, John, would you like some juice and biscuits as you didn't have much breakfast?' She was pale but composed but, as ever, back in charge.

Inside the kitchen Jamie was busy making coffee. He turned as Polly came in and she ran towards him, throwing her arms around her father. He hugged her as she started to cry. Once she had begun it was impossible to stop and Richard took over the coffee making whilst wordlessly handing her a fistful of tissues.

Later, when Polly had finally stopped crying and the children had been distracted by Richard taking them off for a walk with the dogs along the river, which was not part of the formal gardens, Polly and her parents sat at the kitchen table and Jamie explained exactly what seemed to have happened.

'There'll have to be a post-mortem because Roddy hadn't been seeing a doctor but it appears he had a massive heart attack and even if someone had been there nothing could have been done to save him.' Jamie's voice was gentle and Rosie still had her arms around Polly.

The garden door opened again. It was Betty and John Prendergast was with her.

'Forgive me for intruding' he said in his old-fashioned, courtly way 'but I didn't want Betty to drive here herself and she was kind enough to let me collect her. I hope you don't mind.'

'Of course not, John,' Rosie replied 'it's very sweet of you. Look let's all move into the drawing room it's getting rather crowded in here.' By this time Rosie and Betty were embracing, together in their sadness at Roddy's sudden death.

Outside the sun was shining. The teams, apart from the family, assembled to run the Open Day in the Gardens were going about their allotted tasks with quiet determination. Rosie had firmly decided people should not be let down by turning up to the event and finding it cancelled. But the whole day took on an almost surreal quality.

'We've managed to get a flight to Leeds Bradford airport this afternoon, you have quite enough on your plates without having us hanging around.' Nigel said this with great charm but also firmness. John Prendergast offered his driver to take them to the airport and fond, though sad farewells were soon said. Hugh and Virginia decided they must stay on for the time being.

Just when Rosie thought things could not get worse Alistair and Madeleine arrived and she realised no-one had told them about Roddy's death. Alistair parked his car at a rakish angle and bounded, youthfully, he thought, into the house. He was followed by a sulky-looking Madeleine.

Now Jamie took charge again and broke the news, ending with, 'So I don't know what your plans are but I think you can see we are all pretty fraught here and it might be best if you booked into an hotel or bed and breakfast in Edinburgh whilst we get everything sorted out and arrange the funeral.' This did not suit Alistair's plans one little bit and as he had rather burnt his boats with the Montgomeries he felt they could not return there.

'Perhaps we could go to Polly and Richard ...'

'No I don't think it's fair to them either. I'm sorry Alistair, you're welcome to some lunch but you will really have to make your own arrangements after that' was Jamie's firm reply.

'Of course we'll get out of your hair' Alistair replied graciously 'after lunch,' he added.

'In the meantime then may I suggest you and Madeleine go for a drive, or round the gardens and come back around one o'clock?' This was Rosie, it was all getting too much and even Alistair saw that and took Madeleine, who had only so far managed to say she was very sorry at the news, off to have a look at Stobo Castle.

Later when Rosie tried to recall the events of that day her overwhelming memory was of the sheer exhaustion of dealing with all the different branches of the family at once. Charles and Maggie were also staying on for another day and she was glad of her son's quiet strength and Maggie's sweetness, sympathy and willingness to take on any task.

At last the house was quiet. The Lodge had been locked up and Jack was looking after Roddy's dog. He had refused all offers to stay at Whitewalls and insisted he would be 'just fine.'

A post-mortem would be carried out the next day and neither Rosie nor Jamie wanted to think about that. Charles and Maggie had gone off to bed, leaving his parents to have a little peace together. They sat quietly beside the fire Jamie had lit, not because it was cold but because it was comforting. He had persuaded Rosie to have a glass of brandy and after pouring one for himself was beside her on one of the sofas.

Rosie sighed deeply. He put his arm around her shoulder and hugged her close to him.

'Darling girl what a dreadful day you've had.'

'But what about you? Roddy's your father and you must be feeling even worse!'

'Come on, Rosie, you're exhausted, let's go to bed, things will look a bit easier in the morning.'

Edinburgh

Communication between Richard and Polly was minimal for the rest of that day. The twins were both exhausted with all the excitement. Whilst they realised their grandfather had died the reality of it had not really sunk in. With the resilience of young children they had accepted the news and the attendant events by taking it all in their stride.

It was not until after nine o'clock Richard and Polly were able to sit down and face each other, both with very troubled thoughts in their minds. Richard spoke first.

'Do you want to tell me about it? Why you were in bed with that man, how long has this been going on? How many lies have you told?' Her eyes were red-rimmed with crying and she spoke very quietly.

'Richard, I don't know. I can't really talk about this now. Could we please let it rest until tomorrow? I've had hardly any sleep ....'

'I'll bet you haven't' he retorted grimly 'if what I saw this morning is anything to go by but yes, I can see you're not in any fit state to have this out now but I warn you Polly I have never been more angry in my life.' That night they slept in the same bed but with a chilly space between them and they might as well have been on different continents.

Whitewalls

By the end of the week all the arrangements for Roddy's funeral were well under way. Everything had happened quickly and the post-mortem had confirmed he had died of a massive heart attack. Charles had got compassionate leave and Maggie, too had managed to postpone rehearsals. Rosie found it a great comfort to have both of them helping. The more she saw of Maggie, the better she liked her. Polly had been out on her own, quiet and red-eyed which Rosie put down to grief and was in any case too distracted to question her daughter. In fact, Richard and Polly were hardly speaking to each other and being found in bed with David, by Richard was worrying her to distraction. She could think of little else and what she was going to do.

Hugh also proved to be a tower of strength whilst Virginia, wisely, spent quite a lot of time resting and reading magazines and assured everyone she was fine, not bored in the slightest.

They had decided against a small private funeral as Roddy was so well known in the Borders and instead the celebration of his life was to take place in the big church in the nearby town of Peebles. Jamie was adamant, his father would not want people to wear black and equally that everyone would be welcome.

The minister, Andrew Williamson, from the little village church agreed to officiate along with the minister of the Peebles church, Michael Martin. Rosie, Hugh and Jamie chose Roddy's favourite hymns. Jamie insisted on the inclusion of "We Plough the Fields and Scatter the good seed on the land". It was a harvest hymn but neither minister thought it was inappropriate. Jamie would talk about his father's life and afterwards everyone would be invited to the Park Hotel for tea. For once Rosie didn't want a huge crowd at Whitewalls and Polly would not be involved in the catering. Molly was very subdued throughout the proceedings and just got on with helping everyone when and where she was needed.

'He was a good man, the Major, the best, he'll be sorely missed' was all she said about Roddy's death. But it was enough.

Edinburgh

'So you see, Sir Alistair we don't believe you have a strong enough case to test it in court. I'm really sorry but we would not be giving you our best professional advice if we led you to believe there was a chance you could regain the title to Whitewalls and the farm.'

This was a blow. Despite the flimsiness of the evidence Alistair had been secretly reasonably confident of at least getting his claim on Whitewalls to being heard in court.

'Are you absolutely positive, Christian?' he asked not betraying the emotion he was feeling.

'I'm sorry, but yes. I've even spoken informally to one of our senior judges who strongly advised taking no further action. Apart from anything else, the length of time from your divorce until now is against it and your former wife would have to agree to a court hearing, which I think is unlikely. The best thing you can do is to try and build bridges with your family and hope to get back at least some good will.' Realising the lawyer was not to be budged from this very definite position Alistair gracefully rose to his feet, shook Christian warmly by the hand and left saying 'Many thanks for your efforts', hoping he wouldn't get a bill he could not afford to pay. He was very thoughtful as he walked back to the Roxburghe Hotel to face Madeleine.

Whitewalls

It was a beautiful, sunny day with just a hint of a soft breeze. The Douglas family were all at Whitewalls preparing to say their goodbyes, finally to Roddy. Richard and Polly had decided in one of the very few conversations they'd had over the past 10 days to include John and Minty in the service. John had said quite simply 'I really love Grandpapa Roddy, he used to tell me stuff about the horses and I want to be there with everyone else to say goodbye.' Polly's eyes were bright with tears when she heard this, 'besides' John went on 'someone's got to look after Mints and make sure she's not too upset'. This was too much for Polly who practically ran from the room into the kitchen garden. Wordlessly Richard followed her.

'There's something badly wrong there' Rosie said to Jamie 'but right now I don't even have the energy to ask.' 'I agree, but let's leave it until after today before we try and help.'

The Old Church in Peebles was full. The organist played a selection of traditional Scottish music and the piper was standing by. The Douglas family had asked people not to wear black as this was to be a celebration of a long and fulfilled life.

The congregation stood for the first hymn, Love Divine All Loves Excelling, led by the choir; the service was underway. Long afterwards everyone agreed that whilst it was sad they were saying goodbye to Roddy, the occasion managed to be an uplifting one with strong readings - Ecclesiastes and Paul's letter to the Corinthians which ends with the immortal words "and the greatest of these is love".

After everyone had left Rosie and Jamie took the dogs for a long walk along the river and were quietly thankful to have each other and that the day had gone so well. Jamie made sure the Lodge was all locked up, Jack was seeing to the horses and Whitewalls eventually went to sleep in the soft half light of a Scottish midsummer.

Edinburgh

'Leave him, Polly, it's simple now. All out in the open, there's nothing to stop us being together'. They were in David's flat and after frantically making love and clinging to each other as if they were drowning Polly and David were still in bed and having a very serious conversation.

'David, it's not so simple. I have to think about John and Minty, my parents, my family I can' just think about us!'

'Why not? I'm prepared to take on the twins and everything else can be sorted out. I love you Polly. I haven't been playing around and I hope you haven't either. I've never felt like this before about any woman.'

Now Polly realised the enormity of the situation she was in. Whilst she enjoyed the heady sensations of a secret relationship, exciting sex and the feeling of being very special she began to realise the possible cost of it all. He became angry.

'Then I think you'd better go away and think about this and don't keep me waiting!'

She left to go back to Murrayfield and have the most crucial talk of her life with Richard.

They waited until the children were in bed. Richard was still very cold towards Polly and she began to be very afraid that the choice of staying or going might not be hers. Instead of at the kitchen table where most of their important discussions had taken place over the years, they were in the drawing room, seated on either side of the fireplace.

'Why, Poll? Was I not enough for you? Did you think about the children and how all this may have affected them? Bringing him here was a rotten thing to do and I'll be that wasn't the first time!' Her face told him it was not.

'It's hard to explain' she began. 'Everything seemed so settled, as if this was it for the rest of my life. And, no, it's nothing you've done or not done. You're a great husband and father, you work hard, my parents love you; more than they love me, I think. Even Roddy has left you the Lodge and everything. David seemed exciting, different and dangerous but I never meant it to go as far as it's gone.' She stopped, looked at Richard for some kind of reaction. There wasn't any. His face was stern, impossible to read. Then Richard spoke.

'Polly, I've given this whole sordid business a lot of thought. I feel really deeply hurt by what you've done and it has damaged our marriage. I've seriously thought about divorcing you and naming McLean. But I've decided for the sake of the children and your parents to give you another chance.' There was a long silence. Polly felt exhausted.

'Thank you. I'm sorry' was all she could manage to say.

Whitewalls

Rosie came off the 'phone after taking a call from her mother. 'I really thought there could be no more surprises' she said to Jamie as they had their morning coffee in, for once, a peaceful kitchen.

'What's happened now?' he asked mildly.

'My mother and John Prendergast want to come round to talk to us, something to do with my father and the legal case. But I think there's something else, too. So, anyway, they're coming round for lunch, which will have to be pot luck. It's a lovely day so we can sit outside and find out what's happening.' She felt cheerful at the thought of seeing Betty but not quite sure where John came in all this. Rosie was soon to find out.

She really had to admire her mother and her ability still to surprise. After a brief conversation, during which Betty spoke rather more than John. However, he delivered the bombshell.

'You know, of course, that Betty and I have been seeing a lot of each other recently, particularly with her cancer scare and the legal business with Alistair. We are both tired of living alone so I have asked Betty to marry me and come to live with me in Stichill. Now it was Betty's turn.

'I hope you'll be happy for us. Because of Roddy's death, we're planning the quietest of weddings at the Register Office in Peebles then a blessing by Reverend Martin at the village church.'

Jamie recovered from the shock first. He shook John's hand warmly then hugged Betty.

'That's great news'. Rosie burst into tears then hugged both her mother and John. Betty grinned broadly. She was enjoying this.

'There's even more good news. Alistair's dropped his legal case. He was told there was no chance of success. So Madeleine has left him, gone off in a huff back to France now she knows he hasn't any money and apparently she's had a lover in Chambery for ages!'

'Might as well tell them the rest, my dear' John joined in.

'You mean there's more?' Rosie couldn't believe it.

'Now don't get upset or excited' Betty began, 'I really feel quite sorry for Alistair as it turns out even the vineyard and château are only rented and the lease is almost up immediately after the harvest. So he's going back to settle his affairs in France, then I am going to rent him the Tower.'

'You're not, that's too kind, he doesn't deserve it' Jamie and Rosie cried almost in unison.

'Isn't that typical of Betty?' John enquired mildly, his eyes twinkling. She broke in,

'Don't worry, he will be eternally grateful and I will charge him a sensible rent. We'll have a proper contract drawn up!' At this they all burst out laughing, including Betty.

'I'm going to get a bottle of champagne out of the fridge and we'll celebrate this news properly.' With that Jamie went back into the kitchen and soon returned with five glasses and a bottle of Tattinger. Molly had been in the kitchen so he invited her to share the good news. She was delighted, even though it was a turn up for the books and she doubted at their age whether Lady Betty and the Colonel should be getting married. Then, she thought, there'd been so much bad news recently maybe this was the very thing to cheer them all up.

Jamie was still in charge. Once the glasses had been filled, he raised his with the toast

'To all our family, may we be blessed with health and happiness for years to come.'

'Our family' they happily repeated bringing to an end the most turbulent Spring and Summer they could ever remember.

Lightning Source UK Ltd.
Milton Keynes UK
18 March 2010

151570UK00001B/231/P

9 781906 558215